PRAISE FOR *BAGHDAD SOLITAIRE* BY LESLIE COCKBURN

"Fearless and artful, with a Renaissance painter's eye for detail, Leslie Cockburn regales us with the most provoking political thriller to have come out of the Iraq war and its aftermath. Smells, sounds, the clash of cultural values, the vices and virtues of humanity in a war-torn, dismantled society practically jump from the pages to immerse us in an unforgettable story. A great read."

— Gioconda Belli, author of *The Country Under My Skin* and *Infinity in the Palm of Her Hand*

"Hemingway once said that the most important credential for a writer is to have lived an interesting life and to have something to say that the world needs to hear. Leslie Cockburn has most assuredly lived an interesting life, one of intrigue, adventure, romance, trouble, and danger. Her stunning debut novel, *Baghdad Solitaire*, is a thriller that resonates with authenticity and truth, a book that could only have been written by one who had actually lived on the razor's edge of death."

— Wade Davis, author of *Into the Silence*

"Leslie Cockburn brings the eye of a top-notch journalist to this page-turning thriller set in post-invasion Iraq. Rife with intrigue, corruption and cover-up, *Baghdad Solitaire* is so utterly believable you'll wonder if the events she describes didn't actually happen. From the lawless, insurgent-held deserts north of Baghdad to the seething Shiite mosques to the south, Cockburn takes us on an unforgettable journey into a modern-day *Heart of Darkness*. This is suspense of the highest order."

— Scott Wallace, author of *The Unconquered: In Search of the Amazon's Last Uncontacted Tribes*

"A compelling personal account of the conflict in Iraq told by a woman is long overdue. It has finally arrived in the form of Leslie Cockburn's beautifully written page-turner about one woman's quest for truth and understanding amid the chaos and devastation of war. Cockburn brings the depth of her own firsthand experience to her fictionalized character in this authentic and gripping tale."

— Susanna Styron, producer/director of *9/12: From Chaos to Community*

Baghdad Solitaire

———

Leslie Cockburn

Asahina & Wallace
Los Angeles
2013
www.asahinaandwallace.com

FOR ANDREW

1

MOHAMMED BIN SALAH'ADIN sang to ward off *djinns*. The western desert, south of the Wadi Hauran, was thick with *djinns*. They lurked in the dry riverbeds and quartz-sand caves. They kept company with cobras and horned vipers. Some took the shape of snakes or black dogs or even humans. After the bombing began, they took revenge on passing convoys by blowing dust devils right into the path of the cars. If it wasn't the *djinns* causing trouble, it was thieves, out-of-work soldiers, who plundered their old arsenals to prey on travelers from Amman. Mohammed sang to forget his fear of this cursed highway. His friends said his singing sounded like a sick camel in the Jumhuriya Market.

"A sniper will shoot you one day just to stop the noise," his cousin Ahmed told him.

Mohammed ignored the abuse. What did Ahmed know? It had been years since anyone had studied music in Paris or Seville on a scholarship paid for by the country's oil profits. The only knowledge people mastered these days was how to steal copper wire and load a gun. Mohammed felt like a relic from a lost civilization, buried in the muck of the Tigris. Sassanid, Seleucid, Sumerian. Achaemenid, Assyrian, Akkadian. He sometimes thought he was the only one who remembered. For what it was worth, he could sing the ancient songs of the pearl divers.

Mohammed lit another cigarette. He wanted to travel to Andalusia to hear the gypsies sing flamenco, with their hoarse drunken voices cutting the night like broken glass. When the Umayyads migrated across Arabia and Africa to Cordoba, they brought the songs, a kind of howl, of lost love, lost dreams, life's cruelty. Mohammed would sing with the gypsies. For now, he would drive this highway to make a living. Artists had to live.

His huge, tobacco-stained hands gripped the steering wheel. His sandaled foot pressed the gas pedal to the floor. The lapis lazuli worry beads, draped over his rear view mirror, swung back and forth like the hips of Scheherazade, Mohammed's favorite belly dancer, who refused, in spite of the war, to leave Baghdad. Mohammed told her that all of Iraq lay in the soft plain between her hips that stood out like the Zagros Mountains. He played a little game on her tummy, looking for the Tigris and the Zab.

While Mohammed sang mournfully, his passenger sat silently in the back seat, staring at the black desert. Mohammed watched her in the mirror, flicking his lighter to see her eyes, the color of jade, the shade of the tiles in one of Saddam's palace swimming pools. Her hair was dark brown. It reminded him of the stain from a walnut. Mohammed could not see all of it because it was swept up severely into a clip, with wisps around her face like an Ottoman parasol. He could not judge her age because she was *ajnabee*, a foreigner, and he was the first to admit that they all looked alike. Somewhere between 25 and 35, he thought. She was of medium height, though what that meant, now that the Iraqi youth suffered from what the U.N. pamphlets called "stunting and wasting," he could not say. She was tall by comparison, but thin enough to have lived under sanctions. Her wrist, resting under her chin against the dark glass, seemed small enough to break like the porcelain cups Baghdad ladies were selling at the auction house to raise cash for food. He had heard she was a doctor. She looked too weak to amputate a leg. He felt like the ferryman in "Gilgamesh." Why do you come here, he wanted to ask, wandering over the pastures in search of the wind?

* * *

His passenger was absorbed in her own thoughts, deaf to the ancient songs. She was imagining her execution. It was a swift, impersonal killing that fit the reputation of this road. In her mind she saw the gunmen, smelling of cardamom and sweat, dragging her from the car, ordering her to her knees, and shooting her in the back of the head. In her mind, the scene repeated itself, like a low budget al-Qaida video, where the martyr dies in a pool of his own perfume-scented blood and the gruesome pictures are replayed on a loop.

Death was sweetened for the martyrs by the promise of 72 virgins waiting in paradise. She had researched the 72 virgins. The number wasn't actually in the Quran but in the Hadith 2687, collected in the Book of Sunan. The Quran, in Sura 56, was vague on the point. *And theirs shall be the dark-eyed houris, chaste as hidden pearls.* Al-Suyuti, in the early 16th century, wrote, "Each time we sleep with a *houri* we find her a virgin. The sensation you feel each time you make love is utterly delicious and out of this world and were you to experience it in this world, you would faint." But a new analysis in *Die Syro-Aramäische Lesart des Koran* translated *houris* from the Aramaic dialect Syriac as "white raisins," which put everything in a very different light.

"Do you know the American who disappeared?" Mohammed's face was red with embarrassment before he had finished asking the question.

"Yes."

"Is your friend still alive?"

"I don't know."

"Are you really a doctor?"

"Yes." She could see his huge yellow teeth lit by the dashboard.

"There was a woman killed on the Haditha road. She burned to death."

"I'm sorry."

"She looked like you."

Outside, half buried in the sand, there were carcasses of tanks. From the spring, they thought in tandem. From the invasion. Mohammed and his passenger were traveling in convoy, in the second of four white Suburbans, hoping to see the back of Anbar province before breakfast. The doctor had chosen to drive rather than fly because the previous week, *mujahedeen* had fired six missiles at the American embassy charter flight that corkscrewed through evasive maneuvers into Baghdad airport every morning.

Mohammed shared the front seat of the Suburban with Tariq, so thin that every surface of his body was concave, his tendons tight as catgut. He had carefully combed his few strands of white hair across his bald head, in a display of vanity from another time, when King Faisal's court dictated fashion. Tariq ate pistachios. There was a little mountain of shells at his feet. His clothes were coated with ash. In the glove compartment, which he opened to forage for more black-market cigarettes, there were gaudy prints of Shia saints that he pinned up depending on what province the car was passing through. In this part of Iraq, he locked the saints away.

The lead car of the convoy and the chase car at the back carried the security detail, former British SAS men who called themselves Patriots. Their job, for a fee of $1,000 a day, was to defend the convoy from the dangers that lurked in the folds and shadows of Ramadi. The doctor could already see Ramadi's faint lights, powered by jerry-rigged generators, worth a small fortune since the war. Mohammed told her the Americans had promised that the electricity would run 24 hours a day. So far, there was less power than the ministry had managed under sanctions. Worst of all, he said, the American soldiers ordered Iraqi men to lie down in the street so the soldiers could step on their faces with their boots.

"How can the Americans do these things?"

As Mohammed talked, the doctor was trying to think where to hide her American passport. There was a small hole in the lining of the side pocket of her purse where she kept her keys. She shoved the passport through the lining. She placed her Irish passport where it could be easily reached.

In the six months since the "liberation," Ramadi had become a hot zone of resistance against the occupation. Explosives from old ammunition dumps, buried by Ramadi boys in the road, ripped through the thin metal jackets of Humvees and catapulted anyone inside through the vehicle's roof like rag dolls shot from a cannon. Traumatic brain injury was appearing on the patients' charts at Ramstein and Walter Reed. TBI gutted the cerebral lobes as the blast wave traveled at 1,600 feet per second. A secondary wind slammed the soft tissue against the inner skull.

"Doctor, *masmuk*? May I ask your name?"

"Lee McGuinness."

"Guinness. Like the drink. Too strong. It tastes like dirt. You are Irish?"

"Yes."

"You are welcome in Iraq."

"Thanks, Mohammed. *Shoukran.*"

"*Afwan.*"

It tasted like peat, not dirt, she thought. The peaty water from the bogs. Eight hours had gone by since Lee had left the hotel in Amman. She had tried to shape her bags into a comfortable pillow and was dozing fitfully. Her head fell forward and jerked back rhythmically like a metronome, and she was unsure, when she saw a black sedan pull along side at high speed, whether she was dreaming. Her first thought, however unlikely, was that the driver needed directions. Maybe he wanted to point out something wrong with Mohammed's car. As she prepared to roll down the window, the man in the passenger seat, his head wrapped in a black-and-white *keffiyeh*, casually trained his AK-47 on Mohammed. It took over a second for Lee to register what was happening. She groped the seat for the walkie-talkie the Patriots had tossed in her car in Amman, conscious that the man with the AK could mistake it for a weapon and shoot it out of her hand. She was breathing hard.

"They're going to kill Mohammed." She threw herself to the floor, bruising her chest.

"Roger. We see them."

She wedged her ceramic-plated vest against the inside car door to stop the bullets. Sometimes the plates worked and sometimes they didn't. A sniper could find the soft spots.

She counted three shots.

"Doctor. Do you copy?"

She felt broken glass lodged under her collar. The glass was cold and hard. The dry wind, full of sand grit, roared through the car. Mohammed and Tariq shouted in Arabic a mixture of prayers and obscenities. Blood streamed down Mohammed's jowl, seeping into the folds of his heavy neck. Another burst of gunfire was followed by an explosion.

"Yes, yes. I'm here. Mohammed's wounded." The doctor raised her head a fraction to see. She watched the attackers fall back, fishtailing into the desert. She lifted her hand behind Mohammed's head and placed it firmly on the wound to see whether the bullet had found the carotid artery. It hadn't. No gushing. Mohammed groaned. With her other hand she threw him a scarf.

"Hold this against the bleeding. Can you speak?" She wanted to be sure his airway was intact.

"Yes, *tabiba*, I can speak. I can even sing."

The caravan of Suburbans slammed to a halt. The Patriots were out of the cars, spraying bullets into the BMW sedan until the car began to sag and burn. The sound of each bullet echoed across the dunes and wadis, alerting every village and Bedouin encampment from Jubba to Rutbah.

When the firing stopped, Lee grabbed her backpack and ran to the attackers' car. The driver was headless, his blood spurting like a dark red fountain. She looked for the body of the other man, the one with the *keffiyeh*, and found him in an untidy heap in the back of the car, his yawning head wound leaking brain fluid.

"We have to move." A Patriot, rigid with adrenaline, pulled her back from the wreck. She was light, easy to steer.

"That's unnecessary," Lee said coolly, removing his hand. "He's dead."

"We know these *muj*, Doctor. They attacked three convoys and left the passengers stripped by the side of the road. You're lucky they didn't kill your driver. Everyone in the cars," the Patriot shouted to the little crowd, whose faces were ruddy from the heat.

There were faint protests from an evangelical preacher from Denver, who had come to rewrite Iraq's schoolbooks, and a Danish journalist, sent by a Copenhagen daily to investigate civilian casualties. They did not want to leave the corpses unburied, splayed across the blackened wreck. They said it was *haram*, forbidden. Jackals or turkey buzzards, Lee thought, would make short work of the carrion. There must be some kind of buzzard in Iraq. No one made a move to dig a grave. There was no way to clean or wrap the bodies.

Fear was surging through the convoy's passengers, fear of the dark, fear of revenge by the relatives of the dead, fear of the unknown waiting for them at the end of the highway. A pair of headlights approached from the direction of Ramadi, and the evangelist and the Dane dispersed like startled game. Once again, the Suburbans screamed down the highway, straight as a Roman road, a remnant of the once oil-rich country that could pay for the best foreign contractors to roll the tarmac. Mohammed held the blood-soaked scarf to his face. "They were *djinns*, *tabiba*. They can take human form and when they smell fear, they attack. While they are human, *djinns* are vulnerable and can be killed, thanks be to God. They are born of fire and those have returned to the fire."

"I need to dress that wound, Mohammed." She dismissed his ramblings and unzipped her backpack. "You will have to go to the hospital in Baghdad. My friend Dr. Qais will see you. Tell him I sent you."

"God be with you, *tabiba*." Mohammed smiled and felt ashamed that he had doubted her.

II

LEE HAD HEARD THE NEWS that Martin had disappeared 12 days before she boarded the plane to Jordan. She had a visceral reaction, like she was sinking into the cold, bottomless lake up on the Vee, in the Knockmealdowns above Lismore, where she had spent her Irish summers as a child. The shepherds on the Vee said the lake was home to a witch who dragged down anyone who dared to swim there. One summer, her sister dove into the frigid lake on a dare, swam to the middle, and drowned. The water was the color of dark peat. When Lee and one of the boys from Cappoquin dove in to rescue her, there was no way to see where she had gone. Lee herself went limp and began to sink. The boy grabbed her hair. He pulled her to the boggy shore. The muck was spongy underfoot.

Lee felt like she was drowning now. She was in a taxi in lower Manhattan, outside St. Vincent's Hospital, and the Pakistani driver was shouting into his cell phone in Urdu and had the radio at maximum volume to listen to an item about fresh violence in Iraq and a footnote about a missing American.

"Can you turn that up, please?"

"I'm sorry, madam, I can't make it any louder. Some chap's been kidnapped. That's all, madam. Slow news day."

She was gasping for air in the taxi. She opened the window.

"Drop me here, please. Seventh and Charles." She stumbled from the cab at dusk in front of the shop selling Afghan imports.

Martin kept a fourth-floor walk-up on Charles Street, a block from where she stood watching her driver weaving recklessly into the downtown traffic. She had a spare set of keys to the apartment to let the plumber or the cable man in while Martin was away. She walked without thinking to his front door and climbed the century-old wooden steps that needed paint and repair. In Martin's apartment, there was a worn sofa he had found on a tip. The walls were covered with blown-up black-and-white photos of refugees. His bed was an air mattress on the floor next to a dangerously tall pile of books. The refrigerator was bare. There was a second staircase covered in Moroccan tiles that led to the roof, where he liked to sleep in the open air as people did on hot summer nights in Kurdistan. In New York, he was a drifter. His real home was a series of cheap hotels and rented villas in Congo, Kosovo, Kabul, and Iraq, where he ran operations to move humanitarian supplies and build camps.

Lee climbed to the roof. She sat on the bench and smelled the cedar. She looked across the low village cityscape to lights the colors of snow-cone syrup on the Empire State building. She caught her breath and started making calls to aid groups, news desks, State Department friends. Everyone repeated the same few facts. His clothes, his computer, and satellite phone were found in the hotel room. No note. Martin had simply vanished.

With refugees washing over one border or another every year, Martin Carrigan was never out of work. He was approaching 40 and had never married. For the most part he lived like a monk. He had strong blue eyes and the black hair of his ancestors from West Cork, and he was, at times, so calm it seemed his pulse had slowed to nothing. When he looked at you, he made you want to confess. Martin had considered becoming a Jesuit. He took a deep interest in liberation theology. He was a witness from the world beyond the West, a world defined by outrage and desperation. At parties, he lapsed into silence. He preferred the company of people like Lee, who had seen families living in bombed-out buildings laced with mines. They were also from the same tribe, with the same collective memory of the Great Hunger and the coffin ships.

When the U.S. invaded Afghanistan, Lee and Martin had crossed the front lines together and rented a villa in Kabul not far from Chicken Street. Martin knew the country. That October, when U.S. AC-130 gunships strafed the villages of Bori Chokar and Chowkar-Karez, Martin took her there, expecting refugees and wounded. What they found were 93 civilians dead. There were body parts hanging from the telephone wires. When they arrived back in Kabul, dust-caked from the trip, they listened to the Pentagon's official statement: "The people there are dead because we want them dead." There was no apology. The defense secretary added, "I cannot deal with that particular village." There was no explanation. He was a busy man with a lot on his mind.

They traveled together to Thori, where 23 civilians died in a bombing raid, and to Khanabad, where more than a hundred people were killed in what people told them was carpet bombing. Forty more were killed when their mud huts collapsed from a stray bomb near Kunduz. The incident was officially reported as an "error."

Martin introduced Lee to a Pashtun surgeon in her 60s, a tall, defiant woman, who chain-smoked and refused to wear a *burqa* on the grounds that it was an Iranian import and not her national dress. The traditional costume, which she proudly wore, looked like it was out of a 19th-century print of a Swiss milkmaid. Brightly colored fabric. A fetching scarf. The Taliban had chosen not to dismember the difficult surgeon or turn her into the street to beg for alms because she was a cousin of the old king. She was from a powerful Pashtun family. She invited Lee to work with her at a military hospital. Martin had helped arrange it. There, Lee saw the effects of 2,000-pound bombs, cluster bombs, cruise missiles, depleted uranium, and weaponry that mutilated the body in ways beyond imagination. By Christmas, there were 3,767 civilian casualties. Martin gave her a present of diaries from the Great War. He recited Vera Brittain and Wilfred Owen:

If you could hear, at every jolt, the blood

Come gargling from the froth-corrupted lungs,

Obscene as cancer, bitter as the cud

Of vile, incurable sores on innocent tongues ...

Then Martin saved her life. They were returning from Deh Rawud, where 48 people at a wedding party were killed by a B-52 bomber and AC-130 gunship. They had helped move women and children to Mirwais Hospital in Kandahar. At a roadblock on the Kabul Road, a Pashtun tribesman had decided to blow up their car. He had raised his RPG, with its projectile shaped like the onion dome of a Russian Orthodox church, and aimed it with care to immolate them. Without a second's hesitation, Martin opened the car door, hands high, and instructed the man in Pashto to shoot him, not the woman in the car. In the second before the man fired, he recognized Martin. The Pashtun dropped his weapon. He walked up to Martin, embraced him, and ordered his men to slaughter a goat. They baked flatbread and grilled pumpkins. They picked bunches of tiny sweet grapes, all because Martin had once evacuated the man's family to the refugee camps across the border in Peshawar. Without Martin, the family would have been wiped out. It was a debt the man had to repay, just like the debt Lee felt now. The memory of it was charged with the terror of the weapon that nearly fired, the screams that never came, mixed with the taste of *kaddo bourani*, the sweet pumpkin that they devoured after the danger had passed. Coming to Baghdad to find Martin now was the least that she could do. He had saved her life and now she would save his.

Martin had moved to Baghdad in August and refused to evacuate after the car bombings that drove most of the aid workers away. He dismissed as propaganda reports that the war had been won and that the U.S. presence would be simply for the purpose of "mopping up" the resistance still loyal to Saddam. Given the forces unleashed by the invasion, Martin anticipated some 5 million refugees over the next few years, and he wanted to be ready for them, shuttling between Baghdad and Amman and Damascus, urging reluctant officials to think about camps, water, latrines. Everyone knew him, even the *mujahedeen*, and it was understood that his motives were beyond reproach. That much seemed obvious to Lee. She knew that kidnapping was a growth industry in Baghdad, but Martin was a special case. It seemed more likely the work of common criminals who knew nothing of his reputation. It was also possible that Martin had made enemies who wanted to sabotage his mission. In war, there were always saboteurs.

Nearly two weeks had passed since the news that Martin was missing, and the men in the Green Zone, the Americans who ran the war, had maintained silence. Everyone assumed they were negotiating behind the scenes. Lee wanted more than anything else in the world for that to be true. At the same time, she knew that the relationship between the Green Zone and the aid community was strained. The provisional government insisted that aid workers sign papers saying that they would not comment to the press on the roundup of civilians, the arrest of doctors, the dark side of the occupation. Under these conditions, Lee knew enough to think that someone might find Martin inconvenient.

Martin had called her on his satellite phone the day before he disappeared. He told her the latest Baghdad joke about ransom money and camels, and mentioned a close call at a roadblock near Amarah, where he had been questioned for an hour and released. He had dined with Kurdish friends in the new foreign ministry, who had just narrowly escaped being blown up in their offices. Lee replayed the conversation in her mind. If Martin had given her a clue about an enemy he had crossed or a hazardous trip he had planned, she had missed it. Given the bloody scene she had just witnessed on the road, she thought Martin might be dead, mistaken for an Iraqi in one of the unrecorded incidents in Anbar or Tikrit, his corpse hosed down and wrapped tightly in a white shroud.

Martin's colleagues at Project Refugee in Washington saw no need to risk a trip to Baghdad. They relied on government channels. The State Department had given them assurances. The director had spoken personally with the secretary. Finding Martin was a job for people with weapons and helicopters. What could an NGO like Project Refugee do in the face of insurgents? There had been no ransom demand. They would wait for news and do as they were told. Lee, they said, was welcome to do as she pleased. She was a free agent.

She knew that in the Baghdad kidnapping market, Martin was worth a million dollars or more. She also knew that Martin never traveled in a convoy with bodyguards. He hired old cars. He dressed in local clothes and wore three days' growth of beard. He made sure there was never a pattern to his movements.

"If you don't want to be a target," he liked to say, "then don't act like an American." Martin carried two passports, as she did. She was a dual citizen. The Irish were neutral.

* * *

As the convoy reached the ragged outskirts of Baghdad, Lee lit her first cigarette in a year. Her last had been in Kabul. She gagged and stubbed it out, enveloped in the lingering smell. She checked her watch. It was 7 in the morning, Baghdad time, too early to call Naji. She was anxious to see him, to get her bearings in Iraq. They had done their trauma fellowship together in Baltimore, a city half in ruins from arson and neglect that looked worse than Baghdad. Naji Qais had left the States in May, after the invasion, like other Iraqi-Americans who wanted to build the new Iraq. It was the long-awaited moment, the time of return. But his early effusive emails had grown sober and spare. Things were deteriorating. He would tell her about it when he saw her. The smoke stuck to her throat like Saran wrap.

She stared through her smashed window at the neighborhoods streaming by that looked like Los Angeles south of Sunset. She had done her residency at LA County Hospital, where the CT machines were so old she had to mark off the body parts for scanning with paper clips. She thought Baghdad hospitals might be like that. She would ask Naji about the buzzards. The city was low concrete sprawl dotted with defaced portraits of Saddam Hussein, his features mauled by rocket-propelled grenades. There were date palms and hot

21

pink bougainvillea. The yards were full of topiaries. Villas pulverized into rubble still had clipped boxwood peacocks in the front yard.

Mohammed told Lee that some of Baghdad's famous landmarks from the old days, the ones you could find in yellowing guidebooks, existed only in people's imaginations. Baghdadis gave directions like "where the Saddam victory statue used to be" or "just by the old portrait of the boss in blood."

"Saddam's favorite portrait painter dipped his brush in his own blood," Mohammed said with perverse satisfaction, dabbing his wound. "Can you believe that? His own blood. He would paint Saddam and offer it to him as a gift. The painter refused to take any money until the palace forced it on him. The guy was crazy. The whole country was crazy."

There would be no one from the International Committee of Surgeons to welcome Lee. The surgeons' last tour in Iraq had ended badly, in the blast furnace heat of August, five months after the invasion. A gunman had fired an RPG into the Sadr City clinic and left a French doctor and two patients split open like overripe fruit. The patients' families, camped in the halls with their bed rolls and cooking pots, had been incinerated. ICS had decided to pull out. The Red Cross and most of the U.N., suffering their own casualties, left too. Six weeks had gone by since the attack, and Lee had convinced the Surgeons' Committee to allow her to make an exploratory trip, to see whether a joint project with Naji Qais in downtown Baghdad would be less hazardous for volunteers than Sadr City. It was Naji's idea. He needed the money and supplies. His people would take the risk.

The Surgeons' Committee was happy to dispatch Lee to Iraq. She had served as a surgeon in the Afghan provinces of Nanghahar and Ghazni, opening mud brick clinics as the

Taliban retreated in 2001. She was accustomed to risk. The joint project seemed like a sound idea. No one else had come up with anything better.

The committee also knew that the disappearance of her friend Martin Carrigan from his Baghdad hotel room had accelerated her desire to serve in Iraq. Every news outlet was running the story. The name Carrigan was now more familiar to Americans than the names of most of the presidents.

"*Kaif halak*, doctor?" Muhammad asked, turning around and studying her crumpled figure in back. "Are you okay?"

"I'm okay." Lee felt the nausea rising from her stomach. She longed for the privacy of a hotel room. She lay down in the back seat and groaned.

* * *

"Rush hour," grumbled Mohammed, the blood from his wound congealing nicely. "*Allahu alam*."

Lee sat upright, feeling breakable and disoriented. The streets were much dirtier than she expected. There were parts of burned-out military vehicles mixed with old vegetables and Fanta cans.

"Checkpoint." Tariq spoke for the first time.

She could hear his annoyance. The U.S. Army was taking its time today, stopping every car.

As Mohammed's car approached Masbah Circle, Lee could see that there was hardly a woman on the street. One was darting into a shop, wrapped in an *abaya*, the baggy shroud that had once been worn only by poor women in Saddam City. Baghdad women had dressed in short silk chemises and hand-made chunky jewelry. When they walked down Sadoun Street, they wore stiletto heels and big glasses from Chanel. That was all in the past. Kidnapping and rape went unchecked now, and it kept women, even the doctors, behind locked gates. One recent morning in Mansour, a Shia member of the governing council was pulling out of her driveway when the assassins opened fire. No one knew who had done it.

"Hand me some water, would you, Tariq?" Lee wondered whether Tariq had been one of Saddam's infamous Mukhabarat, who spied on foreigners in the old days. Tariq's bloodshot eyes followed every move of the American soldiers blocking the way of the SUV.

The troops looked like a lost intergalactic force, wearing headsets and impenetrable shades, peering down from tank turrets on this shabby Baghdad street. Lee knew that most of the soldiers had been told that their tours of duty in Iraq would be extended. The Pentagon called it "stop loss." She had a letter in her briefcase from an American soldier in Beit Har to his father, Col. Frank, a Pentagon consultant who had earned a handful of medals in Vietnam. Col. Frank was an old friend of Martin's and had driven all the way from Gaithersburg, Maryland., to Kennedy Airport to meet her for a drink before her flight. He had told her about his son. He had handed her the letter as though it contained everything she needed to know. She reread it now, hoping that it would, in some way, lead her to Martin.

Dad,

More and more I wish you were here. The CG has told us that we will be in Iraq for another year. My men are pissed off. Right now they are fighting on the streets of Beit Har. My mortar platoon has been under attack every night. Last week one of our tanks fired up a civilian vehicle with four Iraqis inside, out after curfew. They were scorched beyond recognition. We left the car in the middle of town. Nobody has picked up the bodies...

The soldiers at the checkpoint shouted to the drivers up ahead, who could not understand. "Move it. Pull over. Hey, you. On the double, damn it."

"No problem. No problem." A driver had retrieved the only English he knew. A soldier slammed him against the side of his car.

"Shut the fuck up, Hajji."

There were overloaded buses, vans, and battered pickups packed with Iraqis waiting to be interrogated. One man was forced to his knees in the dirt, his hands tied behind his back with plastic handcuffs that the soldiers called zips, which Lee might have used to tie a garbage bag.

"There has been an attack. Look there." Tariq pointed at an American Bradley armored vehicle upended in the fast lane on the far side of the road. "Bomb." The Pentagon called them "IEDs," improvised explosive devices, which could be detonated by someone in a cotton *dishdasha* and flip-flops.

The vehicle looked like an elephant carcass robbed of tusks. The casualties, if there were any, had been taken away.

Lee felt the tension in the front seat as an American soldier cradling a weapon motioned for Mohammed to stop. The soldier stared at Mohammed's broken window and saw the fresh bandage on his neck. He stepped back.

"Out of the car."

Before Mohammed could move, one of the Patriots jumped from his Suburban and hailed the soldier. Lee could not hear the conversation but saw the soldier's rigid body relax when credentials were presented and the story of the bandits told. The soldier and the Patriot were brothers in arms. Polite and deferential now, the Patriot approached her car.

"We briefed him. He radioed for another unit to move the bodies when they have time. It's all taken care of. No worries, doctor."

As the convoy was waved through the roadblock, she wondered whether the whole morning's episode would be smoothed over, cleaned up, and filed as an "incident" of little note in this war. Any question submitted to the occupation authorities would likely draw the response, "We have no record of that."

Lee felt a wave of guilt and a strong desire for a shower. She wanted to wash away the residue of animal fear from the attack. She should have insisted that everyone stop to bury the bodies. She thought about tracking down their families in Ramadi to compensate them. But then, the families might find her hotel in Baghdad and blow it up.

Once again she picked up the letter. Unfolding it had become like fondling a rosary, and the paper had started to tear.

... The other day, one of our tanks hit a mine hidden in a pile of trash outside our front gate. Whoever hid it knew exactly what they were doing. I ran in a pair of flip-flops to my medics to make sure they were prepared to accept casualties. They were way ahead of me. My scouts are great too. They know how to kick in doors and how to keep the locals from stealing the copper in the power lines.

I need to talk to you, Dad, about the infantry company here. They are stealing money from the locals. I'm not talking about small amounts of cash. I mean a fat bankroll. They take the money during raids. I'm not saying that I care for the Iraqi people. To tell you the truth, I don't. They are our best friends during the day and shooting at us that night. We will never win hearts and minds here.

26

Gotta run,

Your Son

Col. Frank had said that he was worried that Martin had stumbled onto something. When Lee pressed him to speak more plainly, he said he was sorry but he had to get back on the road.

"Go see my son, doctor. He's been there long enough to know."

The convoy turned onto a pot-holed street that led to the Aleem, a small hotel where one of the American television networks kept a bureau on the fourth floor. This was Lee's stop. She was looking for someone there, a friend of Martin's. He was the sort of friend she wanted to see in person without someone listening on the phone line. Col. Frank had told her to be cautious on the phone. Too many intelligence services were monitoring calls. The Aleem's sign advertised a rooftop bar, where guests could smoke a water pipe in a Bedouin tent carpeted with silk pillows. Looking up, Lee saw masking tape binding the windows to protect them from bomb blast. The road ahead was littered with concrete barriers. Men were pouring cement into rusty oil drums. Iraqi security guards argued over where to place the new fortifications. When the bomb went off, she thought, it would be an inside job.

There was a cursory check by the guards under the Suburban's hood and an animated discussion of Mohammed's wound. Lee's treatment was admired. She removed her suitcase that had survived her tour in Kabul, her backpack medical kit, and Thuraya satellite phone. In her bag was a bottle of wine for barter. She looked at the bulletproof vest jammed against the door under the broken glass and knew that she would never wear it. The plates were so heavy they made it hard to run.

"Go to the hospital to have that wound stitched up by Dr. Qais before you head for Amman," Lee told Mohammed, handing him a wad of bills. "Tell Dr. Qais I will stop by the hospital later this morning. *Ma'a salama.*"

"*Ma'a salama*, doctor. Take care of yourself. It is very dangerous here." Mohammed wanted to protect her. She was not like the others, foreign vultures who came to this war for profit.

"I know, Mohammed. I should be ready to head back to Amman in three weeks. You can take me to Petra, and sing for me in the ruins."

"Insha'Allah."

III

THE TALL PICTURE WINDOWS on the ground floor of the hotel had been blocked up with concrete to protect against automatic-weapons fire. In the lobby there was a shop selling old books behind a "closed" sign. She saw a bound volume of Ibn Khaldun, a history of the Umayyad dynasty, and some titles in English — "The Case of the Headless Jesuit" and "Mr. Punch in Holiday Mood" — relics, she thought, of the British occupation. They were probably from an old Baghdadi family's library, sold off under sanctions. Martin told her that after the books and silver had been carted off to the auctioneers, the middle class became so desperate that women ripped out their washing machines and ceiling fans to pay for baby formula and gas.

Two desk clerks watched her impassively next to a handmade sign that advertised a "business center."

"*Marhaban.*" She tried to be friendly.

"*Ahlan.*"

They told her that the elevator was old and slow with barely room for one. Lee could see that it was piled high with silver boxes, so she climbed the four floors to the news bureau, a suite of drab rooms decorated with wanted posters of Saddam. The place seemed deserted, aside from an insistent voice speaking in Arabic on the phone. She followed the voice to a windowless office where she found Nizar Hadithi behind an unctuous smile and a clean desk. He was well fed, unlike most of his countrymen, and his skin had the sheen of high-gloss paint. He wore an alligator shirt and new jeans, pressed, with an oversized belt buckle inlaid with turquoise. He signaled her to a chair with his cigarette and, after a few threatening remarks to whoever was on the other end of the phone, slammed the receiver down and gave Lee his full attention.

"Mr. Hadithi?"

"Yes."

"My name is Lee McGuinness. I am a member of the Surgeons' Committee."

"Welcome, doctor. Please call me Nizar." He leaned back and toyed with a large set of keys on a black plastic Darth Vader chain. "What brings you here?"

"I am trying to restart the Surgeons' Committee mission here." She cleared her throat of what felt like a cup of sand.

"Iraq is very grateful to you, doctor. I'm not sure I am the one to help you with this. May I ask who gave you my name?"

"A friend."

"Someone I know?"

"A friend who is missing. Martin Carrigan."

"Ah," he said, fumbling for a fresh cigarette. "Everyone is looking for Martin. Do you smoke?"

"No, thanks. Martin has told me a great deal about you."

"Really? Good things, I hope," Nizar laughed.

What Martin had told her was that Nizar had been a Ba'ath Party member, a loyal functionary in the old ruling elite whose lucrative racket under Saddam had been extortion. He had demanded huge exit fees from foreigners for the privilege of leaving the country.

Anyone who refused to pay was given an AIDS test with a dirty needle.

"Of course."

"I am glad to hear that." Nizar disappeared behind a veil of smoke.

Lee knew that under the occupation, he was a black marketeer and one of Martin's most useful contacts. Nizar could acquire whatever Martin needed for his refugees.

"Do you have any idea what might have happened to him?"

"I saw him last at the Baghdad Hunt Club. We had some business. He wanted something from me and never turned up with the money."

"May I ask what he wanted? Martin told me how important you are to his work."

"Supplies."

"What kind of supplies?"

"Tents, cooking equipment, that sort of thing. You know he was working with all of these displaced people. Would you like a coffee?"

"Yes, that's very kind."

"Let's go downstairs. We had better walk."

In the gloom of the empty coffee shop, Nizar ordered them Turkish coffee, medium sweet.

"I don't like to talk in the bureau." He tapped out a rhythm on the table with a thick gold ring set with a yellow diamond. "We Baghdadis don't believe in anything anymore. We always wear something to pay the ransom or bribe the border guards."

"Of course." Lee looked at her own bare fingers. She thought she should wear her lapis ring from Chicken Street. "Had Martin made many enemies?"

Nizar laughed. "We all have enemies here, Dr. McGuinness. I dare say even you. There are a lot of people missing in Iraq. Just the other day I heard of somebody asking $250,000 ransom for an Egyptian. Can you imagine? An Egyptian. That's inflation. This war," he said, leaning closer to her, "is all about money."

"Have you heard anything about Martin? Any rumors?"

"Not so far."

"What about your news bureau?"

"They rely on statements from the Green Zone."

"You haven't heard any speculation?"

"My dear." Nizar folded his hands and sat back like an Ottoman pasha. "We've just met. You could be working for anyone."

"I apologize, Mr. Hadithi. Let me show you my ID." Lee rummaged through her purse.

"I have a man who makes those down the street."

Lee considered leaving. Defiance entered her voice. "There are plenty of rumors that Martin is dead."

"Not from a reliable source." Nizar blinked slowly.

"I've come all the way from New York to find him."

"You seem very impatient."

"I'm not sure that we have a lot of time."

"Everything takes more time here. A bit more coffee?"

Lee hesitated.

"I promise, you are not wasting your time. You have to realize that in Iraq, a conversation can cost you a bullet in your head. Let's talk about you for a moment. You must be a very close friend."

"Yes." Lee didn't quite know how to describe her relationship to Martin. "Martin and I have known each other a long time. We were in Afghanistan together."

"Ah. I am at your service, doctor." Nizar bowed. "Martin and I go back a long way, too, to the days when you could still drink a bottle of Johnny Walker Black Label with lunch." He lit another cigarette. "I don't want to offend you, doctor, but what makes you think you will have better luck finding Martin than anyone else?"

"I know him better than anyone else."

"But you don't know Iraq."

"I will rely on you for that."

"I'm flattered, Dr. McGuinness. I think the Coalition Provisional Authority is better equipped, don't you?"

"How are their sources among the insurgents?"

Nizar smiled. "I wouldn't know."

"I have a favor to ask." Lee felt compromised somehow, placing herself in Nizar's debt. "My driver, Mohammed, got wounded on the road and had to go to the hospital. Do you know of someone I could hire for a couple of weeks? Someone who will go anywhere?"

"With an old car like Martin's?"

"Yes, exactly." They both smiled.

"You ran into trouble on the road?"

"Yes."

"Who was your driver?"

"Mohammed bin Salah'adin."

"Ah, yes, I know him."

"How do you know him?"

"He worked for me occasionally. Before the war. I hope he is not badly hurt?"

"No. He will be fine. I took care of him. He worked for you?"

"Every driver who crossed the border did small favors for the government." Nizar smiled. "He is also a distant relative. We are both Dulaim. Mohammed was lucky to have a good doctor in the car. Since you looked after my relative, I will give you one of my best drivers. Sadoon is in the parking lot." Nizar lowered his voice. "He was Republican Guard." Nizar exhaled. "Do you understand what that means?"

"Exceptionally loyal to Saddam and tied to the resistance."

"To protect yourself, doctor, I suggest that you learn to be very discreet. When anyone asks questions, say as little as possible. You have the advantage of being new here and being a woman. People will assume you are less intelligent than you are. Now I have to leave you. We've had a bit of trouble here. Someone has been casing the hotel. Our people chased a car with heavy weapons in it yesterday. They were taking pictures."

"Who are they after?"

"The South Africans on the second floor. They have a contract to feed the U.S. troops. The resistance thinks killing them would help to starve the army."

"Nizar, I'll be staying at the Dar Kebeer." She handed him a piece of paper with her Thuraya number on it. "Call me the moment you hear anything."

"*Insha'Allah.* If they don't bomb this hotel first."

The lobby door opened and a man wearing a safari jacket with dark glasses fastened to a leather strap around his neck strode in and hurried to the elevator. Lee recognized him from channel surfing the news.

"My boss." Nizar tucked her number into his wallet. "He pays in dollars, gives me a *haweeya.* Identity card. Without that, I could easily be picked up as a former Ba'athist by the occupation forces. In exchange, I do logistics. I make his life easier in the Sunni provinces."

"Does he know you're a friend of Martin's?"

"No, my dear. Only you seem to know that. You're not a spy, are you?"

"No, Nizar. I came to you first because you have the contacts to help me. Martin said he couldn't operate here without you."

"Of course. *Ma'a salama*, doctor."

Lee was conscious that Nizar watched her trying to adjust her *abaya*. She knew everyone could tell a Western woman by her awkwardness and her shoes. As Lee turned to leave, she remembered something Nizar had said.

"You said Martin never turned up with the money. Was it a lot of cash?"

"Maybe $10,000."

"Would someone have killed him for that?"

"People kill for much less than that, my dear."

"That's comforting."

"Let's hope for the best, Dr. McGuinness. May I call you Lee? One night, Lee, you must come with me to the Baghdad Hunt Club. They serve the most delicious *masgouf* from the Tigris."

"*Masgouf?*"

"Grilled fish, spiced with tamarind."

She remembered the pungent smell of sewage from the river as Mohammed drove by the bombed-out treatment plant.

"Thanks. I would love that."

IV

SADOON WAS WAITING by his sad little car in the parking lot. He was small and muscular, with the look of a hunted animal. The shadow of a mustache marked him as someone who had prospered under Saddam. Lee greeted him with relief. Perhaps Sadoon knew some of the men in the resistance. He could have access to information.

"Where are you from, Sadoon?" she asked as they maneuvered through the barricades into the Baghdad streets.

"Fallujah." He looked at her for a reaction but could only see her dark glasses and slim face framed by her black *abaya*.

"Oh."

Fallujah was regarded as the most dangerous place in Iraq for Americans. Fallujans even spoke a dialect that few Arabic speakers beyond the town could understand.

"You've been there?" Sadoon was squinting in the rear view mirror.

"No."

"Are you a journalist?"

"I'm a doctor."

"Good. We need doctors, *Wallahi*." Sadoon scowled. "Journalists only tell lies and smuggle carpets."

Lee checked to see that her hair, nearly dark enough to pass for an Iraqi's, was hidden beneath her veil. She was tempted to dye it black. As it was, she could pass for a descendant of the Ottoman rulers and their pale Circassian wives. Settling into the lumpy back seat of the clapped out car, she was happy to be free of the convoy and the Patriots. Sadoon could negotiate the hazards of Baghdad's streets without anyone looking too carefully at his passenger. She would not be mistaken for a member of the Coalition Provisional Authority. CPA staff would never venture out in a battered car. They preferred to travel in armored personnel carriers. Everyone in Baghdad carried a weapon in the glove compartment or under the seat. The ordinary household arsenal included an AK-47. There were no policemen to enforce the law and no law to enforce. The anarchy made Lee feel like a child at a funhouse, spinning in the barrel and sticking to the wall when the floor dropped out.

"Where would you like to go, doctor?"

"Omar Hospital and then the Dar Kebeer."

Two undernourished Iraqis in stolen uniforms were attempting to direct traffic in exchange for tips. Sadoon lurched the car onto the sidewalk and dropped down onto a back street. He studied the bullet-scarred landscape, watching every doorway and parked car for a possible ambush.

"We have to be careful here."

He said the American forces in their gunships ignored the robbery and gang warfare that had spread through central Baghdad since "regime change." They said it was not their mission.

"Sadoon, put my Thuraya on the dashboard, will you? I think I can get satellite reception there. Have you got any music?"

"Yes. Do you like hip-hop? It's from al-Jazair."

"What about Iraqi music?"

"The *oud?* The soul of Iraq. The Wahhabis are smashing them now. They say the music is *haram.*"

"What does it sound like?"

"I don't know the word." He shoved in a cassette and Lee heard what sounded like a lute. Its tone was mournful like Segovia, and given the ancient ties of Baghdad and al-Andalus, the roots were the same.

Sadoon turned abruptly to the left and stopped.

"Uday's palace. Do you want a tour?"

"Not now Sadoon. *Shoukran.*"

Sadoon had driven just inside the entrance of a bombed-out faux Roman villa, its fluted marble columns holding nothing but air. Uday Saddam Hussein was Saddam's eldest son. Lee had seen his picture as a disfigured corpse after a gun battle in Mosul.

"Uday," said Sadoon with a mixture of reverence and pity, "was Mr. 50 Percent."

The president's dead son had cornered the chicken market, so that the price rose to $39 when Iraqi civil servants earned $150 a month. He also cornered the penicillin market and the polio vaccine market. He took a 50 percent cut on every deal.

Saddam's younger son, Qusay, had run the Security Services. In the execution chamber at Abu Ghraib, Lee had heard, there was a noose, a thick one, to draw out the agony of suffocation. Below the trap door, down a short set of steps, there was a gas chamber to complete the operation. But before reaching the gas chamber, victims were cut open, while still alive, to remove their organs.

"Let's go to the hospital, Sadoon." Lee wondered whether any of the doctors at Omar had assisted in harvesting organs at Abu Ghraib.

Omar Hospital was a squat white building with peeling paint, shaded by purple jacarandas. An old tile mural of Saddam dressed as a surgeon, brandishing his stethoscope, marked the entrance. The tiled face had a large shell hole in the forehead. Inside, the stained cement walls were lined with wooden benches crowded with patients. A man with bloody gauze stuck to his eye held the hand of a child with shrapnel in his buttocks. Flies had settled on everyone, probing the open wounds. Lee turned to find a quiet spot in the courtyard where she could call Naji Qais on her Thuraya.

"Lee." Dr. Qais had spotted her from the hallway.

"Naji." Lee's friend was well over 6 feet, with wire-rimmed glasses and dark hair going prematurely gray. He had lost at least 10 pounds since she had seen him last, and the faint lines in his forehead and the crevasses that formed a parenthesis on either side of his mouth had grown deeper.

"Come this way." He led Lee past the families camped out on the bare floor. He touched her veil. "You can wear that for next Halloween. My office is primitive but private."

"Thanks, Naji. I am so happy to see you."

"Sit down. Sit down. I will order some tea." His office had a '50s-era sofa covered in pink flamingos, and a Rolling Stones poster taped to the wall. His desk was piled high with papers, and his computer had a screen saver of a giant lobster from the Baltimore aquarium.

"I saw Mohammed, your driver, this morning. He will be fine in a couple of weeks."

"Thanks so much for looking after him. We had a bad night."

"Yes. You're lucky to be here. Do you take sugar?"

"Today I will."

"Are you still a vegetarian?"

"You have a good memory."

Naji returned with a cracked teapot, cups with mismatched saucers, and a plate of English biscuits.

"We're not very glamorous here."

"Naji, please tell me if you have to get back to the pit."

"I have someone who will cover for me. So, Lee, is it true the Surgeons' Committee might join us at Omar Hospital? We would be very honored, and frankly, we're desperate for help."

"I've proposed it and so far the response is good. If you'll let me observe for a few days while I'm here, I can give New York a better idea of what we can do. You can imagine how concerned they are with security."

"Well, I'm not going to let you observe when we have this many patients. I will put you to work."

"Okay, Naji." Lee laughed. "Fair enough." She sipped the sweet tea. "You should know I am also here to find my friend Martin Carrigan."

"That's a good way to get yourself killed."

"I just need to satisfy myself that the Green Zone people are really looking for him. I need to talk with them myself."

"Lee, don't get ideas about finding him yourself. You're smart and courageous, but you're no match for people who will kill you for a pack of cigarettes. Things are very unsettled here. Promise me that you will tell me where you are going and who you plan to meet."

"Of course, Naji. Is your family all right?"

"My grandparents have left for Amman. My parents are trying to get them visas for the U.S., but no one is being allowed in. My sister is in Sulaymaniyah, working with the refugees there. There is no reason to stay here now. Soon the only people left will be the ones who can't get out. They are queuing up to die."

"What about you?"

"I am here for the duration. We have a human catastrophe on our hands."

"Is the power shortage causing problems?"

"I have bought or stolen every generator I can get my hands on. They break down constantly. The medicine is spoiling. The incubators go on the blink. We really need your help."

"I will do everything I can, Naji. I will be at the Dar Kebeer. As soon as I have made my inquiries about Martin, I will be back."

"Lee, listen to me. We are old friends. This is your first time here. Security is bad, and it's getting worse. Frankly, you shouldn't be here at all. If Martin has been kidnapped and you go after his kidnappers, they will be happy to kidnap you, too. In fact, you are worth much more than he is."

"I'll be fine, Naji."

"I want you to spend as much time as possible right here where I can keep an eye on you. People must understand that you are really a doctor and not a spy."

"What do you mean?"

"If someone thinks you are a spy, they will kill you without a second thought. A foreign woman traveling alone is suspicious. If you are traveling around looking for Martin, at least team up with journalists who know something."

"I will. Naji, I lived in Afghanistan."

"Iraq is more complicated. Believe me, I know."

"Naji. Do you have buzzards here?"

"Yes, we have them. Steppe buzzards and long-legged buzzards. But not enough for all of the dead."

It was late morning when Lee spotted the tower of the Dar Kebeer Hotel.

"*Funduk.*" Sadoon gestured toward her destination. "Your hotel."

The Dar was down a side alley blocked by a maze of barriers and guards with automatic weapons.

"I'll walk from here, Sadoon. Pick me up after lunch, will you? I want to go to the Green Zone. The entrance at the Assassin's Gate."

"Of course. I will be here."

Lee grabbed her bags and said a few polite words to the guards so they would recognize her face and be less likely to shoot her when she returned late at night. At the top of the hotel steps, two more guards flanked the doorway. Behind them was a jewelry shop selling tarnished silver and watches with Saddam's face staring out from between the hands. In the dim hallway beyond, she could make out the front desk on the left and a billboard advertising a Chinese restaurant with a piano bar.

"Welcome, Dr. Lee. My name is Ali. *Sabah al-khair.* A great pleasure to meet you. From now on, I hope you will call the Dar your home away from home." Ali was small and servile. Lee thought he was probably drawing paychecks from several governments.

"*Sabah al-noor,* the pleasure is mine." Lee's command of Arabic was slight, but she was determined to use what she knew.

"Ah, you speak Arabic."

"*Kalilan.* Just a little."

"Most of the journalists here barely speak their native English." The servility had vanished for a moment. "You have a suite in the new wing with a very nice kitchenette. Very nice. You can have Turkish coffee there and, if you want, have some friends over. We can bring you dinner, music, whatever you like. Don't forget the curfew, Dr. Lee. Anyone in the street gets shot after 10 p.m. If you don't mind," the desk clerk added under his breath, "please keep your curtains drawn. I am so sorry, but with the situation, you understand, we have to be careful. It's such a pity to block the beautiful view of Baghdad. Really a pity. But the situation is improving. We think every other hotel in Baghdad will be bombed before the Dar Kebeer. The resistance knows the foreigners here are friends of the Iraqi people. And now a great doctor to help them. Do you need a wake-up call?"

"At two this afternoon. Though I doubt I will need it with this noise."

She could hear bursts of automatic weapons fire coming from different directions in the neighborhood and the steady "whop whop" of helicopter gunships thundering overhead.

They must be looking for someone, she thought, as she walked through the glass doors into an interior courtyard. There were several empty tables on a raised terrace overlooking the pool. She scanned the high wall enclosing the grounds and noted that above the broken glass and barbed wire on the parapet that served as hotel defenses, there were two shabby apartment blocks with balconies that could easily accommodate snipers. She would swim at night.

The journalists were out at this time of day and the foreign doctors and aid workers had been evacuated. In a lounge chair next to the water's edge, she saw a man with a shaved head and torso glistening with tattoos. She wondered whether he was a mercenary for hire.

Her "suite" was decorated in various shades of brown burlap with a cheap shag carpet and Formica tabletop. There was an antique television that provided "BBC World News" updates every hour, and two small bedrooms facing the unprotected street below, where a mob of children was jumping on an old tire. Lee calculated that the blast from a bomb in that street would kill her instantly. She lay down on the bed on the side furthest from the window, as though that would do any good. Before she could kick off her shoes, the power cut out. She waited for the sputtering sound of the generator and fell into a dreamless sleep.

When she awoke in the twilight of the shuttered room, she had no idea where she was. It took several seconds before she could focus on the grating ring of the telephone. She nearly broke her toe on the bedpost as she ran to answer it.

"Dr. McGuinness?"

"Yes, who is this?"

"My name is Hamdoon. You don't know me."

"How can I help you?"

"I have a message from Mr. Carrigan."

"What?"

"He wants you to know that there is no need to look for him. He is very sorry but he is doing some work up north and has no time to see you. He says you should go home."

"Who are you, Mr. Hamdoon?"

"A friend."

"Tell Mr. Carrigan I want to speak with him."

"I don't think that will be possible."

"Where are you? Can we meet?"

"It is not safe for you here." The line went dead. Lee felt an electrical current of fear and confusion rush through her. Who the hell was that? She stared at the phone and then plunged her face under the cold tap. The phone rang again. She grabbed it with wet hands. "Hamdoon?"

"No, Dr. Lee. It's Ali. Your wake-up call. Welcome to Baghdad.

V

B Y THE TIME Lee and Sadoon crossed the Jumhuriya Bridge, it was rush hour. Sadoon's old compact entered the Karradat Mariam district and descended onto al-Saheer. Lee could see the gutted shell of the al-Sinak telecommunications building and the flattened remains of a shopping center. They inched along al-Saheer toward a hive of soldiers and barricades at the foot of the monumental stone arch known as the Assassins' Gate, where Baghdad ended and the Green Zone, the American enclave that covered miles of the central city, began. Foreigners called it Oz.

Sadoon was not allowed to park anywhere near the gate. When Lee stepped out of the car, Sadoon was waved away by the soldiers. As an Iraqi, he was automatically under suspicion. Lee joined the line to enter the zone, standing beside massive coils of concertina wire with the other supplicants. Here, just waiting in line was an act of courage. She was exposed to the wide boulevard and thus was an easy mark for a passing sniper or suicide bomber. Americans without Green Zone credentials were corralled with the local janitors, cooks, and drivers employed inside the zone. In the eyes of the resistance, these Iraqis were collaborators, a label that carried a death sentence. Lee hoped that no one was planning to execute one of them in the next 10 minutes.

"May I help you, ma'am?" The Army 1st Division private manning the guard post looked at her as though she had taken the wrong subway. To Lee, It sounded like "maaaaam." The soldier sort of sang it, with a sustained C and then a rising inflection through an E-flat to a G.

Deep South.

"I'm Dr. McGuinness. I have a meeting with George Plumber."

Plumber was not officially at the top of the Coalition Provisional Authority's organization chart, but he was the man who held sway in the Pentagon. Col. Frank, in their meeting at the Kennedy Airport bar, had been very clear about that. For public consumption, the occupation authority was civilian. Plumber was too close to the military, particularly military intelligence, to want his name printed every day in the papers.

"Credentials?"

She fished her International Surgeons' Committee ID out of her purse.

"Wait here, doctor."

"Is there anywhere a little more protected where I could wait?"

"You have to wait here. Those are the rules. No exceptions, ma'am."

The soldier casually dialed Plumber's office on a cell phone network reserved for the exclusive use of the occupation force. He was not in a rush.

"What was your name again?"

"Dr. McGuinness."

"Irish?"

"Yes."

Lee knew right away from the weary expressions on the faces of the Iraqis behind her that if she was treated with casual indifference, they were experiencing something exponentially worse. Lee pulled out her Thuraya and called Plumber's office herself, dialing the U.S. area code for the Green Zone. Just as it rang, she was hailed by an American civilian, with a buzz cut and Ray-Bans, driving a black Suburban.

"Jump in, Dr. McGuinness."

"Thanks."

"Your first time in Baghdad?"

"Yes."

"Are you enjoying Iraq?" The man had a plastic cord coming out of his collar, attached to an earpiece. He was muttering to someone.

"Very much, thank you."

They drove through the gate up the long allée of date palms to a Deco stone palace the color of sand. The palace was crowned with four massive sculpted heads of Saddam Hussein wearing a pith helmet. Lee stared at the handsome and ridiculous heads, wondering why they had not been dynamited. The escort parked the Suburban in a lot that was packed with shiny new cars and Humvees, and directed her to an outdoor table under the canopy of an ancient bougainvillea. Security officers demanded her passport. She pulled out the American passport this time. In the foyer, under a massive dome copied from the Pantheon, she caught sight of the trim figure of a man she had known years before and had hoped to forget. He wore a button-down shirt and khakis and was unmistakably bearing down on her. Carlton Camp, who she had last heard was working for one of the wildlife cable channels, had been in her class at Yale.

"Hello, Lee. Sorry about the confusion at the gate." He offered his hand. "Everything is a little chaotic around here."

"Not a problem, Carlton. What a coincidence that we should both be here." She had always disliked him. He had worn a bow tie to class and cheated at croquet at the Lizzie. "Are you doing an animal series in Iraq?" Lee hoped to spoil his day.

"No. That's all in the past. I'm with the government now."

"Doing what?"

"Outreach."

"Outreach with whom?"

"The press. Congress."

"Is that like propaganda?"

"Well, that would be a crude way of putting it." Carlton was frowning. "I saw your name on the appointments calendar. So it's Dr. McGuinness now."

"That's right."

"Where did you go to med school?"

"Harvard."

"Trading with the enemy." He smiled a knowing little smile.

"Yup."

"Plumber is finishing up a meeting. Let me show you around."

They walked down a hall crowded with soldiers, contractors, and government staff who inhabited the zone. The notice board to the right of the "mess" advertised a comedian from the Starlight Club in Reno. The sign at the entrance read:

No Weapons Allowed! Pistols Only!

Inside, 300 Americans consumed buckwheat pancakes, chipped beef, and hash browns.

"I want to show you the throne room," Carlton said, pleased with himself, pleased with his proximity to power. "Sit on the throne and I'll take your picture."

Saddam's garish throne stood under a brightly colored mural of Scud missiles.

"Thanks, Carlton. Not today."

"That room over there is where Saddam shot his cabinet minister. Wait 'til you see outside. This is Uday's pool." Carlton cut a trail through army officers and contractors, drying off on lounge chairs after their morning dip. "Pool parties every Saturday night. And this is where I live." In the date groves, beyond the pool, was a trailer park.

They re-entered the palace, passing a sign that read, "We love the Army! Thank you for fighting!" The Green Zone was a land of exclamation marks. Carlton stopped in a sitting room with gold-fringed damask furniture in such bad taste that it could have only been chosen by a decorator from Saddam's hometown of Tikrit.

"Have a seat, Lee." He laughed a dry stiff laugh that he had probably picked up from one of his Washington clubs. "What are the chances that we should both end up here?"

"Yes. What are they?" She let a silence hang in the air.

"Well, the food's good. We fly in everything, including the water."

"Do you get out much?"

"How do you mean?"

"Outside the gates?"

"Oh, the Red Zone. Not much. It's pretty dicey out there. We take R & R in Amman or Kuwait City."

"I'm staying at the Dar Kebeer."

"You always took risks. Didn't you sleep in the graveyard one night in New Haven? On a dare?"

"Yes."

"That's pretty wild, Lee. I remember while the rest of us were drinking at Mory's and camping in the stacks, you went off to live in a village in Africa where no one had ever seen a white person and people were dying of bilharzia."

"Mm hmm."

"You're going to love Baghdad. Listen, if I can help you in any way while you're here…" He handed her his card. "I understand you're a friend of Carrigan's."

"That's right."

"I'm going to let George Plumber tell you what we know. He should be here any minute. Can I offer you a soda or Turkish coffee?"

"Turkish, please."

"How do you like it?"

"Medium sweet."

Carlton strode off to grab a waiter, cell phone to his ear. For some reason, the waiter was wearing a jeweled turban.

Lee sat quietly, like an anthropologist observing Green Zone life. Staffers, fresh from small Christian colleges and internships on the Hill, rushed through the palace halls, wearing headbands and espadrilles, loaded down with briefs and charts, administering a country they had never seen outside the compound walls. She wondered when the last helicopter would lift off from the palace roof and whether Carlton would take the throne with him. She heard a sound, a kind of low bass rumble that penetrated her stomach and that she instantly recognized as a bomb. It was a sound that unfolded over several seconds as the blast's shock waves rolled down the streets and alleyways of Baghdad. She stood up. No one in the halls seemed the least bit concerned. Perhaps it was just the heavy rumble of an M1 tank. Either that, or people here were confident that the bombers in the Red Zone would never come over the walls.

She had been sitting for several minutes when the cadaverous figure of George Plumber filled the doorway. Plumber was 6-foot-5 with bleached blue eyes and pockmarked skin. He wore old khakis and a blazer, a studied grayness favored by men in Washington.

"Sorry to keep you, doctor." He sat down opposite Lee.

"That's quite all right. I appreciate your taking the time." She wasn't sure how to begin. "Mr. Plumber, I've asked for this meeting because Martin Carrigan is missing."

"Yes, of course."

"Martin is a close friend of mine. I'm told you knew his father."

"Yes, we were both posted in London." He said it with so little emotion that Lee could not tell whether Plumber and Martin's father had been friends or enemies.

"You know the International Surgeons' Committee has moved out for security reasons. I'm exploring ways to bring them back. And I'm hoping to learn as much as I can about Martin while I'm here."

"We're doing everything we can to find your friend. This is a very difficult time." His tone was even and indecipherable.

"I was hoping to hear any news you have so far."

Plumber turned stiffly toward Camp.

"Get Dick McCleary in here, will you?"

He retrained his gaze on Lee. His eyes had lost all color and were now gray like his clothes. The effect, Lee thought, was like watching an early TV set with a blown-out color tube.

"Dick has been working on this." Plumber's cell phone rang and he took the call, listening with an occasional grunt of assent, and waited until McCleary entered the room.

McCleary had dark rings under his eyes and lips that curled slightly on the right side in a look of permanent disdain.

"Tell me, Dr. McGuinness, do you know what Martin Carrigan was doing here?" Plumber broke his silence.

"Refugee work. Blueprints for the exodus of civilians if this war continues." She was impatient at having to state the obvious.

"That's what Carrigan told us. When he arrived last spring, he came straight here, to this very room, to get our cooperation. But we've since discovered he's doing some pretty odd things to help poor refugees." A tiny ball of spit rolled around between Plumber's dry lips.

"What kind of things?"

"Training a militia." Plumber gathered up the spit with his tongue and swallowed it.

"Importing weapons," Dick McCleary finished the indictment.

"You're joking," Lee laughed awkwardly. She felt she had taken a wrong turn somewhere. First Carlton. Now this. No one else stirred. "Martin is a humanitarian." She gathered her thoughts. "He is not an arms dealer. And he is certainly not a mercenary. There's obviously been a mistake."

"Apparently he's branching out," McCleary said caustically. He unwrapped a piece of nicotine gum and began chewing it loudly.

Lee was developing an intense dislike for McCleary.

"What makes you think that?"

"We've found his name on invoices and documents captured in an enemy combatant's house in Karbala."

"Karbala? Isn't that in the south? I thought the resistance was in the west and the north, the Sunni triangle?"

"We're having a few problems in the south, too," Plumber said quietly. "The odd troublemaker in the Shia community who is not with us."

"May I see the invoices?" She tried to remain collected and reminded herself that her aim was to leave the palace with something, anything, to work with, even if it was a false lead.

"I'm afraid not," McCleary said with evident pleasure. "Classified."

"The enemy prisoner, is he in jail somewhere that I can request permission to see him?"

"You'll have to go through channels at the 800th MP Brigade for that. Check with Col. Darling."

"May I have the prisoner's name?"

"I'm afraid we can't give you that, doctor." Plumber cut her off. "As much as I would like to."

"Do you know when Martin was last seen?" Lee concentrated on whatever thread she could follow.

"He had a meeting 10 days ago at the Tigris Hotel, where he was staying."

"With?"

"One of Adnan Jabarri's men."

She knew the name Jabarri, one of the Iraqis handpicked by Plumber and his colleagues to take over a "friendly" Iraq. Jabarri was also a prominent smuggler, wanted by several governments in the Middle East for illegal shipments of cigarettes and hashish. There was a warrant out for his arrest for tax evasion in the Emirates, where he had fled Sharjah dressed as a woman, wrapped in an *abaya* with *niqab*.

"Did Martin check out of the Tigris Hotel?"

"No, he still has his room." Plumber spoke slowly. "Though the hotel was bombed about 15 minutes ago. Now that's a coincidence, that we should be talking about the Tigris Hotel."

Lee said nothing.

"Minor damage. A few locals killed." Plumber dismissed the dead with a flick of his long fingers, with skin that made Lee think of a snake ready to shed. "None of our people. The situation here just keeps improving. We've got things pretty much under control, Dr. McGuinness. The Saddam dead-enders are running out of steam. We are close to making a deal with the Shia. Baghdad is safer every day. Services are on the mend. Everyday there is a new school or clinic. I'd like to take you on a tour of our clinics. You would be proud. Iraqis are so grateful for what we have done. We've got an emerging democracy here. A real success story. It's the press who paint a very distorted picture. Dr. McGuinness, this is not Saigon or Mogadishu."

Lee knew from Col. Frank that Plumber had been in both. He had also offered his services to the oil company that had flown the Taliban leadership to Sugarland, Texas, to make a pipeline deal, at a time when the Taliban were beating women with sticks for wearing the wrong shoes.

"Mr. Plumber..." Lee steadied herself. "Are you telling me that Martin Carrigan is working with the insurgency? Why would he do that?"

"Greed, maybe. Politics. It's hard to say why people turn. I believe Mr. Carrigan may sympathize with their cause. The underdog. The occupied. The victims of aggression. He's Irish, after all." Lee bridled. "He's made a bad mistake, doctor. I would like to help him, but the longer he refuses to cooperate with us, the more likely it is the consequences will be severe. Perhaps you can change his mind. You might save his life. Well, I'm afraid we all have to go," Plumber stood up. McCleary and Carlton Camp followed smartly. "Keep in touch. You have our numbers. And if you find your friend Carrigan, don't forget he's a fugitive. Wanted for crimes against the coalition."

"What's that?" Lee asked, beginning to feel sick for the second time that day.

"Treason."

Before Lee could react, Plumber added, "You don't want to be an accessory to treason." The meeting was over. He turned away, but then turned back.

"I believe you grew up in Africa."

Lee looked at him with alarm. "When I was very young."

Plumber nodded. "Please give my regards to your parents."

* * *

They left her with the humorless escort to collect her passport and make her way out of the Green Zone.

"Have a nice day." The escort dropped her just inside the gate.

Lee walked alone back to the war.

VI

THERE WAS A PUNGENT SMELL of modern life on fire: synthetic carpets, plastic lobby chairs, fake leather briefcases, and rubber tires from burning SUVs. The black funnel of smoke from the Tigris Hotel hung thickly over Baghdad. Lee stood by the razor wire, hailing Sadoon from across the traffic. He executed a U-turn at suicidal speed. She wondered what else the Republican Guard had trained him to do.

"The Tigris, Sadoon." She leapt into the car.

"The road is blocked."

"Just get as close as you can. I'll go on foot from there." She had hoped that Plumber would offer her security, lend a helicopter, open his files. Instead, he had stripped her of protection. Martin was a hunted man, a terrorist. Lee wondered whether any of it could be true. Her dislike for Plumber was tempered by his last words. He knew her parents. They had all served in government, a long time ago. Perhaps some residual loyalty to them had made him want to warn her not to be naïve. Perhaps he thought she could be recruited to help persuade Martin to cut ties with whatever faction he had fallen in with. Who else would want to touch this now? The word "treason" was enough to scare away the aid community and State Department, anyone who should have been demanding that Plumber and his Green Zone friends track him down. Her jet lag was coming back in waves, sabotaging her efforts to absorb the information she had just heard. Her brain kept shutting down.

"This is as far as we can go." Sadoon had stopped at a roadblock where the barrel of a tank was trained on the car. Lee groped for her ID and forced herself into the street. The pavement was strewn with bits of metal and dollar bills. She saw a severed foot still wearing a penny loafer. That is not a local foot, she thought. She was filled with dread at the possibility of finding some part of Martin, a hand or a piece of scalp, something that she would recognize. A palm tree in front of the hotel was hung with little clumps of red flesh like Christmas ornaments. One of the soldiers manning the barrier checked her ICS pass and waved her through. There were camera men swarming through the wreckage. The man in the safari jacket from the Aleem had planted himself between a camera and the mess in the street. Lee watched him comb his hair and check the shine on his nose in a compact mirror before dabbing on some powder. She picked her way through hot fenders and broken glass to the yawning hole that had been the Tigris Hotel lobby. There was an electric razor on the floor next to an upturned room service tray and an abandoned satellite phone that started to ring.

She kept telling herself that Martin was not here. The reception desk was too hot to touch. Hotel guests, who had lost pieces of clothing or were soaked in blood, wandered through the scattered body parts looking for their glasses and wallets. An American contractor, whose shredded arm was hanging from a string of scorched muscle, asked Lee for help to find a medic. It was not the time to question anyone about Martin.

"I can help you," she told the man and ran to Sadoon's car to collect her backpack. She returned to find the contractor faint and disoriented from loss of blood. Her own confusion, brought on by Plumber, began to recede. She needed to concentrate now. She knew exactly what to do. The contractor's axillary artery was gushing, and his hand had already gone white and hypoxic, starved of oxygen.

"Try to relax." Lee told him. "You're going to need surgery, but I'm just going to wrap you up a little bit to slow the hemorrhaging. I'm going to give you something to dull the pain."

"I shouldn't have come here."

"Everything will be fine."

"No, I shouldn't have. I needed money."

"Just sit quietly for a little while until we can get you to the hospital." She gave the contractor a shot of morphine and clamped the artery. He would lose his arm. It was better than bleeding to death.

"I never want to see this place again."

"They will medevac you out."

Lee tended to three more of the injured, dressing shrapnel wounds and clamping another artery below the knee on a mangled leg. The smoke stung her eyes. Someone photographed her working. She could hear the motor drive. After ambulances arrived and the wounded had been loaded up or bandaged, she retreated to the car and realized how much she wanted a drink.

"Let's go to the Dar, Sadoon."

"Yes, Dr. Lee."

"Why did they hit the Tigris Hotel?"

"The CIA people stay there."

"Does everyone know that?"

"Of course."

In the fading afternoon light, she watched Sadoon in the rear view mirror. He was smiling, though Lee could not think why, given the dismal scene they had just left. She had an uneasy feeling that the resistance was everywhere in Baghdad, like an undertow ready to drag the occupiers down. She remembered the stories from Saigon of the faithful Vietnamese in the news bureaus, the embassies, and the hospitals who turned out to be senior cadre of the Viet Cong.

"You helped people today, *tabiba*. Iraq is fortunate to have you here."

"Thanks, Sadoon. Listen, I want to go to Karbala tomorrow. We may be there for a couple of days. Can you manage it?"

"Yes. I will tell my wife."

"I will pay an out-of-town rate."

"Yes, of course, Dr. Lee. Whatever you want. Are we going for the festival?"

"What festival?"

"The birthday of the 12th Imam."

She would look up the 12th Imam at the Dar Kebeer. "How many people are expected?"

"Two or 3 million. They have already started walking to Karbala from all over Iraq. Even from Iran and Kuwait. We have to start very early."

"Come at 6:30. I need to make one stop in Mansour on the way. Do you know the al-Bahari house?"

"The date grove?"

"Yes."

"I know it."

By the time she climbed the steps to the Dar Kebeer Hotel, it was dark, and the colony of journalists and soldiers of fortune living there had settled in for the night. The tables around the pool were overflowing with bodies and ashtrays. She smelled olives, sweat, and juniper from the spilled gin. Lee thought she recognized some of the faces in the candlelight from the guesthouses on Passport Street in Kabul. A group of middle-aged Germans looked familiar. There was a long table filled with Americans who had drunk too much and were making expensive wagers on what the insurgents would target next. Two Italian journalists complained to the waiter about the mysterious meat that passed for steak and tasted more like horse. A man roughly her age, English from his complexion, stopped her progress across the terrace. He was tall and lean, with a well-cut black jacket. His face was perfectly symmetrical, with gray eyes framed by heavy lashes that reminded her of sable. She knew they had met before.

"Hello, Dr. McGuinness." He seemed forward and reticent at the same time. "I'm Duncan Hope."

"Did we meet in Kabul?"

"We had dinner together at the Elbow Room. I write for the London *Herald*."

"Oh yes, Duncan, of course. You were with that U.N. fellow. The one caught in the brothel. What ever happened to him?"

"Last I heard he was in Haiti." Duncan offered her his chair and pushed away a jumble of bottles and Arabic salads. She was not his first guest.

"You looked different then." Lee was tired. "Did you have a beard?"

"Yes. It was my Taliban period. Thankfully, that's over for the moment."

Lee smelled the smoke from the Tigris in her clothes. She wished she could have changed her shirt, sprayed with a fine mist of blood when she applied the clamps. Her body felt heavy, the way she felt as a child by the sea when her sister buried her in the sand.

"May I offer you a drink?"

"White wine, please." The waiter was hovering, a holdover from the days when that job held the extra promise of a police informer's tips.

"Gin and tonic, Jamal, and a white wine for the doctor. Take it from my box, the one from the Bekaa. *Shoukran.*"

"Your own cellar?" Lee was impressed.

"Most of what you get here is such plonk you have to make arrangements." Duncan lit an Indian *beedi* and a faint smell of cloves drifted between them. "So, what brings you to Baghdad, doctor? It can't be a new clinic, because all of them have been looted and resold by the contractors."

"I'm here to see whether it might be time for the Surgeons' Committee to come back."

"Do you see that table of Americans? Their hotel was just bombed. They are the Dar's newest refugees. I'm not sure that I would bring anyone back."

"I was there, after the bombing."

"At the Tigris?"

"I went to check up on an old friend and ended up treating the wounded. I apologize for my appearance."

"No need for that. I'm sorry, I thought you might have come to Baghdad to find Martin Carrigan."

Lee sat up straight. "Why would you think that?"

"I remember seeing you two together in Kabul."

"Of course." She had the uncomfortable feeling that he was looking for a story and she was becoming part of it.

"It's a nasty business, this kidnapping racket. The CPA is buttoned up on the whole thing. Not a hint of a leak. There are 20 different groups who might be holding him."

Lee said nothing. Her thoughts darted back to Plumber and what his next move might be, as Duncan speculated on kidnappers in Samarra and Fallujah. Her friend Naji had warned that she needed allies in the press, people who could help her avoid making mistakes. Yet her instinct was to wait to confide in Duncan until she had found some small piece of evidence that the charges were false. "Treason" splashed across a headline would condemn Martin before she had even begun.

"I had a rough time coming in from the border this morning."

"Bandits?"

"Ex-bandits."

"How did they become ex?" Duncan asked casually.

"Patriots."

"Bloody Patriots will get us all killed."

"So it wasn't the first time?"

"Sadly not. A lot of things go unreported here."

She noticed two soldiers in unfamiliar camouflage sitting against the wall, burdened with so much combat gear she thought they would drown if they fell into the pool, the way soldiers landing on the Normandy beaches died in the surf before anyone could shoot them. There was a sharp report of automatic weapons fire just over the wall that echoed around the courtyard.

"That's the Viceroy's fault." Duncan filled Lee's glass.

"Viceroy?" Lee drank deeply.

"One of our illustrious occupation leaders was here this afternoon, dining at the Chinese restaurant. He arrived with two tanks, four armored personnel carriers, a dozen body-guards, and two helicopters. Now the resistance will associate us more closely with the occupation and bomb us. It's his idea of a good joke."

When the second bottle arrived, Lee had forgotten what a bad day it had been.

Duncan lifted his gin. "To the Rapture. *There before me was a white horse, whose rider is called Faithful and True. With justice he judges and wages war.*"

"When do you find time to read the Book of Revelation?"

"Every British school boy goes to chapel."

"There will be plenty of parking places for those of us left behind." She drained her glass.

"Americans are so practical." Duncan looked at her with appreciation. "Do people in the States still believe in this war?"

"Some of them. If our troops are here, it must be the right thing."

"How marvelous to be always right."

"Just like the British. Ladysmith. Ghazni. Kut. Every war, always right."

"You take an interest in British history."

"We could start with the Easter Rising."

"I gather your people were on the other side."

"The Irish are always right, too."

"Which way are you headed tomorrow?"

Lee hesitated. "South to Karbala."

"That's a long way from the kidnappers."

"I want to have a look at the hospital. The Surgeons' Committee is thinking of sending a pediatric orthopedic surgeon there." It had the ring of truth. Lee told herself this little deception was necessary to protect Martin.

"May I join you?" Perhaps her real purpose was completely transparent.

"Of course."

"I'm doing a story on Abbas al-Kufa. I want to see if his people show up at the imam's birthday."

"Who is he?"

Duncan explained that al-Kufa was the rising star of a radical faction of the Shia Muslims, who openly challenged the occupation. As U.S. troops rolled up from the south and Saddam's enforcers fled, several Shia leaders had been murdered in the vacuum of power. Al-Kufa's people were responsible for at least one of the killings. As the wolves tore apart the carcass of Saddam's Iraq, al-Kufa hoped to devour his competition.

"They're expecting trouble down there," Duncan said languidly.

"What sort of trouble?" Lee asked, already numb from the day's events.

"It's not clear. Bombs. That sort of thing."

"Duncan, does the name Hamdoon sound familiar?"

"Hamdoon. No, why?"

"He called me today and claimed to be the friend of Martin Carrigan's. I just thought his name might ring a bell."

"Afraid not. Have you talked to our rulers over in Oz about him? Maybe they'll open up for you."

"I was there this afternoon."

"And?"

"They didn't say much." She poured herself another glass. "What do you know about George Plumber, Duncan?"

"Shall we order some *mezze?*"

Over *babaghanoush, tashi,* and *fattoush,* Duncan told Lee that Plumber was not someone she wanted to tangle with. He was a veteran of every covert operation since the Phoenix program in Vietnam. He had a vicious streak. When he was recruiting *mujahedeen* in the '70s to fight the Russians in Afghanistan, he chose a fanatic who liked to throw acid in women's faces. In Central America, he built death squads that slaughtered priests.

He offered her some pita. "He rarely speaks to journalists. He flies under the radar here. Plumber has power, unquestionably. It's just hard to see what he is doing with it. The CPA, on the surface, is a very weird outfit. Please share this *bamia* with me, Lee. It's too much."

"What do you mean by 'weird'?"

"The Green Zone is a fantasyland. The inmates waste countless hours discussing things like setting up the Baghdad stock market. Twenty-six-year-olds gorge themselves on sex and tequila and forge so many phony overtime hours they can make $40,000 a month. The second floor of the Singapore Sling is a whorehouse staffed with desperate Iraqi girls known as the Muj Hookers. They turn tricks for $10." Duncan ordered more gin and lit another beedi. "At the Lotus Café you can smoke hookahs till 5 a.m. Everyone has a gun. The guy who fixes the photocopy machine has a .45. To what end?"

"What do you think Martin thought of all that?"

Duncan exhaled slowly so that the smoke danced above the votives. "I would say, fairly critical."

"Had he made enemies there?"

"I don't know, why?"

Lee shrugged. "I'm just trying to get a sense of what's going on."

"I'm afraid what's happened to Martin is all too obvious. He was picked up by thugs. Unless, of course, he has gone over to the dark side."

"The dark side?"

"There has been a lot of intelligence activity in the aid business lately, spies posing as aid workers. That could get him in trouble."

"Martin is not posing as anything. He's absolutely committed to his work."

"I was just playing devil's advocate." Duncan drank down his gin. "I'm not sure that I really know anyone anymore."

"What does that mean?"

"Give it a few days."

A long burst of weapons fire brought them back to the war.

Lee rose from the table, her slim frame casting a long shadow from the terrace spotlight. "I'm so tired I can probably sleep through this."

"Lee. I'm sorry if I seemed intrusive about you and Martin. I think I'm actually jealous that you would come all this way to find him."

"We went through a lot together in Afghanistan."

"I lost my wife there not long ago. Just across the border."

"I'm so sorry, Duncan." Lee sat down again. "What happened?"

"She died at Greens Hotel in Peshawar. Eighteen months ago. It was heroin, 100 rupees a gram. She was smoking it, chasing the dragon, as they say, and then she chose to inject it."

"God, how awful. I remember hearing about it in Kabul. A photojournalist, right? I had no idea she was your wife."

"I was the last to know that Sophie was an addict. She was very good at hiding things. I suppose that says a lot about our marriage."

"I'm sure you were both traveling so much."

"Yes, there were long periods apart. And, in spite of my profession, I'm not the most observant person in the world. You see what I mean about not really knowing anyone at all."

There was nothing Lee could say. She felt mean and small and slightly sick for withholding from Duncan what she had learned from Plumber. Still, she would wait. She would find a way to tell him in Karbala.

VII

LEE WOKE UP BEFORE DAWN in a fog of alcohol and Ambien. A helicopter droning outside her window was the first sound of the day, and she peered through the heavy plastic curtain to see a city in darkness. The power was out. She lit a candle by the bed and forced herself to dress. There was little to do but make strong Turkish coffee so that she could think.

She was 5 feet 7 inches tall and had to bend down to see herself in the mirror. Whoever had hung it over the sink was very short, she thought, a traveling mirror-hanger from Sana'a. Arabia Felix. The land of frankincense and myrrh, the golden resin from thorn trees, genus *Commiphora*, extracted when the myrrh gatherers beat the tree, wounded it repeatedly, and let it bleed. Duncan was bleeding. And she? She had a hangover. *Veisalgia*, from the Norwegian *kveis*, uneasiness following debauchery, and the Greek *algia*, pain. By candlelight, her face resembled a thin slab of white marble. Her beauty was the kind that had been fashionable 500 years ago, when ladies whitened their skin with vinegar, chalk, and arsenic. When the arsenic finally ate holes in their skin, they filled the holes with lead. She needed sun. She lived in a world of neon light and rubbing alcohol. She could see the blue veins in her arms like tributaries of a river.

Lee thought about Plumber. After his savage assessment of Martin and veiled threats against her, she wondered whether his men were watching her now. She drank two bottles of water to rehydrate before she sipped her Turkish coffee and listened to the voice of the *muezzin* echoing across the city. Of course the mosques had generators.

Lee walked down three flights of steps in the black stairwell, lit only by the faint glow of her phone, and found her way to the pool's edge. She stood behind the diving board in an oleander bush in what was known as "Thuraya corner," the place with good satellite phone reception. She dialed New York and left a message at Martin's office. She told them that she believed that Martin was still alive. Lee made a second call to the Surgeons' Committee, to report that she had toured Omar Hospital and was planning another visit. She tried to sound optimistic. The dawn light brought heat and gunfire.

Duncan appeared at the far end of the pool heading for the front entrance, wearing another well-cut jacket and white shirt. Lee thought he probably dressed carefully to hide the fact that his world had fallen apart, that he was oozing myrrh. He carried a notebook under his arm along with a satchel of supplies.

Lee directed him to Sadoon's car.

"Sadoon, this is Duncan."

"*Sabah al-khair.*" Duncan's "good morning" was brisk.

"*Sabah al-noor.* You are British?"

"Yes."

"I have seen you before."

"That's very likely."

Lee smiled. "Do you smuggle carpets?"

"I beg your pardon?"

"Sadoon says all journalists tell lies and smuggle carpets," Lee said. The light was playing with her green eyes the way the sun falls on a pond.

"Only a few, in my case."

Duncan told her that he had bought an old shiraz at the auction house to celebrate his 34th birthday. In the morning light, he had blotches of color on his cheeks above a two-day stubble. It was easy to see him as an English schoolboy.

"Why did you become a journalist?"

"Better than working for a living." He told her that Oxford had led to journalism because it was the path of least resistance. His father wrote for *The Sunday Times*. There was a desk waiting for Duncan on Fleet Street the day he had received his First.

"My mother is an Arabist. Her field is art and archaeology of the Near East. It would be surprising, given my parents, if I hadn't ended up here."

The streets were deserted and the balmy wind coming off the Tigris brushed their faces with the scent of incense cedar. Driving down the leafy avenues past rows of faded shops, they were alert for the army patrols. When the patrols fired on civilians, their superior officers usually looked the other way. U.S. military rules of engagement allowed soldiers to fire on anyone who was not positively identified as "friendly."

"Who do you plan to see in Karbala?"

"I thought I would start at the hospital."

"May I make a suggestion?"

"Of course."

"There is a man I think you should see, Ali Husseini. He's a scientist but also someone very important in Karbala. If you want to accomplish anything there, arrangements with the hospital, supplies, whatever you need, he can make life much easier. If there is a trail to Martin Carrigan in Karbala, Ali Husseini will help you find it."

"What?"

"I assume that's why you're going. You don't strike me as the sort of person who would waste time going in the wrong direction."

Lee lapsed into silence. "I should have told you last night." She caught Sadoon's eye in the rear-view mirror. Her voice dropped to a murmur. "Later."

"Seriously, Lee, let me help you. You have to trust somebody here. It can't hurt talking to Ali Husseini."

Duncan told her he had known Ali Husseini ever since the scientist escaped from Abu Ghraib prison in the first Gulf War. He had endured 10 years in solitary confinement, a punishment ordered personally by Saddam. Dr. Husseini had refused to build the nuclear weapons that Saddam badly wanted. The scientist had been tortured. He was hung by his thumbs and forced to listen to the screams of his children in the next cell. The physicist was then placed in an airless cement cubicle the size of a doghouse and expected to go insane. Husseini endured that for 4,000 days.

"He told me the worst thing about solitary confinement was the silence." Duncan said, keeping his eyes on the street. "Husseini remembered the sudden sound of a leaking tap. Each drip became a plucked string, then more strings, pizzicato, then a voice. It was Vivaldi's aria *Sento in seno ch'in pioggia di lagrime*, 'I feel within a rain of tears.' The water falling on stone was the most exquisite music he had ever heard."

Lee tried to imagine that kind of sensory deprivation, the lack of time and light. How easy it would have been to give in to madness.

In the confusion of a bombing raid during the first Gulf War, Husseini was freed by fellow dissidents. They drove out the front gate in stolen uniforms and crossed the desert to a safe house in Kurdistan. They escaped through a mine-laced mountain pass to Turkey, lying under blankets in the back of a pickup, and then to Germany. After that, Dr. Husseini gave up his scientific work and ran an underground railroad of intelligence, food, and weapons for Iraqis trying to flee. There were marshes along the border with Iran — the Qurnah, the Hammar, the Hawizeh — where refugees plied their wooden boats through the tall reeds, and slept on tiny islands of mud, stalked by water rats. Husseini rescued them and guided them to Iran. Saddam discovered what was going on and drained the marshes. The marshes became dust bowls, littered with beached boats and broken beds.

Sadoon followed Lee's instructions to stop in Mansour, and as the houses grew larger, some of them boarded up, he turned down a small street that came to a dead end in a grove of date palms.

The garden of the al-Bahari was an oasis of 10 acres that attracted all of the birds in the city. It was one of the most famous gardens in Baghdad. The *Times* had written a feature about it.

"I want to leave a note." Lee got out of the car and walked down a path of colored pebbles edged with broken terra-cotta pots. The house looked abandoned. Lee smelled lavender. She thought it was worth shoving her note under the door.

Laela,

Are you here in Baghdad? I need your help. Urgently. Rm 310 at the Dar.

Lee M.

Lee had met Laela al-Bahari in New York when Lee came for a show of Laela's work in the Meatpacking District. Laela sculpted and threw pots. Lee remembered the story Martin had told her. During the worst of the air strikes on Baghdad, when the electricity was knocked out and the bombs left signatures like towering thunderheads over the city, Laela had cooked her entire neighborhood's defrosting chickens. Everyone came to Laela's chicken party. They ate by candlelight and smoked hashish to forget the bombs.

During the bombing, Laela was famously the first to notice that the birds flew upside down. Even the insects behaved oddly. While everyone else was running for the shelter, Laela, with her mop of ink-black hair and kohl-rimmed almond eyes, was crouched in the garden, observing bugs. Her sister shouted that she was a bloody fool. "The entire U.S. Air Force is dumping on us and you want to commune with nature." Laela would shrug and bring a beetle with her. Everyone loved Laela.

"No one home." Lee found Duncan admiring the pots.

"It looks like no one has been home for some time," Duncan observed.

"They may be in Beirut." Lee felt sure that Laela could help find Martin if she hadn't left for her family's flat in Beirut. By reputation, she was stubborn, which Lee hoped would bring her back to Baghdad regardless of the danger.

"The Garden of Eden," Duncan said. "It belongs to the al-Bahari family. One of them is an archaeologist. A friend of my mother's."

Lee realized the archaeologist was Laela's sister. Of course Duncan would know her. The sisters were a product of the British school where the al-Baharis and nearly everyone else from Baghdad's upper class were educated before the Saddam years. When the al-Baharis spoke amongst

73

themselves, they used the shorthand borrowed from the British civil servants who had once ruled their country. Baghdad was "Bags." Saddam was "Suds."

"She lives in Paris and is tracking stolen artifacts from the museum."

"I've never met her," said Lee.

"She advises Interpol and the U.S. Army."

"I know Laela al-Bahari. She is an artist and a friend of Martin's. I'm hoping she will have heard something."

"You'll have to introduce me," said Duncan. "The al-Baharis are a remarkable family. They are old Baghdadis. Most of the old families are gone."

"Duncan, now that we're alone, I have to tell you something."

"About Martin?"

"Yes. In the Green Zone yesterday, Plumber said Martin wasn't kidnapped."

"I'm sorry?"

She leaned closer, smelling the cloves from his cigarettes. "Plumber says Martin is on the run. He is arming the insurgency and is now wanted for 'crimes against the coalition.' "

"That's an Orwellian mouthful."

"Plumber threatened me with treason charges if I find Martin and don't turn him in. If you stay with me, you could be thrown out of the country."

"I've been thrown out before. Don't worry about me. I'm just wondering what Plumber is up to. Martin has made a very potent enemy. I suppose next week there will be a press conference," Duncan ran his finger slowly around the painted neck of one of Laela's pots. "And Martin Carrigan's reputation will be shredded. Then when he comes to a bad end, no one will be sorry."

"There is an enemy prisoner from Karbala whose house was raided. Martin's name supposedly turned up in the documents. Could Ali Husseini help me find him?"

"Very likely."

"If we're sharing information, Duncan, and you publish too soon, it could get Martin killed."

"Well that would defeat the purpose, wouldn't it? Then you would never speak to me again."

The route south took them through the slums of Baya where Duncan's radical sheik was gaining converts daily and where one of his clerics had just been arrested. His sermons called for a jihad against the occupation.

"We're near the mosque where the arrest took place," Duncan was studying the streets. "Do you mind if we stop to see how al-Kufa's people are reacting?"

"Not at all."

Duncan directed Sadoon to a neighborhood of modest houses and donkey carts, not far from the Surgeon's Committee's old clinic. Lee and Duncan could see a crowd of 30 or so men milling around on the sidewalk in front of the mosque, wearing cheap sandals and carrying flails.

"On festival days, the devout Shia like to flail themselves for their sins," Duncan explained. On the 12th Imam's birthday, you could see the flails on sale between the children's toys and boxes of nougat.

"Who is the 12th Imam?"

"Born 869. 15 Shaban 255 A.H. Some Shia believe that he is the savior. He will return with Jesus. Park across the street, Sadoon. I won't be a moment."

"With Jesus?"

"Yes. They call him Isa. He is part of the Muslim story."

Duncan approached the congregation so that he could hear what they were chanting.

"With our blood, we will sacrifice for you, Sheik."

He pulled out his notebook. When Duncan questioned the men, their anger flowed in a torrent, their rage at the occupation, their humiliation by the "nonbelievers." They said the Baya mosque had sent a delegation to the Green Zone to negotiate the release of their sheik and the Americans had jailed the entire delegation.

"What happened to them?" Duncan asked.

"We don't know. The Americans are like Saddam. Their prisoners disappear like ghosts."

Not all of them were happy that Duncan was asking questions or that an infidel woman was watching them from the car. The crowd started arguing among themselves about whether or not to talk.

"Nonbelievers!" one of them shouted in Arabic.

It was suddenly still, as though all of the oxygen had been sucked out of the air. The men began throwing stones. They nicked Duncan's elbow and collarbone and bashed the car with sticks.

"Get in the car. Please. Now!" Sadoon shouted.

Duncan fell into the back, just as the back window shattered.

"Go, Sadoon. *Yalla. Yalla.*" Duncan's tone was urgent. "I have no desire to be stoned to death."

"They are angry." Sadoon threw the car into gear.

"What are they saying?" Lee pulled her veil tightly around her face.

"That we are spies."

The car shrieked as the wheels tore away from the curb.

They were facing a high wall.

"Other way, Sadoon."

"Yes, yes, I can see," Sadoon spun around wildly and drove at full throttle into the massing crowd. Bodies flung themselves out of his way and at least two of them were injured.

"That was close. Nice work, Sadoon." Duncan brushed the glass from his jacket. "I'm afraid we've made some enemies."

"I guess so." Lee wondered whether it had been wise to bring Duncan after all.

VIII

IN BAGHDAD, car repairs were carried out in a maze of alleyways, piled high with spare tires, fenders, rusting car doors, and stolen CD players. Since the war, the car markets were choked with thousands of late-model Mercedes and BMWs pouring in from Jordan.

"Who's got the money to buy these cars, Sadoon?" Lee could see that someone was doing well out of the occupation.

"There is money here." Sadoon told them to wait and disappeared into one of the cavernous garages to negotiate repairs with two men sipping coffee on a detached back seat resting on its springs. The glass was refitted within the hour. Money, in the form of large bricks of devalued Iraqi dinars, changed hands.

"Soon we will have to fill the trunk with dinars to buy a piece of bread." Sadoon laughed.

As the sprawl of Baghdad gave way to open countryside, they passed a military graveyard several miles long, full of battered tanks, rocket launchers, and Scuds, most of the rusting detritus that had been Saddam's arsenal. Amidst the wreckage, they could see American soldiers.

"What are they doing, souvenir hunting?" Lee asked.

"Scavenging for metal." He explained that they tacked metal onto their Humvees to protect them from roadside bombs. Troops slid the battered scrap metal between two panels of plywood and secured it with sandbags. Usually the jerry-rigged protection blew apart, which is why they called their Humvees cardboard coffins. Still, there was a chance the scrap could save someone's life.

Just beyond the first U.S. Army check point on the Karbala road, they saw the pilgrims. The men wore white cotton *dishdashas*, the women were wrapped in black *abayas*, carrying huge green banners with embroidered gold inscriptions. Other pilgrims wore black bandanas and carried black flags. There were women with bundles of cooking pots and babies in starched pink dresses. They walked, with 50 miles of hot pavement ahead of them. Soon whole lanes of the highway were clogged with pilgrims. First thousands, then tens of thousands.

"My God." Lee was not prepared for this. She suffered from mild claustrophobia and felt it settling like an incubus on her chest.

"When Saddam ran the place, he forbade these people to celebrate the birth of the 12th Imam." Duncan lit a cigarette. "He ordered anyone found walking across the fields and palm groves of southern Iraq at night to be shot. Karbalans left lanterns and baskets of food along the pilgrims' way. Now they are free to walk down the main highway."

The crowds paid no attention to Sadoon's passengers. They were pilgrims, too. There seemed no other reason to be here. "They think you're Iranian." Lee said with relief. She hoped that Duncan would not notice that she was breathing hard.

"And you're a green-eyed Pashtun." Duncan admired her face, "Like the girl on the cover of *National Geographic*. Turi tribe. Northeast Paktia. They are Twelver Shia."

"Meaning what?"

"The Twelvers say the Mahdi will be the 12th Imam. You are at the right festival." He gave her a censorious look. "I can see little wisps of hair coming out of your *abaya*, doctor. I would fix that if I were you."

The veil was forever slipping back. Lee was finding it hard to control her discomfort as the crowds pressed against the car. "Sadoon, we have to find some other road." She was beginning to sweat.

"You must be warm in that rig." Duncan had noticed.

"Yes."

"We can take the Basra highway and double back." Sadoon honked and gestured energetically to other drivers to let him cut through the tangled traffic until they were on the dirt shoulder and then in the back streets of Hillah. They passed a mannequin on the sidewalk in a lace and tulle wedding dress with bare shoulders.

"They'll be sending that to the Baghdad museum soon." Duncan was picking glass out of the seat.

Sadoon shoved in a cassette of Iraqi music and turned up the volume. "This is *maqam*. Can you hear the *joza*? It's like a violin made of a coconut shell." He was humming to the music, lost somewhere in the past.

"Duncan, I don't want to get you in trouble." Lee was breathing more evenly now, and cracked the window for air. Pale yellow dust filled the car.

"You really think I'm going to let you do this alone?" He watched two Black Hawk helicopters skimming over a plantation of date palms, hunting for insurgents. "I wonder how many months it will take for the Air Force to turn every palm tree in Iraq into a blackened stump."

"I want to show you something." Lee carefully unfolded the letter from the soldier to his father that she had been carrying around like a talisman since her meeting with Col.

Frank. "It's supposed to mean something, but I'm not sure what."

Duncan read it twice.

"Who gave you this?"

"The father of the soldier. I promised him I would go up to Beit Har to see his son."

"You know there was an uprising up there? For two days, the Iraqis took over the whole town."

"Have you heard about soldiers stealing before?"

"I've heard Iraqis say the soldiers search their houses, find their savings under the mattress, and take it. But I've never seen anything like this from someone on the inside. It's kept very quiet. You wouldn't see soldiers doing this if the same thing wasn't going on further up the chain of command." Duncan studied the tense young soldiers in the back of an army truck just ahead. "Sadoon, move away from that convoy. We don't want to get blown up with them." He turned to Lee, who was sunk in thought. "How can you be certain that Martin hasn't turned?"

"It's just out of the question."

"What about his family?"

"His father was with the State Department. Martin grew up in Eastern Europe, Istanbul, and London. His father never spoke to him much about his work."

"That could mean he had State Department cover."

"It's possible." Lee looked away.

"His father might have been in intelligence with a State Department title like cultural attaché."

"Let's say Martin is just posing as an aid worker." Lee was impatient. "What's he doing training a Shia militia to fight the U.S. government? With his background? Not likely, is it?"

"You never know. He might hate his father. Why do you care so much about Martin?"

"We're very close. He saved my life."

"That's a good reason." Duncan threw his cigarette out the window.

"You think I'm in love with him."

"Well, it had occurred to me."

"I'm not. Falling in love with Martin would be suicidal."

"How so?"

"It would ruin our friendship. He has walked away from every woman who ever loved him."

"Commitment problem?"

"Something like that. Fear, maybe."

"So you're not spoken for?"

Lee looked at Duncan with genuine surprise. "No."

"Were you ever tempted to get married?"

Lee laughed. "That's very forward of you."

"That's what happens in wartime."

"Yes, I was tempted. I was engaged once, but my fiancé broke it off."

"Why?"

"Doctors' hours. Travel. He was upset that I wanted to go to Afghanistan. He couldn't understand it."

"He didn't deserve you." Duncan got through to Dr. Ali Husseini on the Thuraya. They arranged for one of Husseini's aides to meet their car on the edge of the city and escort them though the roadblocks of the Badr Brigade. The Badr Brigade was made up of Shia militiamen, armed with AK-47s and black armbands. They were alert for saboteurs and bombers from Saddam's old cadres who might want to terrorize pilgrims on the 12th Imam's birthday. Outside the city, Sadoon negotiated two checkpoints of American troops flanked by tanks. As they reached the suburbs of Karbala, the troops wore a different camouflage. Duncan recognized them as Poles, shipped in by the Americans to make the occupation look more diverse.

At the first roundabout in Karbala, they spotted their escort in a white jeep with the logo of Dr. Husseini's charity. Sadoon fell in behind and was waved through every roadblock. Husseini was well connected. Lee's attention was distracted by something in the street. She pointed to half a dozen men with unkempt beards and white shrouds on their shoulders.

"Al-Kufa's men. Dressed for martyrdom." Duncan looked nervous for the first time. "I hope they haven't heard about our little problem at the mosque. At least we're with the Guardians of the Shrines now. Dr. Husseini is close to Sistani, the Grand Ayatollah."

As they approached the city center, Lee and Duncan could see the massive gold leaf domes and minarets of the shrines of Hussein and Abbas, half-brothers who died in battle 13 centuries before, fighting for the right to succeed Muhammad. People in Karbala all knew that Abbas was killed along the river, just under the site of his shrine, while he brought water to women and children who were dying of thirst. The river was long gone. Now the city's drains were blocked and the shrines were flooded. Lee smelled sewage, rotting vegetation, and mold. From a distance the shrines, strung with festive lights, looked like they were decked with giant strands of pearls.

"Termites are eating away the 1,000-year-old calligraphy carved into the walls." Duncan lit a cigarette. "The city fathers have pleaded with the occupation authorities to do something about it, but there's been no response."

Dr. Husseini's office was a functional modern building piled high with boxes of computers, shoes, and wheelbarrows. When Duncan introduced Lee to the scientist, she was surprised that he was so small and slight. He led them around stacks of mattresses packed in plastic.

"These are for newlyweds who can't afford beds. We're supplying eggs and milk to 5,000 people a week." Dr. Husseini radiated energy, as though he carried around his own small power plant. "And we have a unit documenting Saddam's mass graves. Look at this." He showed them a photo of an exhumed shroud full of tiny bones and a baby bottle. "There was a massacre in the garden of the pediatrics hospital."

"May I have a copy of that?" Duncan asked.

"Yes, of course." Dr. Husseini offered Lee some cardamom tea.

"How is your family, Dr. Husseini?"

"Very well. I've left them in Berlin. My daughter is in school, and my son is about to get married."

"Congratulations."

"Thank you. I don't want them to come back to Karbala for the moment. We have some serious problems."

Everyone assumed, he said, that Karbala was quiet. Aside from the danger of Sunni extremists infiltrating the crowds on holy days, it was a Shia city, badly battered by Saddam and well disposed to the occupation army in their midst. But there was an undercurrent of anger. When Saddam's government fell apart, and all of his apparatchiks scurried into hiding or exile, Karbala had been one of the first cities to form its own government. People voted for their own protection force and a city council. There were no revenge killings against Saddam's enforcers who had persecuted them. There were even town meetings held in the Hussein Shrine for people to talk about grievances. Karbala was a model for Iraq. Everyone loved the idea of democracy. But when the American troops came, they disarmed the protection force and installed Saddam loyalists to run the police.

"Your military feels comfortable with Saddam's men because they know how to follow orders." Dr. Husseini said the Saddamis were seasoned informers and were not bothered by a small thing like changing masters. The decree that former Ba'athists could not hold jobs in the army or police was overruled. The new police chief had served Saddam for 20 years. He was hiring others like himself and had brand-new weapons at his disposal.

"Who is the police chief?" Duncan pulled out his notebook.

"General Yazid."

"You're sure about his past?"

"We have all of the documents from his Mukhabarat file. We also have footage of him beating a man to death. Saddam liked to put these things on television."

Lee knew the U.S. military was capable of this. While doing a research project in New Haven, she had come across a 1983 report from the Department of Justice. The report detailed evidence that at the end of World War II, as the American forces occupied Germany, the Army Counter Intelligence Corps had hired Nazis to gather information on French and Russian intelligence activities in the American Zone.

"They've hired the Saddamis to keep the Shia under control."

"If the resistance is former Ba'athists and the new police force are former Ba'athists, are they one in the same?" Lee saw the downside of arming Saddam's old friends.

"We know that the resistance is smuggling guns into the city and the police force has not stopped it."

Husseini said it was difficult to tell whether decisions were being made in Karbala or Baghdad. "Col. Slay is involved. He has his hands in everything from reconstruction contracts to intelligence. Slay sees to it that any information going up the chain of command to Baghdad is going through him."

"Is he the one ordering raids on people's homes?"

"If Yazid tells him someone is a troublemaker, they raid the house. Two of the city councilors were arrested and their houses ransacked. One of them escaped and is a fugitive now. The other one is in prison."

"Where?"

"We think in Abu Ghraib."

"Abu Ghraib?" Lee was alert now. Plumber had said the prisoner from Karbala, whose documents implicated Martin, was in Abu Ghraib. "Do you know what he's charged with?"

"He has not been charged."

"Has anyone tried to see him?"

"His son went with the family lawyer. They were told no visits were allowed."

"I thought Abu Ghraib was only for ordinary criminals. Thieves and rapists."

"That is what the military is telling the press. But this man is not a criminal. From his prison numbers we know he must be in Abu Ghraib." Dr. Husseini looked at Duncan with a gaze that was steady, unblinking. "Perhaps you can find him."

There was no pleading in Dr. Husseini's voice, only the conviction that Duncan had a role to play and the moral authority to make him want to play it.

"It's difficult to get in. The CPA's standard operating procedure for requests like this is simply to not return phone calls."

The prisoner's name was Ahmed Rubai. He was respected in Karbala, a local businessman with a successful chain of convenience stores. He had served 10 years in Abu Ghraib prison under Saddam for his role in the Shia uprising of 1991 that was brutally crushed. In Karbala it was a badge of honor.

"You know we have an alumni association of prisoners who served 10 years or more." Husseini said with pride. "I just went to a reunion in Baghdad."

Duncan had read about the same phenomenon among the survivors of the Cultural Revolution. They organized reunions in villages where they had been sent as slave labor.

"People trusted Rubai," Dr. Husseini said. Rubai was put in charge of security by the popular city council. He ran the protection force. When 1 million pilgrims flooded the city for Ashura, there were no unpleasant incidents, no killings or bombings. "Rubai worked day and night. Right after the celebration, he collapsed with a viral infection and went into hospital."

The protection force was armed with the Kalashnikovs and handguns that could be found in every Iraqi household. The expectation was that they would be the new police force. Yet Col. Slay insisted that the force should disarm. The weapons were given to the old police, mostly Ba'athists, Saddam's loyal cadres.

"I don't think he really knew what he was doing." Husseini wanted to be fair. "Colonel Slay just found it convenient to use their secret police as a source of information. These were people who were willing to serve him."

"When they ransacked Rubai's house, did they find any incriminating evidence?"

"Talk to his son. He was there when the Americans came. I can arrange for you to speak with him. Not tonight because of the festival. But in the morning. I would like the meeting to be discreet. It's a risk for him to see you. The Americans may think he's a troublemaker too. He is the only man left in the family."

Dr. Husseini looked at his watch and summoned two of his aides. "We have to go now. I have arranged a meeting for you with Sheik Ibn Fattah. He represents the Grand Ayatollah here. He knows you're here too, Dr. McGuinness. He would like to talk about the desperate conditions at the hospital. We can go in my car. It will be faster through the road blocks. Your driver can follow."

IX

THE CITY CENTER was overrun with pilgrims, every building draped with green banners, every sidewalk a campsite for men in urgent discussion, sipping glasses of tea set on upturned wooden crates. Women in black huddled like flocks of starlings. Young boys trotted beside donkey carts carrying grandmothers who could no longer walk after the journey from Nasiriyah or Basra. Food sellers and water vendors set up shop in every available foot of ground not taken up with brightly colored blankets and bedrolls. The smell of seared *kebab* and spiced *falafel* filled the streets. Dr. Husseini had found rooms for them at a pilgrims' hotel overlooking the Abbas shrine.

"I've asked Ali to stay with you." Dr. Husseini gestured toward a man sitting next to Sadoon in his car. "People need to see you with one of us. Al-Kufa's men are very upset with the Americans because of the arrests. In crowds like this, people get overexcited."

Lee wondered how many Iraqi Shiites were called Ali.

The car pulled up next to a side street that was too narrow for traffic. Ali had already jumped out and was negotiating parking places where none had existed. People on the sidewalk parted before him.

"Who is Ali?" Lee asked Dr. Husseini.

"He's a pediatrician."

"A pediatrician commands that much respect?"

"He's a very good one."

Ali greeted them with reserve, placing his long, delicate fingers over his heart with a slight bow and explained in his soft, persuasive manner that they were better off walking. They entered a warren of streets sunk in gloom in the most ancient and decayed quarter of the city. The mud bricks were moldy with damp, and stagnant water lay in pools. Ali explained that the drinking water system had broken down since the war. The city's water was now contaminated with agricultural chemicals from the irrigation system that had backwashed into the canals. Children, sick with typhoid from the foul water, were taken to the hospital only to find there were no antibiotics. Dr. Husseini had been calling doctors in Kuwait to ferry drugs across the border.

They stopped in front of a carved wooden door with a notice board out front full of proclamations.

"*Fatwas*," said Dr. Husseini. "From the Grand Ayatollah. If he wanted to, the Ayatollah could command over half the population of Iraq to rise up against the Americans. For the moment, he is preaching tolerance." Dr. Husseini paused to remove his shoes. "That could change."

The hallway was lined with religious scholars, each with his black turban and translucent skin produced by fasting and lack of sun. Each had a pronounced bump on the forehead just above the bridge of the nose. Five times each day, Dr. Husseini said, the scholars bowed deeply so their heads touched a smooth Karbala stone placed on a prayer carpet.

The center of the house was an enclosed courtyard with rough wooden benches for petitioners who needed a religious judgment.

Today, with the festival, the courtyard was overflowing. Dr. Husseini directed Lee and Duncan to follow him up a set of stone steps, into Sheik Ibn Fattah's receiving rooms, bare of furniture, and strewn with pillows. The sheik could not have been more than 40, with clear olive skin. He wore pearl-gray robes and the thick spectacles of a man who had spent years studying religious texts in Najaf and another decade reading in his prison cell with a single naked bulb. He sat cross-legged under a ceiling fan and waited for Dr. Husseini to introduce his guests.

"*As-salamu alaikum.*"

"*Wa alaikum assalam.*"

The sheik smiled.

"Dr. Ali, I need you to translate for me." Lee was sure that her Arabic would be hopelessly inadequate.

"Of course, Dr. McGuinness."

Sheik Ibn Fattah greeted Lee and told her the story of the siege of Karbala during the uprising in 1991, when Karbalans revolted against Saddam. The revolt had failed. Bombing and massacres followed.

"I watched scores of men, women, and children die." The cleric looked at Lee with an intensity that made her feel uncomfortable. A hot, prickly sensation girdled her waist, under her clothes. "Families were buried alive in their homes. The Americans allowed Saddam to fly his helicopters and fire rockets at us."

Beads of sweat gathered on the sheik's forehead and an attendant adjusted the speed of the fan stirring the heavy air. "Now the American soldiers force people to their knees."

The sheik was agitated about the arrest of Rubai and the other city councilor who was now a fugitive.

"The U.S. administration has put some of the old security services back to work." He turned to Duncan. "These people should have been fired. The Americans issued exemptions to Ba'athists. This is not right."

"The police chief. General Yazid." Duncan flipped a page of his notebook. "Did the Americans know he was a high-ranking Ba'athist when they hired him?"

"I don't know." The sheik seemed nervous discussing Yazid.

"Do they know now?"

"Yes, they know."

"Yazid and his friends are bad people," he said to Duncan, lowering his voice. "They told the Americans that I have weapons. I asked them to come and search the house. Did they find guns?" He gestured around him to the acolytes, who looked barely able to lift a rifle. "No."

"Have you ever heard the name Carrigan?" Lee decided to bring up Martin. It was, after all, why she had come.

"Is he with the occupation?" The sheik looked puzzled.

"No. He is an American aid worker who is missing. When I went to see the authorities in Baghdad, they said he was wanted as a traitor for training and arming a Shia militia that is part of the resistance. They said documents had been found when they raided a house in Karbala. The documents had his name on them. Does any of this mean anything to you?" Lee's voice was steady and firm, as though she was telling a patient that the leg would have to come off.

"This is a lie." The sheik asked for water.

"What makes you say that?"

"We do not have Americans training any Shia resistance force."

"I'm wondering whether the house the Green Zone authorities are talking about is Rubai's," she pressed him, "the councilor who may be somewhere in Abu Ghraib. I'm going to speak with his son tomorrow. Can you help me find the other councilor who is on the run?"

The sheik looked at Dr. Husseini for assurance that this was not a trap.

"Yes, I can arrange it. He will come to you at Dr. Husseini's tomorrow. Now I must tell you, doctor, we need antibiotics, morphine, syringes. The situation here is becoming critical in spite of the talk of reconstruction. You will excuse me now. I must say the prayers at the Hussein shrine. I have a lot of people waiting."

Out in the Karbala streets, it was dark. The electricity was coming on and flickering, giving a strobe effect to the thousands of tiny lights strung across the shrines. The darkness gave Lee and Duncan more anonymity, though they would have to cross a sea of pilgrims to reach the hotel. Lee saw no other Westerners, no soldiers for protection, no journalists for company. It seemed everyone had stayed away for fear of a bomb explosion or violent mobs.

She remembered one night as a child coming on deck on her father's boat off the coast of Maine when it had lost its mooring and was drifting far from shore. She called for him below deck, and her father could not hear. She watched the harbor lights extinguished by a bank of fog and looked behind her to see the yawning black void of open water. Her helplessness, then as now, made her inordinately calm. She wondered how it would feel to be lynched by a crowd of religious zealots in the back streets of Karbala and clawed to death.

"I will leave you here." Dr. Husseini spoke from somewhere in the darkness behind them. The smell of the night was overpowering.

Cardamom, cloves, and urine.

Dr. Husseini touched Lee's arm. "I will expect you in the morning. Please be careful, doctor. A crowd like this is unpredictable. *Ma'a salama.*"

"This way." Dr. Ali led the way back into the labyrinth of passages, potholed and poorly lit. They could hear the sound of chanting. The voices bounced off the stone walls that bound the narrow streets. Lee lost her bearings, unable to tell which direction the sound was coming from. They turned one corner, then another, and found themselves face to face with a procession of men dressed in white shifts bearing a coffin. Some held flaming torches that smelled of kerosene. The fire cast weird shadows on the dilapidated buildings full of squatters who watched from the balconies. The mourners shouted prayers to Shia saints. Intoxicated with grief, the men wailed like a gathering storm. Ali pulled Lee back around the corner.

"This is one of the men killed in Sadr City today." Ali's voice was low and urgent. "The Americans fired on al-Kufa's people outside the police station."

"How many were killed?" Duncan asked.

"Three. Two more were wounded."

"Why did they bring the body here?" Lee pulled her *abaya* across her face in case the funeral procession cast a light on her.

"To circle the holy shrines before burial in Najaf. The dead man is a martyr." Ali was standing absolutely still. "This is the correct way to send him to paradise."

Lee thought about the 72 virgins, or the bowl of raisins, waiting on the other side. The shouting was too overwhelming now for conversation. As the mob passed, they were so preoccupied with the corpse suspended over their heads that not one of them noticed the foreigners in the shadows. It was several minutes before Lee and the others braved the street again, turning away from the martyr's cortege. At the end of a lane that smelled of wet rot, they were blinded by spotlights.

"The Abbas shrine," Ali said with relief. The shrine was ringed by a mass of celebrants like a human skirt.

"*Haqiba.*" A stern teenager with a black armband demanded to see Lee's purse.

"They are searching everyone." Ali spoke softly in English, encouraging her to open it. "Someone tried to bring a bomb into the square this afternoon. He was caught ..." Ali went silent, "... with explosives. There may be others in the crowd."

The boy from the Badr Brigade recognized Dr. Ali and stood at attention. There were two more checkpoints. Inside the cordon, they could see some of al-Kufa's people, roaming in packs.

"If there's trouble," Duncan said quietly, "it's going to be tricky getting out of here." All streets leading on to the broad plaza were blocked with bodies. Some pilgrims, who had walked for days, were stuck out on the highway, huddled around bonfires.

When they reached the hotel, Lee was so relieved she felt almost lightheaded. Ali introduced them to the proprietor, a man with a ready smile and ample girth, who produced keys to rooms that he claimed were his best. Lee wondered what he had done with the pilgrims who had booked these rooms.

"I will leave you now." Ali bowed slightly, placing his hand over his heart.

"We had hoped you could stay with us." Lee's relief disintegrated into fatigue and fear.

"I'm afraid I cannot."

"Dr. Husseini said it would be best if you stayed."

"There is no need."

Perhaps he had some pressing medical business. Lee felt guilty that she had taken up so much of his time.

"How can we reach you?"

"This is my number. I will come back in the morning." He smiled faintly, his face utterly blank. "You will be safe here."

He turned and left.

X

ALI HAD TEMPTED FATE. Uttering the words "you will be safe here" was like walking under a ladder, looking at the new moon through glass, or spilling salt and not throwing the grains three times over your left shoulder and saying *unberufen*. Lee knew it had been a mistake to leave Dr. Husseini's side. How could she have made that miscalculation? Why didn't Duncan object? There were several million people outside in the square, an unknown number of them hostile. The local phone service was unreliable, and there were no foreigners or U.S. troops in the city.

"Does the Thuraya work?" Lee reeled in her unhelpful thoughts.

"Not here. We may have better reception on a higher floor." Duncan walked up two flights of stairs to a small metal door that led onto a gravel roof. Lee could see that he was doing his best to appear in command of the situation, but she knew that things could come apart very fast. In wartime, lessons learned from the last narrow escape did not necessarily apply to the next. Duncan had led her to believe that he was a competent guide. He could read the danger signs. Now she felt unsure. Coming to Karbala had been rash. Duncan was too eager for Martin Carrigan's story, too anxious to break it.

The door to the roof was unlocked. Duncan stepped out at eye level with the shrine parapet, the massive gold domes blazing with light. The shrine's roof was a hundred feet away and patrolled by at least four sentries in silhouette holding automatic weapons. Duncan raised his Thuraya slowly to avoid attracting the guards' attention. They could mistake the satellite phone for a weapon and shoot him. He fell back into the shadows and tested reception. A silent woman and child, who had dragged plastic chairs to the roof for a good view of the festivities, froze at the sight of him.

The noise of the crowd rose to the roof in a steady roar, like the sound of the sea in a conch. Once his phone registered a signal, he inspected the storage tanks, heating ducts, and clotheslines for a possible escape route in case of trouble. To the left, there was a series of obstacles. Nothing insurmountable. He counted five pipes at knee level, roughly 2 feet in diameter. Beyond, there was a short metal staircase leading down to the next roof. At the end of the second roof, he saw a gap of about 3 feet before the lip of a third roof, which was connected to several houses at more or less the same height leading away from the square. They would have to watch it over the gap.

There was nothing more he could do. Duncan found Lee downstairs in a corner room facing the square, with tall windows draped in polyester curtains dyed a depressing shade of tobacco.

"Keep the curtains drawn, Lee. We don't want to be seen by this crowd."

"Is this place safe?"

"We'll be all right. We have an escape route if we need it." He sat down on one of the sorry little single beds, slabs of foam rubber covered in rough woolen blankets.

"We've got company tonight," Lee said, massaging her bare feet on the linoleum floor. "Bedbugs. And cockroaches that look like they've survived a nuclear test. Do you know what cockroaches call your suitcase?"

"No." Duncan stood up and watched as she removed the bedding from one cot and dug two sheets and a towel from her bag.

"The Mayflower."

"I'm sorry?"

"It's a joke." She laughed at him. She had removed her black shroud and her hair fell loosely around her shoulders. Under her thin cotton shirt, the muscles in her back were knotted with tension.

"Lee, come and join me at the rooftop bar."

"English joke. There is no rooftop bar." She made the bed meticulously with hospital corners.

"I have a bottle of Irish whiskey."

"Ah."

Duncan led the way back up the stairs. The chairs were empty and there was no sign of the woman and child. He chose a dark corner for them to watch the ocean of believers below, pressing like a riptide into the square.

"Someone's going to be crushed," he told Lee. "It happens every year in Mecca during the *hajj*, when they walk seven times around the Kaaba," Duncan poured both of them generous drinks and lit a cigarette. "It's always some poor *hajji* from Bangladesh. Did you know that the sacred black stone in the Kaaba that pilgrims must circle seven times is a meteorite?"

"A meteorite?"

"Yes. It's pre-Islamic. People have been circling the meteorite since long before Muhammad."

"Really."

Duncan was her Zephir on the island of the Gogottes, spinning stories, buying time, plotting to save the princess before the monsters turned her into stone. "Archaeologists believe there is another meteorite in Yemen, in the ruin of the Temple of the Sun."

"Who built the temple?"

"Balqis. Queen of Sheba." He took a long sip of whisky. "I saw it when I was visiting a town in the Hadhramaut called Shibam, with ancient skyscrapers made of whitewashed mud. I noticed that one corner of the magnificent, ancient mud house featured in Shibam's only postcard had collapsed. I asked my guide what caused it, and he said the owners had gone off on a trip to Saudi Arabia and left the tap running."

"Is that true?" Lee looked doubtful.

"Of course it's true."

"I don't believe you."

"Don't then."

Lee leaned back to study the night sky. Her veil slipped off in a puddle at her feet. She felt relieved to be unwrapped in the open air.

"Did you know that the whole system of constellations began right here," Duncan told her, "started by the Sumerians, Acadians, and Babylonians, in the Euphrates valley. They recorded the Pleiades, just over there, as early as 3000 B.C."

Duncan took her hand. He gently stroked her fingers. "When Sir Henry Layard excavated the library of Ashurbanipal at Nineveh in 1850, he found a cuneiform tablet, a 21-year record of the planet Venus as she appeared and disappeared in the night sky. The tablet is 3,500 years old, the work of ancient astronomers who served Ammisaduga, a Babylonian king."

"Did it survive the invasion?"

"Layard carted it off to the British Museum. Room 55. Your surgeon's hands are like an archaeologist's hands, probing an ancient tell. I want you to meet my mother, Lee. You would have a lot in common. I'm so happy to find you again. I want to know everything about you."

Lee sipped some whiskey, "Well, I grew up in Africa, and then moved with my family to Virginia. We have a farm in the foothills of the Blue Ridge, a very old mountain range that was once taller than the Himalayas. Geologists say that before the continents broke apart, the mountains were connected to the Little Atlas range in Morocco. There is a forest of white oak and sassafras. Bear cubs raid the cherry orchard, and wild turkeys nest in the hollows. You can hear coyotes at night. In the spring, after a soft rain, we hunt for wild mushrooms. Morels. The mountain people call them 'morals.' They hide under giant tulip poplars near rotting logs and matted leaves and have funny wizened caps. In summer, we watch the fireflies. You can drown in the smell of wisteria and lilac."

"Sounds lovely." She reminded him of English girls in their Wellies, smelling of wet dog. "You know there's an online dating service in England for people like you. It's called Mucky Matches."

"Oh, please."

"Yes. True. Why were you in Africa?"

Lee hesitated, as she always did when asked this question. "My parents were with the government."

"Like Martin's?"

"My mother was making a language map of the Congo. My father was building cattle dips and introducing new kinds of grain. I was in boarding school a lot of the time. After my parents split up, my father moved to New York.

"And what do you do in New York?"

"Art, theater, medicine. My father inherited an insanely big Park Avenue apartment, so he's given part of it to me. He also has an island in Maine. He supports research there on shark hearts."

"Shark hearts?"

"Sharks don't get heart attacks."

"So, if we were more sharklike, we wouldn't get heart attacks."

"That's right. My mother retired from government and now she raises animals in danger of extinction." Lee laughed. She was on safer ground now. "She has Babydoll Southdown sheep, less than 2 feet high, who mow the vineyard; Cracker cattle; Mulefoot pigs; and those crazy goats that fall over in a dead faint when a stranger looks at them."

"Really?"

"If they know you, they're completely relaxed. If they don't, they just keel over. It's a genetic disorder called myotonia congenita. The old goats learn to prop themselves up against the fence."

Duncan kissed her lightly on the mouth.

"That was nice," Lee studied his face. "Should we be doing this?"

"Absolutely not." Duncan kissed her again, a long, slow kiss that reminded her of what was missing from her life in scrubs. She wondered how much Sophie's suicide had scorched whatever love he had to give. "You have an empty glass."

She wanted to sleep with him, though not just yet. Not in Karbala, not in the Mayflower. "I have to tell you Duncan, I was depressed by Husseini and Sheik Ibn Fattah today. I hate hearing how guilty my country is for everything that has gone wrong. Your country is just as bad. Look at how the British behaved at Amritsar. Sixteen hundred rounds of ammunition fired at women and children at close range. The sepoys, strapped to cannons and blown to bits. I know how badly the Pentagon behaves sometimes, but you can't condemn a whole people for that. Forgive me if I seem stupidly patriotic."

"They would be mortified to hear that they had offended you. They don't blame you, Lee. Occupation is an ugly thing."

Duncan ran his hand through her long, dark hair. There was a sound like faint rumbling echoing in the stairwell, people running perhaps, and he sensed that they were no longer alone. Standing in the shadows, framed by the glittering lights of the shrine, was a heavyset, bearded man, with a wide face and enormous eyes, watching them.

"Lee." Duncan grabbed her arm and they stood up in one fluid movement. Lee threw on her veil. The man had vanished.

"Come on. We have to get off the roof," Duncan sprang to the stairs. Within seconds they were two flights down, inside Lee's room, with the door bolted. Neither of them turned on a light or spoke. Duncan pulled back the curtain just enough to see an agitated crowd circling in front of the hotel door and lit a cigarette. Lee could hear him exhaling. There was a loud rapping on the door. Neither of them moved.

"Dr. Lee, Mr. Duncan, open the door please."

"It's Sadoon." Duncan unbolted the lock and found Sadoon panting, drained of color.

"Sadoon, I'm so sorry. Come in please."

Sadoon stood rigid in the dark. "I think we should get out of here."

"Why, what's happening?"

"The al-Kufa people say you are enemies of Islam. You should be driven from the city. They say I am an agent of Saddam. It is not safe here."

"Where is the car?"

"Outside the square, maybe half a mile."

Duncan took another look at the disturbance in the crowd growing like the slow spiral in a satellite image of a storm. "Agents of the unjust rulers," Duncan translated the chanting. "Lee, they're talking about us. We have to go back to the roof."

"But we just saw one of al-Kufa's men up there."

"We have no choice. There are hundreds of his men down there."

"Do you have your *keffiyeh*?"

"Yes." Duncan grabbed the cloth to wrap around his head. They opened the door, checked the fluorescent-lit hall and hurried back up the stairs. A door on the landing opened and closed. On the roof, Duncan led the way over the tangle of pipes and down the stepladder to the next roof. Lee could hear the rising sound of a disturbance below, shouts, banging doors, a woman's indignant voice.

Duncan jumped the gap. "Come on, Lee." She leapt across in a practiced jeté. They paused for Sadoon.

"Dr. Lee."

"What is it, Sadoon?"

"I'm afraid to jump."

"What's wrong?"

"I am scared of heights."

Duncan crossed back and took Sadoon's arm. "We will go together. On the count of three. *Wahed, ithnan, thalatha.*" He flung Sadoon to the other side, where he fell on his knee and cried out in pain.

Lee helped him up. "Sadoon. We have to move quickly. Can you walk?"

"I'm all right."

They had climbed over several rooftops leading away from the square, weaving through drying sheets and satellite dishes, when al-Kufa's men appeared behind them on the hotel roof.

"Don't stop," Duncan whispered as they began looking for a route down. A doorway two houses ahead looked as though it might lead to a stairwell.

"This way." Duncan found the door unlocked. Just before descending Lee saw men backlit by the spotlights on the minarets.

"Come on, Sadoon." She urged him on. The passage from the roof looked like a black hole.

Duncan fumbled for his lighter.

"Oh, God." Lee stopped.

"What is it?"

"I stepped on a rat."

At the bottom of the stairwell, the door was locked.

"We have to break it down," Duncan began kicking.

"Wait." Sadoon was soon bent over the lock, picking it. The door opened.

"That's a very useful skill, Sadoon." Lee thought he must have had another life as a thief. "Which way to the car?"

"Yasar. To the left."

There was no way to run through the mass of pilgrims huddled over cooking fires on the sidewalk. Lee and Duncan had to step carefully around them. Lee, wrapped in her *abaya*, stooped her shoulders and feigned a limp. Being a doctor had its advantages. Observing people and their maladies. She knew how to pass for a sick pilgrim. She took Duncan's arm. In the smoke of the fires, they were just another Shia family desperately seeking salvation. Al-Kufa's men lost them in plain sight.

"This way." Sadoon, wearing a bright green scarf that he had purchased from a street vendor to pass for a Shiite, led them off the broad avenue through a small alley to a city parking lot. There were still attendants on duty, two teenage boys who obligingly took their ticket and returned with the keys. Once inside the car, Duncan locked all of the doors. Sadoon pulled out into the rising tide of celebrants still flowing to the shrines. The car was soon invisible to anyone pursuing them, as the sea of devotion closed behind them.

"Oh, damn," said Lee.

"What is it?"

"My sheets. I left them on the bed."

"Oh." Duncan laughed. "We can send someone to pick them up tomorrow. We have to make a decision. Either we can call Ali and Dr. Husseini to ask for beds for the night. Or we can go straight back to Baghdad and come back for Rubai's son and the fugitive in the morning. By tomorrow the roads should be clear."

"Let's go to Baghdad." Lee was anxious to get away.

"I almost believed you were an invalid," Duncan said with admiration.

"I was very good in anatomy class."

It was midnight when they found an empty table by the pool at the Dar. Someone was playing Brazilian lambada, an improvement on the steady percussion of gunfire. For the moment, Lee wanted to feel safe in this badly defended fortress. She was about to ask Duncan whether he might be able to probe Martin's connection with Adnan Jabarri, the former exile, without raising suspicion, when they were interrupted.

"Hello, Duncan." A tall, bearded Kurd, with pale skin and fine cheekbones, wearing jeans and a leather jacket, was standing by the table.

"Masoud. How wonderful to see you alive." Duncan said it with genuine pleasure. "This is my friend, Dr. Lee McGuinness. Masoud is with the leading Swedish daily. Please join us. Have a drink. I want to hear about the north."

"I was embedded in Beit Har last night." Masoud poured a glass of Bekaa red.

"Beit Har?" Lee gave him her full attention.

"Yes, with a mortar platoon."

Lee's mind was on the letter still folded in her pocket. *My mortar platoon has been under attack just about every night ...*

"There was an uprising up there," Masoud told them. "We were under attack. The resistance was using homemade mortars. When it was over, the troops talked to me for a while about how much they missed home, how much they wanted a hamburger, and wished they could sleep with their girlfriends. Then they raided a house. There is no way the mortars could have come from that house. It was in the wrong direction." The Kurd sipped his wine slowly.

"They found a old man in the kitchen and they hauled him out and started beating him. This man was completely innocent, covered in blood, pissing his pants. He kept pleading with the soldiers. I watched them kick him to death."

No one said anything.

"Then, as if nothing had happened, they went back to talking to me about how much they missed hamburgers. It was demented. They even let me take pictures."

Lee sat perfectly still as Masoud finished his story and his drink. She excused herself, promised to call Duncan in the morning, and stopped to ask the night clerk for a wake-up call, before retiring to her Formica and burlap suite. There was a message waiting for her under the door.

It was from Laela.

Welcome, doctor.

I stayed in this hellhole through the whole bloody mess. Dinner at my place tomorrow. We'll scrounge for something edible.

Yours,

Laela

Lee stood in her dreary kitchen listening to the hum of the generator.

XI

BY THE TIME Lee and Duncan reached Dr. Husseini's office the following morning, it was already 8 o'clock. Rubai's son had been waiting patiently, the way people outside the First World are accustomed to wait, strangers to indignation. He stood in a garden choked with weeds. He was young and frightened and carried two well-fingered passport-size photos of his father, one in his best suit, the other in a hospital bed. The boy could not stop running his fingers across the photos, as though touching the images might bring him back.

"How old are you?" Lee asked gently.

"I am 17."

"Are you his only child?"

"I have five sisters. I look after them, along with my mother."

She studied the boy's father in the pictures, wondering whether he was really the key to Martin's disappearance or whether Plumber and McCleary had laid a false trail. Rubai had a clipped white beard and the hard expression of a man who had long ago given up trivial conversation. He wore the sign of Shiite devotion, a lump on his forehead from repeated contact in the act of prayer with Karbala stones.

"How old is your father?"

"59."

He looked 70.

The boy handed her two documents, worn photocopies of official occupation papers. The first was Rubai's registration as an "Enemy Prisoner of War." The second was his release form, signed by an American colonel, saying Rubai's case had been investigated and dismissed.

"It says here that when he was first picked up, they took him to Camp Bucca," Lee passed the papers to Duncan.

"Umm Qasr, yes." The boy used the name Iraqis knew.

"And he was released?" Lee was patient. She felt closer to Martin's trail now.

"Yes. You can see what the camp commandant said."

She read the form, neatly typed in English.

The Board conducted a preliminary examination of the individual in order to determine whether there was cause to question the detainee's status before a full Tribunal convened under Article 5 of the Third Geneva Convention 1949.

The Board reached the conclusion that there was no evidence to support an assertion that he had committed a belligerent act against coalition forces. It was further satisfied that there were no further investigations that could be undertaken in respect of this individual. In these circumstances, there is no reason for the continued detention of the individual and further investigation into the case by way of a formal tribunal is not required.

The boy waited silently for her to finish reading.

"When was your father arrested a second time?" Duncan asked in Arabic.

"The 2nd of September."

"Are you sure they took him to Abu Ghraib?"

"I have his prison identification numbers. The Red Cross gave them to me."

Now Lee had something that she could use as proof. No one could claim that the prisoner did not exist.

"Have you tried to see him there?" Duncan asked.

"Yes, with a lawyer. We were told we could not see my father."

"Did they say what the charges were?"

"No charges."

Lee could see in his face the despair of the dispossessed. If what he said was true, Abu Ghraib was now housing political prisoners.

"What about the Red Cross? Have they spoken with him?"

"Most of the Red Cross people left Baghdad after the U.N. bombing. I went to the Palestine Hotel to see the ones left behind, but they were busy with other things. No NGOs have been in to see my father."

"May I keep these documents and the prison numbers?" Lee asked.

"Of course."

She handed the papers to Duncan, who suggested the boy might have seen or heard something significant when his father was arrested.

"Were you at your house when the Americans came to take him away?" Duncan asked.

"Yes, I was there."

"What happened?"

The boy said five Americans drove up in a military vehicle at about 2 o'clock in the morning. They drove right through the front door. His sisters began to scream. The men ransacked every room, pulling books from the shelves, and carting away his father's papers. His father ran security for the city after Saddam fell. The Americans said they were looking for guns. His father was in the hospital for his infection, so when the men had finished, they drove to the hospital and took his father away.

"So they took your father's papers?"

"Yes, they took his papers and all of our savings."

"How much was that?"

"$14,000."

"In cash?"

"Yes."

Duncan and Lee looked at each other.

"Have you asked the Americans to return the money?" Lee was not ready to accept that American soldiers would steal.

"Yes. They refused, saying it was money to fund terrorism."

Lee thought there was a chance that this boy had met Martin if his father had some association with him.

"Did your father have any American friends?"

"Yes. Because he was on the city council, my father knew most of the Americans who worked with Colonel Slay."

"Did he know someone called Mr. Carrigan?"

"I don't know that name."

All of this has been a waste of time, she thought.

"Martin Carrigan." Lee said it slowly this time.

"Oh, you mean Mr. Martin. Yes, of course I know him."

Lee held her breath.

"How do you know him?" Duncan said.

"He came to our house many times. My father was happy that Mr. Martin had come here, because my father was angry about the prostitution ring and the stolen cars."

"What stolen cars?"

"Some Americans took government cars and were selling them to make a profit."

"Which Americans?"

"I don't know their names."

Duncan was scribbling notes.

"And the prostitution?" Lee asked.

"My father complained about the women the Americans were bringing in at midnight. This is a holy city."

"Of course."

"He said some Americans were taking bribes for reconstruction contracts when there was no reconstruction. There are big contracts for the Police Academy and the Regional Democracy Center, and someone is stealing the money."

"Have you seen Mr. Martin since your father was taken away?" Duncan barely looked up from his notebook.

"Yes. Two days later. He came to ask questions just like you."

"Did he give you a phone number?" Lee felt she could almost touch Martin now.

"Yes. He told me that if the Americans came again or if anything happened to my family, I should call this number." He carefully unfolded a small piece of paper and handed it to her.

Call Mr. Hamdoon. 914 360 2400.

Lee let a long silence fall between them.

"The 914 code tells us something," Duncan said, filling the vacuum. "The U.S. government gave out that number."

"Do you know Mr. Hamdoon?" Lee watched the boy closely.

"No."

"Thank you for coming here," she said warmly. "We'll go to Abu Ghraib. Please don't tell anyone that you have spoken with us."

"I understand. I hope to see you again. *Insha'Allah.*"

"Yes, *insha'Allah.*"

The boy shuffled off into the morning. Lee did not like to think what could happen to him if his father's enemies got wind of their conversation. As she stood watching the diminishing figure of the boy melt into the harsh desert light, Dr. Ali appeared from the next room.

"I am sorry for last night." He seemed contrite.

"Not to worry, Ali." Duncan stood up to greet him. "The al-Kufa people were looking for trouble and we were an obvious target. Might I ask you to send someone to the hotel for me to pick up a few things belonging to Dr. McGuinness and pay for our rooms?"

"Of course. In the meantime, there is someone waiting. He cannot stay here for long. I think you know the Americans want to arrest him."

"Yes. Yes. Let's go."

Dr. Ali led them through the garden to a secluded corner sheltered by a grove of cedars. The fugitive was checking all possible exits in case Lee was an American agent as well as a doctor.

"Hello, Dr. McGuinness. I spent 11 years in Abu Ghraib prison under Saddam, where, as you can see, I got TB." He spoke aggressively, scything the air with his words. He pointed to his gaunt and sallow face. "I will commit suicide before going to prison again."

"Are you on a course of medication?"

"Yes, but it's too difficult to continue. Soon my TB will be drug-resistant." He coughed a long, hollow cough, full of death and bitterness.

"I won't keep you long. Tell me your name?"

"People know me as Sheik Abbas." His eyes were small and black. They flicked from Lee to Duncan, full of suspicion, the way a bird with a broken wing watches cats.

"You're a professor, correct? On the Karbala city council?"

"Yes. I was running a town meeting at the Hussein shrine. It was an open-to-anyone. At the meetings, people complained about the occupation, and that's why Colonel Slay regarded me as a troublemaker."

"Did he try to arrest you?"

"We were meeting at the city council and Colonel Slay was there. Everyone was upset that the troops took over the university. The students couldn't take exams. Two security men appeared, Americans, from one of those contractors. Slay ordered them to capture me. I ran out the back way and managed to escape. I have been in hiding ever since." He shook his head in disgust.

"What are the charges against you?"

"Terrorism," he laughed dryly. "They said I was 'instigating' against the Americans. Stockpiling guns. I challenge Slay to produce one piece of evidence showing that I received guns. I'm not stupid." Sheik Abbas was short of breath. Lee could hear the rattle of his chest.

"Do you know General Yazid?"

"Yes. We showed his file to Slay. Yazid was a senior Ba'athist. He has blood on his hands."

"Do you think he was picked because Slay and the others are ignorant?" Duncan was trying to understand.

"We told them, don't do this. I'm afraid, doctor, that democracy is only allowed in your country, not in ours." His bile and shame filed the space between them.

"Your colleague Ahmed Rubai was arrested and sent to Abu Ghraib, according to his son. Do you know why?"

"Ahmed Rubai was critical of the black market the soldiers are running here."

"I was told that he was organizing the resistance."

"That's nonsense. The Ba'athists are running the resistance. Go ask General Yazid what he does in his spare time."

"Look, Sheik Abbas." Lee knew that she did not have much time. "Someone has gone missing here. His name is Martin Carrigan. Do you know him?"

"Yes."

"I've come to find him. When I asked the occupation authorities for help, they told me that he is wanted for treason. They accused him of arming terrorists. They said documents were found in a Karbala raid that implicate him."

"Your friend is in a lot of trouble. He's a fugitive, like me."

"You know he's alive?"

"Yes."

Lee sat quietly for a moment, flooded with relief, listening to the wind in the cedars and the sheik's labored breath.

"Dr. McGuinness, I can't stay here. I'm a wanted man."

"Sheik Abbas, please."

"Goodbye, Dr. McGuinness." With that, Abbas rose from his folding chair, coughed a deep, wheezing cough and walked away.

"Wait," Lee followed him through the overgrown garden. "Please help me fix a meeting."

"Dr. McGuinness, did you ask me here to find out what is happening to Iraqis under this occupation or just to learn the fate your friend?"

"I'm sorry. I didn't mean to offend you. If there are false charges against you, we can expose it." Lee turned to Duncan. "Mr. Hope is a journalist."

"Expose the fact that Ahmed Rubai is in Abu Ghraib. Then we can talk."

The sheik's frail figure in the loose-fitting *dishdasha* vanished through a gap in a high hedge of green fig.

"Dr. McGuinness, I think it is time to go." The enigmatic figure of Ali had appeared, and Lee felt defeated. She had come so close.

"Thank you, Ali. Is Dr. Husseini here in the office?"

"He will be gone for the rest of the day."

"Please pay my respects and tell him that as soon as I get permission from the U.S. military, I will go to Abu Ghraib."

"I will tell him, doctor. Shall we go to the hospital now to see what supplies we need?"

"Yes, of course."

Duncan handed him an envelope with $100 in cash.

"For the hotel. Perhaps next time we can stay the night."

By the time they had toured the wards of Karbala hospital and reached the outskirts of Baghdad, a sun like a blood orange was sinking into the Tigris.

"I'm expected at Laela's. Will you come?"

"I wasn't asked." Duncan lit a cigarette.

"I'm asking you now. The food will be a lot better than the Dar."

"Yes, all right. You've persuaded me."

XII

THEY FOUND LAELA in her date grove. Long rows of palms bearing Khadrawy, Medjool, and Amir Hajj dates dwarfed her lithe figure like the pillars in the temple of Karnak. She looked otherworldly walking among them. The moon was rising, casting shadows through the giant fronds, and Laela was talking loudly to her trees.

"Come on now, the termites won't kill you. Just think of them as annoying houseguests. Ignore them."

"Hello, Laela."

"Oh my God, Lee, you startled me."

"Sorry to interrupt. This is my friend Duncan Hope.

"Yes, of course. A pleasure. I was just giving them a little encouragement. The bloody termites the British brought with them when they imported the railroad ties from India are a plague in my garden."

"They are eating the shrine in Karbala." Lee smiled.

"Well, we know these termites are not Shiites then."

"At least your palm trees haven't been bombed." Duncan looked on the bright side.

"Not yet. Touch wood. Soldiers are bulldozing date palms all over Iraq just in case they are sanctuaries for the resistance. Pretty soon Iraq will be naked. Would you like a gin and pomegranate juice?"

"That sounds deliciously sinful." Duncan walked beside her. "Your sister is the archaeologist."

"That's right. I know your mother, Duncan. She came to stay with us in Beirut. She has a dig somewhere in Syria, isn't that right?"

"Yes, near Aleppo."

"The juice is fresh from the garden. Thank God I have all of this, because it's getting bloody hard to get what I want from the market. I'm growing all of my own vegetables and lettuce."

Duncan and Lee followed Laela in the moonlight along a path to the low stone house, washed in color like one of her terra-cotta pots.

"I've got beets, beans, basil, cucumber, aubergine, six varieties of tomatoes, squash, arugula, and sunflowers. I adore sunflowers, don't you?"

"Yes." Lee was intoxicated by the smell of jasmine.

"It reminds me of Tuscany. You know the way they plant the sunflowers in the olive groves so as not to waste an inch of earth."

The house behind the thick stucco walls was cool. Laela slipped off her sandals, and Duncan and Lee kicked off their shoes, thick with dust from Karbala. The floor was made of Laela's painted tiles, decorated with acanthus leaves and papyrus stalks. The walls were lined with books in English, French, and Arabic. There were family photos, some of them dating from the monarchy. The al-Baharis had served as the ministers and diplomats of the king, who served at the pleasure of the British. The family's rise had started even further back under the Ottomans, when highly educated Sunni Arabs were allowed to prosper under the watchful eye of the Turks, so long as they did not entertain ideas of independence. On the wall, there were distinguished looking men wearing fezzes and medals. Ladies wore elegant Edwardian moire and lace over tiny satin shoes, with ostrich feathers in their hair.

"Oh, don't look at that rubbish. It's all gone now. We are just beggars hunting for our next meal. And I hope you will be very pleased about what I found for you. *Masgouf*" — Laela flashed a radiant smile — "fished from the Tigris this morning. The boy was fishing well above the busted Rustamiyah sewage plant. It's clean and absolutely huge. Come and look."

They followed her into the kitchen, which looked like it belonged in a museum. There were storage pots with wide necks big enough to hide a man, and a bread oven, black from constant use, next to an ancient and warped chopping block. In the middle of the room was a long, narrow table, hand-hewn from a giant cedar, worn with generations of hands rolling out flat bread and chopping *mezze*. Rows of copper kettles at least a century old hung from the ceiling, and dried herbs were strung up everywhere. The smell of turmeric and saffron, cumin and cardamom, was overpowering, like a stall at the covered market. A huge black Persian cat sat like a pasha in the corner.

"That's Hammurabi. A prize ratter. He's such an efficient killer he could have worked at Abu Ghraib. He lines up the plump little rat carcasses every morning just outside the kitchen door. So I spoil him with treats." The cat lowered his eyelids and purred.

Laela picked up a serving platter, valuable but obviously mended many times, covered in a cloth.

"Have a look at that." It was flat like a giant sole.

"A magic fish," Lee said approvingly.

"Well, let's make some wishes, shall we?" Laela poured them drinks. "Look at that juice. Like a pigeon's-blood ruby. I wish for electricity 24 hours a day."

Laela maneuvered the fish onto the grill of the ancient AGA and the smell of seared flesh and herbs filled the room. Hammurabi looked expectant.

"Why did you decide to stay through the bombing?" Lee asked.

"Why should I go? Who does this country belong to anyway? It took me days to clean the dust out of the house and the noise made it impossible to sleep. I would get out of bed and just stare at the red sky full of tracer fire and anti-aircraft barrages and feel the earth shake from the bombs. Two of my neighbors were vaporized by mistake. The fog from all of the debris seeped into my bedroom. My bedside candelabra looked like a far-off lighthouse. I taped the windows, but there was still broken glass everywhere, and just as I had tidied that up, looters showed up at the door. I gave them my computer and some of my best pots and one extremely valuable artifact from the oldest library in the world and even fed them my last chicken so they would leave me in peace. Then the U.S. Army turned up shouting all of that 'hooah' nonsense, in hot pursuit of a dangerous terrorist who I think was my electrician, under suspicion because of his white van and his toolbox. I spent a day cleaning the mud from their boots off my carpets. Now taste this." Laela put a fork full of *masgouf* into Lee's mouth.

"God, that's good."

"I think Hammurabi had a small nervous breakdown."

Laela had laid a table in the moonlight with homemade yogurt and cucumbers and mint from the garden, *babaghanoush* from her own aubergine, and grilled pumpkin with nutmeg.

Lee looked up at the night sky and felt as though she was in the dreamscape of a Rousseau painting, the inky green date palms against the stars, Laela's pots amid the garden like ancient Assyrian treasures half-buried in forgetfulness. She saw the Pleiades and could taste Duncan's kiss from the Karbala roof.

"That pumpkin is a recipe from my Afghan great aunt." Laela was silent for a moment and Lee savored the illusion of peace. Then, without warning, an Apache attack helicopter, brushed the tops of the date palms like a dragonfly. Someone in the helicopter trained a searchlight along the grassy floor of the grove, moving steadily toward the quiet garden table like the funnel of a twister.

"I'm just waiting for them to defoliate with Agent Orange or super Roundup." Laela shouted over the thunderous noise. "They hate my trees because they are the oasis of an ancient civilization. Our new masters allowed the great library to be gutted, the museum to be sacked, and now they will destroy my date palms to remove all trace of us Babylonians. To 'fire up' the fertile crescent."

The Apache hovered for a moment above them, enveloping them in wind from its blades, and moved on as quickly as it had come, screaming across the city in search of other prey.

"They fly low and fast to avoid the rocket-propelled grenades. The sound of the helicopters terrifies the children. The U.S. Army spokesman says Iraqis should be grateful. He calls it 'the sound of freedom.' Can I get you another drink?"

"Yes, please." Lee followed her into the kitchen. "Are you really all right, Laela?"

"You know most people in my neighborhood are sick. Many of them have cancer." Laela poured the drink slowly. "Everyone says it's the depleted-uranium rounds. Radioactive shells. We are breathing uranium-contaminated dust. My neighbor was a doctor. A great oncologist, actually. She died without proper treatment. Let's go back outside."

She let the embroidered shawl on her shoulders fall to reveal pale arms the size of a child's. She wore a bracelet of pounded and engraved silver around one of them, in the shape of a snake.

"Laela, I don't think you are eating enough. You look malnourished."

"I'm making up for it tonight, doctor. Now that's enough about me. Tell me about you and our missing friend. What did you mean when you said Martin is wanted for treason?"

Lee fortified herself with a long sip of gin and pomegranate. "I was told by two senior U.S. officials that they have evidence he is arming and training the resistance. They said he is wanted for 'crimes against the coalition.' This seemed completely insane to me, but now that Duncan and I are following up their leads, I realize how little I know about Martin."

"Do you think he's really helping the *shabab*?" Laela turned to Duncan.

"We're talking about a Shia resistance, if it exists. But when we found the son of the alleged terrorist Martin is supposedly involved with, he told us this had nothing to do with the resistance. His father is investigating corruption, and Martin is helping him in some way. American corruption. Which may explain why Martin has so many formidable enemies in the Green Zone."

"Corruption?"

"Yes. All kinds. Prostitution. Black marketeering. Theft. We don't know how extensive it is or how far up it goes. But the fellow he was involved with is now in Abu Ghraib. No family visits, no lawyers, no Red Cross. He's a ghost prisoner and we have to find him."

"Is Martin alive?"

"Yes. I think so." Lee tasted the sweetness of the pomegranate juice at the back of her mouth. "We met with a fugitive today, on the run from the occupation authorities, who says Martin is alive and in trouble. The man didn't trust me much and refused to say more."

"Who is this man?"

"A professor who was running town meetings in Karbala. His story is that he crossed the Americans by asking too many awkward questions about the black market. The other strange thing is that when I first arrived, I got a call in my hotel room from someone called Hamdoon. He told me to leave Iraq. He has a Green Zone phone number. Hamdoon insisted Martin did not want to see me. I discovered Martin had given the name 'Hamdoon' to the son of the prisoner in Abu Ghraib. In case the boy needed help. So Hamdoon is someone he trusted."

"Who else has Martin been seeing?"

"Just before he vanished, he was staying at the Tigris Hotel. He met with one of Jabarri's men."

"Adnan Jabarri?"

"Yes."

"You know he's my cousin. On my mother's side."

"I didn't know that."

"Adnan Jabarri is a mafioso. Mr. 10 Percent. Just like Uday used to be. God knows how many billions he's skimming. Why was Martin meeting with him?"

"I don't know."

"Perhaps he was trying to get Jabarri's protection for refugee supplies." Duncan lit a cigarette. "Unless of course he was investigating Jabarri's role in several billion dollars worth of reconstruction money that is unaccounted for. $2.5 billion in frozen Saddam-era assets, $4 billion from the UN oil for food program. Another $1.3 billion from the banks. No one knows what happened to it. There are no auditors. And nobody knows how much oil is being smuggled out before it hits the refinery, because the CPA doesn't meter the extraction. There are no controls."

"Is it safe to look into this?"

"That's a hard question to answer." Duncan smiled. "I'm not sure that Dr. McGuinness fully appreciates what we're up against."

"What if Martin really doesn't want to see you?" Laela studied Lee, who knew that her hostess was fishing to see whether her feelings for Martin went beyond friendship.

"Then he can call me himself to ask me to leave," Lee said, beginning to doubt herself. "By now everyone in Baghdad knows I'm at the Dar."

Laela let the subject drop.

"I have some really special wine, a pinot noir my sister brought from Paris last year. From the sound of it, you may not be around for long, so we had best celebrate now."

When Laela opened the wine, the air was fragrant with flowers, and the only sound was a full chorus of crickets that drowned out the crackle of gunfire somewhere in Mansour.

"I must light a coil. The mosquitoes are devouring my ankles."

"Laela, I'm so happy you and your garden survived." Lee raised her glass. "When did you last see Martin?"

"Not for ages. I've been in Beirut for the past couple of months, you see. I have no idea what he's been up to."

"This wine is excellent," Duncan said, conscious of how badly his own cellar at the Dar compared. "How is your sister?"

125

"She says I'm mad to be here. But she comes once every three months now with her commission, investigating the theft of antiquities. Every site in Iraq has been looted. My sister says the Brits and Americans are paying villagers to dig up priceless stuff."

"Soldiers?"

"Yes."

"Do they get stopped?"

"Zara has a friend at Kennedy Airport who has caught some valuable stuff destined for the big collectors in New York. She says London and Paris are much more porous. The thieves are shipping goods through Switzerland."

"Is it just pilfering by the troops or something more serious?"

"A bit of both, I think. You should hear Zara in her rages about the buyers outside Iraq who pay millions for objects they have to bury in a closet. The thrill of owning something 4,000 years old is like a drug. Or a curse, I suppose."

"Is Zara coming any time soon?"

"Next week. I will have a party on Saturday. We can invite my Jabarri cousins. Can you buy wine from the hotel?"

"Yes, of course. But it won't taste like this."

"Bring whatever they have in stock. Lee, you must be careful hunting for Martin. What would be his relationship with Jabarri?"

"It could be very complicated," Duncan interrupted.

"If Jabarri found out that Martin was investigating him for corruption, would he take revenge?"

"Of course." Duncan poured a second glass of wine.

"How would he do that?" Lee asked.

"Well, he has the intelligence files on everyone in Iraq. It was the first thing he did after Saddam fell. He went to the headquarters of the secret police and loaded the files onto a dump truck. And because he has the files, he can forge new ones if he likes. He is in a powerful position."

"So if he denounced someone for arming the resistance, would it stick?" Laela asked.

"It might."

"Does he have allies in the Green Zone?"

"Yes."

"Would he be doing business with any of them?"

"I don't know."

"Is it worth finding out?"

"Laela, don't get involved in this. Just because you're Jabarri's relative doesn't mean you can get away with being too inquisitive." Duncan was already feeling protective.

"Yes, I know, I'm only an artist. What would I know about the dark side of Baghdad?"

"People will know that you're a friend of ours." Lee said. "Sadoon, my driver, has seen us here twice."

"Which reminds me that, given the curfew," Duncan said, "we've got to either get back to the Dar now or stay the night. Otherwise some member of the all-volunteer army will shoot us on sight."

"Well, I have plenty of room if you need beds. I can also put up your driver. You're welcome to stay. Lee, I can't understand why Martin hasn't tried to reach you."

"He may think I will lead his enemies to him. Inadvertently, in the blundering way of a friend."

"Are his enemies watching you now?"

"Could be," Duncan took a bite of Tigris fish. "From a very expensive spy satellite."

They ate quietly, savoring the *masgouf* and spiced pumpkin.

"Laela, I saw the *oud* in your house. Do you play?"

"Of course."

"Would you play it for us now?"

"Why not?"

She disappeared into the house, and Lee and Duncan sat under the date palms, trying to sort through the facts they had collected in the past 24 hours, shuffling them like a familiar pack of cards.

XIII

WHEN LEE WOKE UP to the call of the *muezzin* at dawn, she could not remember where she was. From her bed, she studied the vaulted ceiling with its intricately carved beams and a bird's nest in the corner. The window was open, and as she watched a sparrow fly in and out with provisions, she could hear a rooster crowing somewhere below. When she turned her head in search of something to trigger her memory, she found herself staring into the yellow tinted eyes of Hammurabi, who shared her pillow.

The room was sparsely furnished with little more than overflowing bookshelves and an antique desk. She focused with some difficulty on the book titles, which appeared to be histories of the Ottoman Empire. On her bedside table, there was a candle and a bottle of water. The end of the evening came back to her with the insistent whine of a helicopter somewhere overhead. Laela had lit dozens of candles, apologizing for the lack of a generator, and picked up her long-necked *oud* and played until Lee had felt heavy with sleep and excused herself from the table. She left Duncan with Laela. He belonged in Laela's garden, Lee thought, in this strange civilized place, floating on a river of insanity.

There was movement from below, and within seconds, Hammurabi was out the door and in the kitchen, where Lee could hear Laela offering him a fish head. Lee dressed and joined the little party, which included Duncan and Sadoon, greedily bent over Laela's homemade yogurt.

"Morning, everyone. That was a magical evening, Laela."

"You are sweet, Lee. Now before you both go rushing off to find Martin, don't forget about the party Saturday. I will expect you to empty the cellar of the Dar for the occasion and do bring any strays you find between now and then." Laela turned to Sadoon. "You must come, too, and I expect you to take very good care of Dr. McGuinness."

"Of course, Miss al-Bahari. *Insha'Allah.*" Sadoon and Duncan excused themselves, and Lee had Laela to herself for a moment, though at that hour she found it impossible to articulate what it was she wanted to say.

"Thank you, Laela." Lee kissed her lightly on both cheeks. "Thank you for listening last night."

"Lee, it means a lot to me that you came to my poor, desperate country. Even if it was only for Martin."

"I feel so much better having seen you."

"Let me know if you leave town. In case I have to send out a search party."

"I will."

It was quarter past 7 when they emerged from the date grove and set a course across Baghdad to avoid roadblocks on the route back to the Dar. There was no traffic to speak of, and minutes later they were skirting the Green Zone barricades signalling to Iraqis that they were outsiders in their own city. Sadoon was making good time on 14th of July Street heading toward Damascus Square when he suddenly turned sharply away from the fortress walls, down a road west of the zoo that was completely unfamiliar to Duncan.

"Where are we going, Sadoon?"

"You don't want to be near the Green Zone this morning."

"Why not? That road is much better than this. Sadoon, I think we should turn around."

"That way will be blocked."

"Why would it be blocked at this hour?" Duncan's irritation, usually masked by his English composure, was apparent.

"Some problem over there."

"What problem?" Lee disliked obtuseness.

"*La arif.*"

"What do you mean you don't know?" Duncan was angry now. "Sadoon, what's going on?"

Sadoon refused to speak another word until they reached the sentries at the roadblock in front of the Dar.

"I will wait for you," was all he could say as Lee climbed the steps and wondered, all the way to the shower, what had just taken place. By the time she reappeared downstairs, the coffee shop was full and she made her way through a thicket of journalists to a table where Duncan was furiously scribbling notes while listening to a young Iraqi speaking to him in a low and urgent whisper.

"Lee." He half-stood and motioned her to sit down. "I think you ought to come with me to the Green Zone. They may need you over there."

"Why, what happened?"

"A rocket attack. Several rockets hit the Rasheed. There was a delegation from Washington. Two killed, including an Army general. Seventeen wounded." He gave her a knowing look. Both of them knew that Sadoon was somehow part of it.

"What time did this happen?"

"Around half past 7."

"Oh my God."

As they and a few others piled into Duncan's car, Lee was silent. She turned to look at Sadoon parked under the

131

eucalyptus. He was staring straight ahead, his face streaked with sweat. He briefly caught her eye as she motioned for him to stay put. Her expectation from the start, that Sadoon would have useful ties to the insurgency, had not prepared her for this. People were dead and dying, and Sadoon knew all about it. Had he taken the car to pick up detonators? Had his cell phone triggered the launch?

"A senior official of the Defense Intelligence Agency was dressing for an 8 o'clock breakfast meeting," Duncan said to no one in particular. "Between 6 and 8, rockets hit the hotel and blew holes in the concrete. They hit the seventh and 11th floor. Some of the survivors had to wade through deep water in the hall from burst pipes. The launcher was in a trailer, disguised as a generator. Apparently the guards did not think the Chevy pick up towing the trailer was odd because of the blackouts. Everyone needs a generator. I recommend we head straight for the hospital."

Lee sat motionless, conscious now that she and Duncan knew something the others did not. She felt, in some way, complicit.

"*Dottore*, are you all right? You're looking ill." An Italian journalist was lighting a cigarette in the back.

"No, I'm fine. I think it was the fish last night. Caught in the Tigris."

"The river is filthy."

The emergency ward of Omar Hospital was crowded and dirty, with soldiers in their body armor filling the hallways. Lee and Duncan's passes were checked and rechecked until they reached some of the victims of the morning's carnage. Duncan found a wounded security guard who had made the mistake of asking one of the insurgents to move his trailer away from the Green Zone. The insurgent fled just as the rockets streaked out of the back toward the Al-Rasheed, and when they ignited, the security guard was badly burned. Lee remembered the statement of a Pentagon official who had briefed the Surgeons' Committee just before their clinic in Sadr city was bombed. It stuck in her mind like a nursery rhyme.

Intelligence is getting better all the time.

Cooperation is getting better all the time.

Across the forest of IVs in the emergency room, she caught sight of Naji Qais, who had his hand inside someone's leg.

"Naji."

"Lee, just in time. Grab a gown in there. I assume you came here to work," Dr. Qais was splattered with blood.

"I heard you might be short-handed."

The hospital was short of everything: syringes, sutures, sterile gauze, oral rehydration solution, antibiotics, anticonvulsive medicines, oxymeters, syringe pumps, anesthetics, cardiac monitors, plates, screws, drills.

"Dr. Qais, we have a thoracic impalement coming out of the ambulance." A small intense looking woman with thinning hair waited for orders.

"He's all yours, Lee. Selma is your anesthesiologist," he said, pointing to the woman. "She trained in London."

The victim was a middle-aged American with a rusted pipe jammed through his chest. A rocket had landed in his hotel bathroom.

"Respiratory rate?"

"30 breaths per minute," Selma responded with the voice of someone who had seen too much of this.

"Pulse rate?"

"130 beats per minute."

"Blood pressure?"

"70/50."

"Chest x-ray?"

"Multiple rib fractures on the left side with collapsing left lung." He was bleeding, going into shock.

"We're going to do rapid sequence induction using thiopentone and suxamethonium, followed by endotracheal intubation." He would be in a dead sleep before the tube went down his throat.

"Anesthesiologist, I need blood." Selma ran to the refrigerator for whatever O-negative blood they had left. Lee worked steadily, without conversation, removing pipe, shrapnel, and glass. Selma worked by her side, with quick hands and a frozen face deadened from watching the blood drain out of her country.

There were water shortages and generator breakdowns. The first time they lost power, Lee was extracting jagged glass from the man's chest and found herself in total darkness. She felt fear rise in her throat. The anesthesia machines failed. The ventilator failed.

"Selma, I need a flashlight. We need to bag the patient."

"I have a pen light."

"Hold it for me. Is there a portable cardiac monitor?"

"I'm sorry. We are poorly equipped."

The generator sputtered back on and held for an hour before failing again. It was dangerously close to curfew when Lee finally got out of the operating theater. She had operated on five more of the wounded that day. Dr. Qais was waiting for her.

"The American will need a splenectomy tomorrow."

"Let me give you a lift back to the Dar." Naji put his arm around her shoulders. "There's an opening here for you any time. You can see how much we need the Surgeons' Committee to come back."

Although Lee had spent the day somehow washing away her sins, making up for her association with Sadoon, she still felt uneasy about her brush with the insurgency.

"Naji, how big is the resistance? Really?"

"I couldn't possibly answer that. Who knows?"

"Would it surprise you if someone you saw every day was a part of it?"

"No."

"Would you expose them if you knew?"

Naji Qais was silent for a moment. Lee could see he was weighing the cost of revealing himself to a foreigner, even an old friend, who might quote him too freely in the wrong circles.

"Haven't we had a long day? Lee, I want you at the hospital whenever you can come. Day or night."

"Would you come with me to Laela al-Bahari's on Saturday, Naji?"

"Yes, I want to see Laela's new work. Everyone is talking about it. Did she show it to you?"

"Not yet."

"It's a massive sculpture, built of dismantled tanks and anti-aircraft guns. She calls it her weapon of mass destruction. She wants to display it in the lobby of the Rasheed."

By the time they reached the barricades at the Dar, the headlights revealed one lone car and driver still parked outside the hotel. It was Sadoon, who, it seemed, had hardly moved since she had left him.

"You can go home now, Sadoon. See you in the morning."

"What time, Dr. McGuinness?"

"Around 7 will be fine. Sadoon, how did you know there would be an attack?"

"Everyone knew."

"Who is everyone?"

"All the people."

"Good night, Sadoon."

"*Ma'a salama*, doctor."

They both knew that he would not be there at 7, that he would disappear somewhere into the back streets of Anbar Province, in Ramadi, or his hometown of Fallujah until the danger of Lee calling Central Command and identifying him as a conspirator in the rocket attack was past. She could not be sure that he wasn't telling the truth, that the insurgents hadn't alerted everyone in al-Adhamiyah that the attack would take place. She was relieved to see him go, so that she was no longer forced to make a choice that would land him in Umm Qasr or Abu Ghraib, where he would be hooded and stripped regardless of his innocence or guilt. Lee found it unsettling that the head doctor at Abu Ghraib prison was the same man who had served in that job under Saddam. The doctor had claimed in a recent interview in the London *Independent* that he knew nothing of what had gone on at the time. He had never heard the screams.

There were two new security guards posted inside the lobby of the Dar, though how they would stop a rocket was a mystery to Lee. Ali signaled her energetically from behind the front desk.

"Dr. McGuinness. *Masa' al-Khair.* You have messages."

She saw there was one from Nizar Hadithi, from the news bureau over at the Aleem. Nizar's message was urgent. Lee waded through the tables by the pool to Thuraya corner and called.

"Dr. McGuinness." He sounded relieved of a terrible responsibility. "I must talk to you. Please come to the Aleem early in the morning." He would say nothing more.

Lee explained that she might not have a car. "Sadoon had a death in the family." She invented the excuse because she had no desire to discuss what she knew.

"I will find you someone."

"In the future, I need a Shia driver, Nizar."

"I have just the right guy. He used to be a big soap opera star. You can get through any roadblock in exchange for his autograph."

"I will see you in the morning, Nizar."

Duncan was waving his cigarette like a firefly from across the pool. There was a woman in a scant bikini noisily splashing between them. Lee recognized the swimmer as a freelance aid worker studying cancer rates in Baghdad. She made a mental note to talk to her about depleted uranium.

"Lee, you must be exhausted." Duncan stood and summoned a waiter for another chair. The Italian journalist was there, as was Masoud, the Kurd from the Swedish daily. "I have been busy on your behalf and I have found out some things." Duncan touched the side of her face.

"What is it?"

"Just a bit of dried blood. We can wash it off in the pool."

"One of my patients."

The swimmer had left a wet trail from the shallow end and as Duncan gently bathed Lee's face, they had a few moments of privacy.

"Did you go to Sadr City?"

"No, because of the rockets, I had to file early. But listen, I spoke with Jabarri, who wants both of us to come to his place tomorrow. And I also got permission from Colonel Darling of the 800th MP Brigade to go to Abu Ghraib."

"How did you manage that?" Lee was impressed.

"I told him I wanted to interview General Tater for *Gentleman's Monthly* about life in the war zone."

"You're not serious."

Gen. Tater was built like an armored vehicle, with gunmetal gray hair combed into spikes.

"Actually, don't laugh, I think I can sell that story. With the prison numbers and details of our friend from Karbala, I can ask the general questions about him. And, you know, if he hasn't been charged, then maybe General Tater will be embarrassed and release him or at least let somebody see him."

"Did you ask Jabarri about Martin?"

"I did."

"And?"

"He said he can prove your friend is an arms dealer for the insurgents and a black marketeer. Jabarri has told his men that if they find him they should shoot him."

"Oh, Jesus. Duncan, if Martin really is investigating corruption, who do you think he's working for?"

"I've been running through the possibilities in my mind. I know that war has broken out among the intelligence agencies in Washington, and I suppose Martin could be helping out one side or the other."

"A consultant?"

"No, a spy. A very vulnerable spy. There's a name for it: NOC, non-official cover. NOC people work for Fortune 500 companies or investment banks or aid organizations but really have some intelligence mission like tracking weapons of mass destruction or dirty money. They have no diplomatic passport and no protection. Any government is free to execute them."

Back at the table, Lee wanted to ask Duncan about Adnan Jabarri's recent record of kickbacks and bribes, but

Masoud had caught his attention and they were reminiscing about a coup somewhere in the Indian Ocean.

"What was the name of that minister of defense in the Comoros who wore a tuxedo in the afternoon?"

"Dr. Toto."

"Who liked his martinis 'savagely shaken'?"

"He pissed himself when the freedom fighters stormed the island. Last I heard of Dr. Toto, he was in Florida, running a bar in South Beach. The Kon Tiki, I think. Where they serve scorpions for four with floating gardenias."

"Speaking of freedom fighters," said the Kurd, "I was in Sudan last month trying to get an interview with the Black Diamond Movement, when I got a message from the rebel chief saying that he couldn't wait to see me again. I have never worked in Sudan in my life. I thought it was a case of mistaken identity. But when I was ushered in to meet him, I was face to face with the old doorman from the Rasheed."

"You're joking. You mean Mustafa?" Duncan poured more wine all around.

"Yes. It seems that after the invasion here, he fled home and when his relatives asked him what he had been doing all this time in Iraq, he spun a tale about fighting bravely with the insurgents against the American invaders. So they immediately made him deputy head of the local guerrilla group, and when the top guy was killed, Mustafa took over. Now he's a rebel hero."

"Duncan, how much money is Jabarri skimming off oil contracts?"

"Quite a lot." Duncan was examining the label of some questionable wine from the Dar cellar.

"Does he have American partners?"

"With his old Washington sponsors turning up in Baghdad, it's possible. There's a lot of money floating around with no receipts. Billions are missing. Christ, the entire budget of the defense ministry has been stolen. Not just a piece of it. All of it. One billion dollars. And no one in the Green Zone even noticed. Imagine a pile of cash, $1 million in $100 bills, 10,000 $100 bills, and multiply it by another 1,000, enough to fill an entire C-130, and absorb the fact that no one even noticed where it went. The Jordanians say they know of $7.5 billion more that is unaccounted for. Everyone is helping themselves, and the Americans are at the head of the queue."

XIV

LEE MADE A POINT of arriving on time for breakfast with
Nizar, as she knew now that the Aleem dining room
served the best food in Baghdad. The Lebanese chef had
trained in Marseilles and knew how to bake a brioche while
managing a black-market smuggling operation that supplied
caviar from Iran and lamb from Damascus. The atmosphere
was on the grim side, as there were heavy curtains pulled
across the bricked-up windows and old Christmas tinsel
hanging from the ceiling. Nizar was sitting hunched over a
small table by the buffet, muttering into his satellite phone.

"Hello, Nizar."

He waved Lee to a chair while he finished his call.

"I heard you were magnificent in the hospital yesterday.
Why don't you stay here a while and help us back on our
feet?" Nizar handed her a basket that smelled like a Left Bank
street. "Have a croissant, invented by Viennese bakers to
celebrate the defeat of the Ottomans in the siege of Vienna.
1683 in your calendar." He took one and chewed it with
obvious pleasure. "If you're interested, I can get my hands on
a shipment of antibiotics. The military seems to have mis-
placed it."

Just then there was the alarming clatter of machine-gun
fire in the car park, a few feet outside the bricked-up wall, and
every table was deserted. The diners were practiced at this.

They retreated into the kitchen with the Lebanese chef. Nizar cradled his head in his hands.

"It's all because of those South Africans on the second floor. Until they clear out, we will never be left alone."

"I don't buy stolen drugs, Nizar. And by the way, Sadoon knew all about the attack yesterday. We were there, at the edge of the Green Zone just before 7:30, when it happened, and he knew."

"You wanted someone well-informed."

"Not that well-informed."

"Listen, Lee, forget all of that. I got a call from someone named Hamdoon. Do you know him?"

"The day I arrived he called and told me politely to leave. He said that Martin Carrigan did not want to see me and that my life was in danger."

"That's the part I wanted to tell you about. He said there is a contract out on your life."

"Who is he, Nizar? Hamdoon has a Green Zone phone number."

"You have it?"

"Yes. Someone in Karbala gave it to me. And I know that Martin thought Hamdoon was his friend."

"Give it to me."

Nizar dialed and got a female voice.

"Mr. Hamdoon, please. This is Nizar Hadithi."

Lee could only hear Nizar's side of the conversation.

"I see. Would you have another number for him? Are you sure he's out of the country? I just spoke with him yesterday afternoon. Well if you hear from him, please tell him to give me a ring. He has my number. May I ask your name? I see. And which office is this? No, of course I understand. You can't give out that information. Well, thank you for your time." Nizar put down the phone. "That's the last time we can call."

"What do you mean?"

"The next time, the number will be changed."

"What office do you think it is?"

"I have a lot of friends in the Green Zone. We'll find out."

"What did he say about this contract on my life?"

"Nothing. Just that I should convince you to leave Iraq."

"Did he sound threatening, or should I be grateful for his tip?"

"I suppose it's better to get a warning than to just be shot." Nizar licked the remains of the pastry butter from his fingers.

"Could you tell from his accent where he's from?"

"I'd say northern Virginia." Nizar glared at an anemic boy standing at attention in a red uniform that was much too large. "*Qahwa*," he barked. "Do you want coffee, doctor?"

"Yes."

"*Ithnan*." The waiter retreated, trained to fear the Nizars of this world.

"But the man who called me was Iraqi."

"Returned exile. Bad Arabic from too much time in the States. He's part of the colonial regime."

"What do you make of this, Nizar?"

"Well, Dr. McGuinness, it depends on what you and your friend Carrigan are up to."

Nizar ate feverishly while Lee told him what she knew. He raised his massive eyebrows at the words "crimes against the coalition." The news that Martin was accused of training and arming Shia insurgents in the south slowed the progress of his fork until it halted mid-air.

"Your friend is being framed."

"He's keeping company with people who have been asking questions about American corruption."

"Contractors or military?"

"That's not clear. How do you know he's being framed?"

"The Shia would never hire him. They have Iran for guns and training camps. They have no use for an American."

"I met a fugitive in Karbala who says Martin is alive."

"Fugitive from the Americans?"

"Yes. One of the Karbala city council members who was fired by the U.S. Army."

"Can he take you to Carrigan?"

"I'm supposed to get one of his friends out of Abu Ghraib first."

"Good luck, my friend. Not so easy."

"Nizar, how would someone like Hamdoon know there's a contract out on my life?"

Nizar shrugged his ample shoulders. "Informants."

"Why would anyone want to kill me?"

"You are getting in someone's way, doctor. Life is cheap in Baghdad right now."

"Nizar, I know you have a lot of ties from the old days. I would like you to use your network to find out which criminals are getting paid to come after me, and who in the Green Zone is mixed up in business with Jabarri. And who set your old Mukhabarat friends on Hamdoon. Presumably they have infiltrated the palace."

"Of course," he laughed with satisfaction. "I wouldn't know about that."

Lee paid the bill and turned toward the Aleem parking lot. She wrapped herself carefully in her *abaya*, conscious now that every doorway might be in the cross-hairs of a waiting sniper. The gunfire that interrupted breakfast had died away, and she spotted Hassan, her new driver, garishly handsome and already signing autographs. He wore a dark silk shirt with one too many buttons undone to expose his chest, and his unnaturally full head of hair was held in place with some kind of slick gel. He reminded her of an Elvis impersonator. She and Hassan introduced themselves and climbed into his vintage Mercedes.

"This is an honor for me, Dr. McGuinness."

"Likewise, Hassan. I don't often have a film star for a driver."

"Television star, doctor. My show was called *The Thieves of Baghdad*. Like Ali Baba and the 40 thieves sort of thing. Highest rated show on Iraqi TV. I did eight seasons."

"Why are you driving for a living?"

"During the invasion, all of the television studios were destroyed. All of the cameras and sets were looted. My horse was stolen. I'm out of work."

"What happened to your horse?"

"Saladin? He was a beautiful Arabian from the Nejd. I think he must have fed a family for a month. These are hard times."

The traffic was snarled in Tahrir Square and Lee had the first taste of what she later called the Hassan experience. Drivers gave them quick, furtive looks, then stared mercilessly at Hassan's face, the Ali Baba they knew so well, who had come into their homes and kept them strong through the grinding years of U.N. sanctions, when they sold the toaster before the television in order to keep up with the episodes about a man of the people who stole from the rich of Mansour and gave to the poor of Hillah.

"Hassan!" It came from every direction. Women in *hijab*, Iraqi soldiers, men in full beards with turbans and *dishdashas* — they pointed, they whispered, they approached timidly. The traffic became hopelessly stuck.

"Is it always like this?"

"I'm afraid so."

"Do you have any kind of disguise?"

"No."

"Hassan, it's risky for me to attract this much attention."

"Don't worry, Dr. McGuinness. It's okay. If you are with me, they think you are someone from Hollywood, my producer or something. Nobody will touch you. Excuse me for a moment." Hassan, the idol of a generation, signed his name on whatever was presented. A young woman approached with her infant's bib.

"I suppose that's the first time you've signed baby clothes."

"No, I've signed lots of them. I've even signed babies."

When they finally pulled up to the barricade at the Dar, Duncan was pacing on the steps talking on his satellite phone.

"Lee, where have you been? Jabarri is waiting. He hates to wait. Let's go." He was startled by Hassan. "Where is Sadoon?"

"Family crisis. Hassan, meet Duncan."

"*Tasharrafna*. Haven't I seen you before?"

They arrived at the Jabarri compound in Mansour in record time because Hassan simply hailed a policeman parked in an official pickup truck and explained to the officer that he needed an escort.

Within seconds they were racing through central Baghdad in a motorcade, complete with siren, flashing lights, and a complement of men with AK-47s. Jabarri's pack of security men manning the gates looked at the police escort with disdain. Lee could see they were American from their walk, their Ray-Bans, and their water bottles. On closer inspection, they wore ID cards from Rattlecorp. The standard kit for

146

such security men included an array of heavy weapons and knives, radio gear, steel-plated vests, and baseball caps or bush hats.

"They always make me feel underdressed," Duncan said waspishly.

Their arms were often left bare to display biceps that looked both meaty and slack. They were men past their prime.

"All hat and no cattle," Lee said.

"What does that mean?"

"It's just something they say in Texas."

"Sir, I need you to stand right over here, please." Jabarri's guards had fashioned a little holding pen marked with concrete barriers and spray paint where visitors were herded while their belongings were being examined. Hassan, Duncan, and Lee all stood in the pen as the Rattlecorp men went through Lee's voluminous purse. A sleek German Shepherd appeared and began sniffing for bombs.

"Good girl, Veronica."

Veronica seemed to be drooling on Lee's passports, keys, and a few more personal items the security men had laid out in the sun.

"This is too much," she said under her breath.

"If you could just spread your legs, please." Lee's temper was still in check but would not be for long.

"Turn around, please."

The guard seemed to be enjoyed patting her down.

"That is enough." Duncan grabbed Lee's purse. "Otherwise I will tell your employer that Rattlecorp is charging him 20 percent more than the Patriots and Whitewater charge."

"I wouldn't know about that, sir."

"Of course not. Because they pay you less. And not a penny of insurance." Duncan shook his head, "You risk your life every day and see how they exploit you."

The Rattlecorp men looked deflated as they swung open the heavy wooden doors, remnants of old Baghdad that no doubt had been crated up and moved from the old city when it was torn down. They motioned for Hassan to return to the car.

"I'm sorry, sir," one said officiously. "I can't let you inside because you're not on the list. You will remain with the vehicle." The Rattlecorp men had no idea who Hassan was, nor did they care.

"We won't be long, Hassan." There had been quite enough foreplay at the gate. Lee was anxious to get through this interview with a man she regarded as unpleasant and dangerous. Inside the courtyard, the garden looked tired and laden with dust. The roses were rangy and unpruned. There were masses of trumpet vines climbing in wild profusion up the stucco walls. The fountain was empty and full of leaves. Its dry spout ran out of the mouth of a bronze shark. There were weapons lined up against the courtyard wall next to some ivory tusks and a plaster cast that looked like one of Snow White's seven dwarves. Just inside the entrance to the house, there was a life-sized stuffed rhinoceros.

"Ground rhino horn is a very popular aphrodisiac," Duncan told Lee.

"Does it work?"

"I haven't tried it, but I suspect Jabarri has."

They were ushered into a large, undistinguished room with overstuffed chairs lining the walls and badly made stained-glass windows. There were carpets, though not good ones, and the floor was the kind of pink marble found in public restrooms in railway stations. The walls were painted flesh color and the light fixtures had naked bulbs. Lee could see that no one was devoting much time to decorating.

Slouched in some of the chairs at the far end of the room were men in *keffiyehs* and polyester suits, fondling their worry beads. They took no notice of Lee's presence and looked as though they had been waiting for days or perhaps weeks for an audience with Adnan Jabarri. A woman sat separately in her black *abaya* with a child wriggling onto her lap, his small hand turning her face to his in a plea for attention.

"That's Saddam's brother's wife," Duncan whispered. "I bet Jabarri helped himself to her property."

Trays arrived with roasted pumpkin seeds and colas that tasted of rust. Before long they were summoned into a small sitting room with overstuffed leather sofas and samovars. Adnan Jabarri was pacing by the windows, satellite phone to his ear, looking for better reception. He was small and trim with a well-clipped mustache and black-rimmed glasses. His one concession to vanity was an expensive leather jacket. Servants brought in dried figs and Turkish coffee.

"Welcome to my home," he said expansively when he had finished the call. "That was the office of the secretary of defense," he said with a half smile. "Your secretary of defense. He thinks I am a traitor and a spy."

"Thank you for seeing us, Mr. Jabarri. I understand that you are very busy these days." Lee gave him a winning look, suppressing her distaste.

"Not too busy for you. Have we met before?"

"I know you only by reputation."

"I understand you are here to find Martin Carrigan."

"That's right."

"I am afraid he has gone to the dark side. Greed, I suppose. I apologize for the state of my family's house. Saddam's sons took it over and used it as their private brothel. It was badly neglected. I'm building an archive here, a kind of Truth and Reconciliation Center with some very interesting files. A record of all of Saddam's agents, some of them very surprising."

"I would be grateful if you could tell me what you know about Martin," Lee said, hoping to strip her voice of emotion. "He met with one of your people at the Tigris Hotel a couple of weeks ago."

"Your friend Mr. Carrigan was very anxious to do business in Baghdad. Everyone knows that I have the experience and contacts to facilitate business here, so of course, everyone comes to me. It is really very routine."

"He wanted you to help with refugee supplies?"

"Good heavens, no." He smiled at Lee's ignorance of the world. "He wanted me to participate in some illegal business importing weapons for the insurgents. The profit was very high, but as a member of the Governing Council, I have a reputation to protect."

"Which insurgents?" Duncan asked.

"Fringe groups, related to al-Kufa."

"Shia groups?"

"Yes."

"Why wouldn't they just go to Iran?"

"Well, you see" — he lit a cigarette and offered one to Duncan — "Iran, like all legitimate governments, likes to work through cutouts. They have a long history of working with Americans on arms deals. It appears they are working with your friend."

"How do you know that?" Lee was impatient with his assumptions.

"I am rather infamous for my sources in Iran. I am a Shiite, too. Your government is constantly trying to prove that I am spying for the ayatollahs."

"I went to see George Plumber in the Green Zone, expecting his help," Lee said abruptly. There seemed no point in holding back information. "Plumber informed me that Martin is wanted for treason and that there is proof in documents picked up in a raid in Karbala. I think I know who had those documents, but he is in Abu Ghraib."

"As a member of the Governing Council with a portfolio that includes the Interior Ministry and Intelligence, I am privy to those documents," Jabarri said, smiling at her triumphantly. "In fact, I have copies." He reached for an envelope on his desk and tossed it into Lee's lap. "Have a look at that, Dr. McGuinness."

She held it for a moment before opening it, afraid of what she would find. A wave of uncertainty washed over her. The fugitive and the boy might have been lying, to protect secrets that she had no business knowing, a cell of resistance, linked to Iran, arming themselves for an uprising against the occupation. For all she knew, the entire leadership of Karbala was involved. They had been told by the Grand Ayatollah in Najaf to be patient. But perhaps their patience was growing thin. It was feasible that they had convinced Martin to help them, for a nice percentage. It was the sort of risk that he had always wanted to take.

"Lee, do you want me to open it?" Duncan's voice filled the embarrassing silence.

"No. It's fine." She ripped the flap and pulled out three 8x10 black-and-white glossy photographs and a sheaf of bureaucratic forms covered in government stamps. They were Iranian government stamps. The photos were of Martin, wearing a suit with no tie and an English trench coat. He had a few days stubble and was talking on a park bench to a man who was handing him a suitcase. She looked behind them in the photos and saw they were in a park.

"Where is this?" she asked Duncan.

He studied the photo.

"That's Laleh Park in downtown Tehran. It's like Central Park. The statue in the fountain behind them is al-Birunii, a medieval Persian astronomer."

The man with Martin was bearded, in his mid-30s and dressed like an ex-Revolutionary Guard, in a collarless white shirt and European suit. In the package there was an official photo of the man and a description from intelligence files. He was a top official with the Iranian Ministry of Defense.

The forms were end-user certificates, showing arms sold from the government of Iran to a company in Tblisi, Georgia, which had then resold them to a company in Panama City whose managing director was Martin Carrigan. From Martin's company they were shipped, at least on paper, to Aqaba in Jordan, destined for a buyer in Amman. The crates, with the same markings and contents as on the manifests in her hand, were seized by the U.S. Marines in Karbala, Iraq. There was a photo of the crates. Inside there were mortars, shoulder-fired rockets, grenades.

"May I take these?" Lee found it hard to speak. She wanted to go back to the Dar, somewhere where she could think.

"Of course, they are yours," Jabarri said, with a hint of pity. "Feel free to make copies for your newspaper, Mr. Hope. "I'm sorry about this."

"No problem." Lee felt defeated. "Thank you for taking the time to see me."

"What you are holding in your hand is a paper trail, of course. The arms never went to Georgia or Panama. They came straight from Tehran to Karbala, as the personal effects of a large group of religious pilgrims. I look forward to seeing you under better circumstances, at my cousin's party this weekend."

"Laela's?"

"Yes."

"How did you know I would be there?"

"Not much goes on in Baghdad that I don't know." He laughed. "And doctor, I want to talk to you about our urgent need of medical equipment from the States. Perhaps we can work together on that."

Before Lee could answer, Adnan Jabarri was already back on his satellite phone, pacing and smoking.

XV

THE MEN FROM RATTLECORP sat with their weapons resting astride their wide laps like sleeping children. They watched Lee climb into Hassan's Mercedes. Her face was expressionless and her movements mechanical. Lee's innocence, her sense of mission, had been lost in Jabarri's compound. The photographs had changed everything. She could still cling to the hope that the documents were somehow forged, but the photos were irrefutable. Martin had been in that park in Tehran. He was with an official from the Iranian Defense Ministry. Lee felt foolish for coming to Baghdad with such strident conviction that she knew this man, now such an enigma. He and the Iranian official were exchanging a suitcase. This was not the work of a man who devoted his life to refugees. Doubt enveloped her like the black veil she wrapped around her shoulders.

As they drove back to the Dar, Lee could not manage polite conversation. She was silent. Her mind was in Afghanistan, in the garden behind the high walls in Passport Street in Kabul, on the road to Jalalabad where the path down to the Kabul River was mined, at a lunch stop with Christmas decorations in June in the shadow of the Hindu Kush. She was with Martin. She was reviewing each scene, knowing now that he might have been an arms dealer or a spy. Perhaps she, as a doctor, had simply been useful to him as cover. The passion they shared to heal the world, to mend the lives that war destroyed like shattered pottery, was for him just a carefully crafted role. It was a painful revelation. She could see now what she had steadfastly refused to acknowledge. She was deeply in love with the man he had pretended to be.

"Can I buy you lunch?" Duncan lit a *beedi*.

"I'm out of my depth," Lee said as Hassan fell in with his police escort. "I really don't belong here."

"Of course you belong here. For one thing, you've improved my life immensely. Baghdad was dead boring before you arrived. Let's have a bottle of wine and some *mezze* by the pool." Duncan took her chin and, like the child in Jabarri's waiting room, gently turned her face to his. "Lee, have you ever heard the expression, 'Nothing matters much and very little matters at all'?"

"No."

"Well, it's the only wisdom I know. What's important is that you're here, right now, doing the right thing. I don't think you realize what a powerful effect you have on people, Lee. I want to help you, which for me is a very unusual desire." Duncan lit a cigarette. "I am a selfish, grasping journalist, consumed with ambition. You are a genuinely good person. Just being with you is improving me to no end. Cheer up, St. Joan. No matter what side Martin's on, you are on the right side. This is a very important story, Lee. Jabarri has just handed us proof that Iran is arming the Shia insurgency. They are shipping guns to al-Kufa, and Martin is the cutout. Do you mind if I write it?"

"What if there is some other explanation?" Not that she could think of one at the moment. She felt tired and spent, as though she had given hours to a patient who did not make it through. "You have to find Rubai in Abu Ghraib, Duncan. Before you write the story. It's the least we can do."

Back in Lee's dreary suite, the light was filtering through the drawn curtains, and she could hear the rotors of a helicopter gunship slapping the air nearby. She laid the documents and photos out on her Formica table, along with the letter from the soldier in Beit Har to his father at the Pentagon. Children were jumping on the tire in the street below and she switched on "BBC World News" because it was something to do. There was an item from Iraq, the American bombing of another wedding party near the Syrian border, mistaken for a gathering of insurgents. A survivor in a ward at the Ramadi hospital described an American soldier kicking her as she lay in a ditch, playing dead next to her son, his body cut in half by shrapnel. The spokesman for the U.S. military insisted there had been no wedding, even though the survivors were still wearing their party clothes, and the women's hands and arms were stained with henna.

There was enough Turkish coffee for one cup, and she sat down at the kitchen table, under the naked bulb, to look again at the soldier's letter.

PS,

Dad, I got your letters, all of them out of order. The packages arrived. I'm using the fan right now and Mom's cookies were great. I am building my own mess hall. We have to walk a mile to the DFAC, where we eat bad food in dirt up to our ankles. We've been skipping meals, which isn't good because we're getting way too thin. I gave the support company commander two days to work things out. I am fed up with these guys and I will not take any more crap from them when it comes to taking care of my soldiers.

The Iraqis have figured out how to destroy tanks. The other day, a tank was rammed by a civilian oil truck that jack-

knifed and leaked oil onto the tank's engine compartment. The oil went into the pre-cleaner and NBC system and started a fire. The truck driver didn't do it on purpose, but now everybody knows.

I talked with my battalion XO. He actually left his palace to see what improvements needed to be made. I like this guy. We are having generator issues, so it is hard to write letters on the computer, but I would rather do that than take pen to paper. The wind rips the paper out of my hands as I'm trying to write. Going out with my mortar platoon tonight. I want to check out their ambush positions.

Thanks for the cigars.

The power failed. Lee sat in darkness, waiting for the sound of the generator. There was a knock on the door, and she hoped it might be the maid bringing her a towel. She found Duncan, breathless from climbing the stairs. The elevator had stopped between floors.

"I was trapped, Lee. The bodyguards on the second floor had to pry open the doors and pull me out." He walked past her into the room. "I need your passport number."

"Why?"

"Because I am getting you into Abu Ghraib prison as my photographer."

"What?"

"*Gentleman's Monthly* has fixed you up a nice press card. Do you have a camera?"

"Mine isn't expensive enough. No one will ever believe that I am a professional." The generator kicked in like an old lawn mower.

"We'll borrow one. Masoud can lend you something. We should leave the hotel tomorrow morning at 7. Tell Hassan we are going into the triangle."

* * *

There was something hopeful about saying "the triangle," as though the violence could be contained. Their Mercedes crossed into it just outside Baghdad, on a deserted stretch of highway heading west that looked like a newly tarmacked spur on the outskirts of Palm Springs. Hassan passed a convoy that had broken down, and the soldiers, their faces rigid with fear, were fanning out into the palm groves to hunt for attackers who found this stretch of road ideal for detonating bundles of high explosives.

"Abu Ghraib means 'father of a stranger,' " Duncan said as they entered the dirt-packed no-man's-land in front of the prison walls. There were guard towers, concertina wire, and snipers, one of whom had shot and killed a cameraman a week ago for taking his picture. Below, in the dusty forecourt outside the first checkpoint, there was a sad gathering of prisoners' relatives, carrying folded bits of paper with copied photos and identification numbers and ration cards that each of them took in turn to the guards, begging for any scrap of information about their missing brothers and husbands. The soldiers, who could not understand what they were saying, stared at them through wraparound sunglasses as though they were a cloud of insects. The soldiers waved the families away, further into the empty lot where they stood, heads bowed in the sun's glare, not knowing what to do.

A public-affairs officer was waiting at the gate, a short, barrel-chested major who leapt into the back seat with his rifle.

"Good morning, all. I'm Major Boomer. I will be your liaison officer today here at Baghdad Central. I understand that you all are from England?"

"Yes, Major Boomer," Duncan tried to match his cheer. "From London."

"I have relatives from Manchester," Boomer continued. "I have yet to go there, but hope that one day I will be afforded the opportunity."

The car was snaking through a maze of sandbags and razor wire, past nondescript low buildings and tent camps.

"Ma'am." Boomer was eyeing Lee's borrowed equipment bag. "There will be no photographs of prisoners of any kind. They are off-limits. You are here to see General Tater, and you are cleared to photograph him as well as facilities for which you have received prior permission. Let's work together on this."

"Of course, Major." She was delighted with the restrictions. She could get away with hardly taking a picture.

"You American?"

"Yes."

"Where from?"

"New York."

"Oh. Well, everybody. We have arrived."

They were in a parking lot surrounded by Humvees and a wall of wire that formed part of a cage filled with dozens of men wearing orange jump suits. The men shouted at them in Arabic, and it was clear that Maj. Boomer was not an Arabic speaker.

"*Sahafi*, journalist, come over here. I don't belong here. Please contact my family. *Min fadlik*." Duncan veered toward the cage.

"The people we are holding in this facility are Iraqi-on-Iraqi crime. Murderers, rapists, aggravated assault." Maj. Boomer spoke like a docent at the National Zoo. "We don't have political prisoners. We have civilian criminals."

"Hello, ma'am," one of the caged exhibits said to Lee. "I am a surgeon. From Husaybah. Near Al-Qa'im. They arrested me in front of my family. I was beaten on my face and legs.

They kicked my face with their boots, *wallahi.*" His face was still blue with an ugly gash in his head.

Boomer tried to herd his charges away.

"Doctor," Lee heard a familiar voice. She turned and there, in prison garb, was Sadoon, dehydrated and scared, with black circles under his eyes that looked like someone had drawn them with soot.

"Duncan," Lee lowered her voice. "Sadoon is here. Distract Boomer." She approached the fence slowly, as though studying the animals with aimless curiosity.

"Doctor, please get me out of here. They came to my house in the middle of the night. You must tell my wife I am here. We are like the dead. No one can see us. The man you are looking for is here too. Rubai. I know him. Please help us, doctor."

"Hey, over there," Boomer had noticed Lee taking far too much interest. "You with the camera. What's your name?"

"Lee."

"Well, Lee, It's dangerous to get too close to those *hajjis.* You might get hurt. Their friends have been lobbin' mortars at us every night. Two days ago we had to call in the 82nd Airborne. Let's head on over to the hospitality tent and grab some coffee before we meet the general."

"Of course, Major. Are you a *Gentleman's Monthly* reader?" Duncan intervened with concentrated charm.

"No. I can't say that I am."

"General Tater will probably get the cover."

"He'll be tickled with that. He's a ham, all right."

"Where are you from, Major?" Lee took up the slack. She was anxious to repair relations so that he would forget that she had strayed too close to the cage.

"Page County, Virginia."

"Some of my family are in Rappahannock."

"Well, I'll be damned. We're probably related." Everyone began to relax.

"How long have you been over here?"

"Too long, I'll tell you that. This war is killin' me. My whole business just about fell apart. I got nothin' to go back to now."

"What business?"

"Cuttin' hay. I had a lot of clients in Page, Madison, even Clark County. They've all moved on now. You can't wait around for somebody to cut hay. I'm already in hock for my Batwing Bush Hog. Pretty soon I'll have to sell my Kubota."

"You can't sell your tractor, Major. Does your wife have a job?"

"My ex lives in Luray. She works part time at Luray Caverns, operating the stalactite organ during the underground weddings there. Ever heard that organ?"

"Of course. I've always wanted to get married there," Lee said, only half in jest.

"Now you're making me homesick. Lee, is it?"

"Yes. When do you go home, Major?"

"April. Maybe. With stop-loss you never know." His tour, he said, could be extended any time. "You folks wait here. I'll get the general."

Major Boomer left them at the coffee machine in what looked like an airplane hangar draped with camouflage nets. The air was full of dust. Laptops and cables littered rows of folding tables, and soldiers were huddled in groups in their sand-colored camouflage. They watched Lee and Duncan with a mixture of mild interest and distrust, as though by nature, all outsiders wanted to pilfer classified secrets from their screens. They were perfectly justified in this case, because Duncan wanted nothing more than to pull up

Sadoon and Rubai's files and see how the 800th MP Brigade portrayed their crimes. He had Rubai's Abu Ghraib inmate number in his pocket ready for the interview. Lee's camera was loaded with film. All she was required to do was pull it out casually and snap a few pictures. No one was going to inspect her composition.

Just then Gen. Tater heaved into view. He was large and square with a heavy brow and deep-set eyes, the same washed out blue as George Plumber's. There were deep shadows in his face from lack of sleep. He grabbed Lee's hand and shook it with an openness belied by his tight, dry mouth.

The general turned to Duncan. "Let's go for a tour first. I want to take you to Saddam's torture chamber and the hanging cells. A lot's changed around here now. Prisoners are fed and watered. It's a completely different scenario than what they faced before. They were treated, you know, inhumanely. More like animals." He walked with long, confident strides through the prison barracks, followed by attendants who fanned out behind him, waiting for an order.

"Are they allowed visits from their families?" Duncan and Lee did their best to keep up.

"Yes. All of our facilities have family visits at least one day a week. They can come in and sit with them for 15 minutes. Now, this facility right here used to be a machine shop." The general stopped. "Saddam's men would force the prisoners' hands into the machines, which would cut their hands off. When they took prisoners to be executed, they would rip them open and take their kidneys or eyes before they actually executed them. Doctors from the Baghdad Medical Center came here to pick up the body parts. Watch your head."

They ducked through a low door and into a dimly lit cellblock covered with Arabic graffiti.

"Those are prisoners' last words," said General Tater. "Here it says 'Ahmed.' Here, 'Jawad al-Abadi.' Here it says, 'Oh my God.' "

The general took them briskly to the hanging room and the gas chamber before offering everyone some bottled water and folding chairs in the courtyard for the interview. The compound walls were pockmarked with bullet holes and larger scars, the size of portholes, from mortars.

"How often are you mortared?" Duncan asked with some concern.

"Three or four times a week," shrugged the general. "This is a rough area. It's a hostile-fire zone."

As Duncan began questioning Gen. Tater about his prison routine, his preferred R&R hotels in Kuwait City and Amman, his background in military intelligence, Lee tried in vain to imagine herself as a great war photographer, a Salgado or Capa. She snapped 15 or 20 pictures, and each one, she knew, would be worse than the last.

"General," Duncan began. "You have one prisoner here who was originally classified as a prisoner of war. His name is Ahmad Rubai."

"It doesn't ring a bell," the general said earnestly. "We have thousands of prisoners here."

"He was a city councilor in Karbala, appointed by the local people there after U.S. troops took the city. He was arrested and sent to Um Qasr. This is a picture of him. Does that help you at all?"

The general shifted defensively in his chair as he studied Rubai's face.

"No."

"He received this signed release form saying he hadn't committed any belligerent acts. Then he was picked up and brought here. You can see his prison number. His family and his lawyer say they've been denied all access. No information about charges. No visits. Is that possible?"

"Not likely, Mr. Hope. Why would we want to deny family members information about their loved one?"

Maj. Boomer was hovering behind Duncan, drawing his finger urgently across his neck, trying to catch the general's eye. Lee could see he wanted to cut the line of questioning. "Mr. Hope, this is hardly relevant to a *Gentleman's Monthly* profile of the general."

"Do you think, General, that you could find out whether he is here?" Duncan ignored Boomer, addressing Gen. Tater with such politeness and deference that it was impossible to deny him what he wanted without seeming rude.

"Well, if we have a record on this fellow it will say what his charges are."

"So no one is being held here without charges?"

"No." The general lost his composure. "I mean, there's nobody here being held for no reason. This is the first time I've ever heard of this individual. We could certainly find him if he's anywhere in our correctional facility."

"Could we check the computer?"

"That is not normal procedure."

Duncan said nothing.

"Major Boomer." As Gen. Tater addressed him, Boomer drew himself to attention. "Would you take them to the hospitality tent while I check on this?"

"Yes, sir."

Lee and Duncan waited for half an hour drinking instant coffee with spoonfuls of dried creamer. When the general returned, his face looked hard, with deep fissures like a fault line dragging his mouth down to his jaw.

"We've located the individual. I'm not authorized to release any information. His processing is not completed."

"You said that process normally takes 24 hours."

"Approximately."

"But it's been two months."

"I'm afraid that's enough." Maj. Boomer stepped in to protect the general from embarrassing himself. "This was supposed to be an interview for a men's lifestyle magazine."

"Major," said Duncan with authority. "This is a very serious charge. This violates the Geneva Convention. And I might add, we recognized another prisoner in the cage who is most certainly not a common criminal. He is our driver. His name is Sadoon. So you can add him to our list of ghost prisoners that we expect the U.S. military to answer for. I don't only write for gentlemen's magazines. I write for the London *Herald*. In two days, this will be all over the papers in Europe. Here is my card, General, with my email if there are any further statements you or anyone in your chain of command would like to make. Thank you for the tour and a most interesting interview."

Duncan turned and left.

Lee stood with Major Boomer, buffeted by Duncan's performance, as though they had just watched a twister cut a path through the foothills of the Blue Ridge.

"Thank you, Major. I hope you get home soon."

"You bet." Boomer was seething.

"And don't sell the tractor. What's your ex-wife's name?"

"Debbie."

"I'll look her up the next time I'm in Luray."

"Yeah." His face was flushed. "You do that."

Outside the fortress gates, the prisoners' families were still waiting for some word, walking slowly in circles, with no audience but the dust devils.

"Can you believe it, Duncan?" Lee threw on her veil, now caked with dust, "They have Sadoon in that kennel."

She wanted to talk about Sadoon, about the rockets in the Green Zone. But with Hassan listening intently, she was sure that by nightfall Sadoon's role in the attack would be the talk of every coffeehouse in Baghdad. The story would be embroidered in the telling and retelling until Sadoon was elevated to mastermind, and Lee was revealed as his handler from American intelligence. Iraqis preferred complex explanations. They believed in the hidden hand, Abu Naji, the machinations of intelligence agencies bent on sowing confusion and civil war.

"If anyone can get Sadoon out, it's you, Duncan. Thank you for what you've done for Rubai, not just because you've brought us closer to Martin but because the poor guy was clearly going to disappear in there, for months, maybe years. You're a much better man than you think, Duncan. How many Rubais are in there?"

"Your military will never answer that question. They will just lie." He was hunched over his notebook in the back seat, preparing his broadside against Central Command.

"Please don't say 'my military,'" Lee said firmly. "This is not my war."

Both of them saw the black smoke spreading like a bruise on the horizon. It was a mile down the highway, a stretch of road that was deserted because it was known as one of the shooting galleries of west Baghdad. Licks of orange flame were dancing in the distance.

"A car?"

"No, it's a Humvee." Duncan had seen this before. "Part of a patrol. Hassan, be careful. Stay away from them."

Soldiers, some looking dazed, others screaming, were limping out of the other two vehicles. Lee realized that one of them was spraying bullets into the surrounding countryside, pivoting on his heels as he turned 360 degrees to collectively punish whoever got in his way. Hassan's Mercedes happened to be within range. Duncan pushed Lee to the floor.

"Stop the car, Hassan. If you overtake them they will kill us."

No one spoke or moved. They waited, until two soldiers waving M-4 rifles crossed the no man's land between them.

"What the fuck are you doing here?" One of them addressed Duncan. The soldier's rage felt like the shock from an electrified fence.

"Visiting Abu Ghraib." He broadened his English accent so that it could be mistaken for something down Maine, hoping that the soldier would relax among his own kind. "What happened up there?"

"Who's on the floor back there?" he pointed his weapon at Lee.

"I'm a doctor."

"Get out of the car. On your knees."

Lee slowly pulled herself up off the floor and sat straight backed, silent and still. She would not get on her knees for anyone, certainly not this boy with a gun who dared to humiliate her.

"What is your name, soldier?" There was defiance in her voice, and fury.

"Shut the fuck up." The soldier wrenched opened the back door. Duncan could see that this would end badly.

"On your knees. Hands in the air. On your knees."

"Look, I'm a doctor. Whatever happened over there, I can help. Please, I might be able to save somebody's life."

The soldiers smelled of fire. They were breathing heavily, trying to focus on the information.

"Where's your ID?"

She pulled the International Surgeons' Committee pass slowly out of her pocket and presented it.

"Okay. Come on, doctor. The rest of you stay right here. Nobody fucking moves. Do you hear me? Nobody fucking moves."

"Where's my backpack, Hassan?" Lee spoke slowly and evenly, watching the barrels of the M4s.

"In back."

Lee collected her supplies and ran with the soldiers to the scene of the explosion. She moved faster, unencumbered by the heavy body armor, the weapons, and shock that dragged them down. The explosion had been an IED road-side bomb, and the heat was unbearable. One of the men was dead. Another who had been thrown from the Humvee was conscious and in pain. His left leg and arm were broken and his back and side of his head were studded with hot metal. Lee gave him a shot of morphine and splinted the bones sticking at 90 degree angles out of his bloody camouflage trousers. She had enough bandages, but needed something long and straight to hold the fracture in place. She reached for a piece of metal pipe, still hot from the explosion. Before the wounded man drifted off, he was anxious to talk, to bear witness to the events that had left him a quivering mass of blood and burned flesh.

"They had buried artillery rounds. When we went by, they just set if off with a cell phone and blew us into the air. They shot at us with AK-47s. There's three to eight guys. I don't know. I was blown up and —"

"Take it easy. Everything's okay."

A halo of blood was forming around his face on the tar-mac.

"It was organized. They knew what we were gonna do, what we were trained to do. You've got to get me out of here."

There was a crash and a shower of sparks as part of the Humvee's armor fell off its frame. Lee could see that it was plywood and scrap metal, what she had seen the soldiers' scavenging for in the junkyard south of Baghdad.

"Where's Eric? Where's my gunner?"

"He'll be fine, too." Lee looked at the crumpled and burnt corpse slumped behind the M240 machine gun.

"He's my best friend."

"Don't any of you have a radio?" Lee addressed the men sharply. "This man will bleed to death if he doesn't get to the hospital."

"They don't work," one soldier spat. "Shit, they don't work at all."

Lee did her best to staunch the blood from the wounded man's head, which looked like a broken sieve, and dress the superficial lacerations of the others. She was nervous waiting on the empty highway, sprinkled with glass and debris, within sight, she was sure, of the insurgents. There was no separating herself from these soldiers now, no way to say, "I am the good American. The civilian, the doctor. Not like them." Here they were all the same, bathed in sweat from the flames, smelling of diesel and charred flesh.

She was hardly aware of the helicopter until it landed. Small-arms fire erupted from the dense plantation of palms beyond the wide drainage ditch that severed the highway from the attackers' refuge. She watched the rescue squad medics reach for Eric's body in the inferno and saw his toasted flesh come apart in their hands. The chopper crew quickly bundled her morphine-dosed patient onto a stretcher and took him away. She never even heard his name.

XVI

"ARE YOU ALL RIGHT?" Duncan was carrying a large gin and tonic.

"I'm fine. Just tired."

Lee could not remember running down the bullet-swept highway back to the Mercedes, only that she somehow climbed into the back seat and felt the blast of hot wind on her face as Hassan drove at high speed into town. At the Dar, she sat by the pool, enveloped in the scent of singed hair that clung to her blood-stained clothes. She needed a shower, clean sheets, and sleeping pills to wipe away the image of the Humvee's gunner, his blackened hand coming away from his wrist.

"Drink this." Duncan placed the gin in front of her, dropped his shoulder bag, and put his cigarettes on the table. "You're going to have a very good reputation with the U.S. Army." He sat down and admired her.

"What do you see? I'm a wreck." Lee surveyed the damage.

"I see a high, intelligent forehead and cheekbones growing more prominent with every day that you decline to eat another bad meal in Iraq. Your eyes look as though someone has sprinkled copper dust around the iris. You're magnificent, Lee."

"I did what anyone would do." Lee was embarrassed by his praise.

"People get medals for that sort of thing."

"Duncan, I can't stop thinking about Sadoon."

"You mean which side he's on?" To survive in his line of work, Duncan remained neutral, or so he told himself, to keep channels open on all sides.

"Yes. I mean, my instinct is to make a big scene to get him out of Abu Ghraib. But you and I both know he was somehow involved in that rocket attack. He knew something was going to happen. He knew when and where it was going to happen." She took a long, slow sip of gin. "What do you think we should do?"

"He could be just very well informed."

"When I confronted him, he said that everyone in al-Adhamiyah knew. Should I believe that?"

"It's not uncommon for the *shabab* to warn their neighbors to stay away from a target. You don't really know until you talk to people there. Even then, it's hard to say who is a conspirator and who just overheard the plot. If you like, I will go and see his family." Duncan moved a stray lock of Lee's hair out of her face. "Actually, I would do anything for you right now."

"Thank you."

"First I must file my story. Rubai isn't just a stop along the way to finding Martin. If he's being held there as a special prisoner, who else is there? They've been lying to us, Lee, about a prison full of thieves and rapists, and it turns out there's a whole secret cellblock of political prisoners. I need to email questions to Central Command." Duncan smiled. "I'm going to get Rubai out of there. Give me the cameras. I promised to return them to Masoud."

She pulled cameras from around her neck and from her seemingly bottomless bag. "Duncan, what if Rubai has been receiving arms from Martin? What if it's true?" Lee felt guilty for even having such knowledge.

"Then he is a prisoner of war and should be treated as such. He is entitled to visits and humane treatment. We have something called the Geneva Convention."

"Of course. Right." She needed some time alone. "Thank Masoud for me, would you?" she smiled. "I hope I haven't broken anything. I'm afraid I have no future as a photojournalist." A look of defiance crossed her face. "You should know I'm going back to Karbala."

"I thought you were doing the sensible thing and going back to surgery. Don't you think Martin's ties with Tehran make things a little awkward for you? Frankly, he should have been in touch by now. You have no idea what you're dealing with." Gunfire erupted somewhere in the neighborhood.

"Just one trip. I promised Rubai's son."

"Please don't go alone, Lee. Wait until I finish my story. I'll come with you."

"There's no time. Hassan will look after me."

"If you must do it, tell Hassan to bring some of his friends from the Badr Brigade."

The whitewashed apartment blocks beyond the court-yard walls were stained pink by the falling light, and the man with the tattoos reappeared in a chaise longue across the pool. The thought crossed Lee's mind that he might have won the contract to kill her. She left Duncan on the terrace and arranged with Hassan to meet her in the morning for an early start to Karbala and asked that he bring some militia-men, just in case there were any gunmen taking an unfriendly interest. Hassan assured her that in spite of the Friday holiday, he could find security. One of the advantages of Hassan's celebrity was that everyone was ready to do the television star a favor.

Lee slept badly that night in spite of the pills. She woke with the call to prayer, dressed quickly, and joined her escorts at dawn. They were unshaven, heavily armed, and ready to shield her from an enemy she had never seen and could only describe by saying she had been warned to leave Iraq. They would do it because she was Hassan's friend. The brigade men drove recklessly through Baghdad in a double helix, folding back on their path, crashing through alleyways, upsetting chickens, scattering piles of garbage, and terrifying one poor man shaving in the open air with a straight edged razor.

"Hassan, is this really necessary?"

"They have watched a lot of movies," he shrugged. "They know every chase scene. You know the one where George Clooney is in his BMW chasing the Russian mafia through Vienna? They've watched it a hundred times. Everyone here is scared of them."

"Well, that's comforting." When they reached the open countryside past Hillah, Lee called Dr. Husseini on her Thuraya and asked him to arrange a meeting with the prisoner's son. She also asked whether the fugitive, whom she referred to discreetly as the gentleman who dropped by the office, might grant her a second audience. She wanted to press him on Martin. She had fulfilled her side of the bargain. Duncan's story would be all over Baghdad by noon.

The boy was waiting for her where they had last met, in the tangled garden behind Dr. Husseini's charity offices, under the cedars. He was expectant but reserved, accustomed, like all Iraqis, to disappointment. Lee had Jabarri's incriminating documents in her purse, and felt, given the weight of the evidence against Martin, far from certain of the facts. The prisoner's son, standing in front of her in his freshly laundered *dishdasha*, might be an innocent whose

173

father was unjustly jailed by the occupation authorities, or a conspirator who knew that Martin had supplied his father with a cache of weapons to use against the U.S. Army. She told the boy that Gen. Tater had admitted that his father existed somewhere within the walls of Abu Ghraib, and that after two months, he had yet to be charged. When Duncan had followed up with Gen. Tater's superiors in the Green Zone, he had received a terse email that he slipped under Lee's door earlier that morning acknowledging that a special class of political prisoner, in spite of official denials, was in fact languishing in his cells.

"Why can't I see him?"

Lee read the email: "Internees are not permitted visitors for a host of security concerns related to the ongoing circumstances involving parties in armed conflict." She asked Dr. Husseini to translate it for the boy. Rubai's son did not understand. He stared at Lee, uncomprehending.

The arrangement violated the Geneva Convention. She told the boy his father might well be released to avoid further scrutiny of political prisoners. He nodded and said only that he would wait.

Dr. Husseini stood on the verandah, wearing a starched white shirt and charcoal-gray suit. He spoke quietly to the boy and sent him home. His face was drained of color.

"We have just found a new mass grave, Dr. McGuinness. We think that Saddam dumped more than 3,000 bodies there. This is a very important find." The families could now bury their dead, and Dr. Husseini would have the evidence that he and the other Shia leaders needed to build the case that the former dictator had been a mass murderer.

"I apologize for interrupting your work, Dr. Husseini."

"Nonsense, doctor. Come and have a coffee. Tell me about my old home, Abu Ghraib." They sat on a worn cut-velvet sofa surrounded by hundreds of cartons of eggs ready for distribution. An old man, with skin like brown paper, offered Lee Turkish coffee, medium sweet.

"Duncan thinks Rubai will be released," she said guardedly, "simply because keeping him now would be a political liability for Central Command. But I am not convinced that he is innocent. Dr. Husseini, I must talk to you about Martin Carrigan. I have some information about his activities and I don't know enough to distinguish between fact and fiction. Are people here receiving weapons from Iran?"

"Why do you ask?"

"Because Adnan Jabarri gave me documents to prove that Martin is a cutout for Iran, selling arms to al-Kufa's people."

"Really?" Dr. Husseini laughed. "Did Jabarri also tell you that he himself is al-Kufa's partner?"

"What?" Lee sat very still, trying to reconfigure the facts in her mind. The more she wanted the truth, the further it receded, like a palace in the desert that was nothing but sand, a dune shifting in the heat, reshaped by optical illusion. The only reality here was deception. "How is that possible?"

"A marriage of convenience." Dr. Husseini was enjoying her disbelief. He was proud of the complexity of his wretched country in the same way that he was proud that it was one of the oldest cultures on earth. The two went together. "Jabarri is a very shrewd man. He will do whatever is necessary to take power in Iraq."

"But if they are partners and Martin is arming them, why would Jabarri want him arrested?"

"Do you have the documents with you?"

"Yes." Lee spread the photographs and the official-looking papers with Iranian stamps on the table. Dr. Husseini spoke Farsi as well as Arabic. Lee hoped that he could detect

175

something useful, like the name of an official in Tehran or the signs of an obvious forgery.

He studied the photos for a long time in silence.

"Unless these photos have been doctored, they show your friend meeting in Tehran with a senior official. I know the man. I can confirm his identity. He is handing your friend a suitcase. But what's in it?" The scientist was testing the empirical evidence. "If your friend is an arms dealer, buying Iranian weapons, then the suitcase should be full of cash. And your friend Carrigan should be handing it to the Iranian as payment. Instead, it's the other way around."

Lee studied the picture again. "You're right. It seems so obvious now."

The long figure of Dr. Ali appeared and told Husseini that there was an urgent call. "Please excuse me, Dr. McGuinness."

"Of course." She felt parched. What could Martin possibly be receiving in a suitcase from the Iranian Defense Ministry? Was Iran paying him a fee to be the cutout for the weapons? She wondered how long she could take extended leave from her life to chase shadows in Iraq. She had not even begun to consider how she could bundle Martin onto a plane at Baghdad airport without anyone noticing, assuming he deserved to be rescued. One plane a day left that airport, and the place was a tomb except for security men and soldiers, each taking a great deal of interest in the passenger list. Lee was facing a road trip to Amman or Kuwait city or Zakho, with a wanted man who had no interest in even meeting her.

"Dr. McGuinness, we have to go." Dr. Husseini turned and left before she could ask for a glass of water. Lee gathered the documents and ran to keep up, nearly upsetting a mountain of eggs.

"Come with me. Tell Hassan and your Badr friends to follow. At a distance. Tell them there may be trouble."

Lee relayed the message, grabbed her backpack, and climbed into Dr. Husseini's car, an old Lada in desperate need of repair.

"Forgive the car. I don't have the time or the money to fix it."

"What's going on?" She saw that they were headed for the Hussein shrine, with its graceful Ottoman arches poised on top of Corinthian columns, a vestige of the Byzantines.

"Al-Kufa's men have seized the shrine. There are 300 hostages inside."

"Why would they do that?"

"To show people they can take power from the Grand Ayatollah. And to rob the shrine's coffers. There are treasures in that shrine that you can hardly imagine. My father saw them once. He told me there was a solid gold brazier with coals made of black pearls and rubies. Shiites have brought gems and gold to Karbala for over a thousand years. Al-Kufa is enough of a megalomaniac to help himself. He will justify the theft as necessary to carry out the overthrow of the unjust rulers. If he takes possession of the shrine, he'll be able to collect funds from the pilgrims, a nice bankroll for his revolution."

There was a police roadblock stretched across the broad avenue in front of them, and Lee could see that the plaza outside the shrine was deserted. The market stalls were shuttered. They could hear bursts of automatic weapons fire coming from the rooftops.

"The guardians of the shrine," Husseini said gravely, "are firing on al-Kufa. This could easily get out of control." There were no U.S. forces or Polish troops, the face of the occupation, poised to intervene. Dr. Husseini spoke with police at the barrier who rapidly acquiesced to his demand to let them pass.

"How did you convince them?" Lee asked when he returned.

"They know me as the Grand Ayatollah's negotiator. It carries weight in Karbala." There was so much about Dr. Husseini that she did not know.

"Dr. McGuinness, I'm bringing you with me because you are a surgeon. I will stop now if you are afraid because what we're doing could be dangerous for you. Your driver will pick you up."

"Let's go." Lee's response was not so much courage as the quick reaction of a doctor trained to suppress panic. She would enter the shrine even though she found al-Kufa's people terrifying. She thought about her flight across the rooftops only a few days before. She was taking too many risks, she thought, and would pay for it. Still, there was no hesitating now. She knew there was an irrational element in what she was doing and it was tied up with Martin. Dr. Husseini's Lada was already beyond the police lines, careening through a no man's land ruled by snipers.

"Get on the floor," Husseini said in a voice that was void of emotion. Lee followed orders. The Lada was so cramped, she only managed to half squeeze herself under the dashboard. As she did it, she felt the air by her left ear disturbed by a draft and a sound like a cicada. It was only when Dr Husseini had run the gauntlet and was stopped at the massive wooden doors of the shrine that Lee saw the bullet hole in her seat.

"Oh my God, that was close," she said to Dr. Husseini. He was no longer there.

"*Yalla*, hurry, doctor, bring your supplies." He stood in the doorway of the shrine.

Breathing hard, Lee quickly checked that her *abaya* was covering her neck, ankles, and wrists and grabbed the backpack. She passed a clutch of gunmen with black beards and turbans, whose suspicion of her hung thickly in the air between them. She stuck close to the small, trim figure of Dr. Husseini. The massive wooden doors closed behind them and they found themselves in a courtyard that could hold 100,000 people. The thick stone walls were recessed and inlaid with cobalt blue and white tiles. Words from the Quran raced across the tiles, painted and baked over a millennium. On the stone seats, worn into deep hollows from the weight of pilgrims over 30 generations, women in black *abayas* sheltered their children. They had the bad luck of being inside the shrine when al-Kufa's men stormed it, and now they were trapped. The children sat perfectly still, smelling their mothers' fear.

"*As-salamu alaikum*, Dr. Husseini," a large portly figure with an AK-47 strapped onto his shoulder, and a beard that still contained bits of breakfast, greeted them.

"*Wa alaikum assalam.*" Dr. Husseini had a gift for being impeccably polite. He loathed al-Kufa's men. They spat on tradition and dishonored his faith. Their weapons and swagger polluted a holy place. They were responsible for the murder of at least one member of the senior Shiite clergy because they wanted him out of the way. His popularity and temperance had blocked their rise. They operated with the viciousness that is unleashed when a society is torn open by war and left to bleed.

Their arsenal of rifles, grenades, and mortars looked as though it had just been unpacked. There was still grease from the crates. Lee was sure that if Martin was arming these thugs in some clever play to split the Shia block, or simply for profit, then he was not a man she wanted to save.

"This way, doctor." Dr. Husseini directed her to follow him into an anteroom of the shrine. As they entered, Lee saw a makeshift ward with fighters binding their wounds with tourniquets made from curtains. "They need your help here. I'm afraid I've promised your assistance as part of my negotiations for their relinquishing the shrine. I hope you are not offended."

"Not in the least. Will they trust me?"

"As you can see, their wounds are turning septic. They would rather be treated by an infidel, even a woman like you, than have an amputated limb."

He left her in the room permeated with the stench of feces and congealed blood.

She turned to one of al-Kufa's men who was staring at her as though she was a piece of spoiled meat.

"*Ana tabiba.*" She knew how to say she was a doctor. "*Uhibu ma'a.*" She brought an imaginary glass to her lips. "*Ma'a.*" She needed water, and the man understood, in spite of his disapproval, that this was for his broken friends.

Some hours later, Lee had extracted dozens of bullets from shredded flesh, inside joints and a spinal canal, and had used up all of her supplies of morphine, antibiotics, local anesthetic, sutures, and gauze. When she got back to Baghdad, she would have to give in to Nizar and buy his stolen drugs. Lee asked one of the al-Kufa guards to find Dr. Husseini and relay the message that she needed more supplies. Perhaps Dr. Ali could find something. Otherwise, she would simply have to confine herself to ripping up *dishdashas* to discourage the blood and pus. Word came back that all of the supplies in Karbala were spoken for. She knew the hospital was critically short of everything, which meant she was on her own. Dr. Husseini followed the messenger by just a few minutes and ordered her to join him.

180

"We are finished here. There is nothing more we can do. We have to leave."

Lee followed him closely back to the courtyard where they waded through a crowd of hostages in the shape of a fan around one of al-Kufa's enforcers, who was savagely beating a woman's legs with his gun.

"What is he doing?" Lee asked Dr. Husseini in a low voice.

"She is showing too much ankle. Don't interfere or you will be shot. We can do more to help her by getting out of here."

"Barbarians."

Lee felt as though they were moving in slow motion toward the great carved wooden doors that must have been 20 feet high. As they reached their shadow, she heard a voice telling them to wait and saw the same oversized man with his AK-47 and beard sprinkled with *babaghanoush* who had met them as they entered.

"Stop there. Dr. Husseini, We will keep the doctor."

"The doctor comes with me," Dr. Husseini said sternly. "The Grand Ayatollah will be very angry if I leave her behind."

The man must have been three times Lee's width and had planted himself firmly in front of her.

"The doctor has no supplies." Dr. Husseini continued coolly. "She is useless without them. You must let us go or the negotiations will be spoiled. Said al-Kufa will not be pleased."

The man cracked at that and they were released and soon running the gauntlet of snipers outside the gates. They made it through the police checkpoint and did not speak until they had reached the familiar offices where the eggs were being loaded into pickups.

"Thank you for not leaving me."

"I brought you in there. It was my responsibility to get you out."

"Did it go well with al-Kufa?"

"They will vacate the shrine and release the hostages. In return, they want power, more of their people on the Shia list for parliament, a percentage of the take at the shrines. I have to relay these conditions to Najaf immediately. I suspect they have already stolen some of the treasure to sell quietly to reputable museums." He smiled at Lee. "We saved lives today, doctor. I am very grateful for your help. Oh yes, and I have found your friend."

"Martin?"

"Yes, I know where he is. Sheik Abbas, the fugitive you met with the other day, is a man of his word. You followed through on Abu Ghraib and now he has promised to arrange a meeting for you."

"Will you take me there?"

"I would like to, but I am sure you are being watched."

"Can you smuggle me out of here somehow?"

"You would have to leave your driver and bodyguards here. They cannot know anything."

"Fine."

"Tell them you will be in my office for a couple of hours so that they do not become concerned. I want to speak with Najaf."

"Okay." Lee told Hassan and the others that she would be working in the office for a few hours and did not want to be disturbed. When she returned, Dr. Husseini kept her waiting for what seemed like an eternity before reappearing to take her the next step.

"There are three ways we can move you. In your *abaya*, in the bedding for newlyweds that is being shipped out today or, I suppose, in a carpet."

"I don't think the *abaya* will work. I don't move like an Iraqi woman. The carpet seems too obvious. What if I lay down on one of your mattresses and cover myself with quilts?"

"Yes, I agree it's the best. Let's try it. At the other end, wear your *abaya* and dark glasses."

Dr. Husseini waited until the truck had been fully loaded before asking the movers to carry one last heavy pile of bedding and place it carefully on top. Lee thought she would suffocate in the heat of the day under the duvets and plastic sheeting. Not long after the truck pulled away from Dr. Husseini's office, she felt starved of oxygen. She told herself that she had to endure this for only 15 minutes before the switch to the Lada. Dr. Husseini had assured her that the shipment was so routine in Karbala, it would never arouse suspicion. No one would search the truck. She was jolted by several potholes and felt herself slipping. She dug her nails into the mattress beneath her. She was gasping for air, drowning again in the mountain lake.

As she forced her covers off just enough to find a tunnel of air, she saw one of the movers, sitting in the cabin of the truck, flick his lighted cigarette out the window. The glowing butt landed on the mattresses, just beyond her reach, and burned a hole through a plastic cover. Lee lunged for it and the cigarette rolled down a deep crack between the layers of goose down. She watched helplessly for several minutes as it began to smoke. She covered herself and breathed in the stench of smoldering feathers. As they pulled into the aid distribution center, Lee heard shouting and the squeal of brakes.

The movers wrenched their doors open and frantically tried to smother the fire with blankets. The disturbance was attracting attention. She heard more voices. Fear gripped her: fear of discovery, fear that she had been abandoned, fear that she would be blamed. The men began to unload the truck. They carried her quickly, in her soft, downy prison, into the warehouse and dropped her on the ground. After they sprinted off for another load, Lee freed herself, wrapped her *abaya* tightly around her face and chest and searched for a dark corner where she could adjust her veil and wait. Just then, a small child, who had wandered in with her father, following a forklift laden with plastic toys, spotted her.

"*Ingleezee. Amrekee.*" The child pointed.

Lee ducked between tall piles of flour sacks with USAID printed on the side. The tiny girl began to screech with laughter, as though they were playing a game of hide and seek.

"*Ingleezee. Amrekee.*"

The child's father called out to her, and unable to see what she had seen, took her by the hand and led her into the street. Lee emerged dusted in flour, wiped her face on the inside of the black *abaya*, donned her dark glasses, and tried to walk unobtrusively out of the building to the waiting car.

"What kept you?" Dr. Husseini was impatient.

"I was nearly found out."

"We had a small fire."

"It was a cigarette."

"Were you smoking back there, Lee?"

"No. One of your men was careless."

"We have to go quickly. Once we have arrived, you must only stay a few minutes. If anyone takes too close an interest in you, your friend will be dead by morning."

* * *

They drove to a neighborhood on the edge of the desert, with low mud-brick houses, where the garbage went uncollected and water was drawn from the mosquito-ridden canal. Some half-clothed children were playing a game with sticks and string, to which live beetles were tied and flung around in circles. Dr. Husseini led her to a crude door painted with a blue wash and they entered a dark room. It took several seconds before Lee's eyes adjusted and she could see the outlines of three wooden chairs and a table, not quite level, on the uneven dirt floor. There was a broom of rushes in the corner and a cheap tea set on a sideboard. A pitcher of water and freshly washed glasses were on the table in front of her. Dr. Husseini motioned to her to sit. Neither of them touched the water.

They waited in silence. Lee could hear the captive beetles vibrating on their strings and laughter like the delicate sound of glass bells. Then there was the sound of a car pulling up and she realized that they were at a safe house. The door opened and she could make out two silhouettes against the fierce, flat sunlight. One of them retreated to the shadows and stood in silence. He was carrying a gun. The other was Martin. She could feel his presence, even before she could make out his features. The tension in his body filled the shabby room. He wore a long white *dishdasha* and smelled of coffee and sweat.

"Hello, Lee."

"Martin." She stood to embrace him and saw that he wore a beard. As his eyes came into focus, she could see the skin under them looked swollen from lack of sleep. He was tall and now very thin. "I came to get you out of here."

"You don't belong here."

"You look tired."

"I'll be fine."

"Martin, what's going on? I went to see Plumber in the Green Zone. He says you are wanted for crimes against the coalition. Treason."

She heard Martin snort.

"I see."

"They want you for shipping arms to al-Kufa. Jabarri has documents that incriminate you. And just for the crime of looking for you, there is a contract out on my life."

"I'm sorry to get you involved."

"Don't worry about it."

"Do you believe Jabarri?"

"No."

"I knew I could trust you."

"Trust me? Martin, right now, I don't even know who you are. Why did Hamdoon call me on your behalf and say that you wanted me to leave the country?"

"Hamdoon is working for the other side."

"Why did you give the boy his number in case there was trouble?"

"That was before I knew Hamdoon's real allegiance."

"Martin, who are you working for?" Lee was impatient now.

"That's not important now, Lee. Are you here to help me?"

"It's important, Martin." Her voice had a brittle edge. She was angry that he could be so obtuse when they had so little time. They sat down at the crude table that wobbled on the uneven earth.

"I want to take you with me," Lee said suddenly, her voice full of warmth now. "I need to know that you are not a criminal. If you're a spy, I need to know what you are doing." She reached across the table toward him.

"That's not possible right now. But I'm going to give you something to take with you. It's very precious to me, and if you can get it out of the country, it may save my life." He handed her what she recognized immediately as the briefcase in the photographs. "I want you to take it out through Kurdistan. Listen carefully, because I only have a few minutes. In Baghdad, just off Masbah Circle, there's a trading company called Sulaymania. Find Omar Barzani and give him this card. Tell him you want to go to Zakho. To the Guest House. He will pass you along to someone else, who will take you across the Turkish border. Once you are in Diyarbakir, go to the *caravanserai*. Wait for someone to contact you and give him the briefcase."

"How will I know it's the right person?" Against her will, Lee found herself slipping into Martin's scheme.

"He will tell you that he's a specialist in Ottoman manuscripts. That he works in the archives and is translating something about Abdul Kadr. He will thank you for bringing him more manuscripts for his work. Can you remember that?"

"Martin, I'm not a spy. I'm a doctor."

"My life depends on this, Lee. And frankly, so does yours. After the delivery, drive to Ankara, get on a plane and go home."

She had no intention of going back to New York without Martin, but thought this was not the time to argue. He was alive and safe, at least for the moment, and she was relieved there was something concrete she could do.

"If Jabarri or Plumber find out that you have received anything from me, you will be hunted down. Would you rather not do this?"

"I think I'm already a target." Lee surprised herself by smiling in the dim light.

"Yeah." He smiled back at her.

"Martin, how did you get mixed up in this? What about the refugees? Was all of that just a cover?"

"No." He took her hand and held it tight. "You have to trust me. Lee, why did you come here?"

She wanted more than anything to say that she loved him, but did not have the courage to risk being laughed at or casually dismissed or pitied, her feelings batted around like one of the tethered beetles. She brought her other hand to his face in the dark. "You saved my life, remember?"

"Yes."

"Now I'm going to save yours." She had found what she was looking for, surrounded by strangers, in a safe house on the edge of nowhere, and she was about to lose him again.

"Isn't there anyone you're working with who I can contact for you?"

"Not now. Every email, every call, is being monitored by NSA. I wish I could say more but I can't." He brushed a strand of hair from her face. "You are so beautiful."

Within seconds he had embraced her once more and was out the door. There was silence again, except for the cries of small children and the juddering of their little victims, flung round and round in the hot wind.

XVII

"WE HAVE TO GO, TOO." Dr. Husseini's voice was a dry whisper.

Lee had almost forgotten that he was in the room.

"Don't forget the briefcase."

When they were back in the Lada, she realized that Dr. Husseini was also risking his life to facilitate the meeting.

"I can't thank you enough for this."

"Look in the back seat. There is a shopping bag. Put the briefcase in it. We will go back to my office through the garden. As for repaying me, when you are in Turkey, buy the medical supplies we need in Karbala. That will make up for everything."

Lee said goodbye to Dr. Husseini on the front steps of his office. She carried the shopping bag as though it were a souvenir from the *souk*. A small prayer carpet was now wrapped around the briefcase to allay suspicion, and as she rode back to the Dar with Hassan, they discussed the siege and how close she had come to being taken hostage.

"It's just like a movie," Hassan said approvingly. "I would pitch it in Hollywood if I were you. I can play al-Kufa. With one of those fat suits." He laughed, and she knew there was no need to fret about whether or not she had aroused Hassan's suspicions by taking such a long time in Dr. Husseini's office. The silent men from the Badr Brigade had dozed off. Had someone tried to assassinate Lee on the road back through Hillah, it would have been an easy shot. But they made it back just as the regulars at the Dar were ordering their third beers. Life in the artificial island of the hotel was much as it always was. A Russian reporter was showing off her jackknife on the diving board, and a table full of Rattle-corp bodyguards played a hand of poker, their table littered with $100 bills.

Duncan hailed her to his table where Masoud and the Italian journalist were buying each other rounds.

"Hello, doctor." Masoud pulled out a chair. "You are getting around. I hear you have become a photographer."

"No. I've been fired for incompetence."

"Where were you ministering to the sick today?"

"Karbala."

"Did you run into trouble? It looks like the siege was quite hairy."

"I was there, inside the shrine."

"Inside the shrine? You're joking." Duncan lost his balance and nearly fell backwards into the pool.

"No, I'm not."

"How on earth did you get in?"

"They needed a doctor."

"God, you are a piece of work, Lee." Duncan pulled his tape recorder out of his jacket pocket. "Would you mind describing for the rest of us exactly what you saw?"

She told them about the hostages' fear and the fighters covered in gore. She added the detail about nearly being taken hostage herself, knowing that it would make the papers and satisfy whoever was hunting her that she had been too preoccupied with the siege to have time for Martin.

When Lee returned to her room, she had three messages under her door, one from Central Command thanking her for assisting the survivors of the IED attack and another from al-Kufa's Baghdad representative thanking her for patching up the fighters in the shrine. The third was from Naji Qais, scolding her for not being in touch and warning that she had better turn up at Laela's or he would send a search party. Lee was surprised by the thank-you notes and decided to keep them, in case she needed proof of friends in high places to show at a roadblock or to win a stay of execution. She found it unsettling that everyone knew where she lived. She switched on "BBC World News," made Turkish coffee, and stared at the briefcase.

The case was expensive, weathered, and locked. It could be full, she thought, of $100 bills, stolen Babylonian seals, Afghan heroin, detonators. She would have to break it open. It would be prudent, she thought, to have a witness, someone who would then know why, if things went wrong, she had been left mutilated by the side of the road.

Her Dar suite was so sparsely furnished there was no place to hide anything. The balcony behind the glass doors covered in blast tape or the laundry bag, under her shirts might serve. The other option was to leave the case out on the Formica table as the most obvious thing in the room. She took her frequent flyer card off her suitcase along with a few airline tags and tied them to the case to give the impression that it had come with her from New York and Amman. Rummaging though the pockets of her suitcase, she found two Doctors Without Borders bumper stickers from a fundraiser in Manhattan the week before, which she stuck on the case. She left her coffee cup beside it along with a Surgeons' Committee report on top. No one would have the slightest interest in her work. The case was hidden in plain sight. It was the best she could do.

The Internet cafe across the street was the social center of the little neighborhood inside the sandbagged barricade that protected the Dar from suicide bombers. Lee found Duncan deep in conversation with the cafe's proprietor, discussing Baghdad real estate prices and the fortunes being made by contractors selling concrete. In Baghdad, the word "reconstruction" meant concrete barriers to protect against bomb blast. The proprietor dabbled in concrete and security services, and did a profitable business in amphetamines and forged passports.

"Duncan, could I borrow you for a moment?"

"Lee, of course. You know Rahim."

"Hello, I'm Dr. McGuinness. I'm sorry to interrupt. This won't take long."

They walked quickly across the street, a habit that came with fear of kidnapping, and she stopped him at the top of the steps within a few feet of the armed guards inside.

"I have something in my room that I want you to see. I don't want to discuss it while we're there, because I am sure my room is bugged. It's Martin's briefcase. I saw him today at a Karbala safe house."

"What?" Duncan was incredulous.

"No one but you and Dr. Husseini knows, and if anyone else finds out, it will get several people killed, including me." She told Duncan about the strange meeting on the edge of the desert and the locked briefcase. "I want to open it, but I want you to be there."

"Yes, okay."

"We will look at it, and if there's something you want to say, write it down."

"Fine. Lee, my story ran on the front page."

"Congratulations."

Once inside Lee's dowdy suite, Duncan broke his Swiss Army knife on the briefcase lock and had to borrow a screwdriver from a network news crew down the hall to pry it open. The lock finally gave way and he opened the case slowly, as though there might be something poisonous in it, like an Egyptian asp. Duncan and Lee studied the contents in silence. There were transcripts of phone conversations, a detailed ledger of payments of some kind, and bank account numbers. There was a wad of $50 bills, perhaps for the contact in Diyarbakir, a disk of digital photos and a DVD. The contents were light and portable, and it seemed unnecessary to keep them in the briefcase. While Duncan studied them, Lee found a plastic bag from duty free. She motioned for Duncan to transfer everything. He checked the case for a false bottom or pockets, and found two packs of cards and a pair of reading glasses, which he tossed into the bag. Duncan wrote in his notebook. *I want to make copies.*

Lee took some old *New Yorkers* that she had brought on the plane and placed them in the briefcase along with a few pens and a phone charger before shutting it. They left the room without saying a word and took the plastic bag to the little business center in the half-finished new wing of the Dar, which no one ever used. They copied the documents and emailed the contents of the disk and DVD to Duncan's secure account at his paper in London. Given her association with Martin, Lee's email account was too vulnerable to NSA spies. Duncan folded his copies of the documents into a side pocket of his shoulder bag. The whole operation had taken less than 15 minutes.

"Let me buy you dinner. I want to celebrate." Duncan slipped his arm around Lee.

Hassan was waiting by the car, signing autographs as usual.

"Hassan, do you know that little Italian restaurant, the Piazza, near the university?" Duncan asked.

"Yes, I know it."

The Piazza was a small piece of northern Lazio transported to Baghdad in the days when oil money attracted every kind of expatriate, from Italian restaurateurs to Irish nurses. There were 10 tables with candles and checked linens, and rustic farm implements — scythes, plows, and horse collars — tacked to the walls. The owner greeted Duncan warmly.

"Duncan, I have some very special fish tonight."

"The only civilized place in Baghdad. Any news from Bolsena?"

"The weather is good, and the boar hunting is terrible."

"And how is your family?"

"Safely out of here, thank God. You must introduce me to this lady, Duncan. We don't see many women like this in Baghdad."

"She is a great doctor."

"That's good, because this country is very sick."

Duncan and the proprietor negotiated a meal that was not on the menu, and they were shown to a small table in the back room, away from the other two couples who might overhear their conversation, and away from the windows in case there was a bomb.

"Mario, do you have any Brunello di Montalcino?"

"For you, yes. For anyone else? No." He darted off to accommodate the Englishman who was crazy enough to come to Baghdad. Duncan studied Lee across the table as the candlelight caught the green of her eyes, like something wild in the dark.

"Doesn't your family find you a bit reckless coming here?"

"I haven't told them."

"But they knew about Afghanistan."

"Yes." She hated talking about her personal life, the same way some tribes believe that having their picture taken robs them of their soul. "My parents often traveled to dangerous places. They are not exactly in a position to say I can't. In fact, I think they are proud of me."

"I didn't mean to make you uncomfortable."

"Forget it."

An enormous spread of antipasto appeared on the table, and they ate until they could hardly move. When the dishes were cleared away, Duncan brought out the accounting ledger and they studied it.

"This is some kind of code." Duncan pointed to the column of indecipherable names. "And this is what they are being paid."

"Whose is this? Why is it important?"

"If Martin was investigating corruption among the Americans, it may be a key to who's getting paid and where the money is."

"Do you think this money is being paid to people in the Green Zone?"

"I don't know."

"I suppose that would be dangerous information."

"To say the least."

Duncan pulled out the transcripts of phone conversations, thinking that might shed some light on the meaning of the ledger. He handed some of them to Lee.

"Who is Delta?" she asked.

"Who is he talking to?"

"Alpha."

"That doesn't help much."

From what they could decipher, the telephone transcripts referred specifically to an oil deal, a deal worth hundreds of millions of dollars. Both Alpha and Delta were taking a cut. They were negotiating percentages. Delta was someone inside the Green Zone. He was someone in a position to manipulate the numbers in the export accounts. The two of them were sharing the spoils. This was government oil that neither one had any right to plunder.

They finished the bottle of Brunello and realized it was almost curfew. There was a loud explosion like a kettledrum from somewhere across the Tigris, most likely a car bomb, that rattled the Piazza's windows.

"We ought to get back." Duncan told Mario he wanted to see boar on the menu next time and gave him a generous tip. In the car, Lee saw that there was a new moon and wondered how the Irish conceived of the notion that it was bad luck to look at a new moon through glass. The neighborhood around the university looked dark and empty as though the power were out. Just on the other side of the Jumhuriya Bridge, someone had built a fire in the middle of the circle. Hassan was waved through a roadblock, past the barrel of an M1 tank. As he turned onto the narrow street that led to the Dar, Lee heard rifle fire at close range. She thought at first that soldiers were in a firefight behind the car and then realized that Hassan was driving at insane speed to reach the hotel perimeter. There was a car full of gunmen bearing down on their Mercedes. Just as Hassan was pulling away from them, a car darted out of a side street and stopped dead in front of him.

"We're about to be kidnapped," Duncan observed dryly.

Hassan had no intention of cooperating. He drove at full throttle at the car ahead and at the last second swerved around it, taking off the front of the kidnappers car. He did a 360 in front of the concrete barriers where the Dar guards were firing at the kidnappers and Hassan gunned the engine so that they shot through the gate to safety.

"I've always wanted to do my own stunts."

"Come on, Hassan." They raced from the car, across the dark street and up the steps.

"Who was that?" Duncan lit a cigarette.

"This is all my fault." Still breathless from the chase, Lee thought of the contract on her life.

"Do you think they know you went to the safe house?"

"I don't think so. They — whoever they are — were following through on the death threats. Hassan, you definitely have a future in Hollywood. You ought to stay here tonight." Lee felt self-conscious about her bravado.

"I'm just going to check the damage. If the guards wounded anybody, I will try to find out who they are."

"I will tell Ali at the desk to find you a room."

"Buy me a drink, Lee." Duncan was drenched in sweat in the warm evening air. "I want to finish the story of the siege. How many bedrooms do you have in your suite?"

"Two."

"Good. I am moving in. You shouldn't be alone."

Lee asked the barman to send up the best bottle of wine he had and reserved two cases for Laela's party. She followed Duncan to the business center, where he mined every detail of the siege of the Hussein shrine and wrote his story.

"What about the kidnappers? Isn't that a story?"

"Only if they had grabbed us and cut our heads off."

By the time he arrived at Lee's door with his overnight bag, the wine had arrived and she had Martin's documents spread on the table. There was a yellow pad for communicating without entertaining the new Interior Ministry secret police and Green Zone security men who were routinely bugging the Dar. Duncan wrote, *I forgot my reading glasses in my room. Do you have an extra pair?*

I don't have any, Lee wrote. *Wait*. She remembered there had been a pair in Martin's briefcase. They were expensive, in a slim red enamel tube with a rose on the clasp. When Duncan opened the tube, he found the glasses wrapped in thin paper, like the crowns folded into Christmas crackers. He held it up to the light, found nothing, and set it aside.

Then the power failed. They sat in darkness, waiting for Ali to switch on the generator, when Lee broke the silence.

"Duncan, look," she whispered.

There, glowing on the table, was the paper from the glasses tube. They stared at the words written on it with what looked like Day-glo ink. The generator rumbled below and as soon as they had light, the words vanished.

Key to the code? Lee wrote.

Duncan nodded and smiled. *Accounts ledger*, he wrote.

They lit a candle and switched the lights off to read what looked like a riddle:

Napoleon's at Santa Helena
Roosevelt's at San Juan Hill
Josephine's with Cadran
The maid's about to kill.

Is this gibberish? Lee wrote. *Or does it mean something?*

Lee stared at the words for a long time. She was hopeless at literary references, not to mention historical allusions. It could be an obscure poem or some kind of political jingle. Perhaps it was a nursery rhyme. She had no idea what Teddy Roosevelt and Napoleon had in common. Josephine's private life was a mystery to her. Did her maid kill one of her lovers in some famous episode? She had spent too much time studying medical books.

Yes, I see ... Duncan began to write. ... *It's a game of solitaire.*

Solitaire?

Yes. These are all games of solitaire, Josephine, Cadran, Napoleon at Santa Helena, Roosevelt at San Juan, all variations on the game 40 Thieves.

Do you know how to play 40 Thieves?

Yes, of course. Bring the cards. Let's go outside.

Anyone watching them from the terrace by the pool would have thought they had simply brought cards along to pass the time. There was little else to do at the Dar but drink and gamble.

"If I remember correctly, you need both decks of cards." Duncan was delighted to impress Lee with his arcane knowledge of games, the sort of knowledge picked up in boarding school. "There are eight foundation piles, built up in suit from ace to king, and 10 tableau piles, built down in suit. Object, move all of the cards to the foundations. At the start, deal four upturned cards to each tableau pile. Total 40. That's it. Only one card at a time may be moved. That's what makes it difficult. Fill in the spaces in the tableau piles with any card. Deal one card at a time and you can use the top card from the discard pile. It's not an easy game."

"Wait. Who's the maid?"

"I'm sorry?"

"The maid. In the rhyme. The maid's about to kill."

"That'll cost you a dinner."

"Duncan. Didn't I give you a first-hand account of the Karbala siege?"

"Yes, of course. We'll count that in. It's obviously been a long time since you've read *The Thousand and One Nights*. It was the maid who saved her master, Ali Baba, by stealing into the courtyard at night and pouring boiling oil on 37 thieves hiding in their jars. She killed them all. Later she dresses as a dancing girl and stabs their captain with a dagger. Two thieves escape and are never heard from again. Ali Baba gets the treasure. End of story." Duncan smiled with satisfaction. "I believe her name was Morgiana."

The key to the ledger of bribes and kickbacks was somewhere in the cards, if only they could find it.

They knew now that there were two decks in the briefcase by design. Someone was meant to find them and use them. Duncan divided the cards and shuffled them with a mastery that came from practicing as a boy.

"Just wait."

"I'll be upstairs."

He played for the better part of an hour. When Duncan let himself into the suite, he brought a bottle of wine and two glasses. Lee was watching "BBC World News." A sheik had been arrested in Fallujah, and a helicopter had been shot down near the Syrian border with a shoulder-fired missile. She left the sound on full volume as they moved to the table and the ledger. Somewhere in the game was the key to the jumbled names on the ledger, "*Maiddons f1c3, Haters f4c5, Aspeds f3c6, Sculb f2c10 ...*"

She stared at it, like a diagnostician trying to spot a rare disease. There it was, she thought. "Anagrams." She wrote furiously on the pad. *Diamonds f1c3*. Foundation one, card three. *Hearts*: foundation four, card five. Card three from the top in foundation one was the jack of diamonds. They studied the card. There was no obvious clue.

"Hang on," Emboldened by her success, Lee switched off the light. There on the jack of diamonds were the symbols GP9. They cross-referenced each card with the code and came up with full sets of initials and ranks, like a DNA sequence.

"*GP/9. RM/5 Col. NH/14,*" the list went on. The number by each name corresponded to the list of Swiss bank accounts. The accounts held tens of millions of dollars.

"We need to talk," Lee said. "Let's go for a swim."

They changed and collected towels, cigarettes, and the duty-free bag of documents and headed for the pool. There were a few stragglers, fairly drunk, sitting at tables on the terrace. Lee and Duncan claimed two chaises and dove into the dark water, still warm from the sun of the day. On the far side there was a ledge where they sat in privacy.

"This is a huge story, Lee," Duncan was breathing hard. "A friend of mine from the World Bank said something to me last month at the Intercon Bar in Amman. I discounted it as spite. He said, 'We didn't know the meaning of the word "corruption" until the Americans came.' If Martin is silenced, the thieves will get away with it. The 40 thieves. Exposing this is the only way to protect him."

"If you do that, won't those bank accounts vanish into thin air before anyone can be indicted? The whole story will be denied, and Martin will still be prosecuted on false evidence."

"What about the phone records? That's hard evidence."

"Yes, but don't you need an official to say 'Yes, these are genuine'? Remember, on the face of it, Martin is just an American aid worker in trouble."

"We will catch them in the act," Duncan smiled.

"What do you mean?"

"Moving money out of Iraq means moving cash. Shrink-wrapped bricks of cash. We just have to find out how they are doing it." Duncan vanished under water like an otter trolling for oysters. Lee was glad no one had turned on the lights. Looking up at the apartment block beyond the barbed wire and broken glass littering the Dar walls, she could see a form on the fourth-floor balcony, amidst laundry, broken pots, and old machinery, holding what looked like a rifle. She dove and caught Duncan, pulling him to the surface.

"We have to get out of here."

"What's wrong?"

"Look."

Duncan saw the man with the gun. He and Lee moved without a sound to the steps, picked up the duty-free bag, key, and cigarettes from the chaise, and ran for the shelter of the building. The night porter watched them impassively. When they made it upstairs, dripping wet, both of them started to laugh.

For a moment, Lee no longer cared who was bugging them or who wanted to kill them. Duncan found towels and poured them each a glass of wine. They drank and laughed and Duncan threw his arms around Lee in a slow dance of denial that they might not make it through the next day.

"My partner in crime." Lee felt euphoric, released from the blinding pain of her work and the war, the charred bodies, the deception and cruelty, the uncertainty of who Martin really was and what he wanted from her, and the dangers closing in.

"Lee, I have to write," Duncan released her slowly, "While it's still fresh. I doubt either of us will sleep."

"No. I suppose not." Lee withdrew her affection like a school of fish darting behind a reef. She smelled his damp skin and re-entered the zone of fear, where there was a man with a weapon outside in the shadows and a man standing next to her whom she did not entirely trust.

XVIII

I NEED DRUGS." Lee sat nervously at Nizar Hadithi's table and watched him devour another of the Aleem chef's croissants. "I'm compromising my principles, Nizar. I'm willing to buy on the black market. What can you offer me?"

"Iraq has corrupted you, Lee."

"I don't have much choice."

"Now you know how it feels to be an Iraqi." He wiped the butter from his mouth. "The chef has outdone himself today. You must try this."

"The Karbala siege gutted my supplies."

"What do you need?"

"Can you get me morphine?"

"It could be arranged."

"Sutures, syringes, cipro, clindamycin, amoxicillin, doxycycline, oxycodone. Tylenol and gauze. And nothing expired, please."

"Are you looking for a container load or a suitcase?"

"Suitcase. I can't afford more and I will have to carry it with me. Oh, and splint materials, a box of latex gloves, and Gatorade."

"Gatorade?"

"Oral rehydration."

"Consider it done, my friend. Say, $700 in cash. Would you take delivery tonight?"

"Tomorrow morning would be fine." She peeled seven $100 bills from her wallet and rolled them discreetly in her palm to hand across the table. "I'm going out of town for a few days."

Nizar took the money without counting it.

"I have done some investigating for you." Nizar lowered his voice, although the Aleem dining room that Saturday morning was nearly deserted. "Jabarri has some partners in the Green Zone. You have spoken with at least one of them."

"Who is it, Nizar?"

"The man who told you to leave Iraq."

"Hamdoon?"

"Yes. Colonel Hamdoon."

"U.S. Army?"

"I'm afraid so. Colonel Hamdoon is in charge of $92 million in reconstruction funds for the south. A new Army training center. The so-called Democracy Centers in Hillah and Najaf, and the Karbala library. My friends tell me Hamdoon has succumbed to temptation. The Democracy Center funds have gone into a Jacuzzi and a Lexus. He also seems very fond of weapons and has shipped large amounts back to the States. Through Fort Simms."

"For his personal use?"

"Resale, most likely. There's a lot of money in weapons."

"Why would Martin have trusted him?"

Nizar smiled and wiped his fingers with care. "Perhaps Colonel Hamdoon came to Iraq wanting to do the right thing."

"Why would Hamdoon have warned me off Martin? And why the threats?"

"Jabarri may be blackmailing him. Or he may be beholden to your friend Plumber. Or both." Nizar laughed at the thought. "You know how things are, Lee. One of our new ministers has bought himself a palace in Poland."

"And you're in stolen drugs. What else are you selling?"

He smiled slyly. "There is a good market in Afghan slaves. Opium farmers are selling their daughters to pay off debts."

Lee chose to ignore his provocation. "Someone tried to kidnap me last night."

"Yes, I know. Word has gotten around." Nizar lit a cigarette, and the smoke curled around the tinsel hanging from the ceiling.

"Hassan saved my life."

"Yes, he is telling everyone in town about his stunt driving."

"May I keep him for a few more days?"

"Of course."

"And one more thing. I may be traveling through some areas where your old colleagues are in charge. Would it be possible for me to carry some piece of paper that might serve as a *laissez-passer* so that I won't be detained?"

"You are already known, Lee. You have a good name. If the *shabab* pick you up, their superiors will release you. Just leave a little extra time for the road. We're on Middle Eastern time, you know. Oh, and if you come across any civilians who need a doctor, you might stop to help them. You were very impressive the other day on the highway with the wounded soldier. You were being watched."

"Thanks, Nizar." Lee was ready to leave. "I'll remember that. Oh, I nearly forgot. You once said you has a man down the street who could forge my ID. Do you think he could take a look at some documents for me? Some end-user certificates. To see if they're fake."

"I'll see what I can do."

By the time Lee reached Masbah Circle, the traffic was backed up to the Tigris.

"I'll jump out here, Hassan. Meet me at Sulaymania Trading in half an hour."

"I need to take the car into the body shop this afternoon."

"There's plenty of time for that."

Lee was close enough to the Sulaymania entrance not to cause unhealthy interest by lingering in the street, and Hassan was capturing all of the attention anyway. She left the soap-opera star in his battered Mercedes, greeting fans. The trading company was upstairs in a mini-mall, and the place smelled of stale cigarette smoke and linoleum. She sat down in the waiting room and glanced at the year-old magazines and the arrangement of plastic calla lilies. The Irish would say that was bad luck, too. The heavily made-up receptionist, with her *abaya* hanging on the door, was pretending to be otherwise engaged. The phone did not ring.

Lee introduced herself in Arabic and asked whether Omar Barzani was in the office.

"The office is closed. Come back tomorrow." The receptionist replied in English. Her accent was from somewhere in London's East End. She opened a drawer, extracted an emery board, and began smoothing the edges of an inch-long lacquered nail.

"But this is Saturday. Everyone is open on Saturday. I need to see him urgently."

"Come tomorrow." The receptionist shrugged and unwrapped a stick of gum, which she chewed mercilessly.

"What time do you open?"

"We are open between 9 and 10."

"May I leave a message?"

"Tomorrow."

Lee stood silently questioning the wisdom of using the services of the Sulaymania Trading Company. She wondered why Martin would direct her here. Was it a false lead? An elaborate joke? Just then, a thick, bullish figure, with dyed black hair, rushed up the stairs. He was about to disappear down the dark corridor when Lee stopped him, hoping to end the tyranny of the receptionist.

"Mr. Barzani?"

"Yes."

"I'm a friend of Martin Carrigan."

He looked at Lee with an expression that turned from dread to weariness, which was not encouraging.

"Come in, please." He said it with such reluctance that she assumed he must be on retainer, doing whatever chores came his way against his will. "May I offer you a coffee?"

"Please."

Barzani shouted to the woman in Kurdish and they soon had strong coffee and pistachios.

"How may I help you?"

"I am traveling north, to the Guest House in Zakho. Mr. Carrigan said you could be of assistance."

"Do you have a car?"

"Yes."

"You will need to go in convoy."

"I want to travel tomorrow morning."

"Not possible. Not before Monday. You need Peshmerga. Come back Monday. Then you can go." There was a long silence while he flipped his lapis worry beads.

"What time?"

Omar shrugged. "Whenever you want."

"I will be here at 7."

"No problem."

Lee did not feel reassured. Hassan was waiting for her below, and once back at the Dar, she sent him off with cash for car repairs. No one accepted credit cards in Iraq. Lee calculated that if she continued spending money at her current rate, she would be broke in a week. At least in Diyarbakir, she could get a wire transfer.

Her room looked vaguely cleaner than when she left it and seemed otherwise undisturbed. Duncan's things were still in the spare bedroom, neatly folded, and Lee could smell the faint scent of eau de cologne. The briefcase was sitting prominently on the kitchen table. The old magazines and telephone charger were still in place. Martin's documents had spent the day by her side, in the duty-free bag stuffed inside her cavernous purse. She spread them before her to absorb as much as possible about the racketeers who were trying to silence Martin and who regarded kidnapping Lee as acceptable collateral damage. "GP/9." She suspected GP was George Plumber, with an account at #9, which was Credit Suisse in Zurich. It explained why Plumber was so determined to frame Martin. The balance was $23 million, GP's cut from Jabarri, she thought. She noted the bank details and account number in her address book, then sifted through the telephone transcripts looking for the Alpha and Delta exchange about oil. The conversation made clear that Iraqi oil was being left deliberately unmetered, so there was no accounting for oil at the wellhead or in the pipeline. They could steal with impunity.

They discussed the movement of tanker trucks, which she gathered they controlled. Tankers were relieving the oil ministry of its cargo at gas stations where the station owners were paid off handsomely to forfeit the oil. The tankers then turned north to Kurdistan and over the border to Turkey, where the cargo was sold and profits deposited, which meant there was a local agent in Turkey in the ring.

Was Martin's Ottoman scholar a Turkish intelligence agent? Perhaps he was an American based at Incierlik trying to penetrate the black market. Or was Martin selling his information to a foreign intelligence agency, which would use it as leverage? Perhaps the contact was a Kurd who would take the ledger of corruption to Washington as capital to negotiate autonomy.

It was late afternoon before she remembered that she had not eaten all day and that it was a good time to call the Surgeons' Committee, before the office opened, to assure them that she was alive. She was pacing Thuraya corner by the pool before she knew what she was going to say. She got the answering machine. Her message was breezy and relaxed. There was encouraging news but she would have to stay for a few more days to work out details of cooperation with Omar Hospital.

She dressed carefully for Laela's party, choosing an embroidered jacket made from an antique sari that she had found in the Rawalpindi market on one of her missions in and out of Afghanistan. She wore a pendant of blue lapis and beaten silver. When Lee found Hassan, he was leaning on a brand new Mercedes.

"Stolen?"

"My uncle lent it to me, until my old car is ready."

"What business is your uncle in?"

"Import-export."

On the far side of the car, a large, well-exercised man with a black leather jacket and stubble, leaned on the hood, smoking.

"I want you to meet my cousin," Hassan said, gesturing to the man, who bore a striking resemblance to Saddam

Hussein's oldest son. "His father is from Tikrit, so I have Sunni cousins. Everyone in Baghdad has Sunni cousins." Hassan laughed. "I feel more secure with Mohammed traveling with us, after what happened."

Mohammed had some sort of weapon tucked under his jacket, which was bursting like the staves of a barrel.

"*As-salamu alaikum*, Mohammed. It's a pleasure to meet you."

"No problem. No problem." Mohammed was a man of few words. He was preoccupied, already concentrating on the street, watching the man on the corner with the shopping bag, the man reading a paper on the apartment block balcony, the teenagers coming out of the Internet cafe. Mohammed was a human radar, scanning for anything out of place. His body was coiled, waiting for the ambush.

"Are you also in import-export, Mohammed?"

"No."

He had no interest in elaborating, so Lee left it at that.

"We have a big family." Hassan stepped in to fill the silence. "I have 33 first cousins. I even have Kurdish cousins. So you see, Dr. McGuinness, we can't have a civil war. We are all related."

Because of curfew, Laela was starting her party before sundown, and Lee found her hanging the last lanterns from the palms. There were candles floating in the little pond and long tables with white linen in the garden. Laela was wearing a silk dress the color of dried lavender that floated to her ankles. Her feet were bare except for a thin gold ring on one of her toes.

"Just in time."

"Laela, I want you to meet Hassan and Mohammed."

210

"*Marhaban*, gentlemen." Within seconds she had them moving tables, folding ladders, and setting up the bar. "Lee, where is Sadoon?"

"Abu Ghraib."

"Bloody hell. What's he done?"

"I don't know that he's done anything."

"Have you complained to our masters in the Green Zone?"

"Duncan is trying to get him out." Lee noticed that someone had drawn blood from Laela's arm. "Are you all right, Laela?"

"I ache everywhere. Something is wrong with my joints. My doctor took blood tests. Have a daiquiri. I made them with my own limes."

"You might have a virus. You are too thin, Laela."

"My friend Wafiq said he had dinner in Amman with a chap who had the job of blowing up warheads here for the U.N. The U.N. man told Wafiq that he did it without any cement seal to contain the dust. He said there was going to be a lot of leukemia here and bone problems."

"I'm sure your immune system needs boosting. You should go to Beirut for awhile."

"Yes, Lee. It's bad for you to be here, too. There are de-pleted-uranium shells all over Baghdad, with 1,000 times the acceptable levels of radiation. Now, before the guests come, I want to show you something. Close your eyes." She led Lee down a path through the date grove. "Stop. Now open them."

They were in a clearing at the end of the walled garden on the far side of the trees, and before them was *The Weapon of Mass Destruction*. The base was the shell of a burned-out tank with gaping holes, revealing the innards where the crew was likely incinerated. Inside, there were helmets and a radio set. On top, there was a profusion of old missile parts sprouting from the tank, bits of mortars, machine guns, and anti-aircraft guns, draped with old ammunition belts like garlands. It was horrifying, and at the same time — the way she had constructed it — stunning.

"This is fantastic, Laela. What will you do with it?"

"I want to exhibit it at the Rasheed. And if the occupation authorities won't have it, I want to ship it to Washington and install it on the Mall."

"How much does it weigh?"

"A lot. I thought we could ask the U.S. Air Force if we could borrow a C-130."

"Laela, is it safe to have this in your garden? Have your checked it with a Geiger counter?"

"You mean because of the depleted-uranium shells that made those holes in the tank?"

"Yes."

"Your bloody military has dumped over 400 tons of uranium-238 on us, burned DU with deadly radioactive oxides. The physicist from the U.S., who in charge of getting rid of it, says it will last forever. He called it 'indiscriminate for eternity.' Can you imagine? The poor fellow found his own body had 5,000 times safe levels after his tour in Iraq. The half-life of the contamination is 4.5 billion years. The age of our solar system. Every street in Baghdad has little black piles of pure depleted-uranium ash. We are a dying people, Lee. Your military has waged nuclear war against us."

"What time are the guests coming?" Lee couldn't think of anything else to say.

"Oh God, any second. Can you help me with the hors d'oeuvres?"

In Laela's kitchen they found Hammurabi curled up on the counter made from Ottoman tiles, his magnificent tail drumming in anticipation of a quick leap on the Tigris fish.

"Don't even think of it," Laela admonished the cat, which blinked lazily at his mistress. She and Lee laid the tables with the sort of food it takes days to make, homemade *mezze*, Persian rice, *kibbeh*. Lee knew that whatever Laela could not harvest from her own garden, she had spent weeks negotiating for.

"Lou" — there was a shout from upstairs — "you've got to help me, I can't do up this horrid dress."

"It's Zara. Would you be a darling, Lee, and take the rest of this out for me?"

She ferried the last of the spread to the table and poured herself some lemonade scented with rose water. Two Black Hawk helicopters screamed overhead, flying so low that she could hear the squealing of the rotors. She thought they could hardly mistake this for a gathering of insurgents, given the open bar.

The first guests to appear were a pair of French diplomats and a small, tense-looking archaeologist. Lee mixed strong drinks.

"*Kibbeh?*" She offered one of Laela's delicacies to the archaeologist.

"*Shoukran.* Are you a friend of Laela's or Zara's?"

"Laela. And you?"

"I grew up with both of them. Laela's brother was in my class at Baghdad College. And of course Zara is a colleague of mine. This is a bad time for archaeologists."

"The looting, you mean?"

"Yes, on a massive scale. Whole villages are being paid by the smugglers. Our army is involved and so is yours. Soldiers have been caught carrying ancient Babylonian seals through customs at Kennedy. Before long there won't be any archaeological sites in Iraq. Just holes in the sand. Samarra, Hatra, Ashur, Uruk, Babylon, 10,000 years of civilization. Our heritage is finished." He helped himself to another kibbeh. "I am Dr. Zuhair Fareed, by the way. My specialty is something very small but important. It is the oldest library in the world."

"Oh yes. I've heard about your work. I'm Dr. Lee McGuinness."

"You're a friend of Naji Qais."

"Yes."

"You see, Dr. McGuinness, the destruction of these sites is a crime against humanity. Uruk, the birthplace of the written word, with clay tablets of cuneiform writing over 5,000 years old, plundered. The sacred Warka Vase, missing. The walls of Hatra, covered with exquisite hunting scenes of gazelles and wild boar, chiseled off. Samarra, 20 square miles of priceless artifacts with the great mosque and Malwiya, the spiral minaret, the capital of the Abbasid Caliphate, now a hunting ground for thieves. There are people who would like to erase our history. Some of my colleagues have committed suicide."

"Zuhair, are you boring the good doctor with our troubles?" Zara had appeared like an act of God at Lee's side. Lee could feel the electricity all around her, as though there had been a lightning strike or a meteor shower. "I'm Laela's sister. She's told me all about you. Zuhair, pour me a glass of wine, would you, lovey?" Zara was short and compact, and although she wore a dress, it was obvious she longed to take it off. Lee pictured her in baggy work pants deep in a trench.

"So, Dr. McGuinness, I hear you have lost your friend and that my wicked cousin may have put him in the concrete mixer."

"Well, I believe he's still alive."

"Adnan was always a bully. Even as a child. When I was about 7, I climbed a cedar of Lebanon and got stuck right at the top. Adnan, the malevolent little bastard, knew I was up there and just left me to rot overnight. When I finally got down, I was absolutely drenched in pee. I took my revenge. I cut his hair off while he was asleep and covered his face in my mother's red lipstick. When he woke up he thought he was a ghoul, covered in the blood of corpses. Very satisfying. Oh thank you, love." She gulped the wine and squinted at Lee. "I hear you're a rather good surgeon."

"I do my best."

"We could use you here. Half my doctor friends have got fed up and left. They lurk in Cairo or Paris waiting for this madness to end. The ones who stay have a rough time of it. The American soldiers storm hospitals looking for insurgents. They tie up the doctors and beat them."

"I would like to stay, Zara, but I have a life at home."

"Oh, sod that."

"Don't you live in Paris?"

"I do. I commute to Baghdad. But you know, this missing loot is moving all over the world right now. I'm hardly ever out of an airplane. Stolen goodies from the museum are turning up in private collections in New York. All of the best museums are buying artifacts and storing them till they can fake a provenance. Absolutely shameful. These collectors are the most awful people. Having a 5,000-year-old treasure in your Fifth Avenue apartment is like a drug for them. They should all be shot." With that she wandered off to greet the guests.

Lee realized she was still carrying the duty-free bag and quickly made her way to the house. She remembered the bookshelves full of dusty Ottoman histories in the guest room and slid the bag behind some of the books that guests were unlikely to want to read. She was suddenly conscious of someone else in the room and turned to find Hammurabi flicking his tail, watching her with his yellow eyes.

"You wicked cat. You frightened me."

Downstairs she spotted Naji Qais in the crowd and waved to Duncan and Masoud, who had cornered the platter of *kebabs* simmered in yogurt and mint. Beyond them was a phalanx of bodyguards, all in black leather, shielding the diminutive figure of Adnan Jabarri. A little Napoleon, thought Lee. The bodyguards fanned out through the palms and took up positions in the bougainvillea. Lee wondered whether some of the guards had tried to kidnap her. As Jabarri moved toward the bar, everyone took one step back. Now that he controlled the country's intelligence files, his presence reminded everyone that they had something to hide.

Only Zara had the nerve to confront him.

"Adnan, you look dreadful. You are smoking too many of those black-market cigarettes. They're full of arsenic, my dear. Now have a daiquiri. It will do you good." Undoubtedly Zara suspected, or even had evidence, that Adnan was dealing in stolen antiquities when he wasn't stealing oil. Still, she needed him to gather intelligence on his competitors. "Have you met my friend Dr. McGuinness?" She turned to Lee and hailed her over. "Doctor, come and talk to my cousin."

Lee could see that Zara was longing to make trouble. "I know Dr. McGuinness," Jabarri moved like a crocodile floating slowly in her direction. "She was at my house just the other day."

"Discussing medicine?" Zara asked in a deliberate act of provocation.

"No. Dr. McGuinness has a friend who is in a bit of trouble. He's selling arms to the insurgents. You haven't found him yet, have you?"

"I'm afraid not."

"I heard about your performance at the Imam Hussein Shrine. You're a good doctor to have around."

"Thanks."

"There are not many people who could keep a cool head in those circumstances."

"I was too busy to think about the risk. Al-Kufa's people even sent me a thank you note."

"As they should." There was no hint in his manner that al-Kufa was his close associate. "I heard someone tried to kidnap you. It really has reached epidemic levels this outbreak of kidnapping. And the prices are unbelievable. You, as an American, you're worth at least $1 million." He paused to appraise her. "Probably two. These people are common criminals. The scum of Baghdad." He watched her over the rim of his drink. "Are you leaving soon?"

"Leaving Iraq?"

"Yes. I thought that since your friend is a wanted man it would be better for you to steer clear of him and go home. What are your plans?"

"I'm not sure yet."

"Allow me to offer you an escort to Amman."

"Thank you, but I have a driver."

"With bodyguards?"

"Yes. They are very anxious to kill whoever tried to kidnap me." She thought Jabarri's eyes flickered slightly.

"Well, you should be in good hands then. You are wise to leave Baghdad. Everything here is so ..." he searched for the word, "uncertain."

"Lee, I've been looking for you everywhere." Laela looked flushed. "Hello, Alpha," she said, kissing her cousin. "I'm so glad you could come. You are so important these days we hardly ever see you." They spoke English with such fluency that they switched to it out of courtesy whenever foreigners were present.

"Alpha?" Lee asked with more interest than she cared to reveal. She felt exposed for a moment and then relaxed. There was no way he could know that she had Martin's phone transcripts.

"A childhood name. From my school. I'm the oldest boy in my family. Laela, it's time we talked about your art. I would like to help you."

"Oh, Adnan. How wonderful. There is a piece at the end of the garden you must see. It's absolutely right for the Rasheed. Perhaps you could twist some arms in the Green Zone to get it installed. It's called *The Weapon of Mass Destruction*."

Jabarri laughed and ordered another drink. He was accosted by one of Laela's neighbors who owned land in the Green Zone and was anxious for the Americans to pay rent.

"Be careful of my cousin," Laela murmured. "He doesn't like you."

"That's because his men botched the kidnapping. I'm sure that irritates him."

"When did they try to kidnap you?" Laela's huge brown eyes widened.

"The other night just outside the Dar. Hello, Naji." It was a relief to see her old colleague.

"Naji tells me you were a great help the other day at Omar Hospital." Laela looked at Lee with admiration.

"It is a pleasure assisting the best surgeon in Baghdad."

Naji bowed. "You are too kind, Lee."

"Naji, I need to ask your advice. I'm going to be in Turkey in a few days and I want to pick up some supplies for the Karbala hospital. Do you have a contact in Diyarbakir I can call?"

"Turkey? I thought you were coming to work with me."

"I'll be back within a week."

"I won't ask why, Lee. You surely know it's a hazardous trip. If you're going for supplies, you're better off going to Ankara. I will give you a man there who can help you. He can arrange delivery. I should warn you that the Kurdish border police will want a bribe for the shipment. Do you have transport?"

"Yes. With Peshmerga."

"If you are stopped by the *mujahedeen*, just give them the medicine. It will go to someone who needs it. As you will be up there, would you mind bringing in a few things for me?"

"I would be happy to."

"I'll call the supplier and tell him to expect you."

As the sun set over the Tigris, Lee climbed the steps to the flat whitewashed roof of Laela's studio. She wanted to be alone. The river had turned silver, and Baghdad was deceptively quiet. She tried to clear her mind of the war and of Martin. She remembered visiting a family of Copts who lived up the Nile from Cairo, next to some un-excavated pyramids, buried in the sand. Just before sunset, the Copts gathered on the roof to gaze across the dunes toward Saqqara.

The sun was sucked beneath the sand as though the earth had swallowed an egg yoke. As it vanished, there was a green flash, an atmospheric phenomenon of scattered and refracted light. The flash was like a polished emerald, so green that Jules Verne called it the true green of hope.

The lanterns in the al-Baharis' garden reminded her of late summer nights at home with the moths beating against the glass. She wanted to take Laela home with her, away from depleted uranium and gangsters and the occupation.

"Lee, why didn't you tell me about the kidnappers?" Laela was standing on the steps in front of her, waiting for her attention.

"It wasn't important."

"Not important? Rubbish."

"Laela, I want to take you to New York. You can get in to the country as my patient."

Laela studied her, the way she would examine a beetle or a dragonfly. "You can't expect me to abandon my guests." She laughed and shook her jet-black hair. "You need a daiquiri. Where would you take me?"

"To my hospital. To Chelsea. To Luray Caverns, with an organ made of stalactites."

"Calypso's cave. Where I will pine for Ithaca."

There was a commotion in the crowd. The Italian journalist had arrived with the foreign minister, who was short and round and distracted. Laela noticed that the minister's Kurdish bodyguards kept their distance from Jabarri's men.

"We now have enough firepower in the grove to start a small war." Laela led the way to the bar so that she could introduce everyone. Laela and the Italian were soon deep in discussion about galleries in Rome, and Lee was left with the foreign minister.

"I'm told you are going to the North."

Lee was alarmed that her itinerary was public knowledge. "That's possible."

"I come from a village outside Erbil." The foreign minister smiled, exposing his bad teeth and a large dimple in his cheek. "I have a big family. I want to invite you to my house. You must meet my wives."

"I may not be stopping there."

"Do you have an escort for the trip?"

"I do."

"Is it adequate?"

"I hope so."

"I will give you six of my own Peshmerga. They are very good." He looked sober. "A lot of people have tried to kill me."

"I couldn't deprive you of your men."

"No problem. Just let me know when you are going. One day you can take me to dinner in New York. I like Peter Luger in Brooklyn. Those huge rare steaks."

"Mr. Foreign Minister" — Duncan had joined them — "May I offer you some of Laela's famous *babaghanoush?*"

They embraced like old friends. Lee left them reminiscing about an evening after the Kurdish uprising, when they were huddled around a brazier in an Assyrian village during a flash flood. The party had picked up now that the foreign minister had arrived. The simple fact that he had traded the safety of the Green Zone for Laela's garden made everyone feel more secure.

"Who is that man with the foreign minister?" Zara had reappeared. "I know him."

"He's Italian. A journalist. I don't know his name."

"Oh, yes, of course. He was nearly killed in Chechnya. I'm impressed that he managed to drag the foreign minister away from the Green Zone. Our overseers, who import their lobster tails in C-130s, tend to keep the drawbridge firmly shut against the peasantry." She took a long sip of her drink. "Laela's sick, you know."

"Yes, I know."

"I want you to help me convince her to come to France. We have doctors in Paris ready to treat her, and a quiet place in the Cévennes where she can recover. I want to get her out."

"I'll do what I can. When she gets her tests back, I want to see them. I'm leaving the country for a few days but I'll be back in a week, *Insha'Allah*."

"Good."

"Her immune system's depressed. It's most likely a virus."

"The cancer statistics here are not good."

"Wait for the tests."

Musicians began to play the *oud*, the *zamr*, and the *tablah*. Soon, Laela was dancing under the starry sky like a dervish. If she was in pain, she had forgotten it. "Zara, I wanted to mention something in passing," Lee said. "I was inside the Imam Hussein Shrine during the al-Kufa siege."

"I won't ask how or why." Zara laughed.

"The point is that I think al-Kufa's people may have helped themselves to some of the treasure from the shrine."

"That would be quite a scandal."

"It's just something I heard."

There was now a wide circle around Laela dancing in her bare feet, her dress flying around her thin hips like blue flames. "She's exquisite." Duncan was standing beside Lee, lighting a cigarette. "Did you speak to Jabarri?"

"He was menacing, our friend Mr. Alpha."

"Alpha?"

"A schoolboy name. Laela used it."

"That's a bit of luck. By the way, Rubai is free."

"He's out of Abu Ghraib?"

"Yes."

"Duncan, that's fantastic. Where is he?"

"Back in Karbala. We must go to see him tomorrow."

The music had stopped. Laela was on the ground. She had collapsed.

"My God." Duncan dropped his cigarette.

"Duncan, find Dr. Qais."

Lee waded through the crowd to the limp figure on the flagstones. Naji Qais appeared and assured the guests that Laela had fainted, nothing more. He lifted her like a child. The music started up again. Upstairs, the doctors checked Laela's eyes for sign of neurological injury, like a slow bleed into the brain. Laela stared at Lee, trying to focus.

"I feel very old."

"Dancing like that would kill most of us."

"I'm so tired. Please tell everyone I'll see them later."

"I need to you stay awake, Laela." Naji Qais spoke gently. "You may have a concussion."

Lee could see that Laela was having a hard time focusing on them. "What do you see, Laela?"

"It's very dark and fuzzy. I'm sleepy now."

"Look at my face."

"You're in a black hole. I need to sleep."

"Naji, I think you need to take her in for a CT scan," Lee rubbed Laela's cold hands. "Laela, wake up. Wake up. Naji will take you to the hospital. I need you to concentrate on staying awake."

"Laela." Dr. Qais picked her up in his arms. "If you will just climb onto my magic carpet, I will tell you the story of Princess Parizade and the speaking bird, the singing tree, and the yellow water of gold."

Zara insisted that the party should go on. The musicians played until just before curfew, and Duncan convinced the foreign minister to let the party from the Dar ride in convoy with his Peshmerga. Lee stole into Laela's guest room to collect Martin's documents. She removed the books from the shelf and the documents were gone. Her heart began to race. She looked down behind the shelf and saw a corner of white plastic. They had only slipped to the floor.

"What's wrong with her, Lee?" Duncan could see beads of sweat on Lee's face as they got into Hassan's new Mercedes, which he had been polishing most of the evening.

"I don't know. She's had some tests. Naji Qais will do more tonight. Her sister wants to fly her to Paris. She has a Lebanese passport."

"Could it be serious?"

"Yes."

"How serious?"

"I don't want to guess."

She stared into the deserted streets. The power was out in most of the city and it looked like the back lot of a Burbank studio. There was desultory firing somewhere across the river, and ahead of them, parked in the shadows, was a patrol of armored personnel carriers. Lee remembered a Washington hearing on C-SPAN where someone testified that a rocket-propelled grenade could puncture the thin skin of the vehicle, turning its belly into an inferno so that soldiers were cooked alive. She thought of Eric the gunner and Nizar's suitcase of drugs.

"In the morning, I'm expecting a delivery of medical supplies. I want to have it before leaving for Karbala to see Rubai."

"He's not expecting us until noon. Rubai is preparing a feast. Lambs will be slaughtered in our honor. When do you set off for Diyarbakir?"

"Monday early."

"I am coming with you."

"Why, Duncan?"

"I want to. I am very fond of the Peshmerga. I remember one night in Talameen near Sulaymaniyah, I arrived at the house of the local Kurdish tribal chief and found 50 Peshmerga in the courtyard. They were ready for war. There had been a slight to someone's honor, a violation of summer grazing rights for sheep on the mountain that stood between two families. My arrival ruined everything because the laws of hospitality required that looking after an unexpected guest took precedence over going to war. The tribal lord announced that we would all go to a wedding instead. It was in the village square, with sequined dancers, a singer from Las Vegas, conjurers, and everyone firing their guns into the air."

"Did any of the bullets fall back to earth?" In Iraq, the laws of physics were routinely ignored.

"Only a couple of injuries that night. My escort was the most beautiful boy, with his baggy pants and sash of bullets, who had never been out of the mountains. Later I heard that the feudal lord and his family finally had their war. The compound was razed. The boy was killed. The village is no longer on the map."

They said their goodbyes to the foreign minister by the concertina wire at the entrance to the Dar. Lee accepted his offer of an escort to the North, particularly as Duncan was coming and she felt less than confident about the security arrangements of the Sulaymania Trading Company.

XIX

IN THE MORNING, at 8 sharp, a courier arrived with Nizar's suitcase. Lee checked the contents and marveled at Nizar's ability to run such an efficient black-market pharmacy. There was a note inside with directions to a stall in the al-Safafer Souk, "to meet the man you're looking for."

The forger, she thought.

Duncan had spent an hour at the Internet cafe exchanging email with his editor. Lee had asked him to send a message to the Surgeons' Committee office in New York to say that she needed to purchase supplies in Turkey for the Karbala Hospital and hoped they would wire money to the Attaturk Bank in Diyarbakir. Since the Surgeons' Committee offices in Baghdad shut down after the attack on the clinic in Sadr City, Lee's sponsors had been looking for ways to be helpful in Iraq without risk. This was just what they needed for the fund-raising brochure: "International Surgeons Ferry Desperately Needed Supplies Across War Zone to Holy City."

Hassan and Mohammed were waiting in the new Mercedes with a fresh supply of cigarettes, sodas, and pistachios. By mid-morning, they had negotiated six American and Polish roadblocks on the Karbala road. Duncan's plan was to collect Dr. Husseini at his charity so that they could go in convoy to Ahmed Rubai's home, somewhere in the maze of the old city. On the outskirts of Karbala, near the Sunday market, they faced what Duncan hoped would be their last checkpoint. This time it was the Karbala police. There were two black SUVs with tinted windows and a Toyota pickup full of uniformed men in dark glasses with M16s. For some reason Hassan did not command the usual respect. If anything, he seemed to anger the men, who ordered him to wait. The police conferred for several minutes with someone inside the SUV. Something was wrong.

"Where are the documents?" Duncan sensed the danger.

"In my purse."

"Give them to me." He slipped the package of bank records and phone taps under his flack jacket and secured it with his belt. He had clearly carried contraband before. "When I give up the paper, I can always go into smuggling. That should do it."

A superior officer emerged languidly from the back of the SUV. He was heavyset, with mirrored dark glasses and a fat silver ring. He approached with the air of a man who knew that the world had no choice but to wait for him.

"Ali Baba," he smiled broadly at Hassan revealing gold-capped teeth. "I am one of your greatest fans. What are you doing driving around these foreigners?"

"The television business is not so good, sir."

"In the new Iraq you will be an even bigger star than before. Passports please."

Everyone obliged and waited.

"Dr. McGuinness?" the superior officer treated Lee to his metallic grin.

"Yes."

"I will have to ask you to come with me."

"I'm afraid I don't understand."

"My chief would like to see you."

"For what reason?"

"You will have to ask General Yazid."

"But I am late for an appointment."

"I'm sorry, Dr. McGuinness. You don't really have a choice." The officer walked with an unpleasant swagger around to the back of the Mercedes and banged on the trunk. Hassan opened it from the driver's seat and two underfed policemen were ordered to search it. They opened the suitcase of medical supplies and the superior officer told them to transfer it to the SUV.

"*Yalla, yalla.*" He hurried them along.

"Hassan, take Duncan to Dr. Husseini's. Then come and wait for me outside Yazid's office." Lee stepped out of the car to follow her suitcase.

"Please give back my property. I don't want to have to call the Coalition Provisional Authority."

The senior officer laughed. "Please, Dr. McGuinness. Your case will be returned. I hope you are not smuggling stolen drugs."

"I'm afraid I didn't catch your name."

"Just come with me, doctor, and everything will be sorted out."

She was relieved that the imperious policeman was completely uninterested in Duncan and the priceless cargo he had strapped under his ceramic plated vest. He drove off unmolested with Hassan and Mohammed, leaving Lee with the unpleasant prospect of meeting Gen. Yazid and convincing him to return her morphine and antibiotics, which the police could easily sell for a profit.

The office was in a square Saddam-era government building that might have been designed by Mussolini, with a forest of antennae on the roof and American tanks parked out front. The tank crews were sunning themselves in their turrets, eating peanut butter and crackers from their MREs. Lee said hello as she passed by and introduced herself. If she disappeared into Yazid's gulag, the soldiers would give evidence that an American had been seen going into the building. The halls were dark and smelled of mold. She was ushered into a bleak office with orange plastic furniture and a travel poster of the Tyrolean Alps, warped from a leak in the broken air conditioner. She could hear the unmistakable sound of American voices — military voices — peppered with "Yes, sir," and "This way, sir," drifting down the staircase and wondered which general or colonel was conferring with Yazid, delaying her interrogation.

The door opened and a square-jawed American in desert camouflage entered.

"Dr. McGuinness?"

"That's right."

"I'm Major Clapp. General Yazid asked me to translate for you."

"Major Clapp, do you know why I'm here?"

"No, ma'am."

"Are you based in Karbala?"

"Yes, ma'am."

"Who is your commander?"

"Colonel Slay, ma'am."

"Would you mind contacting him for me?"

"I'm afraid I can't interrupt him, ma'am. He's upstairs with General Yazid."

Maj. Clapp said he was not cleared to engage in any substantive conversation. "Everything you want to know is above my pay grade, doctor."

In the end, they sat quietly, both studying the snow-capped peaks in the poster. When Gen. Yazid finally appeared, he was much as Lee expected, a large man with meaty hands who had yet to shave the thick, Saddami mustache that marked him as a Ba'athist. He brushed by her and fiddled with the rusty fan that clattered throughout their conversation. Once the general sat down, he sweated onto the soiled blotter on his desk.

"Dr. McGuinness, I apologize for the inconvenience."

"I would appreciate it, General, if you could explain why I am here."

"I think you know, doctor," he smiled, revealing a missing tooth. Dentistry was not a priority of reconstruction. "We are looking for your friend Mr. Carrigan. We know you are looking for him too."

"I am in Karbala for a meeting with someone else."

"Yes, yes. Your friend Rubai is out of jail. You will see him. I have asked you here, Dr. McGuinness, to give you a warning."

"What sort of warning?"

"If you make contact with Mr. Carrigan and do not inform us, then you are guilty of a crime."

"What crime?"

"Crimes against the coalition."

"General Yazid, are you aware that it is illegal under the laws of the occupation for senior Ba'athists like yourself to be working in the police force?"

"I am the exception." His smile amply displayed his cruel mouth.

"I see. Well I am grateful for your warning, but I can assure you that Mr. Carrigan has proved very elusive. I am leaving the country soon. Your men confiscated my medical supplies. I am a surgeon, General Yazid. I would like them returned."

"Of course, Dr. McGuinness. It was a pleasure meeting you. Enjoy your short stay in Karbala."

Lee stood up to leave.

"You look very beautiful in your *abaya*." Gen. Yazid leered and slowly lit a cigarette. "I heard you were in the Hussein Shrine during the al-Kufa siege."

"That's right."

"You have a taste for danger." He smiled suggestively, and Lee wondered how a man like Yazid, thick-bellied, pockmarked, and damp with sweat, could imagine that women regarded him as anything but vile.

"Not really, General. The wounded needed a doctor, that's all. Please give my regards to Colonel Slay." It was only then that she realized that they had spoken entirely in English, and Maj. Clapp had not translated a word. Lee found Hassan waiting with an excited crowd of local fans outside the perimeter. When she checked the contents of her suitcase to see if anything had been pilfered, she found that half the morphine was gone.

"Damn," she said under her breath.

"Something wrong, doctor?"

"No, nothing, Hassan. I lost something, but it's not important."

"Everybody here calls General Yazid 'the butcher.' He ran the prison camp where they used to beat prisoners to death on television. There was reality TV in Iraq long before America, Dr. McGuinness. They got very high ratings."

Lee sat quietly in back, breathing in the air of Karbala with its smell of saffron and sewage, wondering how men like Clapp could stomach a sadist like Yazid. Duncan and Dr. Husseini were waiting anxiously on the steps of Husseini's office, next to a new shipment of beds.

"How was your interview?" Husseini asked as he climbed into the front seat.

"He didn't seem to want anything. It was harassment more than anything, and there was an American soldier in the room."

"Was Colonel Slay there?" Duncan sat beside her in back and emptied the documents into her purse.

"Upstairs. He never appeared."

"Both Slay and Yazid are responsible for Rubai's arrest." Dr. Husseini said flatly. Neither Duncan nor Lee would doubt his sources. "They are the ones who 'confiscated' weapons from him, the crates in the photos. I think they planted them to stop Rubai's public criticism of corruption. I don't think Rubai is safe here. Thanks to Duncan's story he is less vulnerable than he was before, but that sort of protection wears thin. I am encouraging him to go to Dubai."

"What about you?"

"I have the Grand Ayatollah behind me. People are reluctant to cross him. Even General Yazid."

Rubai greeted them outside his low-built Ottoman house with graceful arches leading to a terrace shaded by vines. The polished stone floor had been worn away over hundreds of years by the traffic of bare feet. There were brightly colored cushions to sit on and *kilims* thrown on the ground. Rubai wore a crisp *dishdasha* and a beard turned prematurely white. His unhealthy skin was stretched over sunken cheeks, and his eyes betrayed the humiliation of two tours in Abu Ghraib. He and Dr. Husseini kissed affectionately, as Iraqi men do. Their years in Saddam's torture chambers bound the two men together. Rubai turned to Lee and Duncan and bowed slightly, lowering his eyes and placing his hand just above his heart.

"I owe you my life. You are always welcome here. My wife has been cooking since yesterday."

Duncan replied with a few lines from a pre-Islamic poem that everyone in Karbala knew, about Bedouin offering water and dates to a traveler lost in the Nejd.

"You are a doctor, am I right?" Rubai offered Lee mint tea.

"That's right."

"You cannot believe the conditions inside Abu Ghraib."

"What do you mean?"

"Men chained naked to the bars, menaced by dogs. I am not a young man. I have a heart condition. They denied me drugs." He cleared his throat as though he was starting to choke. "They forced someone's penis into my mouth."

Lee looked away, thinking that she did not want any part of this war. She wanted to drive to Diyarbakir, board a plane in Ankara, and never come back.

"Why were you arrested?" Duncan filled the silence.

"I was a troublemaker. I was asking awkward questions about the people in the occupation who have come here to make money. They knew I was meeting with your friend."

"Martin Carrigan?"

"Yes."

"Your son told us you know him well."

"Yes, I know him. He is the only one who sees that the corruption is like a disease. It will kill the host."

Rubai's wife and daughters appeared in their black veils and spirited Lee into the house to express their gratitude privately. When Lee returned, she told Rubai about her Green Zone meeting with Plumber and his insistence that Martin was guilty of treason. She relayed the evidence compiled by Jabarri.

"They all claim" — she watched her host for any sign of deception — "that incriminating documents were found in this house when they searched it."

"So we are running the insurgency?" Rubai laughed. "Martin is wanted because he can destroy these people who are after him. This is a war between two factions in your government. A civil war." he laughed again.

"In my government?"

"Yes."

"But no one in Washington has shown any sign of wanting to help him. No one admits they even know him."

"If he's caught he will go on trial in Baghdad," Duncan added. "I suppose it's more likely that he will be shot before he gets to the Green Zone."

"He has powerful protectors here. You would be surprised."

Rubai's son appeared with a brass platter of rice and spiced meat.

"I think you know my son."

The boy smiled. He looked healthier now that his father was no longer a prisoner.

"I was threatened today by General Yazid." Lee waited for Rubai's reaction.

"I wouldn't worry about the butcher. It's the forces above him you need to watch out for."

"Colonel Slay?"

"Yes. And more senior people. His friends in the Green Zone."

"How does Slay fit into this?"

"Selling government property and pocketing the funds, encouraging a prostitution ring. He is one of Martin's targets in the investigation. By no means the biggest crook."

"Someone tried to kidnap me in Baghdad."

"Do they know that you have made contact with Martin Carrigan?"

"No. I don't think so. They know that I am at your house. Why wouldn't Martin come with me out of the country?"

"You are too closely watched."

"No one followed us to the safe house. Will you speak with him soon?"

"Yes."

"Tell him that I am following his instructions. I think I may be the only American friend he has left."

"He has other friends. You will see. Please. All of this food is for you."

"Will you take Dr. Husseini's advice and go to Dubai?"

"Yes I think so. Or Sharjah. I am a businessman. There's always room for exiles like me in the Gulf. My family needs protection. There's no law here. Only greed."

Before saying goodbye, Lee asked about Sadoon. Rubai said they had met in the outdoor cage used for exercise and that Sadoon had been anxious that Lee should contact his family. The family had no access. He wanted them to know that although his jailers played heavy metal and TV commercial jingles all night to deprive him of sleep, he was, at least, alive. Duncan asked whether Sadoon had been questioned about the rocketing of the Rasheed, and Rubai shrugged, saying he did not know. They left him to rest. His chest was rattling, and Lee thought he might have caught a strain of drug-resistant TB from one of his cellmates, like Sheik Abbas. She left some medicine with his son to regulate his breathing and arrhythmia, along with a supply of antibiotics.

Dr. Husseini was anxious to get back to receive a shipment of computers from Kuwait for his teacher-training project. Lee left him with the enigmatic Ali, and promised to be back within days to restock the hospital with whatever she managed to buy. Ali said that in the children's ward, he was seeing new cases of typhoid, cholera, and hepatitis type E.

"We never saw that before the invasion. And now we have polio again. Don't forget latex gloves. And trauma shears."

Even though Lee sometimes felt that her efforts to rescue Martin were inept at best, at least she could supply a few desperate doctors with gloves. She had not lived in vain. She called Dr. Qais on her Thuraya to see whether he had any results from Laela's tests.

"Lee, where are you?" Her old friend sounded tense.

"I'm driving through Hillah."

"Can you meet me at Omar Hospital when you get into town?"

"How's Laela?"

"She's resting." He paused for such a long time that Lee thought they had been disconnected.

"Naji?"

"We're doing X-rays and a biopsy."

"Biopsy?"

"She broke her arm when she collapsed. It may mean nothing. But there is a chance she has MFH, malignant fibrous histiocytoma of the bone."

"That's extremely rare."

"Yes, but we've been seeing an increase lately."

"I see."

"I will wait for you."

"Yes. I'll be there." Lee leaned forward. "Hassan, we need to stop at the hospital."

"What did he say?" Duncan lit a cigarette. "What's rare?"

"MFH. Bone cancer."

XX

LAELA WAS AWAKE when they arrived. She shared her room with five other women. There was no hope of privacy. Laela's hair was spread across the white pillow in inky waves and her face looked scrubbed and drawn. Her broken arm lay across her chest.

"I feel so stupid, behaving like a mad Sufi, whirling until I dropped. Look at my arm. How can I throw my pots? I'm completely useless now."

"It will mend," Lee said with affection. "As will that bump on your head. Naji told me they are doing more tests."

"Yes, it's such a bore. But I should be out in a couple of days. Will you be here?"

"I am going up north for a few days. But then I'll be back. Would you like me to come and stay with you?"

"Yes, Lee. Zara's trying to drag me off to France, but she won't succeed just yet."

"I think you should go."

Laela cocked her head and stared. "Why?"

"Baghdad is not equipped to treat you. There isn't even a proper cast on your arm, Laela."

"What about my garden? What about Hammurabi?"

"Naji will take him. Your palms will survive. Why don't you go to Paris?"

"The paper owes me some time off." Duncan touched Laela's hand. "Why don't we both go?"

"Oh Duncan, are you serious?"

"Yes. We can go to Beaubourg to see art and the Closerie des Lilas to eat sea urchins. I will take you to my favorite shop that sells nothing but mousetraps. We can take the TGV to the south and play boules in the Cévennes. I will take you to a cave with paintings 33,000 years old and a museum for prunes."

She wiped away the day of sickness with her laugh. "My God, that sounds lovely, Duncan. Promise?"

"Promise." He kissed her gently on the forehead.

Lee slipped out to find Naji Qais and Zara in the hall.

"I think Duncan will convince her to leave Baghdad."

"How? My sister is as stubborn as a cart horse."

"He wants to come with her."

"Really? Well I must say, his writing is very clever. And he's rather wonderful looking in that English schoolboy way. But I thought you two were inseparable."

Lee blushed. "Afraid not. Just thrown together by the war."

Naji pressed a piece of paper into Lee's hands. "My list for Ankara. The contact and all his information are there. Call him in advance and he will bring the supplies to Diyarbakir. You will have to arrange transport to the border."

Back at the Dar, Lee had an email waiting from the Surgeons' Committee confirming that they would deposit funds at the Attaturk Bank, enough to cover a truckload of syringes and cipro. The trip would be worthwhile even if Martin's Ottoman scholar failed to show. She was anxious now to get the documents out of Iraq and out of her care. It was only a matter of time before it would dawn on Plumber or Jabarri that Martin might use her to smuggle out incriminating evidence.

That night there were gun battles and explosions all over the city. Just after 3 in the morning, someone fired an RPG within a block of the Dar, and Lee got up to take some Ambien, worn by the combination of fatigue and adrenaline. A wounded cat was caterwauling in the ally. Duncan slept soundly, oblivious to the racket outside. His bags were packed for Kurdistan. Lee was grateful to have him with her in the wilderness of the occupation.

Rummaging in her jacket pocket, she found the soldier's letter from Beit Har. She reread the lines about soldiers helping themselves to money stolen from Iraqis during raids. Who told them theft was acceptable? Beit Har was on the route north. They had time to stop. Duncan could get a story out of it.

The next morning, Omar Barzani of the Sulaymania Trading Company was irritated that Lee appeared at Masbah Circle with six Peshmerga of her own. She explained that the foreign minister's generosity was impossible to refuse. Barzani grumbled that he should have been informed. His men looked suspiciously at the foreign minister's men until they established that they were all distantly related by marriage. Two of them had spent a summer together smuggling televisions and automatic rifles across the mountains from Iran. Contentment spread through the party until they learned of Lee's plan to stop at Beit Har.

"That's a Sunni town," Barzani scowled. "There was an uprising not long ago. My Peshmerga are Kurds, Dr. McGuinness. They are not welcome there. I would urge you to do what Mr. Carrigan said. Go to the Zakho Guest House. Arrangements have been made."

"Fine, Omar. Will you be joining us?"

"No. My men know the way. Please, doctor. No diversions. Once you arrive at the Guest House, you will be told how to proceed from there."

"Omar, what is your relationship to Mr. Carrigan?"

"We are old friends."

The convoy moved out in relative harmony, and the drivers had no desire to stop for anything but roadblocks. Two Peshmerga rode in the car with Lee and Duncan, which put Lee in a cheerful mood. Their lean, handsome faces were wind burned from long mountain treks along the Iranian border. Under the ammunition belts draped across their chests, they had the hard physique of men who had never known sedentary life.

"Sitting next to them," Duncan confided to Lee, "I feel like a domesticated animal."

"I wouldn't worry about that."

Past the outer suburbs of Baghdad, where the landscape looked like the surface of the moon, they saw the first sign of trouble. It was a plume of smoke from a blackened car. As they approached, Lee could smell the burning rubber from the tires and then saw what had happened. Someone had fired on the car for failing to halt at the roadblock. There were American troops in camouflage standing around the wreckage and the half-burned bodies of a mother and five children in the road. All had been shot. On the ledge of the back seat of the burnt car, there was a toy dog, its partly blown-off head nodding on a spring. The soldiers signaled them to keep moving. They did not want spectators to what was known as "collateral damage."

"Criminals," Duncan said in disgust.

Lee felt too nauseous to speak and did not break the silence until well past Kirkuk, past the crumpled bus that had veered off the road with a load of Baghdadis coming to Kurdistan for relief from the war.

"They're not criminals." Lee had to say it. "They are brainwashed. Their commanders tell them that everyone is the enemy. When they go home and remember what they've done here, they shoot themselves."

She lapsed into silence again, as they drove past a sign in the middle of nowhere that read "no photo," past the line of stolen white SUVs snaking toward Erbil. It was only after dusk, when the road began to narrow through mountain gorges, that Lee felt human again, watching the fires on the hillsides flicker in the darkness, surrounded by picnickers barbecuing *kebabs* and singing Kurdish songs forbidden under the old regime, far from the horrors of the Baghdad road.

XXI

THE CONVOY ARRIVED at the Zakho Guest House and was greeted with the news that there was no water or electricity. The manager apologized and promised that someone had been dispatched to find a new generator, as the old one had been stolen. On the dilapidated balcony of Lee's room, she and Duncan sat drinking *arak*. They watched the mile-long line of oil tankers and trucks, groaning with smuggled goods trussed up with sisal, that clogged the border. All of the overheated commerce generated by the war was passing beneath them, including the cargo of the Green Zone profiteers. There was no one keeping tabs on how much oil was flowing out of the country illegally. Duncan said he was sure that anyone cutting open the mounds of burlap sacks could find stolen artifacts and suitcases full of cash.

Beyond the chaotic scene were the mountains that rose above the Turkish frontier like worn sharks' teeth. At their base, the meadows were still sewn with Saddam's mines. A bitter wind off the peaks offered some relief from the stench of diesel.

"You're a good friend, Duncan."

"What prompted that?"

"For taking Laela to Paris."

"She is the essence of 5,000 years of civilization that this war is bent on destroying. It is a privilege to do anything I can for her."

"From the moment I saw you in her garden, I knew you belonged there." Lee was quiet for a moment, gathering the courage to reveal herself. "Are you in love with her?"

Duncan took her face, pink with cold, in his hands. "No. I just want to make her happy. To somehow make amends for all of this suffering. Why don't we both go to Paris?"

Lee said nothing. She didn't know how to answer. When Duncan ran out of cigarettes, they followed the sounds of their fellow guests to a small interior courtyard, where they chose a table under a giant oak that had somehow escaped the purge of Kurdistan's trees by Saddam's men. Kurdish traders, U.N. aid workers, and British mercenaries huddled around kerosene heaters as they argued over the progress of the war, the increase in IEDs, and oil rights in Kirkuk.

"May I get you anything?" Duncan smiled as they both eavesdropped shamelessly. One of the mercenaries was loudly offering shares in the Kurdistan Oil Company.

"Pomegranate juice, if they have it." Pomegranates came across the Iranian border on donkeys.

A man with long, slender fingers covered in lapis rings stood in the center of the courtyard and began eating fire.

"We're in luck," said Duncan. "The Kurds love a good magician. Tribal chiefs often keep them on the payroll." The fire-eater spun torches in the air and doused them, one by one, in his mouth. He approached the table and turned his attention to Lee. She laughed with embarrassment and thought it was in keeping with her strange mission to find this conjurer here, on a night so clear the galaxy looked like a trail of spilled glitter.

The man extinguished his fires, sat, and began pulling eggs out from behind Duncan's ears.

"How does he do it?" Duncan was delighted. The magician then turned Lee's pashmina shawl into a green parrot that affectionately bit the lobe of her ear and spoke the only words of English it knew.

"Hello, mate. What about a fiver?"

"Boudi, you have no manners." The conjurer spoke in heavily accented English, reclaiming the bird and changing pomegranate seeds into coins. It was only when he read Lee's palm that she realized he was the man she was waiting for.

"You will have a long life, two great loves, one of whom will disappoint you." He studied Lee's delicate hand with its tapered fingers like a child's, which Duncan thought must be invaluable for surgery, sliding between organs, hunting for tumors and foreign objects. "You will be met by a driver at dawn. He will take you to the *caravanserai* at Diyarbakir. You will be contacted there tomorrow night. Be ready for it."

The man with the rings moved off to entertain the mercenaries. He made the round flat bread of bulgur wheat in the center of their table levitate, accepted some coins for his trouble, and disappeared. His exit was obscured by a troop of Qadri dervishes whirling around the clientele.

"He's good, that fellow," Duncan observed. "A master of deception. I once had a magician pour a gallon of milk from my elbow. I still can't work out how he did it."

The driver appeared at first light as promised. His car was a Turkish taxi that had seen better days, but had the right plates to get through the Turkish military zone they were about to enter. Hassan and his cousin Mohammed would wait at the Zakho Guest House. The new driver spoke only broken English and Kurdish, so conversation was kept to a minimum.

The passengers slept most of the way through Silopi, Cizre, and the parched landscape famous for its hill towns built of honey-colored stone, some of which had been reduced to rubble in Turkish army raids against local Kurdish separatists. By mid-morning, Lee and Duncan had arrived in the capital of the province, winding their way through the ancient Roman streets, past the black basalt walls left by the Byzantines, to the hotel built for caravans arriving from the desert with their camels 500 years ago. The rooms were low and dark, not much better than a stable.

As they were shown to their quarters, Lee turned to Duncan and said, "The magician was wrong. I have been disappointed in love more than once." She turned away before he could say anything.

They found the Attaturk Bank without any trouble, and Lee was relieved to find that $10,000 had been wired to her by the Surgeons' Committee. She stuffed the bricks of cash as quickly as possible into her purse while the dozen or so people in the bank stared. She could not help but arouse curiosity, as Western women here were scarce. She left the task of finding transport for the medical supplies to their capable driver.

"No problem, doctor. My brother-in-law has a lorry."

The driver offered to hire the family pickup truck at an extortionate rate to carry the cargo back to Zakho. Lee had emailed the pharmacist in Ankara recommended by Naji Qais before leaving Baghdad, and he had left a message at the *caravanserai* promising to meet her there in the morning. The end of his message read simply "cash only."

She and Duncan then proceeded to the governor's office to obtain the necessary signatures to export the drugs. They were obliged to pay a substantial "transport tax," which involved waiting several hours for the relevant Turkish bureaucrats to return from lunch. Lee then filled out multiple forms in triplicate, all by hand, exercising a degree of patience she did not know she possessed.

With the sheaves of paperwork elaborately signed and stamped, they walked through a black-and-white mosque to the bazaar.

"Do you like goat's head soup?" Duncan forged ahead through the labyrinth of the old town. "It is a specialty here."

"I would really just like a beer."

"This way." He navigated the alleyways until they emerged onto Gazi Caddesi and turned into a small cafe with a terrace shaded with vines.

"Two Efes, please."

They sat on *kilims* in the cool of the late afternoon, and Lee was grateful that the incessant rifle fire, the low-flying helicopters, the white noise of Baghdad, were far behind them.

"It's quiet here."

"It's an illusion," Duncan ordered some *kaburga dolmasi*. "Not long ago, you could be arrested here for speaking Kurdish."

"I'm just happy to be out of Iraq for a day."

"How do we recognize Martin's friend?"

"He will tell us that he works in the Ottoman archives and that he is translating something about Abdul Kadr. He will thank us for bringing him more manuscripts."

"What if he's the wrong man? Is there some way we can test him?"

"Even if someone had followed us, how would they know what to say?"

"Informant. A monitored sat phone call. An unguarded email."

"I don't think Martin is careless."

Duncan lit a cigarette. "We are all careless. Jabarri is trying to build a secret police like Saddam's Mukhabarat. They know how to infiltrate, how to bribe and intimidate. I just wish we knew a bit more."

"Well, worst case, we have a backup set of documents in London, assuming your email at the paper is working."

"Is the agent American?"

"I didn't ask. I do think Martin knows what he is doing. The magician was a nice touch." Lee finished her beer. "I need to repack the case at the *caravanserai*, so that everything is just as it was when Martin gave it to me. Do you want to come?"

"There is a carpet dealer not far from here who would be insulted if I didn't stop in for a coffee. Can you find your way back from here?"

"Yes, I think so."

"Right, then."

Almost as soon as he had vanished in the crowd, Lee regretted having let Duncan go. The streets of Diyarbakir seemed somehow sinister without him. The dark passageways, just wide enough for a donkey, which had seemed so quaint, were now menacing. Every face belonged to a kidnapper or an assassin. She was carrying a duty-free bag holding the names of men who would happily arrange an accident to get it back. There were bricks of cash in her purse. She began to sweat. The hotel was four blocks away. Why had she agreed to come here? She was caught up in a game she only half understood. Martin could have handed off the suitcase to a professional who was skilled in evasive maneuvers and dead drops. In Karbala, she thought that he had chosen her because he trusted her. She had wanted to be valuable to him because of a special understanding between them. She wondered now whether that was an illusion, a conjurer's trick. Perhaps there was no understanding. Perhaps she was simply useful. The idea of a bond between them seemed naïve now. He was a spy. He had lied to her. The Martin she had known, the ascetic who devoted his life to the poor and the dispossessed, was a figment of her imagination. The fact was, she was tangled up in a game of espionage and had no protection. If something happened to Lee, Martin's organization would not be compromised. She had no phone numbers, no names. Under torture she would be able to describe only someone claiming to be a magician. Martin was confident of her ignorance, like a stranger asking a good Samaritan to carry a package onto a plane. Lee was expendable. It was rash not to have had her driver follow her in the street. She began to run.

She looked behind her and saw that two men in dark glasses and black jeans had broken ranks with the slow-moving mass of humanity in the market and were dodging and weaving through the crowd to follow her. One of them upset a vendor selling spices. The other had a gun. Lee stole into a doorway and found herself in a Jacobite church where an old woman in a black shawl was lighting candles. The long tapers were sputtering and the light was so dim that the woman did not notice Lee slip into the sacristy, where the artifacts of this sect that refused to believe that Christ was both human and divine had been gathering dust since the Council of Chalcedon.

She could hear the echo of urgent footsteps. If they were not Christian, they might be unaware that the chamber where she was crouching existed. She tried to breathe deeply and think what to do, in spite of the blood pounding in her ears. The men's voices trailed off into the street. She waited for more than an hour, until the pain in her legs was crippling her. She rose slowly and lit a candle to St. Jude, patron saint of lost causes, before making her way back to the gate of the *caravanserai*. The hotel had posted a guard to keep out undesirables, and he viewed her clothes covered in dust and cobwebs with suspicion. When she greeted him in English, he clicked his tongue as though her disheveled appearance was further confirmation of the general decline of the West.

When Lee got back to her room, the suitcase was gone. Her first thought on seeing the empty space where she had placed it was that she should have lit a candle to St. Anthony, just as an insurance policy. The fact that she had left it out conspicuously at the Dar without any problem had made her overconfident. Someone on the *caravanserai* staff had been bribed, no doubt, to hand over her key. Bribed by whom? If the maids were moonlighting for Turkish intelligence, their superiors would have received a request from Adnan Jabarri or George Plumber to search the room. It had been clear from the Jabarri documents that part of the smuggling ring was operating here in Turkey. Local officials might be on the payroll to facilitate shipments. They might also be watching her every move. Her alarm was tempered with relief that she had clung to the duty-free bag, which now looked like it belong to a homeless person. There was nothing of importance in the case, but whoever had taken it would be back for the documents in her hand. Lee was anxious for the Ottoman scholar to relieve her of Martin's burden so that she could be an ordinary surgeon again, an innocent abroad. She proceeded to the courtyard bar, where she ordered a large scotch.

As she sat there recovering from the day, the peace was broken by the shrill voices of 50 American women on a package tour complaining about their bus. Lee couldn't imagine what they were doing in Diyarbakir. Surely they belonged in Istanbul touring the Hagia Sophia or in some overrun resort along the coast buying fake Roman amphora.

From the accents, she placed them from somewhere in Minnesota or Wisconsin. They loudly ordered tables to be joined together so that they could sit en masse within 10 feet of her. As she cringed under the invasion, one of ladies, in a twin-set knit suit and hair that looked like it had been developed at NASA, approached Lee's table. She wore glasses on a rhinestone chain around her neck and was laden with a camera and shopping bags.

"Is this chair taken?"

"No, please. You are welcome to it."

"May I join you?"

Lee wondered how she had offended God. Perhaps hiding in the sacristy was a mistake.

"Of course."

"Where are you from?"

"New York."

"Oh, really?" She smiled, revealing a set of well-polished false teeth. "I go there every year for the new Broadway shows. I'm Martha Sparks," she held out her hand.

"Lee McGuinness."

"What a treat meeting an American in far-off Turkey." She leaned toward Lee. The smell of pancake makeup mixed with a perfume of white ginger reminded Lee of the leis at the Honolulu airport. "We gardeners get tired of each other, you know. We're from the Minneapolis-St. Paul Horticultural Society, and we fight all the time, mostly about who knows more about plants. I'm in a dispute with that woman in the blue pantsuit about a tulip I found growing near the Gate of the White Eunuchs at Topkapi. I say it was cultivated by Sultan Ahmet I. She says it was a cheap Dutch import. Right now no one will sit next to each other on the bus."

"What brings you to Diyarbakir?" Lee had a terrible craving for a cigarette.

"Oh, we're passing through on our way to a monastery. It's a horticultural site because they used saffron crocuses in the mortar. What about you?"

"I'm here to meet someone."

"Gosh, me too. I'm looking for Ottoman manuscripts. I'm working on a project at the archives about Abdul Kadr and I need some more material."

Lee looked into her steady gray-blue eyes under the powdered forehead and tight curls with astonishment.

"May I buy you a drink?"

"Oh, no thanks. I ordered a dry martini at the other table."

"I have something right here that will interest you."

Sparks took the duty-free bag and seamlessly exchanged it with one of her plastic bags from the market. It looked as though she was simply adjusting her load, in the clumsy manner of an aging American lady, who might be suffering from the onset of dementia.

"Gee, it was fun meeting you. Thanks for the manuscripts. Maybe I'll look you up in New York sometime. Bye now, Dr. McGuinness."

Lee had not told her that she was a doctor. She looked down and saw that her bag contained a cheap red velvet fez with gold embroidery and a tassel. She finished her drink and retreated to her room, waving goodbye to the ladies as she left. She pulled out her bottle of Irish whiskey and toasted the ingenuity of Martha Sparks. She looked forward to her coming to New York for the theater, particularly if she could untangle the mess Martin Carrigan was in, before it was too late.

By the time Duncan returned with a carpet under his arm, the Horticultural Society bus had left, and Lee was longing for some *mezze* and *kebabs*.

XXII

"LEE, I FOUND SOMETHING WONDERFUL." Duncan unrolled the prayer rug at her feet. "It's a keyhole rug from Konya. Really old. Look, natural dyes and see the thread count? There is Para-Mamluk detail that is really rare." She had never seen Duncan so enthused.

They chose a table as far away as possible from the Turkish band. Lee told him about her adventures in the sacristy and her meeting with Martha Sparks. Duncan was hugely relieved and, at the same time, bothered by the possibility that whoever stole the case would come looking for its contents.

"I suppose I have to sleep in your room then," Lee said, as though it was more of a duty than a pleasure.

"Yes, we can just about manage," he smiled and ordered some Cappadocian wine. "Mustafapasa."

"What's that?"

"Good peasant wine to keep us awake."

They ordered several courses and were just about to retire when the courtyard filled with soldiers. A large man with slicked-back hair and a theatrical cape emerged from their midst. He was an official of some kind, barking orders in Turkish. Lee asked a waiter who the man was.

"The provincial governor," he said, barely hiding his terror. When the governor saw Lee at her discreet little table in the shadows, he made straight for her, the downside of Lee's beauty.

"Good evening." The governor directed his men to fetch chairs. "You came to my office today, Dr. McGuinness. I am honored." He turned his narrow black eyes, which gave him the look of a large possum, on Duncan. "And you are?"

"I am a journalist, Governor. A reporter from London."

"As you can see, there is no news here."

"Of course, Governor, no news at all. We are only here to shop for carpets. And Dr. McGuinness is grateful to Turkey for supplying the medicine she needs to treat the wounded in Iraq."

"My pleasure. We don't often get doctors here. Mostly oil men." The Governor ordered an underling to fetch *raki*, melon, and feta.

"There must be quite a lot of oil coming through Diyarbakir these days." Duncan lit a cigarette.

"A healthy trade." The Governor smiled, revealing several rotting teeth. "Good for the Turks. So what do you intend to do here?"

"Actually, we plan to leave tomorrow as soon as our shipment arrives from Ankara. We have to get back to Iraq."

"Come see me before you go. There are new regulations, just issued this afternoon, about entering Iraq. I will have to give you another stamp." He seemed pleased to inflict the pain of more bureaucracy. "It won't take a moment. Well, I must be going. Oh, Dr. McGuinness, you didn't lose a briefcase, did you? One was turned into my office today, and I thought it might belong to you. There is quite a lot of cash sewn into the lining, as well as a few personal things."

"It is mine, thank you, Governor. How can I ever repay you?"

"Leave Turkey tomorrow, doctor. And take the famous correspondent from the London *Herald* with you. My compliments." He bowed and left, his men falling in behind him like stones trailing an avalanche. The waiter pursued him with his raki.

"How did he know you?" Lee had underestimated the governor.

"Either Turkish intelligence does its job, or I could flatter myself that he reads my paper."

There was a bitter wind whipping through the streets from Mount Nemrut when they collected Martin's case and applied, once again, for the correct stamps. Every surface of the case had been sliced open with a knife, and the cash, Martha Sparks' per diem, Lee assumed, had been neatly folded into an envelope with the governor's seal. It was more than enough to pay for the shipment of drugs without depleting the Surgeons' Committee funds. Lee thought it was a fair trade for her services that Martin and his organization, whatever it was, should pay to replenish the Karbala Hospital. She and Duncan waited patiently in a seedy room with old copies of *National Geographic* to keep them entertained. Duncan was reading aloud to Lee about Muhammad Gaddafi's interest in existentialism, when the governor filled the room with his bulk.

"Gaddafi's favorite novel is *The Outsider*." The Governor smiled, pleased with his own erudition. "By Colin Wilson. Have you read it?"

"I'm afraid not," Duncan said offhandedly.

"A gap in your education, Mr. Hope. Well, no matter. Everything is taken care of. I wish you a pleasant journey back to Baghdad. By the way, Dr. McGuinness. Are you missing anything from your case?"

"Well, there were some papers in it. Nothing important. Whoever stole the case from my room must have thrown them out. Not to worry."

"I see. Well, good luck then. Don't stop on the road. Eastern Anatolia is full of bandits."

Upon reaching the *caravanserai*, they found their driver's brother-in-law loading bags of medicine into his van. The pharmacist from Ankara was small and nervous and anxious for payment. The transfer took about an hour, and Lee double-checked to make sure that the items Qais had requested were part of the shipment. As she packed her bags, she could see that the room had been searched again.

By mid-afternoon Lee and Duncan were back at the bridge over the Khabur River that divided Turkey from Iraq, their papers in order, peeling off $50 bills for the border guards. At the Zakho Guest House everything had to be repacked in a horse trailer that Hassan had purchased from a relative of the Guest House proprietor. Duncan sent someone to find some Koolit bags that Lee could refrigerate overnight and stuff in the boxes of antibiotics. That night she slept more soundly than she had since leaving the Intercontinental in Amman.

* * *

Before dawn, they gathered their various Peshmerga and left the Guest House by first light. The trip south was slow and cramped, and for most of it, Lee's mouth was clotted with dust. She watched the horse trailer slam into the potholes and prayed there would be something left other than smashed thermometers. Getting through the military checkpoints was onerous, as all of the boxes had to be unpacked and checked. She was impatient. Now that they were on the road to Baghdad, Lee could not stop thinking of Laela, lying in a crowded ward, hiding her fear as she soldiered through her battery of tests, with aging hospital machines that could not be replaced in the last years of Saddam's crumbling regime because U.N. sanctions blocked the importation of something better. It might be diverted to make a weapon of mass destruction. MRI bombs. Dialysis bombs. CT bombs. The insanity of it.

Hassan had taken the Mosul road, following the Tigris past Tikrit and Samarra. The Peshmerga in back were tense, fingering their weapons and watching every movement on the horizon. Hassan's Tikriti cousin, Mohammed, was cracking pistachios. This was his home territory, and he did not like the look of it now. Something was burning. The traffic ahead congealed into a mass of idling cars, and everyone knew that an American convoy must be ahead. Lee made sure that her backpack was accessible and watched as frustrated drivers got out of their cars and paced, smoking and flicking their worry beads. Hassan got out to stretch and climbed on top of the car for a better view.

"I can see the American vehicles. It was a roadside bomb. A big one." He shouted down to his passengers. Dozens of drivers were now climbing on top of their cars, half of them staring at the melted convoy and the other half worshipping Hassan. The fuel fire was starting to blot out the midday sun like an eclipse.

Black Hawk helicopters were circling the wreckage.

"Mohammed, come with me. We're going up there."

"Wait, doctor. It could be dangerous for you."

"Then I will go alone." She grabbed her *abaya* and two of the foreign minister's Peshmerga. Mohammed caught up with her as they sprinted between cars to the ugly fire a half a mile down the road. By the time Lee got there, a rescue squad had landed and was loading the dead and wounded on the chopper. The soldiers had weapons trained on the crowd, which was surging forward, only to be blown back by the dust and debris kicked up by the rotor blades. One of the dead had been blown through the roof of a Humvee and thrown 50 feet from the road. The top of his head had turned to pulp, and the sight of the crumpled body had attracted boys from the nearby village. One of the soldiers, off-loaded from the chopper to retrieve the corpse, panicked and unleashed a round of bullets at the boys. Two of them fell screaming to the stony ground. People ran wildly off the highway, into ditches strewn with garbage, into the sandy waste beyond, into the alleys of the little village with bare shops and malnourished dogs by the side of the road. The wounded boys were carried away, leaving the sand stained red. As soon as the helicopter was airborne, a crowd filled the vacuum in front of the fire and began chanting until their voices were hoarse.

"What are they saying?" Lee shouted to Mohammed.

"They are cursing the Americans and celebrating the bombing of the soldiers. Put your dark glasses on."

Lee was surrounded by 200 Iraqis venting their rage and was conscious that at any moment, the demonstrators might turn on her as a convenient victim for sacrifice. She pulled her *abaya* across her mouth and stepped behind the massive bulk of Mohammed so that she could be mistaken for his wife. Bearded young men in *dishdashas* covered in dust were grabbing souvenirs: twisted bits of hot metal, a helmet, a pair of glasses from the baked Humvees.

More helicopters appeared from the direction of Samarra and, as if to answer the celebrants, unleashed their fury, firing rockets into the little hamlet of breezeblock bungalows and sad-looking date palms next to the road. Houses exploded into flying concrete slabs and the trees, in their freshly swept compounds, were ripped from the earth. A dog was yelping with a broken back. It seemed an act of mindless collective punishment. Machine-gun fire erupted ahead of Lee, but it was impossible to tell who was firing. The helicopters pivoted in her direction, hovering over the men waving their fists in the air at the head of the long lines of paralyzed commuters. Without warning, the Black Hawks rocketed the demonstrators. Lee felt as though her head had been smashed against a wall. Everything was dead quiet, and she knew she had lost her hearing. The crowd reeled back, pushing and shoving in fear like a human whiplash. Everyone who could break free dove beneath the cars. The ones who did not make it screamed for help, like a silent Munch canvas. Lee regained some of her hearing. There was a sound that was more animal than human from the wounded, their *dishdashas* splashed with blood on the tarmac.

When Mohammed turned around, Lee saw that the skin above his eye was torn by shrapnel. She took off her backpack and began treating him, and then others, with manic energy, dressing shrapnel, plugging geysers of blood, disinfecting the gaping holes, suturing flaps of skin, as though to make up for every senseless act of violence in this war.

Soon, Duncan was with her, shouting, "*Sahafi Britani*," British journalist.

"Just stay close to me, Mr. Duncan." Mohammed grabbed his arm. "People know me here." Duncan and Mohammed picked up body parts, dumped Betadine and sterile saline into wounds to clean them, and dispensed water and morphine. Lee showed them how to prepare syringes for local anesthetic. She sent the Peshmerga in relays to the blocked horse trailer for supplies. They worked until they could hardly see, joined by Samarra medics from the Red Crescent, as soon as they could get an ambulance across the road. There were nine dead, including a father with two small children who had been hit as they waved to the helicopters, squealing with pleasure. Duncan counted 33 wounded. He was sure that none of them had been responsible for blowing up the convoy.

Rumors rippled through the eddies of survivors that two of the insurgents had been caught and executed. An American army unit had strapped each body to the hood of a jeep, like slaughtered deer, and paraded the dead through Samarra. When Lee and the Red Crescent medics had loaded the last of the wounded into the ambulances and had exchanged numbers, she barely had time to reach Baghdad before curfew.

"Dr. McGuinness, I am very sorry." Mohammed, the Tikriti, had broken one of his long silences as the Mercedes was once more on the open road to Baghdad. "Next time you ask me to come with you, I will not hesitate. You saved many Sunnis today. Everyone will know what you did."

"Thanks, Mohammed. Don't worry about it."

At the Sulaymania Trading Company, they left Omar Barzani's militiamen with handsome bonuses. Once inside the guarded perimeter of the Dar Kebeer, Lee released the foreign minister's bodyguards with equally generous pay.

"Mohammed, please go see Dr. Qais at Omar Hospital. I don't want your face wounds to get infected."

"Yes, doctor. Hassan will take me."

"There are some boxes here for Dr. Qais."

Lee was grateful to Martin Carrigan for the cash sewn into the lining of his case. Hassan promised to bring his Shia friends from the Badr Brigade in the morning, as escorts for what was left of the supplies to Karbala Hospital. They would have to be paid. Lee said goodnight, too exhausted to say more than that they should meet at 7.

"*As-salamu alaikum*, doctor."

"*Wa alaikum assalam*, Ali. All quiet?"

"A car bomb in Mansour. And a message for you."

"*Shoukran*, Ali." The message was from George Plumber, asking her to call.

"Dr. McGuinness, shall I send the maid for your clothes?"

Lee looked down and saw, for the first time, that she was covered in dried blood. "Yes, Ali. Thanks."

To get to her room in the annex, Lee had to walk through the tables at the poolside terrace. Everyone looked at her as though an untouchable had been permitted by mistake through the cordon at the door. The Italian journalist jumped up and offered her a chair, "You look like you've spent the day in a butcher shop."

"Rocket attack. I'm going to shower. Will you order me a drink?"

"Of course. May I be first with this story?"

"Duncan's filing his piece now."

"You and he are always together now," the Italian said with disappointment.

Lee wasn't sure how to respond. She laughed at the thought that she was generating gossip. When Lee reached the burlap suite, she threw her clothes in a heap on the floor and stood for 20 minutes under a stream of hot water. She turned on her short-wave radio to hear the "BBC World Service" reporting that gunmen dressed in Iraqi police uniforms had kidnapped an Iraqi judge in Mutanabbi. They had climbed the garden wall and shot the security guards in the back of the head. The minister of the interior denied that they were police, saying anyone could buy a police uniform in the market. Besides, he said, the police did not drive mini-vans. Lee wondered whom the judge had crossed.

She found Duncan at his usual table, surrounded by Masoud, of course; the Italian, whose name she finally learned was Stephano; and a German from a wire service, who had silver hair and two bullet holes, he said, in his back. He had once crossed al-Kufa's men in Sadr City.

"Okay, now, what happened you two?" The German offered Lee some Syrian wine.

"Outside Samarra, on the highway, a convoy of Humvees had been hit by an IED." Duncan paused to drink his wine. His story would make the front page. "The rescuers wounded a couple of kids and when the crowd expressed their fury, Black Hawks rocketed them. If CENTCOM claims they have no information on a rocket attack, there were several hundred witnesses. Nine dead, 33 wounded."

"What were you doing in Samarra?"

"Just bad luck."

"At least you missed the car bomb," Stephano said. "At Mansour police station. A bloody mess. They were pulling down body parts from the fig trees."

It was some time before Lee could speak with Duncan alone. "If we wanted to go out to an oil field to see where unmetered oil is siphoned off, where would we go?"

"You're desperate to make friends, aren't you? Rumaila, I suppose, on the Kuwaiti border. There are 1,400 wells down there. It would be safe enough. The Army Corps of Engineers has already sent people in to check for rigged explosives."

"Could we just walk in?"

"I have a friend down at Rumaila. An Iraqi oil engineer. We did postgraduate work at SOAS together — the School of Oriental and African Studies in London. His name is Mahmood Maroki. I can give him a call. But Christ, Lee, think for a moment. These people can make a meddlesome doctor disappear in Rumaila or Baghdad or anywhere they want. Probably even in this hotel."

"They've already tried to kidnap me once."

"Why are you taking the risk?"

"To finish what we've started. I don't know. To do the right thing."

Duncan looked at her and smiled. "I hope Martin appreciates you." He kissed her. "As much as I do. How is Laela, by the way?"

"Having tests."

"Any idea what's wrong?"

"Not yet."

Duncan turned up at the suite after midnight, having filed his story for the paper. The pile of bloody clothes was gone.

"Front page, above the fold. You take me to the best places."

"My pleasure, Duncan. Thanks for everything you did today. It is gruesome work."

"I didn't mind. I finally felt I was doing something rather than just being a witness to all of this."

"You would make a great doctor."

"Like Albert Schweitzer. We could open a hospital. Someplace very remote, on a river. Kisangani or Lashkar Gah. Maybe our hospital should be in Shibam, where they left the water running. Or Baidoa. I hear the Somalis love British jokes. Tomorrow, Lee, I wonder if you would give me Mohammed for the day. I want to find Sadoon's family. Mohammed will know that neighborhood."

"Of course. I will take Hassan to Karbala with the Badr Brigade to unload everything at the hospital. I am going to see Laela. And Plumber wants to talk to me."

"In the Green Zone?"

"Yes."

"What will you tell him?"

"That the Surgeons' Committee has saved a few lives at Karbala Hospital."

Duncan reached for the yellow pad on the table and wrote, *Has he been spying on us?*

Lee wrote back, *Shall we go for a swim?*

They ordered wine by the pool. As Lee dove into the dark water, she felt cleansed of the day's horror and thought about the winter garden she would grow at her mother's farm when she got home. When she came up for air, there was the rattle of automatic-weapons fire somewhere in Marifa. Duncan had poured her a glass of wine on the steps. The air coming off the desert was balmy, and she was thankful to be out of the mountains and the raw Zakho wind. She felt a sense of satisfaction that the handoff of Martin's incriminating documents had gone smoothly. Also, several people would not die from their wounds that night because she had been there on the Samarra road to treat them.

"Duncan, where does the oil go once it's pumped out of the Rumaila oil field?"

"Baiji, to the refinery," he was floating, facing the stars, his arms outstretched. "Or Basra, where it's shipped down the Gulf. There are pirate ports now where the oil goes by night to the Emirates."

"Isn't Baiji near Beit Har?"

"Yes, they are next door."

"Duncan, I want you to come with me to Rumaila and Baiji. We need to find out how Jabarri is skimming the oil. Am I asking too much?"

"Lee, thanks to you, my paper thinks I have magical powers. Why would I refuse?" Duncan glanced up at the balconies of the apartment blocks outside the hotel walls and scanned them for snipers. "I think we should go in. We are too exposed here."

"You are paranoid now."

"It's healthy when someone is trying to kill you." Duncan threw a towel around Lee's shoulders. "What do you think Plumber wants?"

"Probably to scare us. I think we have interfered with his plans to ruin Martin."

"I'm sure he's been in touch with the governor in Diyarbakir."

The welcoming party at the Karbala hospital included Dr. Husseini, Dr. Ali, and the senior staff, who asked Lee to express their gratitude to the International Surgeons' Committee for the contents of the horse trailer. Boxes of antibiotics, local anesthesia, oral rehydration salts, hypertension drugs, morphine, cardiac drugs, anti-psychotics, sedatives, syringes, thermometers, battery-powered monitors, sterile drapes, and latex gloves disappeared into the building where over 1,000 patients, hundreds camped in the halls, waited for medication. Their families, who fed and nursed them, filled the wards with the smell of sweat, cheese, and olives.

"*Hubz wa jubn*," a mother eagerly showed Lee the bread and cheese in her basket.

"*Tayib uhtee.*" That's good, sister.

Lee calculated that her shipment would last a week. Now that Karbala's water was contaminated by sewage and pesticides, the cases of typhoid and cholera were growing exponentially. The city needed a new water system, not a horse trailer. She had set aside the portable cardiac monitors and flashlights for Naji Qais.

"You are popular here, Lee," Dr. Husseini was pleased with his handiwork. "They would bury you in holy ground in Najaf if you wanted."

"Hopefully not yet," she laughed.

"Will you stay for lunch?"

"I have to get back to Baghdad. There is someone in the hospital there I must see. Have you heard any word of Martin?"

"Jabarri is using al-Kufa's people to try to find him. His Army of the Believers is searching every house in the city."

"Are you in touch with the people protecting him?"

"It's difficult right now. Do you have a message?"

"I did everything he asked."

"Good."

"Except board a plane. I'm not going home without him."

"He wanted you to go for your own safety."

"It's not his choice. I can't just walk away now. I cracked the code."

"The code?"

"The documents he gave me were coded. There is a long list of people, including CPA officials, we think, on Jabarri's payroll. That's why they are framing him on the weapons charge."

"Please be careful."

"Dr. Husseini, is the Grand Ayatollah taking an interest in Martin?"

"Why do you ask?"

"I am hoping that whoever is protecting him is powerful enough to keep him alive. I thought that because al-Kufa and Jabarri are trying to spilt the Shia with the seizure of the Mosque and arming al-Kufa's thugs, exposing their corruption might appeal to the spiritual leader in Najaf."

"You understand the situation very well."

"But who is Martin working for at home?"

"I can only speculate. Who is running the occupation?"

"The Pentagon."

"And who would dare go against them?"

"CIA or the Pentagon Inspector General's office."

"Washington is like the late Roman Empire, doctor. There are intrigues, plots. We only get the vaguest outline from here. He is working for people who want to expose the dark underside of this occupation. Why? To discredit Jabarri. To remove him from the scene so that he cannot take over the country by force. To stop this poisonous alliance he has with al-Kufa. What does it matter which faction of your government it is? They are helping us. And now, you are working for them too."

The idea that somehow Lee had joined the team with Martin and the magician and Sparks made her recoil. "I'm just a doctor."

"And I'm just a scientist." Dr. Husseini smiled indulgently. "And both of us happen to be caught in this war."

XXIII

LAELA'S WARD SMELLED OF LYE. The families of her room-mates had settled in for the day, covering nearly every available space in the room with their belongings. Laela's territory was marked by a thin polyester curtain tacked in place by Zara, who had brought her own stool as well as fresh pillows and covers for her sister. There were flowers from the garden and photos of Hammurabi pinned to the wall.

"Lee, thank God you've arrived. We thought we had lost you." Laela was sitting up with her arm still wrapped in the linen dressing and sling. "Zara brought me some caviar, smuggled in from Iran."

"You could use some bulking up. What do the doctors say?"

"They're sending me to Paris. They say I need more tests and everything in this hospital is falling apart. The MRI packed it in while I was strapped inside. I was sure I was already in my coffin. I had to close my eyes and imagine that I was lying under my palm trees to keep from going mad. The banging was insufferable. The nurses finally kicked the thing, like an old dog, to release me."

"Parisian MRIs will have cushioned headphones playing Vivaldi."

"Are you coming?"

"I will stop off on my way home, as soon as I am finished here."

"Have you got the goods on my wicked cousin yet?" she asked in a conspiratorial whisper.

"Let's save that for a conversation at the Brasserie Balzar."

"That sounds promising."

"Zara, is everything organized? Do you need any help?"

"I've got a top bone man in France waiting for her. His mother is Iraqi, and he is very interested in Laela's case."

Naji Qais appeared in the doorway. He had just come out of surgery. "Lee, may I see you for a moment?" Naji had blood tests, X-rays, CT scan, and a biopsy in his folder. "Lee, I'm afraid it is not a virus. I was right about the break. She has malignant fibrous histiocytoma. Primary bone cancer."

"I thought that usually comes from exposure to high doses of radiotherapy."

"Living in Iraq is exposure enough."

"Has it spread to her lungs?"

"Not yet. But it has spread from the bone into the nerves and blood vessels around it. I think the recommendation will be neoadjuvant chemotherapy to reduced the size of the tumor followed by extirpative surgery."

"Extirpative?"

"Yes, at the very least they will amputate."

Lee knew that with Laela's cancer, the amputees were the lucky ones. "What are her chances?"

"Not good. But she will have a great doctor in France. Perhaps he will be more optimistic."

Laela would never sculpt again, Lee thought. No more Weapons of Mass Destruction. No more *oud*. All of the beauty, all of the civilization of Iraq, was inside this one being, and she was dying. Lee forced herself to be calm and dispassionate, dreading what she would have to tell Duncan, acting out the theater of medicine, as she returned to Laela's bedside.

"Well?" Laela's eyes were wide and hopeful.

"You were right about the machines. The tests are a mess. Your French specialist will sort everything out."

"I knew it. A complete waste of time. Zara, we have to go home and close up the house."

At that moment, Duncan appeared from behind the shabby curtain, pale and out of breath. He took Laela's hand and held it for a long time without speaking.

"Hello, Laela." It was a quiet, strangled greeting. "You're going to be fine."

She lay there like an exotic bird, weary from the bombs and the strain of flying upside down. "I'm tough as old boots."

Out in the hallway, Lee turned to Duncan and hugged him for a long time before explaining the tests.

"It looks very bad. She might be saved with amputation. The oncologist in Paris will make that decision."

Lee watched as Duncan walked away and started to cry. He wandered the halls until he was directed, finally, by an old man, blinded by shrapnel in one eye, to the parking lot. Once he found the car, he sat, unable to move, in the back seat, while Mohammed waited. Nothing broke the silence but distant mortars.

Lee found Naji Qais pouring too much sugar into his tea in the cafeteria that had seen better days. She sat down on the cracked plastic chair and sighed.

"Thanks for the supplies, Lee. You're a good friend." Naji smiled. "I would never have imagined you this far from New York. I really think that if we are going to do this joint project, you should come back and work with us. Stay for a year or two. The people here like you. When you get back to the States, you have to send me all of the latest medical books. There isn't enough paper in Iraq to download them. How was the trip north?"

"We were rocketed on the road back. It was terrifying."

"By the Americans."

"Yes, we got caught up in something."

"Casualties?"

"Quite a few. We worked for hours."

"Well I'm glad to hear you haven't been idle."

"Naji, you want me to feel guilty. I have to finish what I came here to do."

"I don't want you to feel guilty. I just wonder if it's the best use of your time."

"Naji, Martin Carrigan has been uncovering massive bribes and theft in this occupation. If I help him, I'm helping you. What if someone in the health ministry stole all of the money earmarked for drugs?"

"Look, Lee, I understand what you are doing. I just think it's dangerous. You are a doctor, not a cop."

"If I don't get him out of the country, Naji, someone will kill him."

"Can't you get help?"

"Who am I supposed to trust?"

As she left Omar Hospital, Lee remembered Plumber. "Hand me my Thuraya, would you, Hassan?" She dialed his number in the Green Zone.

"George Plumber." His voice was cold.

"Dr. McGuinness here. You wanted to meet?"

"Hello, Dr. McGuinness, I just wanted to see how you were coming along. Do you have a few minutes?"

"I can be at the Assassins' Gate in an hour."

"I'll have an escort waiting for you."

Hassan looked puzzled when she hung up. "It's only 15 minutes from here."

"I know, Hassan. I want you to stop at Uday's palace. I want to sit in the ruins for a while."

As she had hoped, they had the place to themselves. She found a quiet sanctuary, amid the columns connected to nothing and the tumbled blocks of white marble, and thought about Laela. Soon she and her garden and her country, which had survived the crushing weight of tyrants, would only exist in memory. The occupation had destroyed a country in order to save it. Laela was collateral damage, an unfortunate statistic, if anyone kept statistics any more. Lee doubted that anyone would ever accept responsibility for what had happened to her. She was like the natives of the New World felled by small pox or the Wampanoag of Massachusetts who died of infectious hepatitis. They were inconvenient history.

At the Green Zone entrance, Hassan was shooed away, just as Sadoon had been, as a "*hajji*" who could not be trusted. Lee joined the line, waiting for an insurgent's bomb, but this time the escort in his shades and SUV was prompt.

"Welcome back, doctor."

"Thanks ever so much." She felt her anger at the occupation, at the carelessness of those who ran it, weighing on her chest.

"Enjoying your stay?"

"Yes, indeed."

"What brings you here?"

"Old friends."

"I didn't know anybody had old friends here."

"Some of us do."

Plumber was already draped over the brocade love seat in the palace reception room when Lee was ushered in. He was wearing white ducks with a light jacket and tie, dressed, she supposed, for a Green Zone diplomatic reception, something with a belly dancer or an ice sculpture and tropical drinks with paper umbrellas. His hand was clammy when she shook it, the unhealthy dampness that complemented his washed-out eyes and bad skin. It was common among diplomats who had served in the tropics, whose skin turned a sickly gray rather than brown in the sun.

"Were you ever in Africa?"

"Three years in Monrovia. Two years in Mogadishu. Not the best years of my life," he laughed in a forced sort of way. "Thank you for coming by." Then, without preamble, he smiled. "Your parents were quite a pair. I know they served in the Congo when Lumumba was assassinated. A nasty business. So many dead. Your parents were so devoted to our country. Unsung heroes. Coffee?"

"Please."

He dispatched an assistant who had been lurking by the door to procure it.

Lee resisted the urge to run from the room. Plumber had probed her weakest spot. She felt as though he had grabbed her intestines and twisted them. "They don't talk about Africa much. I believe what they were doing is still classified. They take that seriously."

"They were working with the rebels. I think that operation was called Project Wizard. That was an ugly war. The scheme to poison Lumumba's toothpaste. The kidnapping, the torture, the firing squad. And then in the end, chopping him up with a hacksaw and melting him in sulfuric acid. We let the Belgians do the dirty work. Expensive war, too, paying all of those politicians with that slush fund to do our bidding. Installing a psychopath like Mobutu. Still, we were fighting the good fight. We did what we had to do. I think both of your parents are legends at Langley. Of course all of that was long before you were born. I bet you remember Kinshasa. Mobutu probably dangled you on his knee."

Her parents had overseen assassinations. They had sown countries with land mines. When Lee was old enough to understand what that meant, she had decided to become a doctor, to cauterize the old wounds forever. Plumber wanted to open the wounds. He wanted her off balance. He was waging psychological warfare. Look at your own family. You are one of us. Your people are just as tarnished as I am. Just as much blood on their hands. We all know you have to break eggs to protect democracy. He wanted her to break.

She refused to give Plumber that satisfaction. She wanted to slap his repulsive face, to scream in fury, but she sat perfectly still, back straight, hands folded in her lap, and breathed deeply. If she could pull a pipe out of a man's chest, she could take this.

"Try this Starbucks." Plumber smiled. "Just off the C-130. All the pleasures of home. Life is not too bad here in the Green Zone. I imagine you've been roughing it a bit in the Red Zone."

"I can't complain." Lee looked up to see an officer in desert camouflage and sand-colored boots waiting to be acknowledged by Plumber.

"Come in, Jeeb. I want you to meet Dr. McGuinness."

"Colonel Najeeb Hamdoon."

"Hello, doctor."

Lee recognized his voice as the caller who had warned her to leave Baghdad, who had said there was no need to look for Martin.

"Colonel, so nice to see you face to face." She remembered what Nizar had said about Hamdoon's Lexus and Jacuzzi, purchased from the reconstruction funds earmarked for Democracy Centers.

"I hope I can call you Lee." Plumber had that strange little ball of spit between his dry lips.

"As you like."

"When we last met, you suggested that we might cooperate to find your friend Mr. Carrigan."

"Well, that was before you informed me that Martin was training the insurgency. I don't have those sorts of contacts. I think Colonel Hamdoon would have much better information. He knew Martin well."

Hamdoon looked uneasy. "I knew him before he turned."

"In what capacity were you working together?" Lee thought that if she steered this inquiry, she could delay being interrogated or trapped.

"We never worked together. He was just a contractor for aid projects."

"I'm told he regarded you as a trusted friend."

"Whoever told you that was mistaken."

"Then why did you warn me to leave Iraq?"

"Iraq is a hazardous place. I think you know that by now. It's my understanding someone tried to kidnap you."

"Do you like sugar in your coffee, Lee?" Plumber wanted to cut off the line of inquiry.

"Black, please, George." Lee smiled.

Plumber winced.

"I hope I can call you George?"

"Of course."

"What progress have you made?"

"I have to say we're stumped. We were hoping you might fill in the blanks. You and your reporter friend have been pretty busy. I would remind you that you are obliged to help us with this investigation."

"I would dearly love to help. But I have given up on Martin. Adnan Jabarri gave me ironclad evidence against him that is impossible to refute. I have to tell you, George, I didn't know Martin Carrigan at all. He is not the man I thought he was, which is very painful for me. I'm off the case."

"What took you to Diyarbakir?"

"The Surgeons' Committee ordered a shipment of supplies for the Karbala Hospital, which is in great need, by the way, of everything from aspirin to blood. I was able to deliver it today. This is something you could follow up on, Colonel Hamdoon, in your reconstruction efforts. It is a tremendous public relations opportunity."

"You haven't tried to meet with your friend?"

"Why would I want to meet with a man who turns out to be an Iranian agent? In any case, I've been preoccupied."

"With?"

"Well, yesterday it was 33 wounded from a rocket attack outside Samarra."

"I think you'll find that was exaggerated." Plumber waved his spindly fingers in the air.

"I counted them myself."

"There are so many incidents that are overblown and misrepresented. Overall, things are settling down. The polls show Iraqis are demanding that we stay."

"Have you been getting out lately?" The likes of George Plumber were not allowed out of the Green Zone without armored escort.

"I'm afraid I'm pretty much chained to my desk."

"Pity. There is so much to see. I wish I could be more helpful."

"Ah, Colonel Slay." At that moment, a man with a buzz cut and graying temples appeared in the doorway. Like Hamdoon, he wore camouflage and walked with a loping gait and fixed jaw. The skin around his eyes was deeply creased from squinting in the desert sun.

"Colonel Slay tells me you've been spending quite a lot of time in Karbala. He keeps me fully briefed."

"I haven't had the pleasure of meeting Colonel Slay," Lee said evenly. "I know him only by reputation."

"Dr. McGuinness, because you met with Jabarri and got a clearer picture of Martin Carrigan's involvement with the bad element here in Iraq, we think that Carrigan may be trying to assassinate you."

"Really?"

"Yes. I have to watch what I say because I'm not sure what's classified and what's not, but the kidnapping attempt looks like it involved some of al-Kufa's people, who are armed by your friend. Therefore, we want you to have a security detail with you at all times. They will advise you where it is safe to go and where you might get killed."

"That's very kind of you."

"I feel responsible for you."

"But I can't accept."

"Why is that?"

"My security is perfectly adequate. And if they quarrel with your men, my men will probably shoot them. I would hate to cause an incident."

"I insist."

"You will have to take it up with the foreign minister. I'm under his protection."

"I see." He looked temporarily defeated. "I couldn't do better than that. The Peshmerga are fine soldiers. I'm sure the foreign minister will be happy to keep my office briefed. If you will excuse me, doctor." Hamdoon and Slay followed closely on his heels. He ordered an assistant to show Lee out.

She found Hassan drawing a crowd by the Assassins' Gate. Everyone on the street was murmuring "Ali Baba." Even after she lured him to the car, the fans blew kisses, threw wadded-up little notes, touched the windshield to absorb his fame.

"Are you the best-known actor in Iraq?"

"I think so."

As Hassan drove over the Jumhuriya Bridge, Lee saw that the river, just past Medical City, looked like it was on fire.

"There's a fire in the Tigris."

"A car bomb in Waziriya. One of the gas stations. It's pouring out from the pumps into the river."

"Why would someone blow up a gas station?"

"Mafia business. A fight over who controls the oil. You know, doctor, some people are getting very rich."

"Hassan, did you ever talk to the guards at the Dar about who tried to kidnap us?"

"Yes."

"What did they say?"

"They had never seen them before."

Hassan stopped the Mercedes so that they could watch the river burn. The oil slick was turning the surface an unnaturally brilliant blue, like a diaphanous skin. Underneath, the dark stain was billowing across the water in slow motion. There would be no clean up, just as the million gallons a day of sewage from the bombed Rustamiyah plant surged unchecked into the river downstream. At that moment, watching the fire dance on the spill, Lee wanted to be by Laela's side, but she would ask difficult questions and Lee would have to answer. The best course was to let Zara take charge and stay out of her way.

"We should go now, doctor."

"I have never seen a river burn."

XXIV

THE AL-SAFAFER SOUK in Baghdad was just off al-Rashid Street at the end of Martyrs Bridge. The sound of the coppersmiths carried for half a mile, as they beat the hot metal with hammers into wide vessels, pots, and platters for the lavish *diwans* people could no longer afford to host. The pounding in the smoky forges echoed through the narrow stalls of yellow brick, pitted with bullet holes from gun battles in the spring. Al-Safafer was part of a labyrinth that led into the al-Bazzazeen market, with its bolts of brocade and polyester, and the rug market, with fine old pieces from impoverished families and gaudy imports from China. Across al-Rashid Street was the Shorjah Souk, which smelled of *baharat* and donkey dung. Stall keepers served spices in brightly colored pyramids, burnt yellow saffron next to purple sumac. Piles of black lemons kept company with embroidered silks and wind chimes under clouds of paper lanterns.

In the back of the Mercedes, Lee was studying the directions Nizar had enclosed in his suitcase of black-market drugs. Hassan and Mohammed, back from al-Adhamiyah, accompanied her as far as the entrance to the market. They drew attention away from her as she strode, wrapped in her *abaya*, into the warren of covered alleys. Mohammed, the Tikriti, followed her at a discreet distance. This was Sunni territory. He blended in with other men wearing black leather jackets and gold rings. Lee stopped to linger with shrouded women, massed like jackdaws in an Irish wood, around the shiny tea services, rose bowls, and jugs. She had been careful to choose a pair of old, worn flats so that her shoes would not give her away. At the first fork she veered right, then left and right again, and began counting the stalls. She was looking for the seventh when a military foot patrol turned the corner and began checking identity cards. There had been an incident that morning, a grenade attack at the Church of Mary Mother of Sorrows in Ras al-Grayyeh, across from Shorjah, and the soldiers, with their translator, were asking questions. They were taking names and searching bags, wanting to know what anyone would have against the Chaldeans, other than that they were Christian. Lee was conscious of the documents in her purse and turned to retrace her steps.

"Hold it right there, ma'am," the translator turned the soldier's words into guttural Arabic. He sounded Egyptian.

Lee froze. "Hi, guys."

"You American?"

"You bet."

"Sorry to bother you. What brings you here?"

"Shopping."

"I mean in Iraq."

"The nightclubs."

The soldier laughed. "That's a good one. I guess you're doin' something we don't have clearance for. Good day, ma'am."

She chose a fork that led to the carpet bazaar and accepted a cup of Turkish coffee from a merchant from Kirkuk, while she flipped through a pile of *kilims*. She could hear the echo of the patrols' voices behind her, punctuated by the pounding of the red-hot anvils and the hiss of hot copper being quenched. She tried to gauge by the sound when they had retreated. As she set out again, she turned in what she thought was the direction of al-Rashid Street and stopped. Every alley, with its stone flags and narrow shops cluttered with goods, looked alike. Mohammed was gone. She tried to establish landmarks, Christmas lights strung across one route, someone selling goldfish in front of a Tabriz stall in another. She began to attract the sort of attention she had tried to avoid. Young men wearing flashy watches, who seemed to do nothing but smoke, noticed her hesitation. She returned to the Kirkuk merchant, as though she had made up her mind to buy, and haggled over a small Kashan carpet. She bargained in Arabic. *Arba'oon? La, la, sadiqi, ashroon. Thalathoon? La, la, ahi, ashroon.* When they had agreed on a price, he sent her down a busy alley, away from the *shebab*, along a path she was sure was leading her deeper into the maze.

Lee turned a corner, and found herself in a dense crowd, flowing in a sluggish current. A hand groped her leg. It was fast and furtive. She was like a swimmer, beyond the breakwater, brushed by a shark. Raw terror coursed through her body. Her claustrophobia raked her chest, shortening her breath. She pictured the amygdala in her brain, where nuclei communicated furiously to produce fear, speeding her respiratory rate, shooting her full of adrenaline. She wanted to rip off her veil. The hand fondled her again. She remembered the man murdered on Waterloo Bridge when the Bulgarian Secret Police fired a poisoned pellet into his leg from a furled umbrella. Finally, she saw a broad beam of daylight pouring in from the entrance gate with Mohammed standing under it. The crowd thinned at a crossroads and Lee could breathe. The groper was gone.

"I got stopped by the patrol," Mohammed scolded her. "Wait for me next time."

"I was disoriented." She forced herself to follow Nizar's careful directions once again. She stopped to buy a vial of frankincense oil and rubbed it on her skin.

When Lee reached the shop, Mohammed fell behind to watch anyone who might be taking an unhealthy interest in their movements. An old man with deep grooves in his face and eyebrows that looked as though they had been burnt off offered to show her some antique pieces in back. Following the slap of his sandals, Lee slipped through a curtain of smoke. They landed in an octagonal room of carved wood with a 12-foot ceiling and bookshelves to the roof. A copy of an Ingres nude surveyed the scene along with an old photograph of Gertrude Bell riding a camel side-saddle by the Sphinx.

There was a large heavy table of cedar covered in paste, ink, papers, maps, and reference books of every description. A man sat bent over his work, attending to some fine detail. He was in his late 50s, Lee thought, with a shock of gray hair standing up from his high forehead and wire-rimmed glasses half way down the bridge of his nose under two jeweler's loupes attached by a thin wire frame.

"*La Grande Odalisque*." Lee referred to the nude.

"Yes, I used to churn those out by the dozen in London." He spoke to her before he saw her, not willing to take his eyes from his work. "She's rather good, don't you think? I also forged Delacroix and Weeks. You could say I'm an Orientalist. Did you bring the documents?"

"Yes."

"Please sit down. Nizar briefed me. I won't be a moment."

"I'm afraid I don't know your name."

"It's better that you don't."

Lee dropped her *abaya* and shook out her hair.

When the forger had finished the work to his satisfaction, he looked at Lee and smiled. "God knows what a woman like you is doing here. Perhaps you have a death wish."

Lee drew Jabarri's documents, which detailed Martin's crimes, from her purse and spread them before him. "Are they real?"

He looked carefully at the stamps.

"The stamps appear to be Iranian. Stamps are very easy to forge. There are many stamped Iraqi government documents floating around, most of them giving precise details of Saddam's nuclear weapons program, forged by Iranian intelligence. The Iranians are good at it." He studied it with care. "But this document is real."

Lee stood up without meaning to.

"This is an end-user certificate from Iran to Tblisi, Georgia. There is an active weapons trade between the two countries and this transaction almost certainly took place. The stamps are genuine."

"What does it say about Mr. Carrigan?"

The forger took his time. He studied a long list in Farsi.

"Nothing. His name does not appear."

Lee returned to her wooden bench, which reminded her of a pew.

"The next two documents mention your friend's Panamanian company. Does that make sense to you?"

"I don't know. He never mentioned it to me."

"The inventory list of arms matches the first document. So only these two would have to be forged. This document is from the Panamanian company to the purchaser in Aqaba, Jordan." He was lost again in concentration. "There is no Panamanian customs stamp on it. Normally an arms dealer would take the trouble to bribe Panamanian customs for the stamp. He would want everything in order. With his presumed connections there, it could be done from halfway around the world. But it wasn't. May I offer you some Turkish coffee?"

"No, thank you. Does that mean it's fake?"

The forger lapsed into silence, and then broke it like a fast at sunset. "What about the shipping office in Aqaba? Where is the Jordanian stamp? Do you know where these documents were found?"

"I was told they came from the house of the recipient of the arms in Karbala, who I believe is now in Abu Ghraib prison, being held without charges."

"But if he had these incriminating documents, why hasn't he been charged?"

"I don't know. The documents were found with Martin's name on them."

The forger pushed the loupes onto his forehead. "Normally people set up companies in places like Panama to disguise their identity — rust-bucket tanker owners, for example, who don't want to be traced so easily. Papers relating to a shipment would only show the company title. Now these documents name your friend as managing director of the company. That is highly unusual. In fact, in my view, not plausible."

"But what about the weapons, there, in the photo? I was told they were discovered by the Marines in Karbala."

The photo showed an open crate with small arms spread on the table.

"I don't see a date on the photo. This could be any arms shipment. Or, it could be arms that were captured by the Marines from fighters here in Iraq."

The forger restored his loupes and held the photo close to his face.

"Well, this is interesting."

"What is it?"

"There is something written on this crate, but it is in the wrong script. Judging from the Cyrillic, this crate came from Russia. This, for all we know, was shipped from Moscow to Saddam's Republican Guard. It could have been salvaged from one of the old arsenals. There are a lot of weapons in Iraq."

Lee was about to ask whether it might be a Georgian crate, when she remembered that Jabarri had said the weapons were never shipped to Tblisi. This was only a paper trail.

"What I can say, doctor, is that one genuine document has been thrown in with two fakes to make the whole thing legitimate. I would guess your friend has nothing to do with this."

Lee left the shop with a large copper tray wrapped in a flour sack tied with heavy twine. Mohammed stayed close to her. She summoned Hassan who had gathered the usual flock of admirers. They made one stop at the Aleem, to give Nizar the copper tray as a gift.

XXV

B Y DAWN THE NEXT MORNING, Lee and Duncan were on the road to the Rumaila oil fields. Duncan had rummaged through the kitchen at the Dar for fruit and bread. They ate breakfast in the back of the Mercedes and admired the rose-tinted desert and the Euphrates beyond. As curfew lifted with the sun, the Basra highway was wide and empty, except for the military trucks traveling up to Camp Victory from Kuwait City. The landscape was now flat and burnt, with giant pylons for electricity, remnants from another time, when Iraq advertised itself as a beacon of progress.

Now this stretch was known for its skilled carjackers, former members of Saddam's Republican Guard. Hassan stopped for nougat and soda at Kut, where the boy at the drink stand had flaming red hair, a descendant of the British regiment that had made a last stand against the Ottomans in World War I near this dusty truck stop. There was a neglected cemetery in the town full of their dead, with pipers and weeping willows carved in the gravestones.

"I saw Sadoon's family." Duncan sat down on a rotting picnic bench. "His wife said all of al-Adhamiyah knew that the Rasheed was a target the day before it was rocketed."

"Did you talk with the neighbors?"

"Some said they knew, some didn't. They are afraid. Sadoon was one of four picked up by the Americans. Your friend Nizar is buying groceries for the families. Does that tell you anything?"

"Nizar has resistance ties."

"Could he be involved?"

"He might be. Or he might just feel an obligation to Sadoon. Duncan, who are we meeting at Rumaila?" Two small girls approached her cautiously to stare at her green eyes. They watched silently as she cleaned the mouth of a Fanta bottle with her shroud.

"The engineer I went to SOAS with."

"Does he know what we are looking for?"

"No."

"Do you?"

"Not really. Criminal activity that matches what we know from the briefcase. Sabotage, diversion, theft. I'm hoping he can tell us where some of these pirate ports are. I know the oil fields cover an area the size of Wales."

Hassan found a small guesthouse in Basra, not far from the old market, with its sagging wooden balconies, and the Shatt al-Arab. For years, the waterfront promenade had been lined with a hundred bronze soldiers on pedestals, the dead from another war, pointing their fingers in accusation across the water to their enemies in Iran. It was one of the most powerful war memorials Duncan had ever seen. The statues were gone. The only remains from the Iran-Iraq war were the rusting hulks of ships, sunk where the Tigris and Euphrates merged in a waterway that smelled rank.

The hotel was close to an encampment of British soldiers who controlled the Basra zone. They seemed happy to have guests, and Duncan had all of the right press credentials. A young officer called Capt. Keane, thin and flushed, with the ease of command instilled at Sandhurst, assured Lee that doctors were always welcome. He invited them to dine any time in the officers' mess. Some English officers from Manchester directed them to the Southern Fields Oil Company headquarters, where they found Mahmood Maroki, a fastidious man in a threadbare suit from a London tailor. Maroki offered them tea.

"Well, Duncan, it's been awhile. I haven't been to any SOAS reunions. Lapsang Souchong or Irish Breakfast?" He was pleased to be able to offer his guests a choice.

"Lapsang Souchong, please." Duncan was parched from the drive.

"I'll have the same." Lee wondered about the water. Maroki could see her hesitation.

"I use bottled water. Do you take milk?"

"Please."

"I get my milk from the British." His smile was sad. He had spent most of his adult life under sanctions and at war. "We barter. I am delighted to meet a friend of Duncan's. How are you, old boy?"

"Couldn't be better, Mahmood."

"Now what brings you to the Southern Fields?"

"We are investigating criminal activity."

"I see." He nervously uncrossed one leg and crossed the other. "Looting or sabotage?"

"Not that sort of criminal activity. We were hoping you could tell us about skimming of oil profits by officials in the oil ministry and by the Americans. And by powerful businessmen who control intelligence." Duncan said it matter-of-factly, as though everyone knew the facts and there were just a few details to fill in.

Maroki looked as though he had just swallowed something unpleasant. "Who did you say you are writing for?"

"I am the correspondent for the London *Herald* and Dr. McGuinness is a surgeon. We are trying to verify facts gathered by American intelligence that we have in our possession. The evidence is very damaging. Millions of dollars worth of oil is being siphoned off from the Rumaila fields, and we know, old chap, that you are involved."

Lee looked at Duncan sharply. Duncan ignored her, lit a cigarette, and exhaled slowly. "May I offer you a cigarette?"

"Please." Maroki looked ill. "Will you excuse me for a moment?" When he returned, his eyes looked bloodshot. He had been sick. "Before we have our tea, may I show you the garden?"

"Of course." Maroki wanted to escape any listening devices in his office. They walked through the drab hallways painted hospital green until they reached a courtyard with dead grass and tangled wisteria.

"Duncan. Are you trying to get me killed?"

"Hardly, Mahmood," Duncan flashed a smile of consolation. "I'm sure you don't want any part of this. And when everyone above you in this enterprise is shipped to Abu Ghraib, we want you to look like the man who did the right thing."

"Abu Ghraib?"

"Yes."

"What do you need to know?"

"The port that Adnan Jabarri is using to ship his stolen oil."

Maroki froze. "I'm sorry?"

"What is the name of the port and how do we find it?"

"I don't know."

Lee pulled a copy of the ledger from her purse. "Let's see, Mahmood Maroki. Ah, you are receiving such a small amount compared with everyone else. Only $50,000 this year."

"How do you know that?"

"I promise you won't be arrested if you help us." Duncan said, with an air of authority that he mustered for such occasions.

"If I help you, I will be a corpse floating in the Shatt al-Arab."

"No, Mahmood. When we are finished, everyone else will be behind bars, and you will have a British visa."

Maroki was silent for what seemed like a full minute "Okay. Across from Umm Qasr, before you get to the channel, just north of Jazirat Bubiyan. There is a harbor. Jabarri's operation is there. It operates only at night. You will need a boat."

"Mahmood, we don't have time to get lost. Let's have our tea and then you can take us. How much oil is moving through Jabarri's pirate port?" Duncan had his notebook out.

"Two-hundred-thousand barrels a day."

"One-tenth of total production this year."

"That's right."

"Don't you think you should ask for a raise?"

Lee and Duncan followed Maroki's jeep through Az Zubayr down to Safwan and then along the Umm Qasr road, past the decaying grain elevators, to the rundown deep-water port that had been the first site of U.S. military "liberation" in Iraq. Someone had just turned the lights on again, after six months of darkness. By the time they reached the boat waiting on the dock, reserved for the chief engineer of the Southern Fields Oil Company, it was after dusk.

"In case you are considering capsizing the boat," Duncan said as he stepped on board, "The information I shared with you, including your name in the records, is already in London."

As Maroki cast off, an American military patrol boat pulled alongside. "Good evening, Mr. Maroki."

"Good evening, Major Dipper."

"Are these people authorized to be here?"

"Yes, Major."

"Can you tell me your affiliation?" He was addressing Lee.

"I'm afraid that's classified, Major." She was pleased with her comeback.

"Mr. Maroki, will you accompany them at all times?"

"Yes, Major Dipper."

"Good to go." Dipper's boat roared off leaving a wake that slapped the launch into the pilings.

"The Americans have a lot to learn about diplomacy," Maroki said, now soaking wet.

"That's something we will never learn." Lee laughed. They motored across the water and turned south toward Kuwait. If Maj. Dipper was so attentive to any activity here, then he was certainly aware of Jabarri's port.

"Mahmood." Duncan saw that the poor man was shivering uncontrollably. "Does Maj. Dipper maintain security for Adnan Jabarri?"

"Yes."

"Officially?"

"Yes, because Jabarri has blackmailed the Ministry of Oil. If they don't let him have his cut, he unleashes al-Kufa's people to blow up the facilities. The Army of the Believers has sabotaged the pipeline to Khor al-Amaya. They attacked the pipeline west of Babylon, they attacked it south of Hillah, they blasted the line that feeds the Daura refinery."

"Take my jacket, Mahmood."

"*Shoukran*, Duncan."

"How did you get mixed up in this?" Lee asked.

"What choice do I have against these gangsters? I have a family in Basra."

Lee could see the hulls of small tankers, the kind used to carry oil in the coastal waters of the Gulf. She could hear the hum of machinery and the shouts of the longshoremen.

"How often do you see Americans here?"

"Often. Sometimes they come in helicopters."

"Military or civilian?" Duncan asked.

"Both."

"I want to board one of the tankers." Duncan had already so terrified Maroki that he was ready to do whatever his old friend asked. "Please don't tell the captain who you are."

"Stop worrying, Mahmood. How long have we known each other?"

The crew was surprised to see a woman accompanying the chief engineer of Southern Fields. On the other hand, they thought, the Americans were capable of anything. The captain was drinking *arak* and reading the latest sports results from Dubai.

"Mr. Maroki." The captain stood bolt upright. "*Ahlan wa Sahlan.*" They spoke for a few moments, trading pleasantries. Duncan took the captain aside to look through his log and records. The captain assumed that Duncan worked with the British government, a liaison, perhaps, at the head office of the Southern Fields Oil Company. Lee knew that Duncan wanted to be able to report, with accuracy, where the oil was being unloaded. According to the log, almost all of it was going to Sharjah. Duncan photographed the log, recording the name of the Panamanian shell company that employed the captain, the Liberian registry of the vessel, and the name of the company on the captain's paycheck. Maroki drank two shots of *arak* in the meantime. His English suit was damp and creased.

Lee was solicitous. "We need to get you home and out of those clothes."

"Yes," said Maroki with embarrassment. "I must admit I am rather miserable."

"Captain, please come stand with Mr. Maroki." Duncan arranged the two men on the bridge and took their picture. No one could deny now that Duncan had been here.

When he parted ways with Maroki back in Basra, Duncan gave him instructions.

"When you are asked about us by Jabarri's thugs, tell them that we presented ourselves as American and European intelligence agents and insisted that you take us to the tanker. Dipper will confirm it, because he was told it was 'classified.' You needn't tell them anything else. Soon, all of this will be public. We will give you full credit for exposing what may be the biggest theft in history."

"And my British visa?"

"How many in your family?"

"Five."

"Do you have a photo of the whole family?"

"Yes."

"Find it tonight and drop it at our guesthouse. I will return the original. And write down everyone's names and birthdays."

"Thank you, Duncan. You are a good friend."

XXVI

"YOU DID WELL, MY FRIEND." Nizar Hadithi was staring down at a plate of *ris de veau*. "You have a good name in Samarra."

"I thought of you, Nizar, out there on that highway. It looked like a slaughterhouse. I promised you I wouldn't neglect the Sunnis."

"Try this." He offered Lee his fork. "Aleem chef's specialty."

"So the news network hasn't thrown you out yet?"

"I make myself indispensable."

"Do they know what you're doing on the side?"

"No one asks me. I am the local hired help."

"Are you expanding the business empire?"

"Oh yes. I've added two new lines. Security guards. I'm supplying armies of them. A thousand dollars a day, I take 50 percent. Not bad. And even better, I'm doing billboards."

"Billboards?"

"In the new Iraq, every billboard in Baghdad will be a Nizar Hadithi billboard. Excellent return on investment."

"The war has been good to you."

"My country is a land of opportunity." Nizar stared with dismay at his empty plate.

"By the way, I'm told you're feeding the families of the Rasheed bombers."

"There's no proof against them."

"Sadoon knew that something was going to happen in the Green Zone."

"He protected you."

"Nizar, I operated on some of the Americans at the other end of those rockets."

"It's an ugly war," he said with a shrug. "But Lee, after what you did for the people of Samarra, we owe you a favor."

"I am here to collect." Lee smiled.

Nizar lit a cigarette, a pirated Iraqi brand called Virgin Paradise. "Whatever you want."

"Tell your friends in the *mujahedeen* that I am going to the refinery at Baiji tomorrow."

"Is that wise, doctor? There is a lot of trouble up there. The Americans appointed a police chief who has made enemies. There was a demonstration that got out of control. Something like 2,000 of the Saddam Fedayeen militia turned up. They got into a firefight with American soldiers. Three Turkish tanker trucks were hit with RPGs. So was the mayor's office. Police headquarters was torched. I wouldn't advise going up there at the moment."

"I need bodyguards from Baiji, and I need a name. Who up there can tell me about Jabarri's operation to truck his stolen oil up to the border?"

"Half the people at the refinery are on Jabarri's payroll. All of the people imported by the CPA."

"What about the other half?"

"Go see the number-three man. His name is Tariq al-Samarai. I will make sure that he is expecting you. I wish you would wait a week or two. It would be better."

"I don't have time, Nizar. And the bodyguards?"

"Tomorrow at the Dar. You must leave early. *Insha'Allah*, you will be there by noon. Go straight to al-Samarai. Hope-

fully your bodyguards will not be tempted to kidnap you."
Nizar smiled behind the smoke of his Virgin cigarette.

"Tell them I'm not worth anything. Plumber wants me
dead anyway. I won't be worth the price of an Egyptian."

* * *

The streets of Baiji were strewn with burnt tires and broken furniture that served as barricades. Someone had ripped
out their refrigerator and used it as a shield for a firefight.
The ice trays were lying in the dirt next to a bloody *keffiyeh*.
Lee could see American snipers crouched on top of the
burned-out police station and machine-gun nests behind sand
bags and concertina wire in the ruins of mortared houses.
Nizar's bodyguards were spread between Hassan's car and a
chase car behind.

"This looks bad." Hassan turned off down a side street.
"We should avoid the center."

Not even the cats patrolled the street. There was an un-
natural silence. The shops were shuttered or smashed.
Duncan sat in the back with Lee, alert and tense under her
shroud.

"We are in the eye of the storm," he said quietly.

Mohammed from Tikrit closely questioned the Baiji
bodyguard squeezed into the front next to him. He was there
so that a gunman might recognize him before riddling the
windshield with bullets. "We have to get out of here,"
Mohammed said, showing fear for the first time. "Go right
and down to the river."

Hassan took a road that made a wide arc around the
front lines of Baiji and rejoined the main highway to the
refinery. The place stank of tar. Around the refinery itself,
there were pools of toxic sludge. Tariq al-Samarai was waiting
in his office. He was tall and lean with bright black eyes and a
mustache. His cheap suit was shiny from wear. Turkish coffee

appeared and he looked expectant behind his neat desk. There were shadows on the wall where he had taken down the government-issue portrait of Saddam.

"Most of the staff is gone. They are afraid of what might happen here." Everyone could hear the distant rattle of machine-gun fire and the sharp crack of the rocket-propelled grenades.

"Have you been attacked?" Duncan asked.

"Saboteurs blew up a junction of the pipeline." Al-Samarai smiled wearily. "They will be back. All of the pipelines meet in Baiji. It is the chokepoint. Do you mind if I smoke?"

"Not at all."

Lee wanted to make him feel comfortable. "Nizar Hadithi sends his regards."

"He is my wife's cousin."

"I appreciate your seeing us on such short notice."

"My pleasure."

"We are here to ask some very sensitive questions." Duncan laid his elegant little tape recorder on the desk. "I hope you will not be offended, but people's lives are at stake. One of your colleagues in the south took a great risk by being candid with us."

"Ask whatever you want."

"We know that large quantities of oil from this refinery are being siphoned off and trucked to the border."

The refinery's number-three manager shifted in his chair.

"We know that Adnan Jabarri is running the black-market operation and has people here and in the oil ministry on the payroll."

Al-Samarai began to cough. "You must be mistaken." He pulled out a neatly pressed handkerchief and wiped his face.

"We also have taped phone conversations with officials in the Green Zone about moving oil out of Baiji." Duncan stopped for a moment to let that sink in. "They are being investigated in Washington. I expect some people will go to jail."

"I am not on Jabarri's payroll." Al-Samarai sat bolt upright. "You must know that he and I are on opposite sides of the political fence."

"A lot of people are being blackmailed."

He was gripping his desk, unsure of his next move. "I must ask you to leave."

He escorted Duncan and Lee out and once in the open air, where there was no chance of a bug in the light fixture or the television or under his desk, his tone changed.

"What do you need?"

"The tanker truck records," said Duncan, "with the identification numbers for the tankers that are carrying his oil."

"It's too dangerous. I have children. I can't help you."

"The money from that oil is buying weapons for the Army of the Believers, Shiite fanatics. The stronger they get, the more likely it is that your family will be massacred or forced into exile."

"How is the oil money buying weapons for them?" Al-Samarai looked alarmed.

"Jabarri and al-Kufa are partners. Your oil is financing their army."

"But they are the radical fringe. They are mad."

"With enough money and arms, madmen can take power. Do you want to continue financing them? They have blown up the pipelines in Babylon and Hillah. They think of Sunnis like you as pollution in the new Iraq. You will be ethnically cleansed." Duncan knew how to be persuasive.

Al-Samarai stood quietly in the shade. He had turned his back, to face the massive pipes and belching stacks of the refinery that was his life. "I will get the files."

By the time Lee and Duncan left Baiji, they had a stack of computer printouts. The light was fading to red on the horizon and given the militias watching the roads for prey, it was too late to risk the drive to Baghdad.

"Mohammed, where is the U.S. Army base in Beit Har?"

"Not far from here."

"The bodyguards can drop us there and sleep at home tonight. They can pick us up in the morning."

"Where will we sleep?" Mohammed knew there were no guesthouses left in Beit Har.

"At the base."

The answer was not what he wanted to hear. "Would you mind if I stayed with the bodyguards?"

"As you like. What about you, Hassan?"

"I will stay with Mohammed."

Forward Operating Base Camp Destiny was in a run-down factory complex with a tent city and several acres of barbed wire and blast barriers. Hassan ran a zigzag gauntlet of concrete filled garbage bins to reach the gate. The last 50 yards, he drove straight at the gun barrel of an M1 tank.

"Slowly, Hassan. So they don't mistake us for *mujahedeen*."

"But our escorts are *mujahedeen*."

"The soldiers won't know that."

Duncan jumped out at the guard post followed by Lee.

"Oh, damn this thing," Lee tripped on her *abaya*.

"You look good in that thing ma'am. I thought you were for real." One of the soldiers spoke from behind a machine gun.

"I'm not for real."

"Where are you from?"

"I'm from New York."

"I was wondering. I knew you weren't a *hajji*, that's for sure."

"Can you tell us where we can find Lt. Randall Frank?"

"Yes, ma'am. Lt. Frank is in his barracks. One moment." The soldier, whose accent placed him somewhere in Alabama, radioed his officer. "Sir, you've got visitors." He turned to Lee and removed his gum. "I don't believe I got your name, ma'am."

"Dr. McGuinness. Tell him I'm a friend of his father's. Where are you from?"

"Montgomery." The radio came to life. "Yes, sir. Dr. McGuinness is here. She says to tell you that she knows your dad." He waited for a response.

"Send her in," the radio crackled.

"I will do that." He looked at the cars full of Iraqis. "I'm afraid they will not be allowed beyond the gate."

"That's fine. They are leaving." Lee walked to the car. "Hassan, give me my Thuraya. If they won't allow us to sleep here tonight, you will have to come and get us."

"No problem. We won't be far. But I would recommend that you not stay here either."

She was touched by Hassan's concern. "We'll be okay. Give me my backpack just in case."

She turned back to the gate to find that she had drawn a small crowd.

"Your escort will be Sgt. Dober. Have a nice day."

Lee and Duncan passed more trash cans filled with cement, and someone rifled through Lee's bag looking for guns and grenades. She had pulled off her *abaya* and brushed her hair. In her tight black pants, she made a favorable impression on the sergeant.

"We don't get many ladies up here. What brings you to beautiful Beit Har?"

"I like the heat."

"Yeah, well, we got plenty of that. So you're just visiting friends?"

"I'm a doctor."

"You're a doctor?" The soldier checking Lee's bag had found the morphine and syringes."

"Trauma surgeon."

"Boy, you fit right in up here," Sgt. Dober said cheerfully. "Maybe you can stick around. There's been a lot of action and we're expecting more."

He led her to a large tent with camouflage netting that filtered the dusk light as though they were walking into a Vermeer canvas. At a long, flimsy table with metal chairs, she saw the officer who had written the letter in her bag. He was thin and sunburned with short ash-colored hair and brown eyes like his father. He was 25 or 26, but there was a deadened look in his eyes that came from witnessing too much death.

"Lt. Frank, sir? Your visitors." Dober left the tent.

"Have we met?" Lt. Frank stood up, slightly dazed by the sight of two civilian strangers.

"I'm Dr. Lee McGuinness. This is Duncan Hope."

"Pleased to meet you, ma'am." He looked more than pleased. "Sir." He shook Duncan's hand.

Lee imagined the lieutenant's father, at the same age, sitting in a tent in the same filtered light in Khe Sanh or Da Nang.

"Sit down, please."

"I saw your father just before coming over to Iraq."

"Oh, yes. He emailed me about you. You're looking for Martin Carrigan."

"That's right."

"I'm sorry, I didn't know you were coming to Beit Har. Frankly, I'm a little surprised. Nobody comes here."

"Your father gave me one of your letters. I wanted to meet you."

"I think that gives you an unfair advantage." He said it in an offhand way, but Lee could see that he was silently cursing his father for sharing his confidences. "So you know how bad things are."

"We would like to stay the night. It's too late to start for Baghdad."

"There's a 99 percent chance we'll be mortared tonight."

"Did your father tell you I was a trauma surgeon? I could be useful after a mortar attack."

"In that case, welcome to Camp Destiny. We have a VIP guest tent that has two cots and a hand towel. MREs are complimentary. The camel spiders jump as high as your knees. Check your boots in the morning for scorpions. Did you ask CENTCOM's permission to come up here?"

"I'm afraid not."

"Don't worry, I'm not going to turn you away. Rules at an FOB like this are different from the Green Zone. Dober?" Lt. Frank shouted for his sergeant.

"Yes, sir." He had been listening outside the tent.

"Take them to the VIP tent. You don't mind sharing?"

"No problem."

"Stow your stuff and come back for the full tour."

The VIP tent was set apart from the rest, with a view of the loading dock of the abandoned factory that had been stripped of every piece of metal or wire by looters. There was a dirt floor and no bedding.

"Lee, are you keeping your purse?" The capacious bag always miraculously had room for more.

"Yes."

"We shouldn't leave the printouts lying around, in case an intelligence officer gets curious," Duncan said, conscious of the penalty for al-Samarai if the documents were to get into the wrong hands. "I'd say Dober is a candidate."

Lee smiled indulgently. "What would I do without you, Duncan?"

XXVII

WHEN THEY ARRIVED back at Lt. Frank's tent, he had changed into his shorts and flip-flops.

"After hours," he explained. "Now for the Camp Destiny tour." The base had a temporary feel about it, like a stage set. It had been constructed in haste and looked as though Lt. Frank had ordered his troops to be ready to leave in a hurry. There were no trailers or Quonset huts. Everything but the tanks could be tossed into a helicopter. They made use of the old hangars for ammunition and an emergency room the medics had cobbled together to stabilize the wounded before they were medevaced. The motor pool was full of Humvees armored with plywood and sandbags.

"Useless pieces of crap. Pardon me, ma'am. They promise we'll have the real thing in a year or so. My men are very reassured by that. I would offer you a beer but I'm afraid we will all be working tonight. Come and see the mess tent. This is my greatest achievement in Iraq."

The sign over the door flap read "The Bellagio." Inside there were plastic tables and chairs with pin-up girls in various stages of undress, and posters of gondoliers on the Grand Canal in Venice. The sound system was blaring the Rolling Stones singing the lyrics from "Highwire," about hot guns and cold, cold lies. Lt. Frank's mortar platoon was playing poker.

"They've had a hard week. Two men lost their legs."

In the attached kitchen tent the cook was making cheeseburgers and french fries.

"I had to raise hell to get a cook for this base. We were supposed to trot over to our infantry company down the road every night for food while the snipers took pot shots at us. We'd get there and find the infantry guys had stolen half of our rations."

"You mentioned them in one of your letters. You said they were stealing money from the people here."

"Have a seat." He chose a table in back under an awning made from a tarp. There was tinsel wrapped around the posts and a dog lying in the dirt. "That's Saddam. We adopted him when his mother was blown up by an IED. Can I get you a Coke?"

"That would be great."

The Cokes were in bottles that had been sitting in ice. "This is a first-class operation. Nothing too good for my people. You asked about the money."

"Well, you said they had a 'fat bankroll' from stealing money during house-to-house raids. Maybe I'm naïve, but I didn't think the U.S. Army was full of thieves."

"I would call it a failure of leadership."

"What do you mean?"

"The troops see what's going on at the top and think, 'Hey, why shouldn't I get mine?' "

"What do they see at the top?" Duncan lit a cigarette.

"You know about the contractors feeding at the trough, getting paid millions for reconstruction that doesn't happen. Then there are the private-security guys, some of them totally incompetent, getting paid seven times what we earn. Not a great morale booster. Beyond that, there's wholesale robbery going on, boxes of cash leaving the country that some of the

Green Zone guys are stashing in their private bank accounts. I actually saw a football game where the contractors were tossing around a ball made of shrink-wrapped hundred dollar bills. This whole war is rotten."

"Doesn't anyone tell the soldiers from the infantry company that they will be severely disciplined if they steal?"

"No. Not in my experience. It's just like, you know, plunder is part of war."

"The fish rots from the head," said Lee.

"Yes, ma'am, you got it in one."

"What about your people?" she asked.

"My people are artillery. They don't go looking under people's mattresses. I've talked to my dad a lot about this. He said in Vietnam there were all kinds of rackets in the military. But it took years for them to really get going — when people were pissed off and ready to get out. Here, it started from day one."

"Not great for hearts and minds."

Lt. Frank shook his head. "I'm afraid the problem is our hearts and minds. We don't have them any more. It's okay to steal. It's okay to shoot whoever you want. People turn into animals. Or they go crazy. We had a private go on a shooting spree and kill nine people, including a couple of kids. He said it was target practice."

"You know that Martin Carrigan is a good friend of your dad's."

"Yes, I do. I saw him a lot growing up. My dad was kind of a mentor to him."

"Do you know what's happened to him?"

"I hear he's wanted for treason."

"Does that make sense to you?"

"No. Unless he's been infected like everyone else and thought he could get even richer arming the wrong side."

"Would he do that? Knowing that you're here?"

"It seems odd to me."

"He was sent here to investigate corruption in the Green Zone. American corruption. Including what's been going on at the refinery right here. He found the evidence, the records, the bank accounts, and now he's in hiding."

Lt. Frank sat very still.

"What do you know about the refinery, Lieutenant?" Duncan asked.

"It's a private cash cow for some very important people. We see the tankers. Refinery staffers have complained to me that Americans are involved, as if there was something I could do."

"There is something, Lieutenant. We are trying to save Martin's life."

"Who wants to kill him?"

"A couple of well-placed people in the CPA. Including a colonel."

"Army?"

"Yes."

A call came through on his radio. "I have to take this."

At that moment Lee heard a sound as though someone was ripping the sky. "Incoming," Lt. Frank said calmly. "There's a makeshift bunker over there. It might save you from a shrapnel wound. If it lands on you, there's not much you can do. If you will excuse me."

Lee and Duncan took advantage of the dugout. The mortars fell at approximately one-minute intervals, and although the shelling was over in less than 15 minutes, it seemed like an eternity. The only damage either of them suffered was a long cut on Lee's leg when she slid into the trench.

"Your war wound." Duncan winced. "Have you had a tetanus shot, doctor?"

"Yes, I'm okay. It's nothing."

They brushed the dirt off of their clothes and climbed out to see what had been hit. A soldier was jogging in their direction.

"Dr. McGuinness, Lt. Frank asked me to escort you to the clinic."

"Duncan, would you get my backpack from the VIP tent?"

"Of course."

There was a fire in the motor pool and a few craters in the barracks where tents had stood. The Bellagio was untouched. The medics were already bringing in bodies.

"There was a card game," explained one of them, "in a tent that got hit. We have one dead and four with shrapnel lacerations. The chopper should be here soon, but that depends on hostile fire."

"I'll do what I can to help you in the meantime." Lee saw that one of the patients had gashes next to one eye and a gaping hole dangerously close to his heart. He was slipping into unconsciousness. She knew that he would not survive the trip to Baghdad. "Would you get me a gown, gloves, and morphine please?"

"Yes, ma'am."

"And a thoracotomy tray." She needed to open his chest. "Or whatever you've got. I have to operate now, so we will need a second helicopter for this one."

Performing surgery in primitive conditions was unpleasant because of the risk of infection and the chance of an error, magnified by the lack of precision instruments. The man was young, in his early 20s, and his body was likely to stand the shock. Before 8 that night he was stable. Lee was exhausted and not at all prepared for what was to come.

"He's ready to be airlifted," she told the medic. "He can survive a couple of hours in the air. Not much more."

"Lt. Frank says no more choppers will fly tonight." The medic looked as tired as Lee was.

"What do you mean?"

"There was an attack on the pipelines between here and Baiji. It knocked out the power in the whole country. And the air around here is socked in with black smoke. The crude oil is gushing into the river. It looks like a volcano erupted."

Lee found Lt. Frank still in his shorts, barking orders into his radio and Thuraya. When he saw her he smiled.

"We could use you full-time, doctor."

"My patient will die without a medevac."

"They won't fly. All hell has broken loose out there. The pipeline junction was hit, and it set off a chain reaction in the power-plant system. My men are fighting fires and insurgents in Baiji. You did what you could."

Lee was too numb to think. "Who is he?"

"I'm sorry?"

"The boy I was operating on."

"Moody Fletcher. He's from somewhere in Virginia. Madison County, I think. That little town near White Oak Canyon."

"Etlan?"

"That's it. I'm going to Baiji as soon as I put my boots on. You're welcome to come."

"Give me two minutes."

Duncan had fallen asleep in the VIP tent.

"Wake up, Duncan. Story of a lifetime. Front page. Let's go." He shot out of his cot and was in the Humvee within minutes.

"The insurgents know these pipelines. They have inside knowledge and a lot of expertise. No matter what we do they manage to blow them." Lt. Frank was watching the dark streets of Beit Har for movement. "I wrote to my father and got a reply. He said I should take good care of you."

They heard shots from somewhere behind them.

"This could be a little hairy tonight. I know you are both used to that."

Lee was sorry that he had such confidence in her courage. At that moment, she had an overpowering desire to be someplace else. She thought about the boy from Virginia and the waste of it all. She knew that there was nothing between her body and the blast of a roadside bomb but a thin piece of metal. There was no armor underneath.

"How do you protect yourself in these Humvees?"

"At first we packed the floor with sandbags. Unfortunately, it didn't work. We pray."

The air was thick with smoke, and Lee could smell the fumes from the oil fire. As they rounded a bend she saw the black wall 100 feet high, backlit by the moon, and the red flames gliding across the river. It was like some Biblical cataclysm. A black tidal wave.

"My God." She began to turn red from the heat.

"The mother of all oil fires. Our friends in the insurgency are good at this." Lt. Frank directed his driver to a spit of land where his men were setting up a roadblock. Some had stripped off their shirts and were just wearing flak jackets. Frank conferred with one of his junior officers, who said the whole area was now cordoned off.

"How long is this going to burn?" Duncan was shouting over the roar of the flames.

"Could be days. The Corps of Engineers has to come in here with choppers loaded with chemicals and smoke jumpers. A team from the refinery will be working all night every night."

The Lieutenant checked two more forward positions. His men had seen nothing. The saboteurs had vanished. "I'd say it was an inside job. Probably someone I know. The weird thing about this war is that the enemy is invisible. It is everywhere and nowhere. I hate this place."

As they were driving back to base, Lee could hear the rotors of a helicopter.

"The medevac."

"Yeah, sounds like he made it. He's a good pilot."

When they turned into the base, the chopper was lifting off. It hovered for a moment, like the magician's levitated bread, then pulled away sharply as the medics ran from the wash. Lee's patient had a chance of survival after all. She would not have to face nightmares of Moody Fletcher's corpse lying on the gurney at Camp Destiny, waiting for the helicopter that would never come.

Lt. Frank invited her to his tent for a beer. "I'm going to tell Moody's mother what you did, and she will invite you to Etlan and shower you with moonshine, corn bread, and peach pie."

"I thought he would die here." Lee sat in one of his metal chairs.

"Losing one today is enough. The man killed was a corporal from Oregon. He played alto sax and died for a poker hand. I have to write the letter tonight." Lt. Frank was taking off his bulletproof vest. "We're sitting ducks on this base, a big bull's eye." His eyes were fixed on a shadow on the wall of the tent. "Sgt. Dober?"

"Yes, sir."

"That will be all, sergeant. You're on front gate duty tonight."

"But sir, I —"

"Thank you, Dober."

"Yes, sir."

Lt. Frank waited until he was sure that Dober was no longer eavesdropping.

"Why did you really come here?"

"If we don't get Martin Carrigan out of the country, he will be assassinated. He has put his life on the line to clean this place up, and now we've done the same. We want you to understand what's going on, Lieutenant. It seems there's a civil war inside Washington, and I'm hoping you are on the right side."

She told him what she had learned so far, including Plumber's threats to charge her as an accessory and Hamdoon's warning that she was a target. She described the meeting with Jabarri and the faked evidence detailing treason. Martin's cache of documents interested him the most. Lee said that she was not clear on which branch of government Martin was working for under the cover of his refugee work, but it was intelligence of some kind. He was a fugitive now, she explained, under protection of the Grand Ayatollah and hunted by the Army of the Believers.

"He works with my father," Lt. Frank said.

"What?"

"My father recruited him."

"I thought your father did missile testing?"

"He did. After he retired in disgust at all of the faked testing, one of his friends brought him back for a special DOD task force. They have their own inspector general. They're investigating fraud in Iraq."

"Are they independent?"

"They act like it. There have always been a few brave people in that building. They have a couple of powerful

311

senators who back them, and friends buried in all of the services. My father thinks corruption is corroding the military. He's not alone. He says there is a direct line between the $600 toilet seat and what's happening in Iraq. You remember the $400 hammers?"

"Yes."

"It's all about money. Scratching the backs of their friends. The procurement guys, the armchair generals, have risen to the top. They don't care about me or my people at Camp Destiny. We're cannon fodder. Their attitude about us is, 'Hey, you volunteered. Take what you get.' They care about what overpriced junk they can buy and sell in my name, some high-tech gadget to see a license plate from space when my guys go into downtown Baiji with radios we bought from Radio Shack. Our body armor is defective, our Army-issue radios don't work. I have guys here who have taken out $700 loans that they can't afford so that their wives can go and buy them night-vision goggles, scopes, and gun mounts. If we get blown up by a roadside mine because there's no ground plating on our vehicles and our fatigues are ripped to shreds, we have to pay for a new uniform. We have to pay. We're short of everything, including bullets. Do you know what they fed us for breakfast during training at Ft. Simms? Two slices of Wonder Bread with gravy. Meanwhile, somebody is getting rich. The contractors are pretty brazen, between the golden parachutes, the brothels, and the corporate jets."

"Why did the task force send Martin?"

"I assume it's because he knows Iraq. He's got civilian cover. And he's a real cowboy." Lt. Frank smiled. "You said he went to Iran?"

"Yes. But why hasn't your father sent someone over here to rescue him?"

"I think he did." Lt. Frank opened another beer and put his feet up. "He sent you."

"I don't understand."

"This is not the sort of environment where you send in a team of commandos."

"But I came on my own."

"Once my dad knew you were determined to come, he didn't need to send anyone else. You're a doctor. People trust you. You are not an intelligence agent who is going to arouse suspicion. You have the perfect cover. You are innocent."

"What about Martin's friends, the magician and Sparks?"

"They may be Defense Intelligence Agency types seconded to the task force. They have some very colorful people over there. In the days of the Soviet Union, my dad's best friend was the DIA guy in Moscow who ran the annual Defense Attaches' Transvestite Ball."

"Why can't they get Martin out?"

"You saw them in Turkey and Kurdistan. If they come into Iraq and are captured, they know a lot of secrets. You don't."

She looked at Duncan, who was smoking quietly in the corner. "What do you think?"

"I don't know, Lee, but if it's true, we had better figure out a plan."

Lee felt flattered and used at the same time. The suggestion that she had been manipulated from the time she left Kennedy Airport made her feel as though she were stumbling around in a blindfold, playing a game that was amusing an audience that she could not see.

"I don't belong here."

"Nonsense, Lee, we are almost there." Duncan stood up. "You're tired. We need some sleep."

"Thank you for your hospitality, Lieutenant. Can we count on your help? "

"It depends on what you mean by help." He gave her his Thuraya number.

"You might have to disobey orders."

"That I won't do."

"I should say, change procedures."

"That might be possible."

"You're a good man, Lieutenant. We'll be out of your way in the morning, as soon as curfew is lifted."

XXVIII

LEE WOKE UP BEFORE DAWN on the narrow cot, with a stiff neck and a mosquito teasing her ear. She rummaged in her case for a Lariam and took one with the last of her water. Duncan was gone. Lee dressed quickly and found him sitting on a crate on the loading dock watching the sunrise. His long legs were stretched out in front of him as the pink light revealed the desert floor. In the other direction, toward Baiji, the air was still greasy with oil smoke.

"How are we going to get Martin out of Karbala, Lee?"

"I heard on the BBC the other day that it was easy to buy police uniforms."

"I suppose so. Are you suggesting that we dress up as police?"

"No. Although you would look great as a cop. I was thinking of an actor."

"Hassan?"

"Exactly. I suspect he has out-of-work friends from the old days."

"What if they are caught?"

"At road blocks no one knows who is legitimate. Isn't it easier to let a car full of police pass than question their identity? Particularly if the police have weapons? Hassan can pick up Martin and deliver him here."

"You have a problem there. Everyone knows Hassan."

"Not with a beard and a paunch. Presumably, he is skilled in the art of makeup. When he's finished, he and his friends will all look like General Yazid's men."

"What about the *mujahedeen?*"

"Duncan, we have several *mujahedeen* in our cars. Hassan can arrange to bring one of them along on the raid to smooth the way back through the checkpoints. The question is how we get from here to the border."

"So long as you're willing to vouch for me as a doctor, Lt. Frank can call in a Black Hawk medevac." Duncan smiled at the simplicity of it. "They will take a team of doctors with their patient and can fly 360 miles. Sparks can pick us up on the other side."

"Who is the patient?"

"Presumably Martin will cooperate. If not we can ask one of our *mujahedeen* to shoot him."

"Oh, that's clever."

"Just to wound him."

"Are you jealous, Duncan?"

"Of course I am."

"What if the medevac insists on taking him to Baghdad?"

"There are a lot of things you can't treat in Baghdad, doctor. We're going to alter procedure on the grounds of a condition that requires emergency treatment in Turkey."

"I'll have to meet once more with Martin. Would you like to come? Last time I hid in a shipment of newlyweds' mattresses."

"That could be interesting."

"It was very interesting when it caught fire."

When they reached the gate, Hassan, Mohammed, and the *mujahedeen* were waiting. They were anxious to move the cars away from the base. For the Iraqis, it was like being too close to a leper colony.

"You all take care now." Sgt. Dober was there to say goodbye. "Oh hey, Dr. McGuinness, don't take this the wrong way, but I'd say those bodyguards look a little suspect. Some friendly advice. They could be bad guys. Watch your back. Goodbye, ma'am."

"Good luck, Sergeant." Lee wondered who Sgt. Dober was spying for.

Hassan negotiated three American roadblocks on the road out of Beit Har. In each case, Lee's mention of Lt. Frank and Camp Destiny elicited a respectful "Yes, ma'am."

"If we make it back this far with Martin, the American roadblocks could be a problem." Duncan was looking for all of the holes in the plan. "Lee, ask your friend Lt. Frank to meet us with an escort."

"How was the base last night?" Hassan sounded as though he knew the answer.

"There was a mortar attack. I operated on a boy and saved his life."

"The people in Beit Har told us it was revenge."

"For what?"

"Some of the soldiers killed an entire family the other night, including an old man and a 3-month-old child."

"I see."

"We were happy you were not hurt."

"It was luck."

Lee was thinking how to delicately broach the subject of the Karbala raid when Duncan came straight to the point.

"Hassan, where do we buy police uniforms?"

"What kind?"

"Like General Yazid's in Karbala."

"I know the tailor who makes them. He would do us a favor. How many do we need?"

"Ten should be enough."

"What are they for?"

"A performance. Sort of living theater."

"Someone's performing in Baghdad? Why wasn't I told?"

"It's in Karbala, actually. We would like you to play the lead." Duncan explained in Arabic what he and Lee had in mind.

"So this guy is up against General Yazid, some fat cats in the Green Zone, Jabarri, and the Army of the Believers?"

"That's right."

"I like him already. General Yazid tortured my uncle. He was a cleric, who had just finished his studies in Najaf. In one of his sermons, my uncle spoke out against Saddam's ban on the pilgrims coming for the 12th Imam's birthday. General Yazid came for him in the middle of the night. The bastard drove nails into my uncle's head. All of the Shia hate him."

"I'm so sorry, Hassan. I had no idea."

"It was a long time ago. As for Jabarri, his men treated me like scum the other day. They are all mafioso. They are bleeding Iraq. And the Army of the Believers is a plague of locusts."

"Will you do it?"

"Why not? Would you mind if I asked one of the cameramen from my old show to film it?"

"No. It's a nice touch."

They spent the rest of the journey to Baghdad going over details. Hassan said he would have to find an SUV and a pickup to look like the usual complement of police. His cousin could arrange it.

"I need identification and weapons," he said. That would require Karbala contacts. Duncan would pay a visit to Dr. Husseini and Dr. Ali. He would find a safe house that could be used for the raid.

Hassan would supply his own disguise and choose the actors, while Mohammed would take charge of the Baiji *mujahedeen*. He thought he needed four or five men. If things went wrong, they knew how to shoot. Lee's job was to make sure Martin was waiting for them and willing to go along. Discussion was cut short when it was time to pray.

The vehicles stopped. Hassan, Mohammed, and the *mujahedeen* grabbed their prayer rugs and walked several yards into the desert. They knelt, facing Mecca to the southwest, and touched their heads to the sand. Hassan had brought a Karbala stone. They sat up, reciting from the Quran and bowed again, oblivious to the convoys of tanks, supply trucks, and Humvees rumbling past on the highway. When they had finished, the men rolled their prayer rugs and returned to the cars.

"We need a Thuraya and two walkie-talkies." Hassan was already looking forward to one of his greatest roles.

"That can be arranged," Duncan volunteered. He knew the shops in Baghdad that did a brisk business selling phones and electronics to mercenaries and militias. He opened a bottle of water, which he hoped had not been refilled and resealed by the boy at the roadside stand. "Water, anyone?"

"I won't, thanks." Lee imagined aquatic protozoa gutting her before the raid.

After prayer, Hassan's cousin Mohammed joined the *mujahedeen* in the chase car to brief them on the plan. By the time the Baiji insurgents delivered Mohammed back to the Dar, they were anxiously asking when the fitting was for the police uniforms.

"Tell them we will call," Hassan told Mohammed.

"They are laughing that we are inviting them into a Shia city to be the police. Just like the old days."

"Tell them not to discuss it with their wives. It will take two or three days to organize everything. If word gets around, we will fail, and the Army of the Believers will murder their families."

"Yes, doctor. They are not fools."

Duncan took Hassan to the Thuraya shop and the British Embassy, where Duncan managed to convince his friend the ambassador to grant visas for Mahmood Maroki of the Southern Fields Oil Company and his family of five, without saying why. The ambassador and Duncan were fellow OGs, Old Glenalmond boys, from the same Scottish boarding school. There was a bond between them that went beyond the Foreign Office and Fleet Street and was just strong enough to secure the visas. Duncan knew that he would be asked to return the favor. If the Green Zone fell to the insurgents, and the helicopter failed to land to evacuate the staff, the ambassador might need help from someone like Duncan, who knew the Red Zone well, and could smuggle a desperate diplomat out of the country.

Lee greeted Ali behind the front desk at the Dar Kebeer. He seemed relieved to see her.

"Back at last, Dr. McGuinness. We missed you last night."

"Forgive me, Ali. I should have told you that I would be out of town."

"You have messages." There were two, one from Naji Qais and one from Adnan Jabarri. Lee debated whether or not to respond to Jabarri and decided that it was best to act as though they were on the same side. He had revealed the truth and she had believed him. Her excuse for staying in country was medical. She had decided to reopen a clinic. She would ask for his support, the "Jabarri Wing for Oncology," perhaps. Her first call in the bushes of Thuraya corner was to Naji Qais.

"Lee, where have you been?"

"I went up north to see a friend."

"Laela left by road this morning to Amman. She and Zara fly to Paris tomorrow. Laela wanted to say goodbye."

"I wish they had waited a day."

"Call her in Amman then. I have the number. She is at her cousin's house. It would cheer her up a lot."

Lee took the details and called Amman only to hear an unfamiliar answering machine. Her message was warm and brief, asking Laela to email her details in Paris so that Lee and Duncan could find her. While she still had a signal, she dialed Jabarri and gave the impression that she was happy to hear his voice.

"Doctor, how good of you to call. You told me you were leaving Iraq. I was surprised to hear that you were still with us."

"I have decided to reopen the Surgeons' Committee clinic. It will take several days to decide on a new location, and I would like you to consider being a donor. I thought you might like to endow a cancer wing."

"That's very ambitious."

"Given the skyrocketing caseload, with so many patients unable to fly abroad, Iraq is in desperate need of it. Will you consider it? It will, of course, be the Jabarri wing."

"Let me think about it. Where would this new center be?"

"There are several possibilities. As an Albert Schweitzer donor, our highest tier, you would have a say, naturally. Coming from a great Shia family as you do, perhaps the new oncology wing should be in Karbala. There is some land across from the hospital there."

"How large a contribution are you looking for?"

"I think five or ten million would go a long way."

"That's very steep, Dr. McGuinness."

"The right equipment is very expensive. Think of this as your chance to give back to Iraq what Iraq has given to you."

"Would the clinic use my shipping company to import drugs?"

"We can certainly discuss that."

"By the way, doctor, were you in Basra a few days ago?"

"No, I have been in the north."

"A couple of intelligence agents were questioning my people there. One of them fit your description."

"I'm not an intelligence agent, Mr. Jabarri. There are so many of them here, an American woman with dark hair is pretty common."

"A beautiful American woman."

"I have several witnesses who can vouch for me in the north. I was treating patients at Camp Destiny."

"Okay, I'll think about your clinic. And you think about my company for importing the drugs."

"The Surgeons' Committee would be very lucky to have you as a partner."

Even a telephone conversation with Jabarri made her feel unclean. She stood under the shower for 20 minutes and fell asleep in her dingy suite. When she woke up to the sound of gunfire, it was already dark. She dressed and selected a table by the pool where she ordered a large vodka.

"No vodka today, doctor."

"What have you got?"

"Johnny Walker Black."

"That will do."

Duncan appeared, loaded down with his satchel of note-books and tape recorders. He fell into a deck chair. "Our friend Mahmood Maroki was nearly beaten to death."

"What?"

"Some goons thrashed him within an inch of his life."

"It must be Jabarri. He just asked me if I was in Basra posing as an intelligence agent. Did you get the visas?"

"I hope so. But Maroki may not live that long."

"Duncan, what about that British captain? Keane, I think it was. Can't he offer protection?"

"I'll ask. I wouldn't count on the British army." He sank into silence.

"I'm sorry, Duncan. Jabarri is a monster and we have a chance to stop him. We're uncovering a scheme to steal billions of dollars here. We have to talk to people. Maroki was on his payroll, remember?"

"Bloody hell, Lee. We have to take care of the people who give us information. The next one will end up dead."

"I appreciate your lecture on ethics, but there is a con-tract out on my life. My friend is about to be executed. There is no time for niceties. I am doing my best."

"We're in over our heads."

"That is the truth."

"The difference between us, Lee, is that I am not suici-dal. My instinct for self-preservation is intact, and I do not see the point of dying for Iraq. Do you?"

She felt spent and sorry that she had argued with him. "I'm overtired, Duncan. Which hospital is Maroki in?"

"Basra Teaching Hospital."

"I will visit him tomorrow."

"Lee, you act like you have mad cow disease or some-thing. The last thing Mahmood needs is a visit from you. Do you want him pulped again? We must arrange to get him out of here and fast."

"Of course, you're right, Duncan. Could the Ambassador at least send a car for Maroki's family?"

"I'm trying to arrange everything."

"Duncan, Laela left for Jordan."

"By road?"

"Yes."

"She might have said goodbye."

"I have her number in Amman."

"What is it?" Duncan took the number and seemed too defeated to argue any longer. He turned and walked away.

Lee retired upstairs, unfit for company. Room service, such as it was, arrived with Arabic salads and a bottle of Syrian wine. When Lee turned on the sad little television and flipped the channels, she found reruns of Hassan's old show. She watched for a while and fell into a doze, no longer noticing the steady pulse of weapons fire somewhere in the city.

XXIX

THE FOLLOWING MORNING, Lee found Dr. Husseini at his
charity. He was presiding over rows of young women in
abayas sitting behind recently unpacked computer screens.
"Teacher training," he said with satisfaction.

"This equipment is excellent. From donors in Kuwait.
All free. Come have a coffee in the garden."

She knew that it would take time to convince Dr.
Husseini that her scheme for Martin's rescue had a chance of
success. In the meantime, Hassan set out to negotiate with
the Karbala police tailor for the uniforms. As far as the tailor
knew, Hassan was ordering costumes for the first post-
Saddam war epic. His cousin was already outfitting a pickup
with a second-hand police siren.

"Al-Kufa's Army of the Believers was here last night,
hunting for Martin Carrigan." Dr. Husseini looked drawn.

As he said it, Lee was relieved that she had escorts from
the Badr Brigade sitting outside. "I have to see him again."

"You take your coffee medium sweet?"

"Yes."

"The situation is not good. I would advise against it."

"Dr. Husseini, I've found out much more about what
Martin was doing here. We cannot afford to wait." She told
him what she had learned in Umm Qasr and Baiji, and laid
out the plan for the police raid on the safe house and the

medevac from Camp Destiny. She needed his help for the ID cards and weapons. He could take advantage of the fact that every Iraqi household had at least one or two rifles. There were enough weapons for a platoon within a block of the charity. Beyond that, they needed the safe house and Martin's consent. "I can't get him to agree, Dr. Husseini, unless I see him."

"I will see what I can do. You know I have to contact Sheik Abbas in order to make the connection."

"I understand. I can't thank you enough. If we get him out and expose the fact that Jabarri and some of his friends in the Green Zone have been looting this country's coffers, not to mention arming al-Kufa's fanatics, it will make a difference."

"I know, Lee. You don't have to explain. I have to ask you, though. Why are you taking these terrible risks? Is this all for Martin or is it something else?"

"It's for Martin. And for me. Atonement, maybe. For things that happened a long time ago. I have to prove that there is such a thing as a good American."

"You don't have to prove that."

"Dr. Husseini, how can I put this? My family was involved with intelligence. They weren't the ones who put Saddam in power, but their colleagues did. They would justify it. They would say it was the right thing at the time. They might even justify what Plumber is doing to Martin. Condemning him as a traitor, for exposing the dirty secrets of this war. The acceptance of criminal behavior in the name of the greater good is like a disease. Pretty soon everything is acceptable. Assassination, torture, theft. What next? Mass graves? Like Saddam? This is my fight as much as it is yours. If I can see Martin tomorrow, we can stage the raid the following night."

"It will take a week to prepare for this. Your own people won't be ready. Two or 3 a.m. on a Friday morning would be best. When Yazid or Slay orders a raid, it's usually in the middle of the night. The real police manning the roadblocks will expect it. But if we do it in the early morning hours of a Friday, they will be in a holiday mood, grumbling that they are on duty when everyone else is enjoying the weekend. They will be just a little less attentive."

"Do you know someone who can do the ID cards?"

"Dr. Ali has friends."

"I have been meaning to ask: Is Dr. Ali really just a pediatrician?"

"Dr. Ali fought against Saddam in the marshes. Very few people had that kind of courage."

That explained the deference in the streets the night of the birthday of the 12th Imam. Dr. Ali was a resistance leader in the old Iraq. No one in Karbala would ever forget that.

"Why did he leave us the night we stayed in the pilgrim's hotel?"

"He had a problem to attend to. Someone smuggled a bomb into the square."

Lee thought in hindsight it was better to be abandoned and chased across the rooftops by al-Kufa's men than to be blown up in bed. "Can we travel in a shipment of mattresses tomorrow? Duncan would like to come."

"Yes, I will arrange it. You are already in costume." He gestured toward her black shroud. "You can come with me. I am looking for a second wife." She shot him a look of reproach.

"Lee, it was a joke."

She realized that Dr. Husseini did not know what excuses she had given for being in Karbala at all.

"If anyone asks what I am doing here, I told Jabarri that I am opening a new Surgeons' Committee clinic in Karbala. I asked him to contribute."

"Were you telling him the truth?"

He caught her by surprise. Dr. Husseini had some moral hold over her that she could not quite explain. Perhaps it was just being in the presence of someone who had spent 10 years in solitary confinement because he refused to be complicit in evil. She felt inadequate beside him. Not yet fully human.

"I suppose it's possible."

The following day she and Duncan, who had spent the evening drinking single malt whiskey with the British ambassador, were folded into the shipment of mattresses, sucking in goose feathers from the duvet, their faces, wet with sweat, fused to the hot plastic. In the midday gloom of the aid warehouse, there was no curious child threatening to reveal the presence of strangers. Duncan threw on a *dishdasha* behind the flour sacks, straightened his *keffiyeh*, and walked to Dr. Husseini's Lada affecting a limp. Nothing was more normal in Iraq than infirmity.

This time they drove to the center of the city, a neighborhood of modest mud-brick houses crowded behind the Abbas shrine. The streets were patrolled by the shrines' guardians, who wore heavy black beards, ammunition belts, and AK-47s. They looked more ascetic than al-Kufa's Army of the Believers. Their belts were cinched tight to extra holes punched in the leather. Their foreheads had the telltale mark of the Karbala stone. None of them even glanced in the strangers' direction. In the old car, with no security guards, they were invisible, people of no consequence. On a narrow side street, a block behind the shrine, they entered a dark hallway that smelled of rotting garbage and walked into a courtyard, with laundry strung between the balconies of what was once an elegant Ottoman house. The magnificent woodwork was cracked and chipped. The paint was barely visible. They walked up a narrow interior staircase, onto a small roof that overlooked the golden dome of the shrine. As they stood looking out over the city, Lee felt someone behind them.

Martin was blinking in the light, his lithe frame in an old *dishdasha* and sandals. His eyes, squinting against the glare, looked like the Irish Sea on a fine day. He seemed so diminished that it was hard to imagine that he was being hunted as a dangerous man. Watching him adjust to the light like an animal that has been in hibernation, Lee thought of the risks she had taken on his behalf. In the end, the role she had assumed, to expose the false charges against him and the greed of those who wanted him dead, had taken on a life of its own. It was her own quest now, to right the wrongs of this war, to make up for her family's past. Standing there on the roof, Lee realized that she hardly knew Martin. He was too skilled at discretion. She remembered the magician's prophecy that she would have two great loves and one would disappoint her.

"Hello, Martin." She embraced him. "You know Dr. Husseini. This is Duncan Hope. I think you met in Kabul. He is a journalist for a London paper."

"Thank you for coming." His days of hiding had hollowed his cheeks and left his skin chalky. His black hair, falling out of the side of his *keffiyeh*, was long and unruly. Whereas Lee felt awkward in Iraqi dress, Martin seemed at ease, like T.E. Lawrence or Richard Burton. The fact that he was a fugitive who would be forced, at any moment, to vanish down the steps or over the rooftops infused the little gathering with the same heightened meaning as an ordinary day for a condemned man.

"How did it go in the north?"

"I wasn't expecting an Ottoman scholar like Martha Sparks."

"Which Sparks did you meet? Martha has several identities."

"The matron on a gardening tour."

"Oh, that's a good one. She got the case?"

"She got the contents. With the reading glasses, of course. Duncan and I broke the code."

"So you read the ledger?"

"Yes. And we have managed to gather more evidence from the pirate port near Umm Qasr and the Baiji refinery."

"So you know how sensitive it is."

"Yes. Martin, why did you take on this mission?"

"You know George Plumber. He betrayed my father a long time ago. Do you have a cigarette?"

Duncan fetched one from his bag. Martin took it and inhaled slowly, as though he had finally reached an oasis.

"When they were both stationed in London, my father was running operatives behind the Berlin wall in East Germany. To further his own career, Plumber sabotaged the network. He said the Soviets had infiltrated with their spies, which was a lie. Plumber wanted my father to fail. The funding was cut off, contacts were cut loose. All of the people my father worked with were exposed and sent to the gulag. My father never recovered. The Chinese say revenge is a dish best eaten cold."

Lee thought how similar they were, with these old scores to settle. Martin wanted revenge and she wanted absolution. Irish Catholics. She smiled.

"When Plumber was sent to the Green Zone and I found out that he was taking kickbacks, I was ready to do anything to get a conviction. You can see what he's done to me. He's trying to destroy me, just like he destroyed my father."

"Martin, since our last meeting the situation has become more urgent. Jabarri tried to kidnap us. One of our informants was nearly killed this week. I've been threatened by Plumber. It seems your friend Colonel Frank expects me to get you out. So I have arranged that in a week's time, you will be arrested by the Karbala police. They will not be Yazid's police. They will be ours. We will transport you to Randall Frank's base. You will be medevaced to Turkey."

"Randall?"

"Yes, Lt. Frank is working with us. Right now the Army of the Believers is hoping to assassinate you before we get you out of here. Martin, are you listening? Can we count on you to go through with this?"

"How is Randall?"

"He survived a mortar attack the other night and seems in good spirits."

"Yeah, you can count on me." He turned to Duncan. "Are you coming?"

"Yes. I'm writing the story. Would you like a pack of cigarettes to take with you?"

"Please."

"We must be going." Dr. Husseini broke his silence. "The raid will take place here in the early morning hours of next Friday. Wait for us on the roof."

"I'll be here. What if Yazid's people come first and I don't know the difference?"

"Ours will be led by an actor," Dr. Husseini continued. "His name is Hassan. He is a star, famous for his role as Ali Baba. Perhaps you have seen him."

"Oh, right. This should be entertaining."

331

"I am recommending to your hosts that you be moved to Najaf for a few days to attend one of the great religious schools. No one will find you there."

They had reached the bottom of the staircase when Lee heard American voices coming from the street. "Don't be alarmed." Dr. Husseini urged them on. "Remember what you look like. You are Iraqi. An American patrol is routine."

"We have no papers."

"If they question us, let me talk. You're a woman. They expect nothing of you."

As they entered the street though the carved wooden doors, Duncan could see that the patrol had blocked off the crossroads to their left. Dr. Husseini led them to the right. The little band walked slowly, speaking in low tones in Arabic, as though the troops were no concern of theirs. The Lada was parked on the far side of the patrol and Dr. Husseini led them on a wide circle through the crowded streets to get there. Lee felt sure that at any moment she would be exposed. As she turned the final corner to reach the car, she saw four soldiers in camouflage and shades questioning people in the street. They had interpreters. Her instinct was to break into a run but Dr. Hussein had his arm firmly locked with hers. She feigned a limp.

"Hey, you there." The Marine pointed to Dr. Husseini. "You."

Dr. Husseini looked behind him to see whether someone else was being summoned. "Are you addressing me?"

"What's your business here?"

"We are visiting relatives."

As the marine spoke, a look of recognition passed over his face, which changed his tone to something between reverence and exhilaration at being in the presence of celebrity.

"Hey, I saw you on TV. Aren't you the guy who negotiated with al-Kufa's guys at the Shrine?"

"That's right."

"That was awesome. It was like something out of *The Seven Samurai*. You should be prime minister of Iraq. Really, that was amazing. Those guys are nuts. Go right ahead. It's an honor, sir."

"Thank you. Come along, Zawjati." He took Lee's arm and hustled her past the men before coming back to escort Duncan. "By the way, who are you looking for?"

"A terrorist, a foreigner. We've got the neighborhood sealed off. We'll smoke him out. Not to worry. Is your wife all right there? She looks a little unsteady."

"She has been ill. There isn't enough medicine here."

"I'm sorry about that. You know, it's such a coincidence meeting you. I was just in the States on my home leave and I saw you on the news. I was channel surfing. You were talking about how the Iraqis didn't trust us. They thought we weren't really trying to help them free themselves but had another agenda. We wanted the oil. American companies wanted to make money. And there was this mutual mistrust between us. And we didn't really know who to talk to. That's right, we don't. We feel totally isolated. But I thought, watching you on TV, I could talk to that guy. And here you are walking in the street. Like Gandhi or something. You could do something for this country. Stop everyone from cutting each other's throats."

"I would like to do that. I'm afraid we must be going."

"You take care now. And keep up the good work."

Lee was relieved that they could finally move on. She was sure the soldier was going to rally his friends to meet the celebrity who had been on the network news. Out of the corner of her eye she saw a Humvee pull up with an officer who looked like Maj. Clapp, the translator who failed to translate a word for Gen. Yazid. Sweat was dripping down her face under the *abaya*.

"Oh, sir."

"Yes?" Dr. Husseini stopped.

"Do you know when you'll be on TV again?"

"I'm afraid not."

"I was hoping my mom could Tivo it. Well, have a nice day."

They were free. Clapp was too preoccupied with his men to notice. The only others allowed to pass through the barricades were some mourners carrying a coffin. They told the Marines' translators that they were taking their dead to Najaf, the Shias' holy burial ground.

XXX

L EE WAS RELIEVED to see the guards at the checkpoint outside the Dar. She was conscious that each of her escapes was narrower than the last, and the Dar gave her at least the illusion of sanctuary. Her excuses for staying in Baghdad were wearing thin. Plumber had the power to pick her up as an accessory to treason whenever he liked. He could manufacture evidence. The extra days of preparation for the raid meant she would be delaying her departure with no apparent purpose. She would have to put in time at Omar Hospital and do some fund-raising for the clinic.

For now, she was back in her little refuge, her grim fortress where she could at least pretend there was such a thing as safety in Iraq. Ever since the Tigris Hotel had been bombed, the false sense of security Lee felt driving through the Dar barricades was somehow less convincing. She saw a freshly laid wall of sandbags. Hassan's Mercedes maneuvered the ever-growing obstacle course with 10 police uniforms stuffed under the red leather seats.

"That man is a genius." Hassan was praising the police tailor as the security men checked for bombs on the under-carriage of the car. "He's like one of those Hong Kong guys in a hole in the wall with an old sewing machine. Overnight service. The buttons, the seams, the insignia, perfect. On my next show, he is definitely in the costume department."

As Hassan pulled up under the eucalyptus, Lee saw a familiar car idling in front of her. The man behind the wheel was young but deeply lined from lack of sleep. He wore a mustache and a sullen expression.

"Sadoon." Lee threw open her door and rushed to his car. His face was transformed at the sight of her.

"*As-salaamu alaikum.*"

"*Wa alaikum assalam.*"

Duncan followed her and shook Sadoon's hand. There was an awkwardness between them.

"How did you get out?"

"Nizar Hadithi convinced the news network to complain to Central Command. They said they would do a big story. I never fired any rocket at anybody. So why was I in Abu Ghraib? The guys who did it went back to Fallujah. The Americans already know them."

"Come inside, Sadoon," Lee was flooded with relief. "Let's have a drink."

"I will follow you in. I want a word with Hassan." Duncan could see that the television idol was already besieged by three fans from the Internet cafe in thick glasses and headscarves. "Hassan, give me two minutes alone. Where will you rehearse?"

"One of the old studios. It's a wreck, but we will find space. I will tell the actors that this is a film with an American producer who is bringing in some independent backing. Given these lean times, I will convince them to do it for a percentage rather than money up front. Can you give them a per diem?"

Duncan knew that Lee still had cash from Martin's briefcase and the Surgeons' Committee wire.

"Of course. Let me know if your uncle has any problems with the cars."

"They will look 100 percent authentic. Including the plates and registration."

"Hassan, if you have any doubts and want to pull out, just say."

"I'm enjoying this. Why shouldn't I do something for my country? I have more reason to do this than any of you. Now if you will excuse me, I have to meet my cameraman."

Lee and Sadoon had chosen a table on the upper terrace on the far side of the pool. On a chaise longue below them at the water's edge was the man with the tattoos. Lee was happy to see his well-oiled skin and shiny bald head, for his bizarre presence gave some ballast to life in Baghdad. As everything fell apart around her, the man with the tattoos would remain anchored to the chaise. In the falling light, he was reading a magazine for extreme skiers. The rest of the tables had yet to fill up with journalists and mercenaries. There was one couple trading confidences, an Iraqi she knew worked for the Human Rights Office, and a British correspondent who spoke in whispers.

Lee made room for Duncan without interrupting Sadoon as he described his life in an Abu Ghraib cell. Lee could see from Duncan's intense interest that he would file the story that night, another front page, probably. He questioned Sadoon about torture.

"We stood for eight hours at a time with bags over our heads." Sadoon was uneasy. Lee saw that sweat had broken out on his face and he could not sit still in his chair. "They left the lights on all night in our cells. We were mortared. When we asked the guards to move us to a safe place, they refused. Prisoners were wounded. Everyone said we were used as a human shield. Then there was the music."

"What music?"

"They played the theme song from *Barney*."

"The children's show?"

"Yes. They forced us to strip. May I have some water?"

"Of course." Lee poured him a glass.

"They forced us to do things."

"What things?"

"To touch ourselves."

"I'm sorry?"

He was struggling for the word and leaned over to Duncan, because he was a man, to confess it quietly in Arabic.

Duncan felt ill even repeating it. "He means masturbate."

There was an embarrassed silence.

"They took pictures. They threatened to send them to our families."

Sadoon would be scarred by his treatment for life.

"I'm sorry." Lee looked down, and Sadoon turned away.

"What did they want from you?" She hoped that Sadoon would finally explain his role in the Rasheed bombing in a way that would absolve him of guilt.

"You have to understand, doctor. I know the men who fired those rockets. One of them is my cousin. I have over a hundred cousins, and he is one of them. But I was not working with him. He warned me the night before that something was going to happen so that I would stay away. He knew that I drove around the city day and night for my work. But he did not tell me what they were planning. I did not know they would attack the Rasheed. And doctor, you must understand, the Americans already know who those *mujahedeen* are. In Abu Ghraib, no one even asked me about them. Not once. *Wallahi.* I swear."

"What did they ask you?"

"They wanted to know if I had smuggled Saddam Hussein into the bureau at the Aleem."

"The news bureau?"

"Yes."

"Why would Saddam go there?"

"The interrogators thought that the network was hiding him in order to do an interview. They wanted me to say that I had brought him there. Because I am from Fallujah, they were sure that I must have helped arrange it."

Lee remembered that Nizar had joked that the Aleem Hotel had been cordoned off for hours by soldiers who came to search the offices for Saddam. They even probed under the beds. Nizar had laughed at the absurdity of it.

"At least you're out of there," Duncan said. He lit a cigarette. "Can I order you a Coke, Sadoon?"

"Yes. With ice."

"How is your family?"

"Better, now that I am home."

"Will Nizar give you a paid vacation?" Lee would see to it that he did.

"Yes, *tabiba*, he is helping me. I wanted you to know, Dr. McGuinness, that I am not a terrorist. That morning, when we were driving outside the Green Zone, I wanted to protect you. Because you are a doctor. You came here to help us."

"Thank you, Sadoon. I'm sorry if I misunderstood."

Lee left the two of them poring over the details of his arrest and detention without charges. Who would treat Sadoon's post-traumatic stress from masturbating while being photographed? Perhaps Lee could add a wing to the clinic. In the oleander bushes at Thuraya corner, behind the diving board, she called the number she had for Laela in Amman. The woman who answered said that Laela and Zara had left for the airport hours before. Lee felt a stab of disappointment. She wanted to hire a car and cross the border. Laela was dying.

Since satellite reception was good, Lee decided to call the Surgeons' Committee and Martin's office. It was still morning on the East Coast.

"Lee, is that you?" It was the voice of the director's assistant, who had never been particularly friendly. "Are you all right?"

"Yes. I'm fine."

"Any news?" The assistant's eager concern told Lee that the trip to Iraq had given her added cachet with the Surgeons' Committee.

"I'm staying for another week or so to work on plans for Omar Hospital. A truckload of our medicine made it from Turkey to Karbala. The people of Karbala are extremely grateful to the Surgeons' Committee."

"I'll pass that along. Be safe, Lee."

Lee could not help laughing. Be safe.

She called Martin's aid group, who were hungry for news and indebted to Lee for whatever she could find. She relieved them of their guilt.

"I just wanted you to know that everything is as well as can be expected at this end. There is no news about Martin, except rumor. The latest is that he has signed up for religious instruction."

"Really? That's so unlike him." The voice on the other end was confused.

"My battery is dying. I'll call again in a few days."

When she returned to the table, Sadoon had gone to al-Adhamiyah, and Duncan was examining his notes.

"I called Amman. Laela's gone."

"Oh, blast."

"Don't worry, Duncan. They will contact us from Paris."

Lee walked up the two flights to her suite and poured herself a large glass of wine. She switched on the BBC, which was showing a special on the water gardens of Bangkok. Lee dug the computer printouts from Baiji out of her bottomless purse. She spread the documents on the Formica table. Adnan Jabarri's tanker trucks were marked in Arabic with initials. Looking at the log, she knew that some of them had passed beneath her en route to Turkey, as she and Duncan sat drinking *arak* on the balcony of the Zakho Guest House.

Lee heard a sound from the balcony, on the other side of the heavy plastic curtains, as though someone had kicked a terra-cotta pot. It might have been a cat. A few seconds later, there was a faint scratching noise near the lock on the sliding glass doors. The intruder was trying to jimmy it. If he had heard her moving around, he intended to do more than search the place. Hiding in a closet to satisfy her curiosity was likely to end badly if she were facing an AK-47. She gathered up the printouts, stuffed them into her bag and slipped out of the suite. Before the door was closed, the gunman had throw back the curtain. He wore a police uniform.

Lee ran down the two flights of concrete steps, to the pool terrace now crowded with customers. The policeman would not pursue her there. She walked quickly to the front desk, where there were two well-armed security guards and Ali.

"Ali, there's a militiaman in the hotel. Somebody's death squad, I think, dressed as police. Over in the annex, third floor. My room."

One of the hotel guards spoke into his walkie-talkie and sprinted in the direction of the room. As Lee stood with Ali, three more men in black leather ran past.

"Ali, I have to change rooms. What else have you got?"

"Well, Dr. McGuinness. I can give you the Honeymoon Suite, with a round bed and mirrored ceiling." Ali coughed. "Some of the mirrors fell down in the bombing."

"I need something that faces the front of the hotel. Not the back."

"The Liberation Suite."

"Liberation?"

"It used to be the Saddam Suite."

"Did he ever stay in it?"

"No. We kept it ready for him." Ali shrugged.

The Liberation Suite was decorated almost entirely in gold paisley wallpaper, with chiffon swags wrapping the windows, the canopy beds, and the occasional tables. Everything was wrapped, thought Lee, like something by Christo and Jeanne-Claude. The sofa was gold velvet dotted with cigarette burns. There were silver polyester pillows that smelled of men's hair pomade. Below the balcony of the Liberation Suite, the front entrance of the hotel was blocked off and well lit. Security was good.

Ali looked at her hopefully. "I will give you a 75 percent discount. Please, doctor, don't tell the other guests what happened."

"I'll take it, Ali. Would you send someone to collect my things? Mr. Duncan will also be staying here."

Ali blushed. "Of course, doctor."

He left her with the key. After the break-in, Ali gave Lee a sulky security guard to watch the Liberation Suite. Lee was careful now not to travel around Shia neighborhoods without at least two men from the Badr Brigade. She had guards with ties to Tikrit in the Sunni zones. In mixed neighborhoods, she brought both.

Her first concern was Mahmood Maroki, now in the British Ambassador's residence, recovering from his beating.

Maroki's arm, which had snapped when his assailants cranked it up behind his back to hang him from the ceiling, was mending. The cuts on his face were neatly stitched, like a railway yard with multiple tracks. The bruising around his ribs and stomach was slightly less livid, the blue outlines shrinking like a receding tide. He had some internal bleeding which could only be monitored properly when he reached London. In the meantime, Maroki's wife and children had camped around his bed.

Knowing that her trip to the Rumaila oil fields had brought on the attack made Lee feel enough guilt to want to buy a flail. Maroki had a more pragmatic view. He had survived, he had a ticket out of Iraq, and his family would not die of cholera. His children would not be brain-damaged by a car bomb. The Maroki family could eke out a living in North London and one day go to Libya or the Gulf to work in the oil fields. Duncan would keep his promise to make Maroki a modest hero, the bureaucrat who stood up to the mafia. It was a popular theme, even if it almost never happened, and might land him a few minutes of fame. Maroki had no regrets.

Lee cautioned the ambassador that Maroki should not be moved for at least three days. The ambassador complained that the Maroki family cooked at all hours and listened to Arabic hip-hop. Lee called Duncan, who appeared as soon as the Baghdad traffic jams allowed, and deftly put the Ambassador's concerns to rest. Duncan brought the subject around to the next reunion of their old school and Duncan's plan to host a small gathering for OGs at the Reform Club in London, to which the ambassador was naturally invited. The dangled invitation and a stray remark about possibly offering to sponsor him for club membership had the desired effect. The man could not have been more helpful. Duncan gave clear instructions on where Maroki should be admitted for treatment in London, in a private room with bodyguard. He would visit him in a week's time.

"Duncan, why are you a journalist?" Lee waited until they were in Hassan's Mercedes to ask.

"Why not?"

"Shouldn't you be at the Foreign Office or running a country estate somewhere in Scotland, with shooting parties on the weekend?"

"I prefer to be in the wild."

"Because?"

"People are more noble."

"More savage."

"Well, yes, if you mean militias in Congo wearing fetuses around their necks as trophies. But I still like it best when there's no government at all. Freedom is a powerful drug. No passport stamps, no traffic lights, no scheduled airlines, no laws, no accountants, no social order. I can smoke all I want and my friends can put their weapons in the overhead compartment."

They called Dr. Husseini from the car. Before leaving Karbala, they had agreed that all satellite phone conversations would be couched in discussions about the clinic. Lee wanted to find out whether Martin's funeral procession had evaded Maj. Clapp.

"Have the medical supplies I ordered been delivered?"

"Your supplies have arrived, Dr. McGuinness."

"I will be down soon to look at more clinic sites. Shall we go back to the last one we looked at or do you have something better in mind?"

"Let's look at that one again. I think I have persuaded the landlord to give you a good price."

The safe house would remain the same. Hassan would have no problem finding his way to the old Ottoman house. He and his men would collect the guns, Karbala registration papers, and ID cards from a pickup point outside the city, one of the old drops for food and lanterns for the pilgrims coming to the birthday of the 12th Imam. Dr. Ali was in charge of that.

XXXI

BACK IN THE GOLD HAZE of the Liberation Suite, Lee paced and cracked pistachios. She and Duncan, mindful of the bugging devices, reviewed the plan outdoors, looking for flaws. What happened if they were challenged by Yazid's men? What if the actors discovered that the raid was real? It was more likely they would think it was all part of the production. Hassan had drilled it into the cast that everything had to be done in one take. If things deteriorated, the *mujahedeen* among them would take over. Lee wanted to be with them. What conceivable role was there for her?

"We could be prisoners." Duncan had the epiphany one night at the Piazza restaurant after Mario, the proprietor from Bolsena, presented them with another bottle of Brunello.

"Prisoners?"

"Yes, Lee. We must find some handcuffs."

"You mean flexi-cuffs. What exactly did you have in mind?"

"The police will raid the Dar and arrest us, flex-cuff us, and force us into the back of the SUV, before proceeding to Karbala. If anyone is watching in the middle of the night, it will look as though we had been forced to give away Martin's hiding place."

"Interesting."

"Aren't you glad you didn't evict me from the Liberation Suite?"

"Why would I do that?"

"Perhaps I'm too presumptuous."

"In what way?" Lee sipped her wine.

"Well, I've hardly left your side for the past several days."

"I thought that was so you could get on the front page." She laughed.

"Well, yes and no." Duncan lit a cigarette. "You see, Lee, I think you're extraordinary. I haven't exactly declared my feelings because, frankly, I thought you were in love with Martin."

"What makes you think I'm not?"

"I'm not sure."

"What about Laela?"

"She is dying. You know that." Duncan ordered more wine. "Look, if we get out of this alive, and I'm not convinced we will, I want you to stay with me."

"Here in Iraq?"

"Here, yes, London, anywhere."

"It's 15 minutes to curfew."

"Oh, fuck."

"We can continue this in the Liberation Suite."

They did not bother to turn on the light, leaving the cavernous rooms half in shadow, half bathed in the light from the spotlit façade of the hotel. They kissed and undressed at the same time, feeling their way to the bed and getting tangled in the chiffon. They fell on the satin coverlet that was carefully chosen to impress Saddam, had he ever bothered to patronize the Dar. Their lovemaking had the urgency of two people shadowed by death, every touch electrified by the danger that saturated the air around them. Each of them knew that this encounter could easily be the last, interrupted by an assassin, watching from the dark apartment block across the street. When they finally sank into a sleep deeper than anything pills could deliver, they had defied the war and found peace.

When morning came, Hassan's police force was ready. It was Thursday. Mohammed and the *mujahedeen* had alerted their friends along the route north to let their convoy pass unmolested. Nizar Hadithi had supplied the flexi-cuffs and given his blessing to the *mujahedeen*'s mission to get Lee safely to Camp Destiny.

Lee arranged to have lunch with Stephano. She found the Italian journalist at a table by the pool with a bottle of Lebanese wine.

"Stephano, if anything happens to Duncan and me, I want to you call his paper in London and convince the editor to open Duncan's email. He has sent some backup documents to himself for protection."

"That sounds ominous."

"It's a card game."

"A card game. You mean like poker?"

"Yes. It's called 40 Thieves."

"Like Ali Baba?"

"Right. It's a code. When you break it, publish the story."

"What could happen to you?"

"We might be arrested. I don't know."

"And if you don't get arrested?"

"We hope to leave the country tomorrow night. If we succeed, I will call your Thuraya. Duncan will file his story on Saturday for the Sunday paper. He will give you whatever you need for a front-page story Monday."

"Are you coming back any time soon?"

"I'm thinking of opening a clinic in Karbala."

"You are a glutton for punishment."

"First, I'm going to Paris to see Laela."

"How is she?"

"Not well. Are you Catholic?"

"I'm Italian. Of course I'm Catholic. I have a saint in my family."

"Pray, then. Perhaps your saint can perform a miracle."

* * *

It was an hour before curfew when the Karbala police turned up at the Dar and asked Lee and Duncan to come with them for questioning. Hassan had a Ba'ath party gut and mustache. He had transformed the Sunni *mujahedeen* into Baghdad police, all with forged identification, to evade any questions about why the Karbala force was poaching on Baghdad territory. In the back of the SUV, with the pickup trailing behind, the two prisoners were hooded and cuffed. The *mujahedeen* had brought their own weapons, and in a moment of paranoia, Lee thought they might want to use the police raid as a cover to kidnap them. She prayed that Nizar ranked high enough in the resistance to keep the men in line.

As Lee could see nothing, she asked Hassan to give her a running commentary. The cars slowed to a halt on the outskirts of Al Marifa, somewhere along Qutaiba Ibn Muslim.

"Check point. Americans. Let me handle this. Hello, sir." Hassan struck just the right deferential tone. "Baghdad and Karbala joint task force, sir. Terror squad. We have suspects for questioning, sir."

She could just see the gleam of what must have been the soldier's flashlight.

"Ok, you're good to go." It was easier getting out of Baghdad than entering it. The soldiers were more interested in who might be coming anywhere near the Green Zone with a bomb.

"We made it, doctor. Next stop Hillah."

The Hillah checkpoint was just at the end of the congested city center, where Hassan took advantage of his police siren to scatter the crowds. He finessed the checkpoint. Lee could tell that he was hitting his stride as a terror squad officer.

"The next one won't be so easy. We will be facing General Yazid's people. First, we must find Dr. Ali."

"Hassan, I can't breathe in this hood," Duncan mumbled. "Why don't we just put them on at the checkpoints?"

"Sorry, Mr. Duncan. You wanted authenticity."

It was a clear night that smelled of saffron and cumin from the roadside stalls. Lee, her hood rolled up, could see the lights from kerosene lamps in the mud-brick towns set back from the highway. The headlights picked up the rusting tanks from Saddam's defense of Baghdad, upended on the side of the road. Black Hawks were patrolling the date-palm groves, spotlighting for insurgents.

Dr. Ali was waiting along the old pilgrim's way, a dirt road in the cane fields north of the highway. As Hassan approached, down the rutted track in the pitch dark, Dr. Ali flashed his lights. When the vehicles pulled up beside him, the old resistance leader was standing by his SUV, tall and serene, as though all of his nerves had been surgically removed. He calmly directed the transfer of the rifles and documents, needed for the last checkpoint, without once glancing at the helicopter that was crisscrossing the sky above them.

By the time the helicopter spotlighted them, throwing a disconcerting shaft of light on the vehicles, the convoy was moving back toward the highway. When Lee heard the helicopter fly low overhead, its wash flattening the cane stalks, she felt fear grip her chest, as though she was back in Samarra, about to be rocketed. Whoever was inspecting from above was satisfied with the police markings on the vehicles and the uniformed men in the pickup. The spotlight was turned off and the thunderous noise receded.

They would make it through the Karbala outer perimeter minutes before curfew, which meant less scrutiny and better odds.

"Put the hoods on."

With Yazid's men, Hassan spoke in rapid Arabic, as though he was a busy officer in a hurry. He flashed both Karbala and Baghdad credentials, covered with impressive stamps, and explained curtly that this was a joint terror task force operation, which, of course, they were not cleared to interfere with. He dropped the names of Clapp and Slay, as well as their general, to insure maximum pain if the men made the wrong decision.

"We're in. Hoods off now."

"You're a great actor, Hassan."

"You can tell me that tomorrow. We have a long way to go."

Dr. Ali was following at a discreet distance. When the convoy approached the offices of Dr. Husseini, Ali's car took the lead. He opened the side gate to allow the police vehicles inside the courtyard. Hassan did not want his cast sitting in the street for the next four hours before the raid, in case they aroused suspicion, or worse, attracted Karbala police looking for companionship. Once behind the tall metal gates, Hassan parked under the portico. If anyone at the checkpoint had radioed headquarters with a query about the special task force — unlikely given their desire to get off duty for the Friday weekend — the evidence had vanished without trace.

"Welcome back, Lee." Dr. Husseini welcomed her at the door. "Shall I cut you loose?"

She was still flex-cuffed and making a vain attempt to control her *abaya* with her teeth. "Yes, please."

There was a table full of Arabic salads for the actors and for the first time, Lee noticed the cameraman.

Hassan, flush from his victory of negotiating the checkpoints, was keen to introduce him. "Dr. McGuinness, this is Walid. We did over a hundred episodes together."

Although it had been hours since sunset, Walid wore shades pushed up on his balding forehead. His uniform for the evening was a black leather jacket, a gold chain with "no war" in Arabic, and tight jeans.

"Glad to have you with us."

"Shooting this will be a challenge. I really wanted time to light the safe house. Hassan said that wasn't possible. I have to do the whole thing with a Frezzy light, so it will look a little raw, but that's okay for action stuff."

"Where did you train as a cameraman?"

"I'm a DP actually. I trained at USC."

"Oh."

"I'm best known for Hassan's show, but I shot a couple of low-budget independent films in Brazil. Tonight is really wild though. Hassan says we have to do the whole thing in one take."

"Yeah. No question about that. Have some *mezze*." Lee directed Walid to the food and went to find Dr. Husseini. He was alone in his office, hunched over his report on Saddam's mass graves.

"I'm sorry to disturb you."

"Come in, Lee. Have a seat. Just push those books aside."

"If things go as planned tonight, I won't see you for awhile. I just wanted to say thank you."

"Is the clinic just an excuse? I thought you might be serious. You know the situation here will only get worse."

"I know."

"In a civil war, the clinic will save a lot of lives."

"You're very persuasive, Dr. Husseini. But I am going to Paris to see Laela al-Bahari. She has bone cancer."

"I can see that you are fond of her. I knew her father."

"Yes."

"Come back with her when she has finished her treatment."

"I will try." The fact that she might never come back hit Lee then and knocked her into silence.

"I didn't mean to probe."

"No. It's fine. I know that if things go badly tonight, it will mean problems for you."

"Don't worry about me, Lee. I have powerful friends. I am proud of you for what you are doing. You are no longer a tourist observing other people's suffering."

Lee laughed. "What am I now?"

"One of us."

At 2 a.m. sharp, the gate of Dr. Husseini's charity opened, and the police convoy moved out into the broad, deserted avenue. There was a stiff wind blowing sand into the city, and broken palm fronds occasionally slapped against the car. Old scraps from the shops, brown paper for wrapping fruit, dried husks, and empty cigarette packets scuttled along the sidewalk. The first roadblock guarded access to the Abbas shrine.

"We can go around that." Hassan ducked down a side street to circle around the rear of the shrine to the old Ottoman house. "Okay, this is it. *Yalla, yalla.*"

Hassan pushed Lee and Duncan roughly out of the SUV and forced them to walk ahead of his men. Two sentries were left behind with the vehicles parked on the curb with their lights flashing. The neighbors would not want to inquire too closely. The walls in the dank entryway, lit by the Frezzy light, were caked with black mold. Hassan shined a torch behind his prisoners, and the lights cast unsettling shadows in the abandoned courtyard. They found the stairs, so rotten that one broke under Lee and she fell to her knees. The noise was masked by the wind, whipping through the latticework of the termite-infested balconies.

Nothing moved on the roof.

"Martin. I'm here. With Captain Hassan." She thought he could not hear her because of the wind.

"Mr. Carrigan. This is Captain Hassan. You are under arrest." No one in the neighborhood could have missed that.

With growing horror, Lee thought that Martin had already been captured. Even worse, he might have stood them up, out of lack of confidence or as a cruel joke. She closed her eyes to keep out the sand that was already stinging her face and lining the roof of her mouth. She spat. "Martin, we don't have time for this." She was sorry that she had ever conceived of this ridiculous piece of theater. It was going to land all of them in Umm Qasr or Abu Ghraib.

"Take off their handcuffs." The disembodied voice came from somewhere in the darkness. "And throw down the guns."

Lee realized that Martin believed what he saw, that they were in police custody, brought here as bait to reel him in.

"Hassan, do as he says. Quickly."

He cut the flexi-cuffs and ordered the men to drop their rifles. Martin appeared from behind a pillar.

"Thank God, Martin, we have to go now."

"How do I know you're not working with them, Lee? The last time you came, I had American soldiers searching every house for the foreign terrorist."

"Are you suggesting we led them to you? Don't be absurd. Do you want to get us all killed? You can fade back into the shadows but we are stuck here. In a few minutes we will have General Yazid and Major Clapp booking us for crimes against the coalition. Is that what you want?"

"I want to get out of here alive."

"Martin," Duncan weighed in. "Everyone of these men in uniform will be tortured tomorrow unless you get in the car now."

He succeeded where Lee had failed.

"Yes, I understand." Martin fell in behind him and they raced down the stairs, praying that they did not collapse, and fell into the SUV.

"All of you put on the flexi-cuffs." Hassan was nervous now. "Get on the floor."

Martin waited until Lee and Duncan had cuffed each other before he could bear to give up his freedom. Hassan tore through the narrow streets, his lights flashing. He kept the siren in reserve. The gale wind was blowing anything that wasn't tied down. Old boards and paint buckets were flying into the road in front of them. The sand was gathering in little dunes against the stone walls.

"Police checkpoint. Hoods on."

Martin reared back as a mock guard tried to drop a black cloth over his face.

"Put it on now." Duncan, with some difficulty, helped him adjust it.

"Everybody hold on." Hassan switched on the siren. He must have terrified the skeleton crew manning the barrier, between the siren and his emphatic orders that the joint task force had three fugitives wanted for crimes against the coalition. He was taking the prisoners to Abu Ghraib. The men waved the convoy on without a word.

"Hoods off."

They flew along the broad boulevard that led to the edge of the city. Careening around the roundabout, they nearly sideswiped an M1 tank..

"Hoods on fast. Americans."

Hassan slowed to a respectful crawl. Lee could see the flicker of flashlights bouncing around the SUV.

"Papers, please."

She heard Hassan produce the beautifully forged documents.

"Where are you headed?"

"I have three fugitives wanted for crimes against the coalition. Top-security prisoners. I'm with the joint Baghdad-Karbala terror task force. My orders are to take them to Abu Ghraib."

"Where did you learn your English? It's pretty good."

"Fort Simms."

"Oh, yeah?"

"I did a training course there."

"When did you do that?"

"Last May."

"Wait here, officer." Lee could hear the soldier having a long conversation. The wind and the hood muffled the words. "My sergeant says we'll take the prisoners." He opened the back door, exposing their hooded and flex-cuffed bodies sprawled on the floor. "Tell your men to unload them."

"But I have orders." Hassan had a note of panic in his voice.

"Who from?"

"General Yazid and Colonel Slay."

"Slay?"

"That's right."

"May I see them, please?"

Dr. Ali's documents man had used all of the right stamps. It was probably an inside job.

"Hold on."

There was a second-long exchange with his sergeant. Meanwhile, Lee could hear footsteps and the indistinct sounds of other soldiers surrounding the cars.

"Who's that guy?" Their interrogator was back.

"Task force cameraman." Hassan made it sound like an official post.

"How ya doin' sir?" Walid spoke in his best American accent.

"Why does the task force need a cameraman?"

"With these sensitive cases" — Hassan was making it up as he went along — "we need documentary evidence that there was no mistreatment."

Hassan had a gift for improvisation. Another long pause made Lee lose confidence. She had a terrible sinking feeling that the soldier would radio Slay. Their only hope was that it was now after 3 a.m. and he might not want to risk the repercussions of waking a superior officer in the middle of the night on a weekend.

"Good luck, you guys. You can go."

The door slammed. A mile down the road, they had cleared the Karbala city limits and were on the open road.

"All clear, everybody. For the moment."

"Nice work, Hassan." Duncan was happy to breathe again.

"I was sure that soldier would drag all of you onto the pavement. He would have had quite a shock ripping off your hoods."

"Perhaps we should wait to joke about this until later," Martin said. "Somebody light me a cigarette."

XXXII

ON THE OPEN ROAD, Hassan drove at top speed. He slowed briefly for two more checkpoints, but in the no-man's-land between Karbala and Baghdad, local police had no interest in stopping a large group of armed men who were either senior officers, who could have them fired, or insurgents, who would shoot them in the head. When Hassan reached the Baghdad ring road, and took Highway 1 to Taji and Tikrit, Lee made a call on her Thuraya to Lieutenant Randall Frank.

"Oh-six-hundred hours. I have a wounded man and will need medevac."

"Roger that."

They had agreed that their satellite phone conversation should be short and to the point to avoid attracting interest from the dozen agencies monitoring Iraqi calls. On the outskirts of Taji, Hassan stopped the car.

"What's wrong, Hassan?" Duncan had no desire to stop anywhere along the route.

"New plates."

"I'm sorry?"

"We have to switch the plates. Karbala police don't operate up here. We're from Baiji now. I have everything we need. Just be patient."

Duncan could see that Hassan had put far more effort into the planning than he had.

At the Taji checkpoint, where they faced two M1 tanks, Hassan flashed his Baiji credentials. He had adjusted his story to fit the region.

"We have three insurgent fugitives wanted for the Baiji refinery fire. Our friends here from the Baghdad police terror task force helped us raid their safe house in Waziriya. None of our people were killed, I'm glad to say."

"May I see their papers?"

The Baghdad IDs were displayed.

"Have a good evening."

The cameraman asked Hassan why he had changed the story line.

"You already have enough in the can. I'm just ad-libbing."

The first dawn light spilled across the plain and Lee opened a window for air. There was still sand in her clothes from the storm. She could hear the sound of the *muezzin* from Mashada calling the faithful to prayer. *Allahu akbar.* Martin and Duncan had fallen asleep. Lee felt drowsy and cramped. She tried to move her leg muscles to avoid a blood clot. The British Airways coach class exercise video was running through her head. By the time they reached Tikrit, it was daylight. The road ahead was blocked.

"*Mujahedeen.*" Hassan slowed the car respectfully.

Mohammed, a native of Tikrit, shoved his head out the window. "*Habibi.*" A term of endearment coming from the Baiji police confused the well-armed gang in the road until they caught sight of his face. "I know these guys. We were in school together." Mohammed explained, to their great satisfaction, that he was on the run. They joked in Arabic about how much the prisoners were worth as hostages. They said there had been so many kidnappings that it was no longer a sellers' market. Prices were coming down but for the three of us they thought $2 million would be a good price. One million for Lee alone.

"Mohammed, let's go."

"Be patient, doctor." He replied that they might get the $2 million but Gen. Nizar Hadithi, Lee's protector, would cut their balls off. They demurred and let Hassan through.

"General?" Lee sat up straight.

"You didn't know? Nizar Hadithi is a *mujahedeen* commander. A very powerful one."

She thought back to his *ris de veau*. "You're sure that he's a commander? I thought he was just in touch with the resistance."

"I'm sure. So were those men in the road."

Lee remembered the day she first ran the gauntlet of the Aleem Hotel oil drums, filled with fresh concrete, thinking that if someone bombed the hotel, it would be an inside job. Of course, Nizar knew all about the South Africans on the floor below who had the contract to feed the troops. She thought about the fact that Gen. Hadithi had the Green Zone completely penetrated. George Plumber was shrewd enough to know that as occupiers, with the likes of Nizar recruiting insurgents, they could never win the war. They could only profit from it.

Lee reached in back for her doctor's bag and woke Martin.

"What is it, Lee?"

"I need to bandage you."

"Why?"

"To get you a medevac out of here, you have to be severely wounded. I think we'll give you a nasty head wound and two bullets in the groin."

361

She wrapped his head until he looked like something out of the Egyptian Museum. Hassan turned off the highway toward Beit Har. The roadblock that had worried Duncan, after the bombing of the pipeline, was now gone. With their Baiji plates, they were local, above suspicion. No one in the street questioned their movements. Their convoy pulled up to Camp Destiny nine minutes early. Lee jumped out, no longer cuffed, and relieved to be standing.

"We are here to see Lt. Frank, please."

"You're the doctor."

"That's right. I have a wounded man with me so I would appreciate some help. I will need a gurney from the clinic."

"Okay, doc." Lee heard the lieutenant acknowledging her on the radio. "You're cleared ma'am. These Iraqis will have to wait here."

"I understand."

The medics appeared and lifted Martin gently from the SUV.

"Duncan, will you take him in? I want to say goodbye to Hassan."

"Yes, Lee."

She gave Hassan a kiss. "*Ma'a salama, habibi.* When I come back you will once again be a star. Hassan, will you be all right getting back to Baghdad?" She felt unsure about dispatching him without her.

"Yes, doctor. Without the curfew, it will be a piece of cake. The SUV and the pickup will travel separately with Baghdad plates."

"I'm not sure when I will be back." She gave Hassan a wad of cash.

"Soon, *tabiba.* If you need me, just call."

"Take care on the road. And, Hassan."

"Yes, doctor?"

"It was a great performance."

"Thanks, friend. Next time. And *tabiba?*"

"Yes?"

"I'll do a live show to benefit the clinic."

"Thanks, Hassan. *Insha'Allah.*"

She found Lt. Frank leaning over Martin's wrapped body, trying to make out what he was saying under his bandages.

"Let me cut away some of that tape from his mouth." She had wanted to make him pay a small price for his reckless stalling on the Ottoman roof.

"Lee, is this really necessary?"

"Well, Martin, unless the medevac pilot believes you are near death, he's going to fly you straight back to Baghdad into the arms of George Plumber."

"Are you angry with me?"

"I was just irritated when you were so pigheaded back there. We've all gone to a lot of trouble for you."

"I'm sorry. I was nervous. You're amazing, Lee. Thank you for everything you've done. Randall — I should say, lieutenant, thanks for working with her."

"It's not exactly a hardship, sir. Welcome back, doctor."

"Lieutenant." She was sorry to leave him behind in the inferno of Beit Har. "Is the oil fire under control?"

"Yes. It took nearly a week."

"I said you might have to change procedures?"

"I'm listening."

"As a surgeon, I am ordering you to have the medevac deliver him to Cizre, Turkey. Is it within Black Hawk range? The reason is lack of facilities in Baghdad for massive cranial trauma. Otherwise, you will be responsible for the patient's death."

"It's hard to argue with that. It's within range. I've always been very fond of Mr. Carrigan." The lieutenant radioed to check on the status of the medevac he had ordered for six.

"I have one more favor to ask. Martin will give you the number of Miss Martha Sparks. She is expecting us and needs exact details of arrival. As she is a Pentagon employee, you should be able to expense the call."

"I would say so."

Lee left the two of them to catch up on their shared history. Duncan was having his first coffee of the day and a cigarette at the Bellagio.

"May I join you?"

"Of course, Lee. That was quite a ride."

"I admit I was terrified." She was attracting interest from the mortar platoon.

"I didn't like those *mujahedeen* in Tikrit. I don't fancy being kidnapped."

"Aren't you flattered that someone would pay so much for you?"

"You command twice the price. Better resale value as a slave."

They heard the drone of the medevac approaching the landing zone.

"We should go."

The helicopter was taking on fuel as Martin was wheeled out by the medics and transferred to the luxurious mobile hospital on board.

"Goodbye, lieutenant. We would have failed without you."

"No problem, doctor. And thanks for saving that boy from Etlan. I told his mom how to find you."

"I'll be ready for the moonshine and peach pie."

On board, the pilot gave Lee headphones so that she could hear him over the roar of the rotors.

"Welcome to the UH-60Q medevac. We have state-of-the-art environmental control systems, cardiac monitoring, oxygen and suction systems, IV solution storage, patient monitoring, and neonatal isolettes."

She wondered how many soldiers gave birth on board. "How long to Cizre?"

"Depends on the weather in the mountains. Shouldn't be long. I'll let you look after your patient. Is the Brit a doctor?"

"He specializes in rocket and mortar injuries."

"Great to have you both aboard."

Lee fussed over Martin, hooking him up to an IV, monitoring every vital sign she could think of and checking his bandages.

"Lee, I'm sorry I lost my faith in you on the roof."

"Forget it."

"Why have you done so much for me?"

She could not bring herself to tell him that she had loved him. His indifference had changed that.

"I'm doing this for me," she said offhandedly.

"What do you mean?"

"Cleaning out Jabarri's mafia will make a difference," she shouted over the engines. "I care about this country. I suppose Plumber will get off. He will be offered immunity to testify before some Congressional committee. Isn't that how it works?"

"We have him cold, and I will push hard for prosecution. My father would have wanted it." He lay back on his litter. "Back in New York you can dine out on this."

Lee turned away and studied the earth below, buckling into leathery folds like an old man's skin. As they approached Mosul and the mountains, she saw the Tigris below and the northeastern spur of Syria, where the pilot was careful to avoid the airspace. The helicopter skirted Zakho, and she thought of those nights on the road to Diyarbakir, when Duncan and she were inseparable. He had become so much a part of her life, like a perfectly grafted tree. She watched him across the row of jump seats, headphones on against the roar, bent over a book about ancient Persia, his hair falling over his eyes.

There was an SUV and a minivan waiting by the landing pad with several Turkish soldiers standing guard. The minivan had "Turkish Delight Tours" printed on its side. Martha Sparks stood in the doorway. She was much as Lee remembered her, but without the wig and dentures. Two bodyguards stood in place of the gardeners. The men took charge of Martin, moving him onto the bus, without the formalities of immigration or customs. "Wait," Martin called to Lee from his stretcher. "Just one thing."

"What is it?" Lee was unsure what to expect.

"I'm going back to refugee work, Lee. I'm going to be the man I was when we first met. When we both believed in something."

"You don't have to say that, Martin. I'm proud of what you've done."

"You saved my life, Lee."

"You saved mine too, remember? You'd better go."

"How can I find you?"

"After you've arrested some of your friends, I'll be back. Do me a favor and tell Jabarri that part of his punishment is giving a large donation to charity."

"Any particular charity?"

"He will know."

XXXIII

MARTHA SPARKS came out to say hello. She wore autumn colors and a sensible straw-colored bag with matching pumps. "Doctor, on behalf of all of us, I want to thank you. Should you ever need help in the future, we are happy to be of service." Sparks handed Lee her card, which was blank except for her name and an email address. "By the way, what did you do with the money in the briefcase?"

"A shipment of medical supplies and per diems for 10 police. A makeover for one pickup and SUV with sirens, and forged IDs for everyone."

"If you ever get bored with medicine, doctor, give me a call. We could use you. As for you, Mr. Hope, write what you like. Just keep my name out of it. You can print that we found a tanker truck at the Zakho crossing, stuffed with shrink-wrapped dollar bills. Quote me as a Western diplomat."

"A pleasure, Ms. Sparks." Duncan shook her hand. "I hope our paths cross again."

"We are not out of the woods yet. Some local Turkish officials are involved. It's best if I take Martin with me. You two have an SUV to take you to the airport in Ankara, where you should go straight to the first-class lounge. My people will be there to watch out for you. These are tickets for a 3 p.m. flight to Frankfurt. Row one. From there, you go your own way."

"Thanks."

"Time to mount up." Sparks liked punctuality. Turkish Delight Tours sped off the field.

"Are you sorry you're not going with him?" Duncan avoided looking at her.

"No." She closed her eyes to shut out everything she had once hoped for. "Let's go to Paris."

When they reached Ankara, their driver paid several airport officials to avoid any last-minute snags. Martha Sparks was thorough. In the lounge, Lee could not detect which of the passengers were Sparks's agents. She was grateful they were there, for she knew that Turkish intelligence could appear and ask them to come for questioning. It wasn't until they were on board the Lufthansa flight and the door had closed that she began to decompress from Iraq.

Before the plane even got off the ground, Duncan was writing his story. Lee left him undisturbed and calculated that with the time change, they could catch an early evening flight to Paris and be with Laela in time to take her to the Brasserie Balzar.

At the Frankfurt airport transfer desk, surrounded by passengers who had missed connections, both of them looked like they had slept in their clothes. Duncan, shambolic at the best of times, was laden with the documents and notebooks to tell the story of over $1 billion stolen in Iraq.

"I promised Stephano you would help him with a story for Monday." Lee wanted to talk about anything but Martin. "I said we would call."

"Tomorrow morning, after my paper comes out, I will send him what he needs." They found the lounge and poured themselves strong drinks. "After all of this is done, I will miss you terribly, Lee."

"Miss me?" She thought for a moment that she had not heard him correctly.

"Yes."

"I don't understand. I thought you wanted to be with me."

"You're still in love with Martin."

"How can you say that? I would have never invited you into my bed."

"Lee, I'm sorry. I'm not blind. Maybe you had forgotten for a few nights. Also, before anything else, I have to see Laela."

"I see." There was nothing more to say.

"Are you coming?"

"Yes, of course."

"Are we friends?"

"Don't be so pedestrian, Duncan." She wondered whether male DNA was missing genes for feelings, for loyalty. She thought some medical researcher could get a dissertation out of it. "Does it mean anything to you, what we've been through together? What you said to me in Baghdad?"

"Look Lee, you are beautiful, you are brave, and you just happen to be in love with someone else. Could we put all of this aside just long enough to look after someone we both care deeply about?"

"Yes, go ahead and put me aside, Duncan. Of course I loved Martin. But that's in the past. Are you so afraid of committing yourself that you can only love a woman who's dying?"

"That's cruel."

"Who's being cruel here? Yesterday we were supposed to spend the rest of our lives together. Now that you have your story, you can file me away with your old notebooks."

"No, Lee, that's not it."

A group of German businessmen was watching them with interest.

"What is it then?"

"One day, Martin will come back and you will leave me."

They finished their drinks in silence. Duncan's cell phone rang and he could see from the number that it was Zara's Paris cell.

"Hello, Zara." Duncan's eyes were fixed on Lee as he spoke.

"You're bloody lucky to be out of there." Zara's voice was loud enough for half the lounge to hear. "We thought you were about to appear on some *muj* video in a *dishdasha* pleading the cause of the resistance. When will we see you?"

"Tonight."

"Will you stay with us?"

"Yes, of course."

"Is the doctor with you?"

"She is."

"Good. I want to buy her Champagne and talk about the ghastly cancer."

"I promised Laela I would take her to Balzar." Duncan stuttered slightly.

"Right, darling, I will book it for you. Now when you get to the Rue de la Santé, you punch in one of those codes which I cannot for the life of me remember. Oh wait, here it is, 1842. Go behind the apartment block into what looks like a secret garden. You'll see a gate and the house is in there, behind the forest of black bamboo. I'll have a martini waiting."

* * *

When Duncan punched in the code, he and Lee were in the entryway of a Belle Époque apartment block that served as the fortress wall for the much older houses behind. They found the wooden gate and the bamboo garden beyond, dotted with brightly painted pots. There, at the door was Laela, even thinner than when they had seen her last. Her eyes looked like enormous dark pools now, and her broken arm was hidden under a cashmere shawl. Her chalk-white skin was almost translucent, and the dark arc of her brow reminded Lee of the sculptures looted from Egyptian royal tombs.

"I've been waiting for you." She smiled a broad smile. Lee watched the fear and betrayal that had consumed Duncan for days banished in an instant.

"I apologize for taking so long."

"Welcome to the house of exiles." She kissed Duncan so softly, it was like being brushed by a moth.

The hall was cluttered with shards of broken pots: Zara's archaeological specimens, the fractured evidence of a civilization for which there was no present except in Zara's memory. The sitting room was lined with books overflowing onto the floor on the Ottomans, Assyrians, Babylonians, Sumerians. There were catalogues from the Baghdad museum, of treasures looted and smashed, and framed photos of digs, where the dirt had once been scraped with toothbrushes, now desecrated by thieves.

"One olive. Shaken." Zara handed Duncan the martini.

"Wonderful, thanks."

"You must be knackered."

"Nothing Paris won't cure."

"What about Martin, Lee? Is he alive?" Laela looked more beautiful than Lee had ever seen her look, like a prize tea rose in full bloom.

"We got him out just in time."

"Lee, you are marvelous."

"Duncan, too." It was Lee's peace offering. She felt ashamed for thinking of herself, when Laela's life was ebbing away.

"Was Martin a spy after all?"

"He was there for a special task force digging up bribes and kickbacks. Your cousin Adnan Jabarri is in trouble. He has a senior American official on his payroll, depositing millions into his Swiss bank account. We smuggled out his ledger."

"Very brave of you, Lee, but Cousin Adnan is a slippery customer," Zara weighed in. "You can't extradite him. He is blackmailing every Iraqi in the government with his intelligence files. They will do exactly what he tells them to do. And anyway, your government loves criminals. They have a weakness that can be exploited. Greed."

Lee thought of Jabarri, demanding that she buy drugs for the new clinic through his company. He could not resist the easy mark, she thought, buying expired drugs and charging her full price.

"You may be right. But it will all be public on Sunday, thanks to Duncan, which will cramp your cousin's style."

"Our wicked cousin is ruthless. He is a survivor. Like a rat after a nuclear test." Laela smiled knowingly.

Lee thought Plumber fit the same description. Perhaps it was impossible to dislodge him. There would be an inquiry with a reprimand and a promotion. He could land a sinecure in Kabul. Or he might join one of the consulting firms lining the Beltway, gorging on government contracts.

"Laela, we promised you dinner." She seemed almost too frail to leave her secret garden, but within minutes, they were all packed into a taxi, tearing around the corner past the old prison walls toward the Seine. The air smelled of damp houses, baker's yeast, and strong coffee. They sat in a banquette where Lee watched Laela pick at some fish from across a table crowded with chopped baguettes and Champagne.

"I have a new doctor."

"The bone specialist?"

"Yes. He did groundbreaking work at the Curie Institute."

"Did they play Vivaldi in the MRI?"

She laughed. "I requested it."

"What does he say, Laela?" Duncan looked down at his plate.

"The cancer has spread beyond my bones. It is eating me alive. Like a weapon of mass destruction. Sometimes, at night, I think I can hear it. He told me to get my affairs in order."

"No chemotherapy or surgery?"

"He says there's no point. I should enjoy what life I have left."

"You should have a second opinion." Lee said it in her most professional voice.

"I've had three second opinions. They all treat me as though I am already a ghost."

"Let's all go for a walk along the river." Zara wanted to change the subject. "Are you strong enough, Laela?"

"Yes, I'm fine tonight." She smiled at Duncan. "I'm so happy you are here. I no longer feel condemned."

The air had turned cold and Duncan gave her his coat. They could hear the music from the *bateaux mouches* as they watched the black water, strung with reflected light, slap against the embankment. The Ferris wheel at the Place de la Concorde dwarfed the city like something Oldenburg would sketch for a giant hamster. The lights on the Eiffel Tower were using more power than all of Baghdad.

"How is your arm?"

She pulled back her shawl. "I chose a purple cast."

"It suits you."

"Can we go to the shop with the mousetraps?"

"First thing," Duncan said, lighting a cigarette. "It's near Beaubourg."

Laela faltered and stopped. "I'm so sorry, everyone. Please take me home. I am starting to ache."

Her pain came in waves, and she had a medicine chest full of painkillers to manage it. Laela was determined not to succumb to the invalid's life, and the next morning she was up and dressed by 7. They took the metro to Les Halles and Duncan bought her coffee and flowers, while they waited for the shop to open.

There was a kiosk selling international papers and Duncan found his story, "Corruption Scandal Rocks Baghdad's Green Zone." He had a large piece of the front page with a photograph of the ledger and an extract of the phone transcripts. The ship's log from Umm Qasr and the photo of the captain were all there. Mahmood Maroki and his family stared out from the portrait labeled "the whistle-blower." The oil tanker printouts got prominent display. Duncan quoted an anonymous American investigator on the central role of George Plumber, whose Swiss bank account number was there with his balance. When Plumber tried to transfer the funds, Sparks would be ready for him.

Lee felt as though a weight had been lifted now that everything was public. At the same time, she felt strangely detached. Laela was dying. Everything else paled beside that fact.

The mousetrap shop was musty and dim, with the traps displayed as though they were in a 19th-century museum. The proprietor was small and bent, delighting in demonstrating his contraptions. They were beautifully made little cages of thin wire mesh, with metal doors that drew back ready to spring on the mouse who followed the cheese. There was no cruelty. No broken mouse legs or severed tails. The mouse was comfortably housed and forced to wait until the owner took him out to the river to release him.

"Do people really buy these?" Laela was delighted.

"Mademoiselle, I have been in business for over 50 years."

"Don't the mice just come back?" she asked.

"No one knows. But there is no agony. And no bad smell. Just the pleasure of good hunting."

They ate sea urchins that night at the Closerie des Lilas and ended the night at Deux Magots. The next day, Laela collapsed. Her doctor insisted on rest and forbade her from traveling to the south. Lee made soup for her and read her the papers. She slept long hours, and Lee emailed the Surgeons' Committee in New York to extend her leave. She explained the circumstances. They replied that they were reading about her in the news, which made them more indulgent.

Lee got word from Martin that he was being debriefed in Rome but would be home the following week. There would a small ceremony in Washington in his honor. Lee was on the guest list. Col. Frank offered her a plane ticket. She knew then that she had no intention of going back. Her place was on the Rue de la Santé. She cooked and read aloud, and did what she could to ease the pain. Whenever Lee found a butterfly or a beetle in the garden, she brought it to Laela, and the offering gave her endless pleasure. There was a nightingale in the garden that insisted on singing day and night.

"It's a recording, isn't it?" Laela asked, like a knowing child. "You have it on a speaker in the garden."

The day Laela died, Lee booked a ticket for Jordan. She and Duncan stood on either side of Zara as she buried Laela in a pretty graveyard in Montmartre. Laela was wrapped in a *kafan* of pure white cotton. Zara, looking small and defeated, threw three handfuls of earth into the grave. The thud of the dirt was almost more than Lee could bear.

When it was time to go, Lee climbed the stairs to the third floor of the house on the Rue de la Santé, and packed the few clothes she had bought in Paris to see her through. Duncan appeared in her doorway. They had hardly been alone together during the long weeks when death hung in the house like an unwanted guest. Since their exchange at Frankfurt Airport, Lee had withdrawn from Duncan, sure that her attraction to him had been dangerous for her, as though she had passed through an electrical storm or a firefight.

"What are your plans?"

"I'm going back to Baghdad. To open the clinic."

Duncan lit a cigarette. "I suppose Martin will come back now that Plumber's been recalled."

"I don't know."

"I'm told Jabarri's been packed off to Kuwait and General Yazid got a green card and a ticket to Detroit."

"You're not serious."

"Yes. Look, I'm sorry about what I said, Lee. I've never been very good at expressing myself."

Lee stopped folding and packing and sat on the bed. She motioned for him to join her and kissed him lightly on the cheek. "Don't worry about it."

"There's something I want to say."

"What is it?"

"Lee, I don't want to lose you."

She looked at him and the words wouldn't come, the words to say he had lost her already. "We've been through a lot."

"Yes," Duncan turned away. He helped Lee with her suitcase and Zara filled a bag with fruit and nougat for the trip.

* * *

Lee flew to Amman. Mrs. Osman of Osman Deluxe Travel sent her to Baghdad with Mohammed bin Salah'adin, whose throat wound had healed nicely.

"What about our trip to Petra, *tabiba?*" Mohammed thought she must have forgotten.

"We will have plenty of time, Mohammed. *Insha'Allah.*"

In Baghdad, she found her way to Hassan. He escorted her to his car as if he had been expecting her.

"Welcome back, doctor. Where to?"

"The garden of the al-Bahari."

The outlines of the garden were there, so she knew she had come to the right place. The date grove had been bulldozed and set on fire. There was nothing but blackened stumps. Lee found shards of broken pots and looked in vain for *The Weapon of Mass Destruction*. It had been towed away somewhere or looted for scrap. The vegetable garden had been trampled and the pomegranates lay squashed, their bright red seeds scattered over the earth. She sat amid the broken palms and closed her eyes. She could see Laela, under the rising moon, talking to her trees. Lee stayed there for a long time. Somewhere in her mind, she heard the sound of an *oud*.

"*Tabiba*, the curfew." Hassan was waiting.

ACKNOWLEDGMENTS

There are a few people who must be thanked. My editor, Robert Asahina, took great care with the manuscript and is surely one of the finest editors in publishing. I was privileged to work with him. Robert Wallace threw his weight behind the book and had steadfast faith in the enterprise. Ruth Graham showed a keen eye for detail. Bill Broyles, writer, editor, and former Marine, gave me the courage to forge ahead. Wade Davis gave me his enthusiastic endorsement. Scott Wallace took time for a close reading and made important suggestions from his own experience in Baghdad. Dr. Corinna Franklin scrutinized my medical details and terminology. Peter Matson offered excellent advice. Susanna Styron cast her critical eye on an early draft. Matthew Hoh, veteran of the State Department and the Marines, gave me an insider's look. The late Selma al Radi, a legend in the world of archaeology, gave me encouragement from the very start. Lastly, my husband, Andrew, sustained me throughout. Together, we traveled the length and breadth of Iraq on several trips between 1991 and 2003. I was there as a correspondent for PBS *Frontline*, a writer for *Vanity Fair*, and a producer for CBS *60 Minutes*. This is a work of fiction. But there are times, I would argue, when fiction delivers the greater truth.

ABOUT THE AUTHOR

Tao Ruspoli

Leslie Cockburn lives in Washington, D.C., and
Ireland. This is her first novel.

AW

Asahina & Wallace
Los Angeles
2013
www.asahinaandwallace.com

CPSIA information can be obtained at www.ICGtesting.com
Printed in the USA
LVOW12s1911110913

352006LV00008B/1176/P

9 781940 412009